Delayed Justice

Keiko Palmer

STRATTON
—PRESS—
Publishing Life

DELAYED JUSTICE
Copyright © 2019 **Keiko Palmer**

All rights reserved. No part of this book may be used or reproduced by any means, graphic, electronic, or mechanical, including photocopying, recording, taping or by information storage and retrieval system without the written permission of the author except in the case of brief quotations embodied in critical articles and reviews.

Stratton Press Publishing
831 N Tatnall Street Suite M #188,
Wilmington, DE 19801
www.stratton-press.com
1-888-323-7009

Because of the dynamic nature of the Internet, any web addresses or links contained in this book may have changed since publication and may no longer be valid. The views expressed in the work are solely those of the author and do not necessarily reflect the views of the publisher, and the publisher hereby disclaims any responsibility for them.

ISBN (Paperback): 978-1-64345-599-0
ISBN (Hardback): 978-1-64345-602-7
ISBN (Ebook): 978-1-64345-715-4

Printed in the United States of America

Acknowledgment

My dear friends, who eagerly await my novel each time, often encourage me to write more, and do not mind critiquing:

Beverley Hescock, Julie Stasick, Amy Brock, Liliane Arens,
Kay Dalton, John Mason,
Etsuko Crissey (journalist),
James Monte Jr. (librarian),
Hilde Klinger, Helga Boerke, Kuniko Cordell, Al Thomas,
Jane Theodore, Michiko Lewis, Etsuko Norman,
my family, and dear friends in Japan.

Contents

Prologue 7

Chapter 1: The Ninth Birthday 15

Chapter 2: Biloxi 24

Chapter 3: Jefferson and Marie........................33

Chapter 4: Jake and Eunice 42

Chapter 5: A Hermit 51

Chapter 6: Almost Like Siblings......................60

Chapter 7: Love at First Sight.........................69

Chapter 8: Alan and Yuri.................................78

Chapter 9: Yuri's Decision 87

Chapter 10: Secret Engagement 95

Chapter 11: Tom Rousseau 103

Chapter 12: A Kid Detective............................112

Chapter 13: Mom's Birthplace.........................120

Chapter 14: Jeffery and Paula..........................129

Chapter 15: A Sewing Basket 138

Chapter 16: Mom's Marriage...........................147

Chapter 17:	My Birth Secret	155
Chapter 18:	Biological Mother	163
Chapter 19:	Okaasan	172
Chapter 20:	Going Home	181
Chapter 21:	Gregory Dubois	190
Chapter 22:	Paula's Letter	199
Chapter 23:	Most Wanted Fugitive	208
Chapter 24:	Katrina	217
Chapter 25:	After Katrina	226
Chapter 26:	Secret Relationship	235
Chapter 27:	A Long Story	243
Chapter 28:	Became a Lawyer	252
Chapter 29:	The Trial	261
Chapter 30:	Delayed Justice	271
Epilogue		281

PROLOGUE

When my mother asked me what I wanted for my ninth birthday, I did not hesitate to say, "Mom, for my birthday, can we go to see a real beach? Sharon and Toby just came back from Miami. I wish I could see the ocean. She said the ocean water tastes salty and the big waves move back and forth without stopping. Mom, have you tasted the ocean water before?"

She did not answer. She was busy cooking dinner for our houseguest, Tom Rousseau. They grew up together on St. Charles Avenue in New Orleans. He had been looking for Mom for years. Finally, he found us here in North Georgia. As he was having a business conference with his vendors in Atlanta, he asked Mom if it was all right to visit us, so Mom invited him for dinner tonight. It only takes him one hour from Atlanta to Gainesville.

My birthday is coming in a week. Most of the time, I celebrate my birthday at the lake beach with Sharon and Toby. However, this year, Mom is thinking about something special for my birthday because I would be nine—the last one-digit number. She is philosophical about my being in the ninth year of my life.

She reminded me that next year, my age would be a two-digit number just like hers. She probably thinks that my innocent childhood would be gone after this year, and I would become an obnoxious or rebellious teenager in a few years, just like other children she know. She often begs me jokingly not to grow up too fast as though she wants to enjoy my sweet and adorable childhood more.

I have seen the blue ocean and the white-sand beach many times on TV, but I could not imagine the ocean water tastes salty and the big waves move back and forth without stopping as Sharon says.

I know all about the lake beach because we live closer to Lake Lanier and swim there during the summer. I know the lake water is not salty and there are no big waves in the lake. Mom's hometown is New Orleans, but I never visited there, so I do not know if New Orleans has the ocean or if she has ever tasted the ocean water.

By eavesdropping on conversations between Mom and Grandma Margaret from time to time while I was growing up, I learned a lot about her family who had lived in New Orleans. Mom and Grandma Margaret were born in the Dubois mansion on St. Charles Avenue in New Orleans, and each of them grew up at the same house.

Before I was born, Mom's only sibling, Uncle Alan, was flying my grandparents from New Orleans to Atlanta to get them tested at CDC for a possible poisoning because they both became mysteriously ill in the office. They had a doctor's appointment on that day, but they never made it to the hospital. His aircraft disappeared in the wooded area in Georgia. After several days of search, the burned aircraft and three mutilated bodies were found. The FAA investigation concluded a fuel leakage led to the explosion.

While the FAA investigation took place, the bodies remained in a funeral home in Atlanta. After the investigation, when Mom called the funeral home, she was told the bodies were already cremated; three boxes of ashes were shipped to the Dubois Import Company's corporate office. The company paid for the expenses.

The funeral home could not tell exactly who ordered the cremation, but the payment came from the Dubois Import Company in New Orleans.

The company had two lawyers. Those two lawyers ignored the existence of the only remaining family member, Michelle Dubois, who was supposed to take care of the deceased, but they never contacted my mother, Michelle. Those lawyers had her parents' will and all other company's business documents in the office, so she went to see them at the Dubois Import Company.

When she arrived at the corporate office at the warehouse, she could not believe what she saw—the entire office and warehouse were emptied. The office building was left open as though the cleaning crew was scheduled to clean it. The sign Dubois Import Company in front of the warehouse building was taken down, and all the heavy crates of merchandise in another warehouse building also vanished. Obviously, a premeditated larceny had occurred.

Michelle assumed the lawyers were behind this criminal thievery—a multimillion-dollar larceny. She could have hired a criminal lawyer or a detective to investigate the disappearance of the family business and locate the lawyers' whereabouts, but she did not know where to start. She simply became a penniless orphan who just obtained an MLS degree.

The Dubois' family friends Jake and Eunice Rousseau were shocked and heartbroken to learn about their neighbors' deaths in an airplane crash. However, without the will of Jefferson and Marie Dubois or the legal documents of the Dubois Import Company, they too did not know where to start and how to help Michelle Dubois.

Their only son, Tom Rousseau, was a corporate lawyer in Chicago, and they thought that Tom might be willing to take the case, but they had not spoken to him for some time since Tom's refusal to take over the family business.

Shortly after the disappearance of the Dubois Import Company, Mom was evicted from the family mansion on St. Charles Avenue, so she moved to her brother's antebellum mansion in Biloxi, but again she was about to be evicted from there too.

With her desperation, she called Aunt Margaret in Georgia and explained everything—the death of her parents and brother, the disappearance of the family business, and the eviction. Aunt Margaret was sobbing on the phone. She probably realized she now had no blood relatives except her niece, so she immediately took her in.

I asked Mom once where I was born—New Orleans, Biloxi, or Gainesville. She jokingly said, "In a hospital." So I figured I was born after Grandma took her in, so it had to be in a hospital in Gainesville. Mom told me my father was also killed in an airplane crash before I was born.

Aunt Margaret's brother was Mom's father, Jefferson Dubois. When their father, my great-grandfather, started an import company from scratch, he wanted all his family members including his daughter, Margaret, to help him, but she eloped with a Creole who was a park ranger and moved to North Georgia.

Therefore, Aunt Margaret's father practically disowned her and refused to see her or talk to her. However, some years later, she heard her father's sudden death from her husband's cousin who owned a funeral home in New Orleans.

When Aunt Margaret came to bury her husband, Mr. Turner, in New Orleans, she came to the Dubois mansion on St. Charles Avenue to see her brother, Jefferson.

He was very happy to see his sister again. She was introduced to his wife—her sister-in-law, Marie, her nephew, Alan, and niece, Michelle. She stayed for dinner with the family and reminisced about her childhood with them. My mother, Michelle, was in high school and liked her aunt instantly.

After that, Mom wrote to her faithfully for years and let her know about her family and her school including her college because Aunt Margaret was the only relative on her father's side in the United States. Some relatives on her mother's side lived in France.

When Mom heard from Tom Rousseau yesterday—many years later—she probably thought the superpower above her sent someone who knows the law to help her. I was very sure she would tell our houseguest, Tom, everything tonight and get his legal advice on her family tragedy that happened many years ago.

*   *   *

My best friend Sharon and her brother Toby live a block away from our house. Sharon's mother, Ms. Norma, was born in the same house where Sharon and Toby were born. When Ms. Norma's mother passed away, the house was given to her, so her husband, Chris Gordon, made the house much bigger before Sharon and Toby were born.

Delayed Justice

Grandma Margaret and Sharon's grandmother were very good friends and had lived in the same neighborhood for years. They helped each other after they lost their husbands. Sharon's grandmother died before Sharon was born, so she did not know much about her grandmother.

I was lucky because my grandmother took care of me while Mom was at work. I knew Grandma Margaret was not my real grandmother, but to me, she was always my real grandmother. When I started school, she walked me to the bus stop every morning; after school, she met me, held my hand, and we walked back home together.

Sharon's father, Chris Gordon, rarely stays home because of his job. He is an eighteen-wheeler-truck driver who travels long distances for days and weeks. Whenever he is home, he always takes us kids to McDonald's for ice cream.

When Chris Gordon takes a long vacation from his job in the summer, he drives his entire family to Florida every year. I always wished I had a father like him who could take Mom and me to the beach. Mom does not say much about my father, but I think my father died without knowing Mom was pregnant with me. Because of it, she used her maiden name to name me, Lily Dubois.

Mom was browning pork chops. Finally, she put the pork chops in the oven with some assorted vegetables. She is a very good cook and always cooked healthy food for us, especially for Grandma Margaret because she was diabetic.

"Mom, did you hear what I said...what I want for my *ninth* birthday?" I emphasized *ninth*.

She nodded, "Yes. Let me think about it for a while."

"Mom, Sharon said it will take two days to get to Miami. They spent a night in the hotel on the way to the beach."

The phone rang, so Mom went to the living room to answer it. Mom and I were already dressed nicely for the guest.

I went out to the front porch and sat on Grandma's rocking chair. My feet hardly touched the floor, but I managed to rock myself. The evening breeze was very nice on my face. My thoughts went back to Sharon and Toby, who just came back from a summer vacation.

Sharon has light-brown hair. Mine is dark brown, almost black. We both are at the same height and wear long straight hair. Her brother, Toby, is only a year younger than we are but short for his age and always looks frail. Sharon and I are often told to keep an eye on Toby whenever we are outdoors. We do not mind it at all because he behaves well just like us.

Because of their father's frequent absence, Toby is not exposed to the boy's stuff, such as playing basketball, baseball, and the games that boys would prefer to play. Besides, there are no boys in our neighborhood, so we treat Toby as one of us.

He does not mind being one of us. We jump rope most of the time at the driveway. Toby is very good at it. Whenever Toby is outdoors with us, his nose runs constantly for some reason. Ms. Norma showed Toby how to blow his nose with tissue, but Toby just let it run. He looked yucky. Sharon and I wiped his nose with tissue often.

One time, we told Toby to blow his nose just as Ms. Norma did. He blew tons of yucky stuff that overflowed to our hands; we both screamed and ran straight into the bathroom to wash off our hands. When we came back, Toby thanked us with a big smile. He was really a nice kid.

When they came to play at my house, we played Barbie. Toby was able to change Barbie's skirts, tops, pants, and even panties just like us. He braided her hair better than we did. I did not have Ken, but I had three Barbies. After we dressed them up, we played house. Toby imitated a girl's voice. He was funny. Sharon and I laughed a lot. Anyway, we were almost like siblings.

While I was rocking the chair, I switched my thought to Grandma Margaret. I remembered her gentle smile on her pale face and her brownish-blonde hair just like Mom's. Once I asked Mom why my hair color was so dark, she just smiled and said, "I will make your hair just like mine when you get older."

One day, when I was in the first grade, Mom was called by the hospital in the middle of the day. I remember Ms. Norma picked me up after school, and I stayed with Sharon and Toby for several nights.

I was told that Mom had to take Grandma back to her hometown, New Orleans. I thought Grandma was visiting her relatives.

At Sharon's house, I did not forget to brush my teeth before bedtime. I slept in Sharon's big bed with her. Toby came over and wanted to sleep with us, but Ms. Norma put him in his own bed.

Mom came home alone without Grandma three days later. I did not ask her where Grandma was. I thought she would be home soon after visiting more relatives in her hometown. For a while, I was all right without her, but a week or two weeks later, I could not stand it any longer because I missed her so much. I asked Mom to call her on the phone and tell her to come home soon.

Mom made me sit on the sofa and explained where Grandma went—heaven—where no one could call or talk to her. I did not understand what she meant and why Grandma had to visit heaven. I was angry with Grandma because she went away without saying goodbye to me, and now Mom was telling me that I could no longer see her or talk to her. I cried loudly like a spoiled brat and kept screaming, "I want Grandma now!"

Mom let me cry on her shoulder for a while and finally said, "Grandma will be watching over us from heaven, and she will always live in our hearts. I know you miss her very much. So do I, but we must be strong, help each other, and live happily. That is what Grandma Margaret wanted us to do—be happy. We will always remember her and her kindness." Mom held me tightly and we cried together. On that day, I learned about *death* and *heaven*.

Chapter 1
The Ninth Birthday

After Grandma's passing, my mother started working at my school as a librarian. Before that, she had worked for the women's college in Gainesville with her MLS degree as a librarian.

Mom probably made more money in college than in our public school, but we both were very happy because we went to school together and came home together. Because of it, I did not have to ride a school bus anymore. Moreover, we both had the same summer and Christmas breaks.

When she started working for the public school system, she had to attend a weeklong conference in Atlanta every summer. She drove to Atlanta early in the morning and came home in the afternoon. Ms. Norma kept me with Sharon and Toby all day until Mom came home. Ms. Norma did not mind having me at her house because we kids got along well.

If the Gordon family had to be on a long summer vacation during Mom's conference, I was sent to a nursery school for a week. I did not like it because there were many toddlers and crawling babies all around me, so I told Mom that I was old enough to stay home alone, but she did not think so.

While Ms. Norma was growing up, Grandma Margaret was like her aunt. After Mom moved into Grandma's house, Ms. Norma and Mom helped each other to take care of their babies. By doing it, they were bonded like sisters.

After Grandma's death, Ms. Norma helped Mom a lot—babysitting me or picking me up from school from time to time when Mom had some faculty meetings. Ms. Norma was tall and chubby, but Mom was rather short and lean.

Over the years, when Grandma Margaret was alive, the Gordon family and my family celebrated Christmas together just like a family. Mom and Ms. Norma took turns to cook Christmas dinner. When it was Mom's turn to cook, the Gordon family ate dinner with us in our house. After dinner, we walked to their house, ate Ms. Norma's desserts, and exchanged Christmas gifts.

Chris Gordon was an expert on making eggnog. He let the children taste it. It was very sweet, but he told us the kids we're not supposed to drink his eggnog, so he made milkshake for the children instead.

One Christmas day, when Grandma had too much eggnog, she could not walk straight. I thought she had a diabetic reaction because of too much sugar intake from eggnog, but I learned later that she was intoxicated from the eggnog. Mom had a hard time holding onto her chubby waist to walk her home. I walked behind them carrying their pocketbooks and Christmas gifts. Grandma was singing "White Christmas" all the way home. Indeed, I remembered we had a white Christmas on that day in North Georgia.

During the summer, whenever Sharon and Toby left for a long summer vacation with their parents, I often wished I were already a grown-up so I could earn a lot of money like Chris Gordon and drive to see a real beach in Miami with Mom.

Since I was not a grown-up, I usually satisfied myself by daydreaming—Mom and I have a two-room suite in a nice beach hotel in Miami. The beautiful white-sand beach is seen from the window. In the evening, we dress nicely and sit in the outdoor café close to the beach so we can hear the sound of waves while we eat. We see the full moon over the ocean. After dinner, Mom takes a bubble bath like a wealthy lady or a movie star. I take a bubble bath in my room like a young princess. We wear pretty summer robes and enjoy the sea breeze at the window while watching the full moon over the ocean. Mom tucks me into a big fluffy bed, kisses my forehead, and then I fall asleep like a Sleeping Beauty.

Although Grandma Margaret left the house to Mom after her passing, Mom had to pay all the bills—water, electricity, gas, food, gasoline, property tax, city tax, school tax, home insurance, and car insurance.

When Grandma was alive, she paid most of the bills from her social security income. Mom bought groceries, my school clothes, shoes, and made car and insurance payments. When she had some money left, she bought some nice dresses for Grandma and even for Barbies, but now she barely made ends meet every month. That was another reason I wished I were already a grown-up so I could help her financially.

While rocking Grandma's chair, I tried to figure out how I could help Mom financially so we both could see the ocean in Miami on my ninth birthday.

I tell Mom not to buy any birthday gifts this year; instead, she must use that money to buy gasoline for the trip. On the way to Miami, we eat Mom's good sandwiches to save the restaurant money and sleep in the car to save the hotel money.

At Miami Beach, I taste the ocean water and witness the magical waves to satisfy my curiosity. If possible, we both swim in the ocean and ride the big waves together.

On the way home, we finish the remaining sandwiches at the rest area and brush our teeth before snuggling into the car to sleep. If Mom would agree to my trip plan, I could get to see the ocean for the first time.

Suddenly, I was startled by Mom's voice. "Lily, where are you? I need your help."

Mom wants me to set up the table with three cloth napkins and three sets of everything including Grandma's elegant Thanksgiving china. She comes to the dining room to see what else we need on the table. As we have never invited a male guest alone in the past, I was curious.

"Mom, how well do you know him?"

"Who?"

"Our houseguest."

"Oh, Tom. We actually grew up together in New Orleans, but we have not seen each other for ages. We lost contact when we moved here. When Tom's mother, Eunice, was buried, his father, Jake, learned that the funeral director, Mr. Turner, was a cousin of Grandma Margaret's husband. Grandma Margaret and Mr. Turner were buried in the same cemetery. That was how Tom found out our whereabouts. Tom's mother, Eunice, was my mother's best friend. They traveled to Paris together many years ago. They also met each other for lunch almost every week for years. I heard she was heartbroken when my mother died and stayed home like a hermit for a while."

Mom put the salt and pepper set on the table.

"Anyway, several years ago when his mother, Eunice, was dying, Tom came back to New Orleans to help his father, Jake, in the family business so his father could spend more time with his mother. Their longtime housekeeper was already gone to Mexico to take care of her own sick mother. Now Tom took over the family business and became the president of the Rousseau Export Company. He bought an antebellum mansion in Biloxi with the money his mother left for him."

She looked around the table and continued. "My brother, Alan, and Tom were best friends from primary school to college. They graduated from the same college in New Orleans. After college, Tom went to Chicago to pursue his law degree. My brother worked as a pilot for several months, but he decided to work for my parents. Alan became the vice president in the company, and our family vacation home in Biloxi was officially given to him because he was the heir to the Dubois Import Company, but it was mysteriously stolen after his death."

She went back to the kitchen and brought a bowl of salad. As I did not have anything else to do, I decided to sit and listen to Mom. She changed the subject to her best friend, Yuri Tanaka.

"Let me tell you all about my best friend, Yuri Tanaka. She was a daughter of my parents' longtime friend in Japan. My parents graduated from the same college with her father. In fact, my entire family including my brother and I graduated from the same college. My parents sponsored Yuri Tanaka to attend the college with me. I was thrilled to have her in our house. We became like sisters. She wanted to be an accountant. I wanted to be a librarian. We went to school together and studied together. My family really adored her."

Again, she went back to the kitchen to check on her pork chops and came back.

"We drove to our family vacation home in Biloxi almost every weekend and studied a lot there. Alan and Tom often came and studied too. They were two years ahead of us in college. We feasted on Yuri's Japanese cuisine almost every weekend. The first summer when Yuri was with us, her father invited all of us including Tom to Japan. We rode a bullet train and visited many places. I would never forget how fast the bullet train went. After Yuri and I finished college, she wanted to stay and take the CPA tests, so she extended her student visa for another year. I was getting a master's degree in library science."

She went back to the kitchen and stayed there for a while.

I shouted, "Mom, do you need any help?"

"No, I am all set." She came back with a cup of coffee, sat with me, and continued talking, but she changed the subject back to Tom.

"Let me go back to Tom. We lived only a block away from each other just like Sharon and you. We saw each other almost every day and grew up together like blood-related siblings. After Tom became a lawyer in Chicago, he landed a job in a big law firm. By then, he was already married to a lawyer who went to school together. Later I found out his wife was my brother's old girlfriend who desperately wanted to marry Alan when they were in high school. My brother refused because he was too young for marriage. Besides, he did not like her possessive personality as well as her obsessive jealousy. I did not tell Alan, but I found out she was a big-time gold digger and a social climber. She only dated the sons of the wealthy families on St. Charles Avenue. I think Alan was her first target. Tom was probably targeted as well. Anyway, six months later, she divorced Tom."

"What is a big-time gold digger?"

"Sorry, I did not mean to talk about someone like that. Don't tell Tom what I said about his ex-wife." Mom did not explain what a big-time gold digger was, but I figured she was not a good person.

"Why did she leave him?"

"At that time, Tom rejected his father's offer—take over the family business. See, normally a gold digger wants to marry a person with millions of dollars. She probably figured that she could not be a rich man's wife in the future because Tom would not take over the lucrative family business, so she left him and then came back to Alan, hoping he would take her back. She knew he was already the vice president in the Dubois Import Company, and certainly he would become a wealthy man in the future."

She sipped coffee and continued. "Anyway, she begged Alan for a job. My brother was a compassionate man, so he decided to hire her as an assistant lawyer to their company lawyer until she was able to land a real lawyer's job in the city. Nobody knew why she approached Alan, but I suspected she was going to use her movie-star-like beauty to marry Alan later. That is how a gold digger would do. Alan was already married at that time, so I did not worry about him. One day, he finally told her about his marriage. Can you imagine how disappointed she was?"

Mom did not say whom Uncle Alan married, but I figured who she was because I saw a picture of their engagement. Not long ago, I accidently found an old album inside Mom's dresser. I forgot what I was looking for, but in the bottom drawer, I saw an old album hidden among her old clothes.

I did not mean to invade her privacy, but I became very curious. As Mom was out for a walk, I sat on the floor to peek into the album without taking it out of the drawer.

In the large album, all the family pictures were displayed neatly. I recognized my grandparents and Uncle Alan because Mom had their framed pictures on top of her dresser along with my school pictures.

I saw some pictures of Mom standing in front of the Eiffel Tower with her brother and a young man. She was probably in high school. I had never seen any of my mother's wedding pictures with my father. In fact, I did not know what my father looked like because she told me she lost all her wedding pictures and my father's pictures when she was evicted from her family mansion in New Orleans. As she was so reluctant to bring up the subject of my father, I stopped asking.

I saw several pictures of Mom with a man. They were smiling at each other lovingly. I wondered if that man was my father, but when I saw another picture with three other people's names listed—Alan Dubois, Yuri Tanaka, and Tom Rousseau—I realized the man was Tom Rousseau, and the young man in front of the Eiffel Tower was Tom Rousseau as well.

I also saw some pictures of them with Yuri in front of a temple in Japan. There were many pictures of Uncle Alan and Yuri Tanaka. Some pictures showed Uncle Alan kissing Yuri Tanaka affectionately. Another one showed Uncle Alan holding Yuri's hand and putting a ring on her finger, and under the picture, it said, "Engaged." Apparently, Mom took those pictures because I recognized her penmanship.

I did not see any of their wedding pictures, but at the very end of the album, I saw two sealed envelopes—one was addressed to Michelle Dubois and the other one was to Yuri Tanaka Dubois. Yuri Tanaka had the surname Dubois. That was how I figured Uncle Alan married Mom's best friend, Yuri Tanaka. I heard the door. I closed the album in a hurry, pushed back the drawer quietly, and tiptoed back to my room.

I knew about Uncle Alan and Yuri Tanaka, but I could not ask Mom anything about them, such as what happened to Yuri Tanaka after she lost her husband. If she said Yuri Tanaka married her brother, Alan, then I could ask many questions. I must wait until she would tell me more about them.

I could not ask Mom much about Tom either, but as I saw the pictures of Tom and Mom with their affectionate smiles, I became curious about their relationship. *Were they lovers when they were in college?*

Mom had another sip and continued. "Without Alan, the gold digger had nothing—no hope of being a wealthy wife. Her ego was down, so was her social status. After four or five months later, Alan and my parents were killed in an airplane crash." Mom sighed and continued.

"My speculation is—after poisoning my parents in the office, they called CDC in Atlanta to make an appointment. Knowing Alan was a pilot, they got a Cessna for Alan to fly. I drove my parents and Alan to the airfield. They were already there and looked so loyal and sympathetic, but I believe they had already tampered with the Cessna by then. After the tragedy, without my consent, they called the funeral home to cremate the bodies of my parents and Alan. They probably tried to hide the evidence of the poison by cremating them. I am glad Tom is coming today. I hope he can help me find those crooks."

The doorbell rang. There stood a nice-looking man with a beautiful smile. He dressed nicely with a tie and a brown jacket. He looked a little older than the picture I saw, but he was still handsome. He was holding two gift boxes.

As soon as he walked in the house, he bent over slightly, gave me a box, and whispered, "Lily, Happy birthday!" and shook my hand, and then turned to greet Mom with another box. He hugged Mom tightly as though he missed her so much and for so many years.

When he turned to me, he told me to open the present to see if I liked it or not; if not, he was going to exchange it. When I opened the box, I screamed aloud because I saw Barbie's long party dresses in three different colors. I wondered if he knew I had three Barbies. Mom probably told him those three Barbies needed new dresses.

I went to hug him and said, "Thank you very much. I really like them. My Barbies never owned long party dresses before. Thank you."

"You are welcome." He said it with a smile and hugged me back. Tom gave Mom a box of assorted chocolates. I remembered Mom used to buy a box of chocolates and hid it in her bedroom because she knew Grandma could devour a whole box of chocolates in few minutes. Grandma was diabetic, so Mom had to keep an eye on her sugar intake. After Grandma's passing, she stopped buying chocolates—she probably felt guilty for hiding the boxes from her when she was alive. However, I knew Mom loved chocolates.

Her pork chop dinner was delicious as usual. For dessert, she served cheesecake and the assorted chocolates that Tom gave her. I picked two pieces of chocolates and ate them with milk. Tom got a slice of cheesecake and devoured it, and praised how delicious it was.

Mom is a good baker and cook. From time to time, she let me bake cookies, but I was not taught to make cheesecake yet. Grandma Margaret was always thankful because Mom cooked delicious balanced meals for her.

Mom looked beautiful with somewhat rouged cheeks. Her large white-collar blouse made her very elegant, and she looked like a high-society lady. Tom Rousseau looked mesmerized by Mom's beauty.

Tom kept saying I looked just like Uncle Alan. Mom glanced at me and just smiled. I wondered why he did not say I looked like my mother. Well, I was not as pretty as Mom was, but I looked all right. Tom was probably right. I looked more like Uncle Alan with long eyelashes and hazel eyes. Mom had green eyes.

I was getting very sleepy, so I excused myself to brush my teeth. I thanked Tom again for the birthday present. Mom followed me, helped me change into a nightwear, and tucked me into bed. She kissed my forehead and said, "I will talk to Tom to see if we can stay in his mansion on the beach. Remember his beach house is in Biloxi, not in Miami, but you still could see a real beach and taste the ocean water. Your dream might come true on your ninth birthday. Sleep tight and have a wonderful dream." She kissed my forehead one more time and left.

My dream on that night was indeed wonderful—I saw the bluest blue ocean and the big white waves. At the end, I was riding big waves with Mom and Tom Rousseau.

Chapter 2
Biloxi

When I got up early in the morning of my birthday, Mom gave me a birthday present—a big wooden jewelry box. She knew I wanted it badly because I did not have my own. I used her jewelry box to store my necklaces and earrings so I would not lose them.

As my ears were pierced when I started school, I've needed a jewelry box for a long time. I thanked her and removed my necklaces and earrings from her box. The jewelry box has a carved flowery design on top and several tray drawers that could store many more earrings, necklaces, and bracelets.

"Lily, it is going to be very hot, so wear these pink shorts with a white top. Make sure to wear sandals."

"Mom, do I need tennis shoes?"

"No, sandals and thongs would do okay on the beach."

I put on pink shorts and a white top first and wore white sandals. Mom and I carried our own suitcases to the car and put them in the trunk. A big ice chest was filled with drinks, some sandwiches, apples, oranges, and a cake box. After she shut the trunk, she went inside the house again, brought a pillow, two beach towels, and a box of books, which we checked out from the library yesterday. She put them on the back seat.

"I almost forgot our books." Mom and I are bookworms. Sharon and Toby are bookworms too. Mom took us to the local library every week. One day, on the way home from the library, she asked us what we would like to be when we grow up. Toby said he wanted to be a truck driver just like his father, but his father told him to go to college to be someone important, so Toby did not know what he wanted to be. I told Mom that I wanted to be a librarian just like her, but she said I should dream bigger. Sharon said she wanted to be a scientist. In the end, Mom told us to keep reading, making good grades so we could go to college, and the college education should be the key to our success in the future.

She put plenty of sunscreen lotion on my face, arms, and legs before putting a seat belt around me. After checking the front door and the kitchen door, she sat in the car and sipped some coffee, and then put her mug next to my juice bottle on the drink tray. After she found a pack of chewing gums from her pocketbook, she said, "Coffee and chewing gum will keep me awake when I drive."

She gave me a marked highway map and said it would take at least six hours to get to Biloxi, and I would be her navigator with the map. After passing the city of Atlanta, we were on I-85 toward Montgomery, Alabama.

When we stopped at McDonald's on the highway exit somewhere in Alabama, she bought a large cup of coffee to refill her mug. We ate some sausage biscuits for breakfast in the car. She showed me where we were on the map before driving off to the highway. Soon, Mom turned to I-65 toward Mobile, Alabama.

"Lily, Tom will be ordering your favorite pepperoni pizza to celebrate your ninth birthday. I told him you love pepperoni pizza. I bought a birthday cake—your favorite chocolate cake."

"Yum! I really love pepperoni pizza with lots of cheese and chocolate cake with milk. I am glad Tom came to see us. Otherwise, I would never get to see the ocean. Does Tom really live on the beach?"

"Not exactly. In Biloxi, the scenic drive divides the beach and the homes. All the homes including Tom's antebellum mansion are on the coastal banks that are like small hills. In order to get to the beach, you have to go down the hill, cross the scenic drive, and then to the beach."

"What is an antebellum mansion?"

"It is a style of big old homes. Antebellum means before the war—before the Civil War. Biloxi was once a resort place for the wealthy plantation owners and merchants in the south. Antebellum mansions usually have two stories with tall pillars in front of the house. After the Civil War, some were converted to hotels, some were remodeled, and some remained the same."

"What happened in the Civil War?"

"I am glad you asked. All Americans including the children should know about the American Civil War, which happened exactly 130 years ago from this year, 1991. It started in 1861 and ended 1865. When Abraham Lincoln became the sixteenth president, he wanted to abolish the slavery, but the eleven Southern slave states retaliated because they wanted to keep their slaves in their cotton fields, sugar cane fields, rice fields, and other agricultural fields. Therefore, they declared secession from the United States of America."

"What is *secession*?"

"It means to withdraw from the government. They did not want their states to be in the United State of America anymore, so they formed their own government called the Confederate States of America and elected their own president. Abraham Lincoln as the president of the Union government did not believe in the secession to divide America into two countries. In the midst of his negotiation with the Southern states, a United States military fort in South Carolina was attacked by the Confederate soldiers."

"All the military forts belonged to the Union government?"

"Yes. There were many federal properties, such as military forts, undeveloped government lands, mountains, and forests in the South. Therefore, Abraham Lincoln ordered seventy-five thousand Union soldiers to reclaim and protect the federal properties in the South, and at the same time, he tried to reunite the American people under one nation just as before, but the Confederate government stubbornly resisted and fought against the Union soldiers from 1861 to 1865."

The traffic was not bad at all on I-65—no one was in front of us and only a few cars were behind us.

"The total casualty was over six hundred thousand out of fifty million US population at that time. It was the most devastating and heartbreaking war in the American history because the Americans were killing each other—the enemies could be their old classmates, distant cousins, and relatives. When the Union won the war, Abraham Lincoln proclaimed the emancipation of the slaves in America by dismantling the Confederate government and reunited the Southern states just as before, but each of the eleven states reluctantly rejoined the Union, and the state of Georgia was the last one to rejoin. If the Union government did not win the war, the slavery system could have remained the same or America could have been divided into two countries."

She fumbled to get her coffee mug and sipped.

"Shortly after the war ended, Abraham Lincoln was assassinated by the Southern rebels. They had had tremendous animosity against the Northern Yankees and Union soldiers for many generations."

"Biloxi and New Orleans were with the Union or Confederate?"

"Biloxi belongs to the state of Mississippi, and New Orleans belongs to the state of Louisiana. Those states were with the Confederate government. In fact, Confederate president Jefferson Davis had lived in Biloxi for many years, but died in New Orleans."

I learned the names of all fifty states and their capital cities in school, such as Atlanta is the state capital of Georgia, Baton Rouge for Louisiana, and Jackson for Mississippi, but I did not know Biloxi belongs to Mississippi and New Orleans belongs to Louisiana until Mom told me.

My mother is a walking encyclopedia. She answered all my questions in the past, even in science and math. Being a librarian, I guess she has to be knowledgeable about every subject. Being a bookworm probably helped her accumulate more knowledge over the years.

"My brother, Alan, used to own an antebellum mansion in Biloxi. That mansion had been our family vacation home for generations. After Alan became vice president of the family business, my parents gave the mansion to him. If Alan were still alive, you should be the princess of that mansion."

She talked without thinking. I did not understand why I should be the princess of Uncle Alan's antebellum mansion. I glanced at her. She was looking at the road obliviously, probably reminiscing about her family. She sat up straight, fumbled to reach her coffee mug, and tried to have a sip.

"Whoa, it is empty. I must get some more coffee. I also need some gas. Lily, thank you for having a conversation with me. Otherwise, I would fall asleep on the wheel."

I heard something about a car accident on the radio once—a driver crashed through the guardrail, went over the cliff, and got killed. The police reported that the driver probably fell asleep on the wheel. I was tired and sleepy, but I was determined to stay awake for Mom and let her talk more so she would not fall asleep.

When we stopped at a gas station, she gave me some money to buy a large cup of coffee for her and a can of soda for me. I used the toilet, washed my hands first, and then bought our drinks.

After filling up the gas tank, Mom went inside to pay—the payment by credit card at pump was not invented yet in the early '90s. I refilled her coffee mug while waiting for her. She thanked me and sipped coffee before she started the engine.

"By the way, Tom told me Biloxi is becoming a casino city soon, probably next year in 1992. He thinks that Mississippi will definitely benefit from this move. See, Mississippi has been one of the poorest states in this country. The gambling industries could provide many jobs to the city and bring lucrative income to the state."

"What is a casino city?"

"A casino city is a gambling city like Las Vegas—a casino is a building for gambling. People bet money on games in the casino, but one problem Biloxi has is that the state only permits the gambling activities on the water. All the hotels in Biloxi are built on the coastal banks away from the water. Therefore, if the hotel owners want a casino business, they have to build their casino buildings separately on the water. That would inconvenience the hotel guests because they have to cross the scenic drive to gamble."

I did not understand what Mom was talking about. I thought she was repeating what Tom told her. The only thing I understood was that Biloxi would be a gambling city like Las Vegas soon. Mom realized she was talking to a child.

"Sorry, I talk too much. Anyway, Tom said Biloxi started building the casinos along the shore. Lily, find Highway 90 or Beach Boulevard along the coastline in Biloxi. That is the scenic drive I am talking about."

"I found it. Highway 90 goes all the way to Gulfport. Does the beach go with it too?"

Mom nodded. "Yes. I think the beach is about ten miles."

"A real beach? Ten miles? I can hardly wait to see it! By the way, Mom, Tom is such a nice person. I really like him. Was my father as nice as Tom?"

Mom got quiet, but she finally said, "Let's not talk about your father right now. I will tell you all about him when you grow older. Right now, let's have fun in Biloxi, but we must get to our destination first. Keep an eye on the road map, Ms. Navigator!"

My mother was very upbeat. She did not want to bring the subject of death on my birthday. She just wanted me to be happy, so I saluted to her. "Yes, Captain Dubois!"

Along the highway, we stopped at the rest area several times. Mom was stretching out her arms and legs before using the restroom. We ate her good sandwiches while resting. I did not know how many hours she drove, but I was increasingly getting tired as though I was the one driving the car, so I kept asking, "Mom, are we there yet?"

I noticed the trees along I-65 looked short, skinny, and malnourished. In North Georgia, we have many trees that look healthy, well nourished, green, and tall, especially where we lived.

In North Georgia, all the hardwood trees look gorgeous with green leaves during the summer. In the fall, the leaves change colors to yellow, purple, red, pink, and orange. The hills and mountains look just like huge flower gardens.

However, we have a kudzu problem along the mountain highways in North Georgia and all the way to the Smoky Mountain in North Carolina. The kudzu vines crawl over the trees and form a big green patch with layers of leaves that look like a green blob in a monster movie. In the warm seasons, they thrive wildly, but in the cold winters, its vines and leaves shrivel like dead plants.

However, as soon as the spring arrives, the leaves and vines reclaim the territory and grow wildly again. The layers of wide leaves could cut off the sunlight and suffocate the trees to death. The forest workers would clear the kudzu patches from time to time, but they grow right back. No one seems to know how to control the growth of kudzu.

One day, after we visited some friends of Grandma Margaret in North Carolina, Mom was driving on the mountain highway in the dark with the headlights on, Grandma sat in front with Mom, and I was in a car seat in the back. All of a sudden, I saw a green monster covering the front part of Mom's car. I was so scared that I closed my eyes and screamed. Mom and Grandma were startled by my scream. Mom stopped her car on the roadside instantly and checked me out by asking, "What happened?"

I kept saying, "A green monster," while pointing to the front windshield. By then, I did not see the green monster. Later, when I got older, I realized that the green monster I saw was a huge kudzu patch at the side of the highway.

In spite of the kudzu problem, the beautiful foliage in the autumn is just breathtaking. Each tree looks like a bouquet of flowers. Mom and Ms. Norma never failed to drive us children to see the autumn leaves every year. We often bought apples and pumpkins on the way home.

When we turned onto I-10 at Mobile, Alabama, I started seeing patchy marshlands along the bridge. Mom told me those marshland swamps are called *bayou* in French.

She also said some people in this bayou region have French surnames because French ancestors once owned the south of the bayou region including New Orleans and Biloxi in the eighteenth century. She said our surname *Dubois* is a French name—her father's family, Dubois, was from France.

She talked about her mother, Marie, and her aunt Marianne who were born in Paris as French. Mom and Uncle Alan spent every summer in Paris and learned how to speak French with their grandparents who were language professors. Mom did not mention the trip to Paris with Tom and Uncle Alan, but I knew it from the photos I saw in the album.

We took the exit ramp to the city of Biloxi and crossed a lagoon by a bridge. At the end of the bridge, a big water body appeared. *Wow! Am I looking at an ocean?* "Mom, is that the ocean?"

She nodded. As Mom turned to the scenic drive, I just kept staring at the ocean.

The ocean did not look like the one I saw on TV. I did not see any big waves and the water was somewhat murky, not blue at all. It looked just like Lake Lanier. Mom said the ocean is on the Mississippi Coastal Sound with the shallow bottom. That is why the water is not clear and waves are quiet.

I was not disappointed. I did not care about the waves and the color. I was just happy to see an ocean and a real beach for the first time. The beach was seen endlessly along the scenic drive. The sands on the beach were white and plentiful, unlike the lake beach.

I begged Mom to stop at the beach because I wanted to taste the ocean water to see if it would taste salty or not. Mom did not mind it at all. She U-turned and parked her car along the beach.

I took off my sandals and stepped out of the car onto the sands. All of a sudden, I felt a burning sensation under my feet. I screamed and hopped like a mad rabbit all the way to the wet sand area. Mom was laughing. She probably forgot to warn me about the hot sands in the summer.

I scooped up the ocean water with my hand and put it in my mouth. Wow! Sharon is right! It is salty! When I spitted it out with a noise, Mom was again laughing. I waded into the water to see the waves. The waves were small and quiet, but indeed, they moved back and forth without stopping.

When we arrived at Tom's antebellum mansion, he came out to welcome us at the driveway. He helped us carry our suitcases upstairs. The mansion was humongous with many bedrooms. I saw many antique furniture throughout the house. Mom and I each got a room upstairs.

That evening, I had the most wonderful birthday party with Mom and Tom Rousseau. It was like celebrating my birthday with a mother and a father. They sang the birthday song for me, and then I blew nine candles.

My ninth birthday was something like a dream came true. It was unbelievably special because I saw an ocean and a real beach, tasted the ocean water, and saw the magical waves for the first time.

When I could not eat any more pepperoni pizza or cake, I begged Tom and Mom to take me to the beach. They made me wear the rubber thongs to protect my feet from some broken glass on the beach.

They held my hands from each side like the parents who would help their young child cross the street. I took off my thongs at the wet sand area and gave them to Mom. I was so happy that I started hopping, dancing, skipping, prancing, jumping, twirling, and even flipping like a crazy little creature. They were laughing at me.

The moonlight was so bright that we did not need a flashlight. Mom and Tom seemed to be enjoying the evening breeze while walking behind me. I wished they would hold each other's hands, but they did not. Finally, I heard, "Lily, it is time to go back." I hopped back and joined them. Again, they held my hands to cross the street.

I took a shower, brushed my teeth, wore a summer nightwear, and shouted aloud at Mom and Tom from the second floor, "Good night! Thank you for the party. I had the most wonderful birthday party ever."

Mom stood up to come toward me, probably to tuck me in, but I yelled loudly, "Mom, I am not a baby anymore! I will tuck myself in. Good night." The bed was huge and comfortable. I was moving around as though I was swimming in the ocean and then fell asleep.

Chapter 3
Jefferson and Marie

Jefferson's father, Richard Dubois, had lived all his life on St. Charles Avenue, and so did Richard's father, Daniel Dubois, who had a big furniture business, which included antique furniture.

The Dubois family had inherited their ancestors' wealth from the sugarcane plantation before the Civil War. With their wealth, one of the ancestors built the mansion on St. Charles Avenue and the antebellum mansion in Biloxi. As family tradition, those homes were given to the heir who was willing to take over the family business in each generation.

Richard Dubois was the only child of Daniel Dubois. Therefore, he was the heir to the family fortune. When Richard was young, his mother passed away. Daniel Dubois remarried several times, but divorced at the end.

After graduating from high school, Richard married a daughter of his father's friend. The married couple took the mansion, and Daniel moved to the guesthouse in the backyard.

Richard worked for his father after his marriage. He was a hardworking son and loyal to his father, but he was somewhat retarded and had no social skills to greet the customers at the store. He would rather sit at the desk to do bookkeeping instead of meeting the customers.

Daniel was a dashing young man when he was at Richard's age. He charmed many young girls before he married one. At the store, he always smiled. His tone of voice was peaceful and soothing to the customers as well as to his employees.

Even though Richard knew he was not cut up to be a salesperson, he tried very hard to learn the family business. Moreover, he loved his father and his own family a lot. His wife gave him a daughter, Margaret, first and a son, Jefferson, two years later.

When Daniel Dubois became ill, he sold the furniture business and gave the money to Richard. When Daniel handed Richard a check, he emphasized that his son must multiply the money by starting a new business of his choice.

He repeated, "Remember to multiply this money. Keep the fortune in the Dubois family." Several weeks later, Daniel passed away quietly. By then, Margaret finished high school, but Jefferson was still in school.

Richard bought a warehouse in the shipyard to start an import business from scratch and expected his entire family to help him, but Margaret eloped with a Creole and moved to North Georgia. His wife left him for their neighbor's husband. He was devastated, but he never showed his emotion to anybody.

Richard worked long hours every day alone, seven days a week; he was obsessed with what his father said—to multiply the money and keep the fortune to the Dubois family.

Jefferson missed his mother and sister very much, especially at the dinner table, but he understood how they felt about his father. Richard Dubois was a difficult person—stubborn, introverted, hardly smiled, no social skills, and very stingy. He had no charms and paid no attention to his attire—he dressed like a farmer or a laborer. He was stout, bald, somewhat ugly, and looked older than his actual age.

Jefferson helped his father after school, even on the weekends. He realized he was the only family his father had. Whenever he saw his father who was hunching over the desk in the office, he felt tears in his eyes for some reason.

Jefferson and his father worked late every day. Jefferson had to prepare dinner. His father did not believe in hiring a housekeeper or eating out. Therefore, whatever Jefferson cooked, his father ate it.

At the beginning, the only cooking he knew was to boil eggs; therefore, he made egg sandwiches for dinner. Gradually, Jefferson learned how to cook; he was able to grill steak and fry chicken, but most of the time, especially when he was tired, he made ham or turkey sandwiches. His father never complained.

After graduating from high school, Jefferson wanted to go to college in the neighborhood. Richard did not like that because he needed his son to be in the office all day. Nevertheless, as his son promised to work for him after school and on the weekends, he finally paid for Jefferson's college.

* * *

Marie Dupont worked twenty hours a week in the library. She was a foreign exchange student from France with a scholarship, but she needed some spending money, so she worked.

She shared a small apartment with another foreign student and worked in the library between classes. Her work was to put the returned books back to the bookshelves.

Marie learned about Melvil Dewey, who invented the Dewey Decimal Classification system. He was born in New York in 1851 and worked as a librarian in a college library. His invention was first adopted by the Library of Congress. In the early twentieth century, his invention of the decimal indexing in ten categories was widely used in the American libraries. Later, it was adopted in the libraries all around the world. He died in 1931. Although his invention (DDC) is still used throughout the world including American libraries, the university libraries in the United States now use the Library of Congress Classification (LCC) system.

There were neither computers nor scanners in use in the libraries at that time; the librarians had to put each catalog card into the book pocket before shelving the books.

One day, Marie had a mount of books on a cart. As she was short, most of the time, she used a folding ladder to reach the top shelves, but on that day, she could not find the ladder, so she did her best to reach the top shelf, but the top shelf was still too high.

When she stepped on the ground shelf to reach the top shelf, she was able to reach it, but all of a sudden, all the books on the top shelf came down on her like an avalanche of books.

Marie was hit on her head by several heavy books, and her body was flat on the floor and buried under tons of books. A tall boy who was passing by came to rescue her by removing the books from her face, chest, and abdomen in a hurry. After that, he tapped on the girl's face lightly to see if she was okay, but she did not respond, seemed to be unconscious and not breathing; the boy did not hesitate to do a mouth-to-mouth resuscitation, which he learned from a CPR class.

After several tries, the girl opened her eyes and looked around the people who came to see the commotion. When she opened her eyes, her beauty mesmerized the boy. He still felt her soft plump lips for some reason. It was his first time to touch someone's lips with his lips. The girl did not know what happened because she was unconscious for a minute or so. She had no clue someone did mouth-to-mouth resuscitation to revive her.

All the audience helped put books back on the shelf for the girl. The boy was already gone. Nobody realized someone saved the girl's life, or at least brought her breath back.

After the mouth-to-mouth resuscitation, the boy often became aroused thinking about it and wanted to touch her lips with his lips again, or if possible, he wanted to kiss her.

He started looking for the girl by walking around the aisles in the library. If she was there, he pulled a book from the shelf in front of him, pretended to read. Jefferson was shy like his father, but looked sophisticated with his handsome face unlike his father.

One day, when Marie could not find the folding ladder again, she bravely asked a tall boy who was reading a book in the same aisle, "Excuse me, would you kindly put this book on the top shelf for me?"

The boy's dream came true. He almost ran to help her and saw her beautiful face again. She had the smoothest skin with rouged cheeks, the most beautiful green eyes with long eyelashes, and her lips were plump and sexy.

For some reason, the boy's body was tremulous. He wanted to ask her if he could kiss her, but that was too much, so he just smiled.

She thanked him with a beautiful smile. Oh, he wanted to hold her and give her mouth-to-mouth resuscitation again, but instead he courageously introduced himself.

"I am Jefferson Dubois. What is your name?"

"Marie Dupont."

"Are you French descent like me?"

"Yes, but I am a real French native—a direct import from France. I am an exchange student with a scholarship."

"Wow! You must be very smart." Jefferson was so tall that he was actually looking down at her when he talked, but Marie did not mind because she grew up with a tall father and a tall sister. She and her mother were short.

As Marie came to another book that needed to be on the top shelf, she asked Jefferson again. Eventually, Jefferson helped her put all the books back until the cart was emptied. After that, Jefferson often met Marie in the aisle.

One day, Jefferson bravely asked her out to eat beignets at Café Du Monde. As she said yes, he called his father on the phone in the library and told him he would be a little late. Jefferson knew he had to finish many invoices that day for the next day's shipment.

In his car, Jefferson explained to Marie that he had to work after school every day and even on the weekends. Marie was very impressed by his determination to finish his college by working seven days a week.

After they ate beignets, he took her back to her apartment. She thanked him by kissing both of his cheeks, just as French would do. Jefferson was aroused. In his car, he touched his cheeks and thought about her plump sexy lips.

Richard's business was growing. He was able to hire two clerks to do invoices. The clerks had to depend on their old-fashioned typewriters or their own handwritings to complete the numerous invoices. Again, there were no computers in the office yet.

As Jefferson was even-tempered and had a likable personality unlike his father, the customers would not talk to anyone else but Jefferson when they had some problems with their purchased products or invoices. He listened to the customers and tried to find the best solution for the problem, which could be a full refund. The customers were always satisfied with Jefferson's generous solution. His father did not like that, but Jefferson ignored his father's penny-pinching attitude.

His father did the accounting book. Even though he did not have any training on accounting, he learned the basic bookkeeping skills in high school; besides, he wanted to keep an eye on every penny he and his son made.

Despite having no social life, Jefferson met a Japanese exchange student, Masaki Tanaka, in class, and they became very good friends. Their major was the same in business. As they were taking the same subjects most of the time, they met in the library and studied together, but Jefferson still could not hang around with Masaki after school.

Jefferson finally told Masaki about his father who owned an import business and why he had to work for him seven days a week. He did not want to tell Masaki about his mother and sister, but he did. Masaki became very sympathetic and volunteered to help Jefferson whenever he had the time.

One weekend, Masaki came to the office. The office was inside the tall warehouse building that was enclosed with the wooden panels at the corner and had no ceiling. Masaki saw several desks with typewriters and telephones.

"Dad, this is my friend Masaki Tanaka, an exchange student from Japan. He came to help us today."

His father did not say anything, but nodded several times and kept working on the accounting book. As Jefferson had already alphabetized the customers' names from the invoices, Masaki volunteered to make an address book.

Masaki Tanaka and Marie Dupont became Jefferson's best friends. Marie often came to see them at the study table when they were in the library. Occasionally, they went out together to Café Du Monde for beignets before Jefferson went to work.

One day, when Jefferson was in the last semester of his senior year, his father passed away quietly in the office. Jefferson was at school. Richard did not have a heart attack or anything—he just died. One of the clerks found him dead at his desk. She thought he fell asleep because he had worked for long hours that day. The coroner said he died from extreme exhaustion or stress, which caused his body system to shut down. It was a natural cause.

Jefferson was devastated, but he made sure his father was buried in the Dubois family tomb in the cemetery. Masaki, Marie, few friends of the family, and his office clerks witnessed the burial. Neither his sister nor his mother came. Jefferson simply did not know their whereabouts.

Masaki and Marie followed Jefferson to his house on Saint Charles Avenue after the funeral. The mansion was humongous, but it looked old with their ancestors' antique furniture that reminded Marie of a haunted house or a ghost house.

Jefferson had never told Marie about his family situation, but he decided to tell her everything—how his mother and sister deserted his father and why he felt obligated to work for his father seven days a week, but now he did not know if he could handle the family business alone. He thought about selling the business.

Masaki and Marie convinced Jefferson to keep operating the family business. If he could survive for six months until his graduation, everything should be all right. They also promised to help Jefferson every day. He was so grateful that he offered them free shelter in the mansion. The three of them lived together, went to school together, and worked seven days a week in the office for six months together.

In the office, Marie did the bookkeeping as her major in school. Masaki sent the business flyers to the customers by using the address book he made. The hired clerks were getting orders on the phone and making invoices during the workdays.

On their graduation day, Jefferson proposed to Marie and she gladly said yes. Their wedding took place in the city hall before Masaki Tanaka went home to Japan.

They spent their honeymoon at the antebellum mansion in Biloxi; Jefferson told Marie about the mouth-to-mouth resuscitation in the library and confessed it was his love at first sight.

"How many times did you kiss me when I was unconscious?"

"I did not kiss you. I did mouth-to-mouth resuscitation. Well, probably three times, and then you opened your eyes like Snow White."

Marie confessed she fell in love with him when he followed her around in the library. On their honeymoon night, they made the most passionate love anybody could ever imagine.

Marie changed her student visa to a permanent resident visa with her marriage certificate. After she passed the CPA tests, she became the official accountant for the Dubois Import Company.

Because of Masaki Tanaka's help in Japan, the Dubois Company imported exclusively from Japan. They imported cameras, watches, clocks, video games, televisions, portable radios, Nintendo games, and other high-tech products.

Jefferson hired a professional builder to build a second floor using two-thirds of the loft in the tall warehouse building. The newly built second floor became the corporate office. By then, they had a dozen employees.

Another warehouse building next to the corporate office was purchased to store the merchandise. The antebellum mansion in Biloxi and the family mansion on St. Charles Avenue were refurbished. Each mansion looked new and the company was growing.

However, Jefferson still had the habit of going to the office to work on the weekends just as before. Marie did not like that at all because she was afraid that her husband might die young just like his father did from the exhaustion or stress, but as Jefferson's workaholic blood had long resided in his body, he could not help it. He had to go to the office seven days a week.

Marie had a good idea. One day, she told her husband if he promised not to go to the office on the weekends anymore, she would give him a surprise gift. Jefferson was curious. The surprise gift could be something he's been wanting since he was a child—a sports car, perhaps?

One day, he told Marie that he was not going to the office on the weekends anymore. Therefore, Marie drove him to their vacation home in Biloxi and showed him the surprise gift. As the gift came with Marie's plump sexy lips, Jefferson's entire body became instantly aroused.

After that, Jefferson could hardly wait for the weekend to come. His workaholic mind was cured, but he became obsessed and increasingly greedy. He wanted more gifts from Marie each time.

Because of his greediness, Marie gave a birth to a son, Alan, and two years later a daughter, Michelle. Marie hired a live-in nanny for the children and a full-time housekeeper for her so she could keep working for her husband.

Chapter 4
Jake and Eunice

The Rousseau family had a family business—an export company—exporting major staples such as flour, soybeans, rice, and potatoes to the nearby Caribbean islands. After Jake took over the family business, he expanded the business to Central America and South America. He only had half dozen employees, including his faithful longtime accountant who had worked for his father for many years and now for him.

His secretary did the international tariff and some legal work with the help of her lawyer husband. His hired clerks were all bilinguals—fluent in English and Spanish—because they dealt with the Spanish-speaking countries. Two did the invoices. Another two did the customer services and troubleshooting. Jake's family business was not as big as Jefferson's business, but the company was steadily lucrative.

Jake and his wife, Eunice, were high school sweethearts in the public school system. After graduation, Eunice moved away to Kentucky with her parents and seven younger siblings. She wanted to remain in New Orleans to go to college just as Jake was doing, but her parents were too poor. In fact, they had been on welfare as far as she could remember.

After Eunice moved to Kentucky, Jake missed her a lot, but he could not do anything about it. Instead, they wrote to each other. Eunice got herself a job at the department store in Louisville and found a roommate to share an apartment.

A year later, her roommate was married and moved away. Eunice was stuck with the rent, but at her workplace, she met a man who was just divorced and looking for a place to live, so she let him move in. At first, they were roommates in separate rooms, but later they lived like lovers sharing the expenses.

Before Jake's college graduation, he thought about Eunice as his wife, so he went to see her, but Eunice was living with a man. He came home heartbroken, but he wrote a sincere letter to Eunice, telling her how he's been in love with her all along. She wrote him the same.

Jake went back to Louisville, Kentucky, and brought Eunice back to New Orleans and married her. Jake moved out of his parent's house without telling them about his marriage and rented a one-bedroom apartment. As Jake was still in college, Eunice got a job at a gift shop to help pay the apartment rent.

When Jake's parents found out about their son's secret marriage, they demanded for Jake to bring his wife to their house; they were surprised to see Eunice because they knew her all along when Jake was in high school. They became very happy and offered Eunice a job in their family business.

After Jake's college graduation, his parents bought a mansion on St. Charles Avenue as their wedding gift as well as Jake's graduation gift. They knew their only child, Jake, would take over the family business after their retirements.

When they moved into the mansion, Eunice was on top of the world. She felt as though she was Cinderella. She recalled her family's poverty while she was growing up.

Several years later, Jake's parents retired. Now Jake was in charge of the family business. Eunice tirelessly helped Jake in the office. Mostly, she organized the files of invoices, customer contacts, legal documents, and other important documents.

As there was no such thing called a computer in the office at that time, Eunice became a computer. She could pull out any files that Jake or other employees wanted.

After they worked late in the office, they often stopped at the French Quarter to dine instead of cooking at home. They had a wonderful marriage and enjoyed managing the family business together.

Years went by. Jake's mother passed away first, and a year later, his father passed away. Jake and Eunice were grief-stricken for a long time because they were genuinely the nicest parents. Every holiday, they came to spend a night with them at St. Charles Avenue. Even though Eunice had no sign of having their grandchildren, they never complained.

After twelve years of their marriage, Eunice finally got pregnant. They almost gave up on having their own heir, but they were blessed with a baby boy. Jake actually cried in the hospital when he saw the baby.

However, after the childbirth, for some reason, Eunice became ill, complaining about aches and pains. She rapidly lost her weight and looked frail and sickly. Jake took his wife to see many doctors, but they found nothing wrong with Eunice. Finally, her primary doctor suggested for her to see a psychologist because she might be suffering from some kind of psychological trauma due to the childbirth.

Eunice refused to see a psychologist and refused to take the medicines the doctor prescribed for the aches and pains. She knew they could be highly addictive. She rather wanted to tolerate the pains instead of getting addicted. Besides, she felt better whenever she lay in bed. She eventually moved to the guestroom next to the master bedroom upstairs so she could sleep for many hours without her husband's bother.

Jake kept hiring many housekeepers to care for Eunice and the baby, but they kept quitting. Jake took many days off from work to care for them himself. As the baby was colicky, Jake had to get up during the night to take care of the baby. He was exhausted.

Jake checked with many acquaintances, especially with his employees in the office to see if they knew someone who would be interested in child care as a live-in housekeeper. He was willing to pay a lot more money than other families would pay and with a free furnished guesthouse to live in.

One of his Spanish-speaking clerks in the office told him that her sister-in-law, thirty-something years old, might be interested in the job. She lost her only child and her husband in a car accident a year ago. She came from Mexico, married the clerk's brother, and lived in New Orleans for years. She owns a car and has a proper resident visa.

Teresa Mendoza gladly accepted Jack's offer. She was very happy about living in a guesthouse free of charge because she had a difficult time paying the apartment rent after her husband's passing.

The day before Teresa Mendoza was supposed to move in, she came to meet Eunice and the baby. She noticed that the mother and the baby were suffering from malnutrition.

Jack showed her the guesthouse, which was separately built in the backyard. It was spacious with a king-size bed, a small sofa with a TV, a dresser, a closet, and a bathroom with a shower just like a one-bedroom apartment, but there was no kitchen.

When she moved into the guesthouse, she immediately started cooking balanced meals for the mother. For the baby, she patiently fed him the baby formula until he emptied it. Teresa served the mother three meals in bed. If the mother refused to eat the meals, she spoon-fed her forcefully.

Later, the mother was ordered to eat the balanced meals at the kitchen table three times a day. She did not like getting up, but she was afraid to be spoon-fed forcefully, so she reluctantly came to the kitchen table in her nightwear.

Eunice was never hungry, but if she did not eat, the housekeeper would spoon-feed her even at the kitchen table, so she had to finish her plate each time.

Gradually the mother and the baby gained weight and no longer looked like a pair of malnourished refugees. The more the mother gained weight, the lesser she complained about aches and pains.

When the baby became colicky from teething during the night, Teresa moved the baby crib to her guesthouse so Jake could sleep better. Teresa remembered her young son's teething and missed him a lot. Her son died at the age of three.

The mother stopped complaining about her aches and pains, but Teresa noticed she developed some kind of phobia. She refused to go outside. Teresa had to do all the shopping—grocery, baby clothes, diapers, and even the mother's panties.

Eunice was afraid of being in a crowd—she became a hermit. Because of it, her driver's license expired, and she had no desire of renewing it or no interest in driving her car. Jake gave his wife's car to Teresa when her old car croaked.

Jake treated Teresa like one of his company employees, giving her the weekends off. Actually, Jake did not want her to get too tired and quit. She was godsend to save his wife and son. He needed her.

On the weekends, Jake fixed breakfast and dinner for his wife and son. As Eunice was afraid of going to a restaurant for dinner, Jake did not have any choice but to cook every meal and ate at home on the weekends. He did not mind cooking. In fact, he started enjoying it.

When Tom became a toddler, Jake took him out every weekend to explore the city, especially the French Quarter area. Most of the time, the toddler was on Jake's shoulders. He loved the view from the top of his father's head. He giggled loudly when his father tickled his legs. He sat on his father's lap when they rode the streetcar.

When they got off, again Tom sat on Jake's shoulders. They walked around the French Quarter to buy some T-shirts; at Jackson Square, they saw many street performers, and sometimes, they walked the Riverwalk to see the Mississippi River.

At lunchtime, they tried a different restaurant each time at the French Quarter, but for dessert, they always walked to Café Du Monde to eat French doughnuts called beignets. The toddler loved beignets better than ice cream. The father always ordered some beignets to go for the mother who also loved them better than ice cream. Most importantly, they never forgot to pray in the Saint Louis Cathedral before they hopped back onto the streetcar.

As Tom had such a nice time with his father on the weekends, he wished every day was the weekend day. During his father's workdays, he was lonely. His mother would be resting in bed. Teresa would be cooking or cleaning the house. Most of the time, TV was Tom's companion.

Teresa spoke English without any problems, but she could not write or read English well. Eunice did not think about teaching her son the basic reading skills since she was ill. Therefore, Tom did not know how to read a book or count numbers before he started school.

On the contrary, Alan and Michelle Dubois had a nanny who taught them alphabets, words, basic reading skills, and adding, subtracting, multiplying, even dividing numbers. When Alan started school, Michelle had the nanny to herself. They spent a lot of time in the library together. Michelle became a bookworm.

When Michelle started school, her nanny went back to England. Michelle felt as though her most important person died and was buried. She cried in bed for many days after she left.

At school, the teacher recognized Michelle's advanced level in reading and math; she made Michelle a teacher's helper so she would not be bored in the classroom. Michelle really liked it. She helped her classmates patiently with reading just as her nanny did. She always imitated her nanny's British accent when she helped her classmates. Her classmates liked her British accent.

Alan Dubois and Tom Rousseau were in the same class and became very good friends. Alan often helped Tom with his schoolwork. Tom was always thankful. He liked Alan because he never intimidated him or never acted superior over him.

The behavior or attitude of Alan and Michelle came from their nanny—she always told them to be humble, to be genuinely compassionate, and to be generous to others without expecting anything in return or not to wear any superior attitude. That was why Alan's help was always genuine and did not intimidate Tom.

Eunice no longer felt aches and pains. Moreover, she no longer wore a nightwear during the day, but she was still a hermit. The people who did not know Eunice at all probably thought she was leading the luxurious lifestyle of a wealthy wife who lived on St. Charles Avenue.

Eunice's dark secret was never revealed to anyone. Jake and Teresa kept it to themselves. Therefore, nobody knew Eunice had not been out of the house for eight years after her childbirth. Tom was too young to recognize the fact of his mother being a hermit.

Eunice took all kinds of vitamins Teresa gave with the balanced meals. Her aches and pains were gone because of Teresa's care, but she knew Teresa could not do anything about her being a hermit. It was up to Eunice to cure it.

Even though she was a hermit, she was physically normal. One night, after Tom was tucked in and Teresa retired to the guesthouse for the day, she decided to sleep with her husband. When she snuggled into Jake's bed, he was startled at first, but waited to see what she was going to do. As her soft silky hands started caressing his naked body, he was instantly aroused.

When Eunice realized Jake was fully aroused, she made him turn toward her and maneuvered him to his forgotten heaven in silence. Jake felt tears in his eyes for some reason. Their lovemaking was so passionate that both of them felt tremulous afterward.

As it happened every night, Jake became somewhat obsessed with sex. At work, when he thought about their passionate lovemaking with his vigorous movements, his trousers felt heavy, and he had to run to the bathroom to release it. Eventually, Eunice moved into their master bedroom and slept with Jake every night. Their sex life was just out of this world.

Nevertheless, Jake was very careful about getting Eunice pregnant again, so he used protection every time. He did not want his wife to repeat the dreadful childbirth again.

When Tom found out where Alan lived—on St. Charles Avenue, a block away from his house—he begged his parents to meet the Dubois family.

Eunice was reluctant, but Tom insisted his mother come. Courageously, she decided to walk a block to meet the Dubois family for her son's sake. When she thought about meeting the neighbors, she was already trembling and perspiring.

It was the first time for Eunice to be out of the house after so many years. Her palms were sweaty, and she felt aches and pains in her body again. Her heart was pounding. Jake understood her phobia, but he wanted Eunice to try many new things to overcome her phobia so she could lead the normal life she used to have. Jake walked with Eunice by holding her hand.

Delayed Justice

Tom looked very happy because his mother was coming with him this time. She had never attended the PTA meetings or any kind of school events in the past. Instead, Teresa came to school.

Alan came to the door and looked surprised. He called his parents to the door. Marie and Jefferson Dubois welcomed them and invited them to the kitchen table.

Jake introduced his family. "This is my wife, Eunice Rousseau. I am Jake Rousseau. Tom begged us to meet you since we live only a block away. We hardly know anybody on St. Charles Avenue. It is very nice to meet you."

Jefferson introduced his family including Michelle. Marie offered coffee, but Eunice asked for a glass of water. The rest had coffee. Eunice had to take a deep breath periodically while they were talking. She had a quiet smile on her face, but her heart was pounding aloud. Jake caressed her hand under the table from time to time.

Alan asked Tom to come upstairs to see his room. Michelle followed them. Alan's room had many toys that Tom had never seen before. He saw Transformers, mechanical robots, Rubik's Cube, and Nintendo. Michelle was watching them quietly while standing against the door. Alan showed Tom how to play a Nintendo game. When it came to the Rubik's Cube, Michelle sat beside Tom on the carpeted floor and showed him how to line the colors.

Tom asked Alan how they got all kinds of high-tech gadgets or toys. Alan explained that some were sample merchandise from his father's import business. Some were bought at toy stores.

Tom had never been to a toy store, or a bookstore. Teresa was always cleaning and cooking every day. Tom followed Teresa around and tried to help her in the kitchen, but most of the time, she let him sit on a stool to watch her cook. She was too busy to think about toys or books for Tom.

While listening to Marie's soothing voice, Eunice's heart somewhat calmed down—her palms were no longer sweaty. Eunice could not pinpoint what it was, but Marie had some kind of magical personality that made Eunice feel at home.

The children were very quiet upstairs. They seemed to be getting along. Tom was actually learning how to play each game from Alan and Michelle. Tom was speechless when they completed lining up the colors of the Rubik's Cube in seconds.

Downstairs, the parents were getting along well too. They liked each other. Jake noticed his wife looked very relaxed, and the redness on her face was gone. Jake thought to himself—getting together with the Dubois family might cure his wife's phobia? He was glad he came to see the Dubois family.

Therefore, he decided to invite the entire Dubois family to his house to have dinner the following Saturday. Jefferson and Marie gladly accepted the invitation.

Jake was a great cook, but Teresa was the one who had to get all kinds of ingredients and food such as fresh vegetables, fish, and meat. As Jake was going to boil crawfish, some corn on the cob, and make a pot full of gumbo by using his mother's recipe, Teresa was again asked to go to the grocery store for Jake before she went away for the weekend.

CHAPTER 5
A HERMIT

The following Saturday, when the Dubois family came, Jake had already boiled enough crawfish in Cajun style and steamed more than enough corn on the cob. Gumbo was ready as well.

A large folding table for the adults and a small one for the children were set up in the sunroom. A tray of crawfish with sweet corns and cups of gumbo were already on each table.

It was the first time for the children to eat crawfish, so Jake, as a native New Orleanian, instructed the children how to eat crawfish. He was talking loudly like a schoolteacher.

"Children, being New Orleanians, you must learn how to eat crawfish by following the steps. Look at me and imitate what I am doing. First, hold the head with the fingers of one hand and hold the tail with the fingers of another hand." Jake went around the table to see if each child was holding the crawfish correctly or not.

"Now, twist the tail to separate from the head. Siphon the juice from the head before discarding it—the juice is very tasty, isn't it?"

All other adults including Marie were busy eating crawfish already.

"Now, concentrate on the tail part. Pinch the very end of the tail hard with the thumb and index finger, pull the tail meat out with other fingers, and eat the meat. Yes, you are doing very well. Please eat as much as you want. I still have a lot more in the pot. Remember we live in the bayou state, known as the crawfish capital. This is our heritage. You must know how to eat crawfish correctly." The children looked very serious when pulling out the tail meat.

Jefferson invited the Rousseau family the following Saturday. He grilled prawns for the adults and hamburgers for the children. They took turns to get together almost every weekend.

One weekend, when the families were together, Marie asked Eunice to eat lunch with her at the French Quarter the following Wednesday. Eunice gladly accepted without thinking about her phobia. It was too late to tell Marie.

Eunice knew almost all the restaurants in the French Quarter because she and Jake often dined in the different restaurants after work. It was many years ago, but she still remembered the location of the restaurant where she was supposed to meet Marie.

The morning of the luncheon day, Eunice's anxiety was sky-high. She was shaking. Her whole body was perspiring, and she felt aches and pains in her body again.

Teresa let her drink two cups of chamomile tea and told her to take deep breaths many times—she seemed to be calming down. Eunice always listened to Teresa because she trusted her more than she trusted her doctor. Teresa saved Eunice and her son's life from malnutrition.

She knew Teresa read many medical and vitamin books in Spanish. She also befriended some Spanish-speaking pharmacists in the drugstores. Whenever she had medical issues, she would visit them and get free advices. Because of Teresa's genuine concern and care for Eunice, she called Teresa, Dr. Teresa from time to time.

Teresa walked Eunice to the streetcar stop and said, "If you feel nervous, take a deep breath. Do not order coffee or tea. Order a glass of water."

In order to avoid people's eyes on the streetcar, Eunice stood against the window and looked out the symmetrically planted Southern oak trees along St. Charles Avenue. When it came closer to the French Quarter, she looked up at the skyline of the city, but her heart was still pounding hard and her body was tremulous. When she got off the streetcar, she took a deep breath and walked through the crowd with her head down—try not meet anybody's eyes.

When Eunice arrived at the restaurant, her cheeks were red and her whole body was tremulous. Marie thought she looked very pretty with her rouged cheeks. She did not know the redness came from her phobia.

While eating lunch with Marie, Eunice began relaxing. Marie wanted to eat lunch with Eunice every week. Eunice was hesitant first, but she agreed. She was determined to overcome her phobia. She wanted to be normal. Teresa and Jake were very happy about her decision to eat lunch with Marie every week.

Marie was eight years younger than Eunice was, but she had much more life experiences than Eunice had. Eunice was genuinely interested in Marie as a friend and very enthusiastic about learning from Marie, especially about the foreign countries, which were always fairy-tale places for Eunice. When Marie described the beauty of Paris, Eunice wished she were there, but she did not think her dream would come true because of her phobia.

As Eunice grew up in poverty with many siblings, she did not have any exotic experiences whatsoever. When she married Jake and started living in a mansion on St. Charles Avenue, she felt exotic. She was on top of the world until the illness struck her and put her in the dungeon for eight years.

When Marie wanted to know Eunice's childhood, she honestly told her about her family who had been on welfare as far as she could remember—her father was a laborer and mother was a homemaker with eight children including Eunice. She had to babysit her younger siblings after school and never been out of the state until she moved to Kentucky with her family. She also explained how Jake brought her back to New Orleans from Kentucky and married her.

She also told Marie that her family used to live on the farmland outskirt of New Orleans before her father got a construction job in the city. Eunice rather liked the life on the farmland because she was able to grow some vegetables in the backyard and pick tomatoes and some fruits. She loved to gather fresh eggs for breakfast every morning. They had many chickens and a pet pig named Nancy in the backyard.

Eunice told Marie about a story of their pet pig. "We had a pet pig named Nancy. She was a plump white pig and very friendly. The pig usually stayed in the pigpen, but whenever my younger siblings were in the field, she followed them and played with them like a dog. The children loved Nancy."

Eunice had a sip of water and continued. "One day, my mother cooked delicious pork chop dinner for the family. Everybody ate plenty. After dinner, one of my siblings shouted, 'Nancy is gone!' All of the children including me went outside to look for the pig in the dark, but we could not find her. My parents told us they had to sell Nancy to get some grocery money. As I was the oldest sibling, I figured out that the pork chop dinner was Nancy."

Marie did not know whether she should laugh or cry, but when she heard Eunice's laughter, she laughed too.

Marie liked Eunice's honesty. Eunice liked Marie's humbleness and compassion. They genuinely became lifelong friends. Eunice's phobia was getting lesser and lesser each week. In the end, she was not afraid of people in the crowd anymore—there was no redness on her face, no perspiration on her forehead, and no sweaty palms. She was becoming normal just like before. Because of it, she started going to work with Jake several days a week and ate lunch with Marie once a week.

One day, Eunice decided to tell Marie all about her hermit life and phobia at lunch. "Marie, have you heard of the illness called a social phobia or anthropophobia?"

"No."

"Well, I suffered from the illness after Tom was born. I did not go outside because I had a fear of meeting people or being in a crowd. In fact, when I met you at your house, it was my first time being outdoors after eight years of my hermit life."

Marie looked shocked and did not know what to say.

"Marie, if you did not set up our luncheon meet, I should still be suffering from my illness. In the beginning, I had a hard time meeting you in the restaurant. I was shaking, perspiring, could not breathe well, my face was red from the anxiety, but I made it each time. It had been my dark secret. You may not know it, but you helped me overcome my illness. Thank you."

Marie was still speechless, but nodded several times as though she was saying, "You are quite welcome."

Delayed Justice

Several weeks later, Marie asked Eunice if she wanted to go to Paris with her. Marie knew Eunice's dream was to visit Paris. Eunice emphatically nodded with teary eyes. No words came out of her mouth because she was too excited.

Marie told Eunice about her parents—her father was a language professor at Sorbonne University, so was her mother. Her parents educated their daughters with many different languages at home. They spoke English, German, Spanish, Italian, and their native language, French.

Every summer, they sent Marie and her older sister, Marianne, to a different country, such as Germany, Spain, England, or Italy to learn their languages. That was how Marie became an exchange student with a scholarship in English to the United States.

Marie's parents weren't considered wealthy in France, but had enough money to send their children to a different country every summer for language training. They probably believed that the children should be exposed to different languages and cultures so eventually they would learn to respect different ethnic groups and their cultures.

Marie had not visited her sister since her father's funeral a year ago. Her mother passed away a year before him. Now she only has her sister in Paris. Marie wants to reunite with her only sibling, and at the same time, she wants to show Eunice her birthplace, Paris.

Marie helped Eunice get a passport. Jake was so happy that he did not mind paying for the first-class ticket for Eunice. Jefferson did the same for Marie.

On the departure day to Paris, as the husbands were at work and the children were at school, Teresa volunteered to take both to the airport.

When Teresa helped with luggage at the airport, Eunice saw tears in Teresa's eyes, so Eunice embraced her and told her not to worry about her illness anymore because Dr. Teresa cured her. Teresa smiled big and drove off.

Marie and Eunice sat side by side in the first-class cabin. When the plane ascended, Eunice was mesmerized by the bird's-eye view of the beautiful sunset over the ocean for the first time. After the airplane reached above the orange clouds, the sky was getting darker.

A flight attendant asked them what they wanted to drink. Marie helped Eunice order a glass of red wine just like hers. Each table was covered with a white cloth. Both ordered steak. It was served with assorted vegetables. They both enjoyed the dinner with a glass of red wine.

A movie was shown on a big screen, but they did not bother to put earphones on. Instead, Eunice asked Marie to teach her some greetings in French. The pronunciation was hard, but Eunice learned some greetings, important phrases, and words in French.

Marie's sister, Marianne, came to the Charles de Gaulle Airport to pick them up. She was very tall unlike Marie. Eunice's height came between them like a ladder.

Marianne's big house was on the hill of Montmartre. The two-story house was modern with many windows. The brick wall around the property seemed to keep privacy and safety. The house had no garden, but many flowerpots were placed nicely on the large terrace on the second floor that overlooked the beautiful city down the hill.

Marianne's husband was an international architect and traveled all over the world. He was in Hong Kong when Marie and Eunice were in Paris. Their only daughter was in a boarding school in Nice. Therefore, Eunice did not meet any of Marianne's family members.

The three girls chatted in English while eating lunch. Marianne resembled Marie in many ways and spoke English very well. After lunch, Marie decided to show Eunice the Sacré-Cœur Cathedral on the hill of Montmartre. It was a short walk.

Marie was Catholic. Eunice was raised in a Baptist family, but she did not agree with the church's stand on certain issues, such as no alcohol drinking and no gambling, yet some of the churchgoers and preachers were alcoholic, so she stopped going to church. Therefore, she was nonreligious.

The Sacré-Cœur Cathedral was dark inside like a haunted house. Eunice came outside immediately, but Marie stayed inside for a while. Eunice was gazing at the vast city from the hill while waiting for Marie.

The next day, they rode a Métro to see the Notre Dame Cathedral. The entrance to Notre Dame was crowded with the tourists, but Marie managed to take Eunice inside.

As Eunice knew of the famous Notre Dame de Paris and saw it on TV many times, she finally realized she was indeed in an exotic city called Paris. She was almost in tears. She did not want to miss any details of Notre Dame while she was looking around.

Marie explained softly, "*Notre Dame de Paris* means Our Lady of Paris. The Gothic design you see here originated in France, but you would see many Gothic buildings and churches throughout Europe."

The stained glass windows reminded Eunice of the Saint Louis Cathedral in Jackson Square at home, but the Gothic design on the interior and exterior of Notre Dame were much more intricate and classier than the St. Louis Cathedral in New Orleans.

She asked Marie why all the walls, statues, and pictures looked so dark. Marie answered that the smoke from the candles they used for centuries caused it. Now they use the electric candles throughout the church except the altar candles.

She explained more about Notre Dame. "During the reign of Louis XIV, Notre Dame's major alteration was completed. Louis XIV was born in 1638, died in 1715 at the age of seventy-seven. He built the palace called Versailles. He used lots of French people's tax money and labor to build that palace."

"Did Marie Antoinette marry Louis XIV?"

"No. She married Louis XVI, a grandson of Louis XIV. When we go to Versailles, I will tell you more about Marie Antoinette."

As some tour guides were explaining all about Notre Dame including Louis XIV, Marie stepped aside and talked more softly.

"Let me tell you more about Louis XIV. When his father, Louis XIII, died, he was only five years old, so his surrogate father and his mother ruled the country until he became sixteen, and then he was officially crowned. After his marriage to Maria Theresa of Spain, he decided to build Versailles in the most grandeur and opulent manner because he wanted to show his power to the French people as well as to other European kingdoms."

After Marie walked Eunice to the side of the church altar, away from the tour groups, she continued talking.

"Even though the French people were very angry with Louis XIV for spending so much money on Versailles and Notre Dame, the Gothic design of Notre Dame and the magnificent architectural design of Versailles became the genuine French culture that every kingdom and people in Europe had envied."

Marie explained further. "Louis XIV actually held the title of King of France for over seventy years from the age of five, but his actual reign was for fifty-five years. He was a handsome Casanova who had seventeen illegitimate children and four from his marriage during his life of seventy-seven years. Because of his lavish spending on his personal matters and his palace, Versailles, the French Revolution was looming against the absolute monarchy. However, the absolute monarchy continued ruling France until the year of 1792. Louis XVI was the king of France at that time. I will tell you more about the French Revolution later."

After several days of touring the city including the Louvre, Arc de Triomphe, and the Eiffel Tower, they took a train to Versailles with a knapsack full of food, a bottle of red wine, and a picnic blanket. Marie asked Marianne to come with them, but she decided to stay home and have dinner ready for Eunice and Marie.

When they arrived at the entrance of the palace, the line was too long, so Marie took Eunice to the garden entrance. Eunice was mesmerized by the grandeur of the palace and the humongous garden that was symmetrically landscaped with gorgeous flowers, numerous statues, fountains, and the neatly mowed lawn along the lake a mile away down the hill.

They walked to the lakeside; there were many local people or probably tourists sunbathing, boating, and children frolicking. When Eunice sat on the blanket, she was actually facing the magnificent palace on the hill. She felt as though she was a princess in a storybook, picnicking on the lawn of the palace.

While eating sandwiches with wine, Marie started talking about Marie Antoinette. "Let me tell you about Marie Antoinette. She was a daughter of the Austrian empress named Maria Theresa, who was the ruler of the Habsburg Empire in Austria and ruled the country for forty years. The empress had sixteen children. Most of her children were sent out to marry the royal families in Europe. Marie Antoinette was one of them, marrying Louis XVI. French people did not like her because she was not French. Besides, she was spoiled and had no empathy for the poor people in France. She enjoyed a lavish lifestyle in Versailles while French people were suffering from poverty."

After sipping wine from a cup, Marie continued. "The French Revolution started in 1789 and ended in 1792, and within three years, the French monarchy that lasted a thousand years was officially abolished. Louis XVI and his wife, Marie Antoinette, were guillotined in 1793. However, when Napoleon I came to power, he wanted to be elected as emperor of France in 1804, so he became the emperor, but he was forced to abdicate ten years later in 1814 and was exiled to the island of Elba. French people did not like the emperorship or any monarchy structure for the country anymore."

"Did Napoleon die in Elba?"

"No, he did not. A year later in 1815, Napoleon Bonaparte escaped and reclaimed his emperorship to lead the French military forces to fight against the British forces at Waterloo. The Hundred Days is known as Napoleon's final bid for power, but he was defeated. After his second abdication, he was exiled to St. Helena, a small island in the South Atlantic Ocean, far away from France. He died there in 1821, at the age of fifty-one. Of course, there were some political struggles among the descendants of the kings and of the emperors for many years in France, but eventually, France became a republic country."

Eunice's visit to Paris was unbelievably wonderful. She was very grateful to Marie because she was able to see the beautiful city of Paris. Furthermore, she learned the history and culture of France from Marie.

After Marianne embraced Eunice at the airport, she kissed her on both of her cheeks and told her to visit her again. Marie and Eunice waved at Marianne at the departure gate.

Chapter 6
Almost Like Siblings

After school, Alan and Michelle had cookies and milk while finishing their homework at the kitchen table. After homework, they wanted to read books but did not have any more library books at home. Their English nanny used to take them to the neighborhood library to check out many books, but now she was not with them. She went home to England. No one would take them to the library. The housekeeper would not do it. Their parents were still at work.

One day, Alan called Tom on the phone to see if his mother could take them to the library. Tom knew she would not drive, so he asked Teresa. She did not mind it at all. The children checked out many books on that day. After that, Teresa regularly drove the children to the neighborhood library.

Tom often walked or bicycled to Alan's house to get help on his homework. The three of them did their homework together at the kitchen table. Alan helped Tom most of the time, but as Michelle was able to solve Tom's homework, she helped him too.

Michelle was very patient and compassionate like her nanny. Every time she helped Tom, she imitated her nanny's British accent. Tom liked her accent and felt grateful because his grades were improving. Eventually, he became as smart as they were.

After homework, the children read in the living room without turning on TV. Tom was becoming a bookworm just like them, and he was no longer lonely. Michelle and Alan became almost like his own siblings.

Delayed Justice

However, when Michelle and Alan went to Paris to stay with their grandparents for the summer, Tom missed them a lot and wished he were with them in Paris as their sibling.

After their grandparents' passing, they stopped spending the summer in Paris. Therefore, during the summer, they played Nintendo games together, played ball at the nearby park, checked out many books, and read.

They three continuously studied and hung out together. When they became teenagers, Michelle was like their pet dog because she followed them everywhere. She rode a streetcar with them to see some events at the French Quarter, followed the Mardi Gras parade with them, ate beignets at Café Du Monde, and walked the Riverwalk along the Mississippi River to see some events and riverboats. The boys did not mind having Michelle because she was neither a whiner nor a nagger.

Michelle felt very safe with the boys because they were like her own secret service agents who would protect her from any danger. If the boys wanted to play a ball game at the park, she did not mind keeping their jackets while they played. She would sit on the lawn beside their jackets, read a book, and wait for them patiently.

Tom was often mesmerized by Michelle's beauty and intelligence. When he reached his puberty, Michelle became the subject of his wet dreams, but he kept his feelings to himself. Besides, she was too young.

Tom and Alan attended a private high school in the neighborhood on St. Charles Avenue. As they both were in the different homerooms, they hardly saw each other on campus.

When Michelle entered the same high school two years later, Alan and Tom were already seniors. She too did not see Tom much at school, but the three were still bonded like siblings.

Tom was quiet and somewhat timid. He was not as tall as Alan was, but he was tall and lean. His handsome face always wore a gentle smile. Whenever Michelle pictured Tom, his gentle smile came to her mind.

Alan was also handsome, tall like his father, smart, outspoken with a great sense of humor, and was very popular among girls. One particular girl who had a mature figure with a beautiful face and blonde hair was interested in Alan. He was flattered because of her beauty and was proud to be with her. She was once crowned as the most beautiful student in school and was known as the beauty queen.

Alan spent a lot of time in the beauty queen's apartment after school. They seemed to be getting along well for several months, but later, Alan started avoiding her because he could not stand her obsessive jealousy—if Alan smiled at another girl, she would explode hysterically. Additionally, Alan felt threatened when she started talking about a marriage.

When Alan stopped seeing her, the beauty queen became desperate to get him back. She started calling Alan at home many times after school. Alan feared answering her phone calls, so he pleaded his sister, Michelle, to answer the phone.

He honestly explained to his sister about his messy relationship, which involved sex. Michelle asked him if she was pregnant; he said no. He also told her where the beauty queen lived and the name of her aunt's gift shop in the French Quarter.

Michelle agreed to answer the phone for her brother. The beauty queen was very rude and practically interrogated her to find out where Alan went and whom he was with. Her frequent phone calls came in before her parents came home, so they did not know anything about the beauty queen. Of course, Michelle kept her brother's problem a secret from her parents. Because of her frequent phone calls, Michelle decided to see her face-to-face at school and told her not to bother her brother because he was not interested in her anymore. Michelle thought she was going to cry, but instead she shouted, "You all go to hell!"

The beauty queen's insane actions such as stalking Alan and embarrassing him in front of his friends continued. So Michelle decided to investigate her background for the sake of her brother.

She went to the French Quarter. Michelle talked to the storeowner next to the aunt's gift shop, who was the property owner of the several stores including the aunt's gift shop.

Michelle asked, "Do you know the aunt and her niece next door well?"

She said yes.

Michelle told her that she was investigating the niece's background for someone and squeezed a fifty-dollar bill into her hand. When she saw the money, she nodded several times with a smile and agreed to answer Michelle's questions.

"Why did her niece come to live with her aunt?"

"They told me her parents died in a car accident, but I was told by a friend of mine that her parents were put in jail for killing a police officer during a sting operation on their drug smuggling. They were sentenced to life. Since the girl was a minor, they put her in the state foster care facility in Gulfport, but her aunt got the guardianship to take her in."

"Can her aunt afford to put her niece in an expensive private high school? Does she make a lot of money from her gift shop?"

"No. She can hardly make the monthly rent from her shop, but I think she is paying her niece's tuition from her big divorce settlement. She used to be married to a wealthy man and lived in a big house. Now she lives in an apartment with her niece. She told me the tuition is her investment. She wants her niece to marry a son of a wealthy family on St. Charles Avenue so her investment could multiply. She knows that private high school is exclusively built for the wealthy families' children. She is confident that her niece could catch one of the wealthy families' sons. Her niece is very pretty and smart. She has a movie-star-like beauty."

"Did she catch anybody wealthy yet?"

"Yes. Several months ago, she brought her niece's boyfriend, whose name is Alan something—I forgot his last name. He is from a wealthy family on St. Charles Avenue. After the young ones left, she came over and told me that they were engaged to be married. She did not tell me when their wedding would take place, probably after their high school graduation, but I felt sorry for the husband-to-be because he would never know his wife-to-be and her aunt are big-time gold diggers."

Michelle now understood why the beauty queen was so desperate to marry Alan. She thanked the storeowner for answering the questions. She thanked Michelle for the money.

Michelle assumed the aunt and the beauty queen researched on the wealthy families and their sons on St. Charles Avenue who attended the private high school. Perhaps, on their list, they had Alan Dubois, Henry Thompson, Tom Rousseau, and so forth.

Alan might have been the first target. The aunt was probably very happy when her niece brought Alan to the gift shop to meet her. Later, when she learned that Alan was trying to break up with her niece, she probably told her to move on, but the beauty queen was desperate to get Alan back because she was probably in love with him by then.

The aunt certainly did not allow her niece to waste time and probably gave her the next boy's name and telling her to work harder. Michelle assumed the beauty queen was trained to be a gold-digger and a social climber at an early age for the sake of her aunt's investment. The beauty queen's phone calls stopped. Therefore, Michelle decided to keep her findings to herself.

* * *

When Alan and Tom graduated from high school, the both sides of parents decided to give the boys a trip to Paris because they wanted their sons to learn their French heritage. Marie arranged their stay with her sister.

Marianne lost her wealthy architect husband a year ago to cancer, but she still kept her big house for her daughter's family who would come to stay with her around Christmas and for some long holidays. Her only daughter married after college and now lived in Nice with her husband and three children.

It would be Tom's first trip to a foreign country. He was extremely excited. His father, Jake, visited his relatives in Paris with his parents when he was young. His mother, Eunice, went to Paris with Alan's mother, Marie, a decade ago. Alan and Michelle spent every summer in Paris for their language training. It was a long time ago.

Even though Alan and Michelle stopped going to Paris for the language training, their mother, Marie, was like her parents—she made her children speak French with her at all times. Therefore,

Michelle and Alan understood French and could converse in French without any problems.

Michelle really wanted to go to Paris to see her aunt, Marianne, again and explore Paris with Tom and Alan. She never begged before, but this time she did.

Marie called her sister to see if she could have Michelle too. Her sister said, "Of course." The last time she saw her nephew and niece was when her parents and husband were still alive, so she was very happy that they were coming to see her again.

Tom was so ecstatic to learn that Michelle was coming with him. When he thought about living with Michelle in Paris for two weeks, his body felt warm. It was like his dream would come true.

On the airplane, Tom sat at the window side; Michelle sat between Alan and Tom because she was tiny. Tom was staring at the ocean and the clouds, but all he could think about was the girl sitting next to him. Every movement she made, Tom felt aroused. He wanted to hold her hand or sit very close to her body, but instead he closed his eyes and imagined Michelle's plump lips.

After everybody finished dinner, the cabin lights were turned off. Alan was fast asleep. Michelle was dozing off, and her head was tilting toward Tom's shoulder. Tom's heart jumped, but at the same time, he felt happy to have her closer, so he let her head rest on his shoulder without moving.

He was tempted to touch her face and her dainty hands, but he was satisfied with the warmth of Michelle's head on his shoulder. Tom, too, fell asleep against Michelle's head. They both looked like young lovebirds or honeymooners who were flying to the most romantic city in the world called Paris.

In Marianne's humongous house, each teenager got a room. The two-story house was modern. The brick fence around the house had an iron gate that opened to a two-car garage.

Marianne said to the teenagers at the kitchen table, "I put plenty of breakfast food in the refrigerator, so fix your own breakfast. Does any of you know how to fix breakfast?"

Tom raised his hand. "I learned how to make fry or boil eggs, sausages, pancakes, French toast, even omelets. I will be glad to cook breakfast for all of us every morning." Tom did not tell them, but he watched Teresa cook. Sometimes she let him cook his favorite cheese omelets. As a child, instead of watching TV alone, he rather wanted to help Teresa. Eventually, he learned how to cook breakfast.

Teresa was like his surrogate mother. She toilet-trained him when he was a toddler and showed him how to lift the toilet seat before urinating in the commode. She also taught him how to iron his own shirts and trousers when he became a teenager. Most importantly, Tom became an expert on breakfast because of Teresa.

Marianne looked relieved. She used to have a housekeeper who prepared the meals for the family and cleaned the house every day, but now, as she lived alone, she had a part-time housekeeper to clean the house twice a week. She did not like to cook, so she had lived on vegetables, cheeses, fruits, nuts, and occasional restaurant meals, but she ate well.

The next morning, Tom made pancakes, cheese omelets, scramble eggs, and bacon. Michelle got up early and made French crepes too. Marianne was very impressed with the teenagers who were so well behaved and could even cook delicious breakfast. She called Marie on the phone.

"Marie, do you know Tom could cook delicious breakfast? Tell Eunice how well she taught her son to cook. Michelle could make French crepes better than I could." She also told Marie that Michelle and Alan had not forgotten the French language. They spoke French with her every day.

Alan did not cook, but he was determined to be a good tour guide for the teenagers. He studied the guidebook and learned where to take them. When they went to the Eiffel Tower, Alan, the tour guide, explained everything about the Eiffel Tower. They took many pictures of each other in front of the Eiffel Tower.

They enjoyed the view from the top of the Eiffel Tower. The matchbox-like buildings below fascinated the teenagers, and again they took many more pictures. After the Eiffel Tower, they crossed the bridge over the Seine river to Trocadero. From the hill of Trocadero, they saw the panoramic view of the Eiffel Tower.

One day, they browsed around the artist square at the back of the Sacré-Cœur Cathedral at Montmartre. They watched some artists who were drawing portraits of the tourists and some who were selling their own paintings while working on their easels.

At Montmartre, Vincent van Gogh and Paul Gauguin worked and roomed together in the late 1800s. The teenagers decided to walk all the way down to the blue-door apartment of Vincent van Gogh, who lived there before he was sent to an asylum because of his mental illness. The apartment was still standing and livable with the historic sign above the blue door.

The following day, after the Louvre tour, the teenagers decided to walk from Tuileries Garden all the way to Arc de Triomphe. At the garden, they bought some ice cream, sat on a bench, and watched the people walking by.

Michelle noticed that Tom was taking many pictures of her, so she playfully made faces at him or stuck her tongue out at him. Whenever Michelle touched Tom's arms or scratched his back playfully, just as she did to her brother Alan, Tom wished he had enough courage to kiss her plump lips, but he realized she was only sixteen—still too young. Besides, her brother, Alan, was watching him.

They crossed the Concorde to the famous street called Champs-Élysées and finally to Arc de Triomphe. They decided to climb 280 steps to see the 12 merging avenues from the top. The steps to the top were narrow and steep, but they did not mind climbing. The 12 symmetrically merging avenues to Arc de Triomphe were something awesome to see.

Several days before the children's return to America, Marianne decided to drive them to Giverny—Claude Monet's village—about fifty miles from Paris. She explained proudly about the French impressionist painter Claude Monet while driving.

"I am sure you have seen Claude Monet's paintings. If you have not, I would buy you some postcards of his paintings."

Marianne was turning the corner near the village. "Anyway, when Claude Monet fell in love with the village of Giverny, he decided to rent a house for his family and worked. In 1890, he purchased his rented house and the vast land in front of the house. By then he was famous and rich. He carefully landscaped his front yard by rerouting the water from the nearby river, planted ten thousand spices of plants and flowers, and made a beautiful water garden. You will see many water lilies under the Japanese bridge. He was fond of Japanese sumi-e. You could see them in his house as his collection. After his death in 1926, his house and the water garden were opened to public."

After she parked her car at the parking lot, the teenagers and Marianne walked several blocks to the ticket office. It was crowded with many tourists. While touring the water garden and Monet's house, she explained more.

"Because of Monet, Giverny became the artist colony. Even American impressionists came to paint in Giverny in the early twentieth century. Even to this date, many artists from all over the world come to paint here. They sell their own paintings to the tourists on the streets. After we finish this tour, let's walk around the village first, and then I will take you to Monet's church and his family tomb."

At the narrow street on the way to Monet's church, Tom bought two paintings—one for his parents and another one for Teresa—directly from the artist with his autograph. Marianne said jokingly, "Keep the receipt and compare the price when the artist gets famous in the future."

It was time for the teenagers to go home. Marianne had tears in her eyes when she embraced each of them at the airport. "Please visit me soon so I can have wonderful breakfast again." The teenagers nodded with smiles and waved at Marianne.

Chapter 7
Love at First Sight

Tom and Alan decided to go to the same college in the neighborhood where Jefferson and Marie graduated from many years ago. Jake graduated from the same college, but it was way before they graduated.

While Jefferson and Jake were playing golf, they talked a lot about their children. They were very happy about their children's decision to go to the college in the neighborhood. Marie and Eunice talked about their children a lot at lunch too.

Jefferson told his son, Alan, that he would pay for his tuition and books for four years as long as he would remain living with them and learn the family business after school each day. He also told him he would pay him generously for his time at work and would give him the weekends off. Jefferson had never had the weekends off when he worked for his father. Alan liked his father's promise.

Alan actually wanted to be a pilot in the future, but he did not tell him. He was planning to take flying lessons on the weekends soon. Nevertheless, he was interested in the family business as well. That was why he decided to major in business.

Jake made the same kind of deals with Tom just as Jefferson did with Alan. Tom agreed to work for his father after school and remain living with his parents and Teresa.

When Tom told his father he wanted to be a lawyer in the future, Jake assumed Tom would stay in New Orleans to work as a lawyer. He was rather proud of his son who wanted to be a lawyer and would be using his legal knowledge to take over the family business later.

Tom did not tell his parents, but the family business did not interest him much because it was so repetitive and boring.

After high school, Michelle, too, decided to enter the same college as her brother did. Her father did not ask Michelle to work in his office, but he would not mind paying for her tuition, books, and allowance. However, she was to remain living with them while going to school.

Michelle was never fond of the aggressiveness in the business world. She rather liked the peaceful atmosphere in the library, so she decided to major in library science. As she was a bookworm, naturally, being a librarian in the future was her genuine choice.

* * *

Michelle spent a lot of time in the local library during the summer after her high school graduation. She read books, which she missed reading while she was in high school. Now she was ready for college. The school would be starting in a week.

It was Saturday. Masaki Tanaka would be arriving from Japan with his daughter, Yuri Tanaka, who was going to the same college with Michelle. Jefferson and Marie could hardly wait to see their lifelong friend Masaki Tanaka. They had not seen each other for twenty-something years.

Michelle went to the airport with her parents in their big family car. On the way to the airport, Michelle learned a lot about Masaki Tanaka and his daughter, Yuri Tanaka, including his wife, Emi Tanaka, from her parents. Since they often wrote to each other over the years, they knew everything about each other.

When Masaki Tanaka went back to Japan after his college graduation in New Orleans, he landed a manager's position in a small clothing company. Several years later, Masaki was able to buy the company with the help of his father, who made a fortune from his real estate business in Osaka. By then, Masaki was able to manage the entire company as president.

He had a dozen employees in Osaka at the beginning—now two hundred. He just bought the Tokyo branch and wants his daughter to manage it after her college.

His company makes socks for all ages, underwear for all sizes, pajamas, nightwear, T-shirts, and other casual clothing including aprons. He has a factory in Osaka, now another one in Tokyo.

The year when Masaki bought the company, he married a schoolteacher named Emi, who was actually a classmate in high school. They honeymooned in Sydney, Australia, for a week. Emi did not speak English, but she was very proud of her husband who spoke English fluently.

They took a dinner cruise at Sydney Harbor, saw a show at the Opera House, and climbed the Sydney Bridge all the way to the top with a tour guide and a dozen climbers. From the top, they saw one of the most beautiful harbors in the world with the site of the Opera House. Because of Masaki's fluent English, they saw every corner of the city without hiring an interpreter.

Emi did not tell Masaki, but if she ever had a child, she wanted Masaki to speak English to the child so their child could become bilingual. She also wanted their child to be educated in the United States in the future, just as her husband was. She believed English should be the universal language.

When Yuri was born, Emi resigned from school and became a mother and homemaker. She insisted Masaki speak English to the child, but he was too busy every day with his company.

Emi was anxious to start her daughter's bilingual education in her early age because she believed the children could learn the language faster than the adults could, but there were no language schools for the small children.

Therefore, she looked for an exchange student from a college nearby. Luckily, she found a female student from England who was studying Japanese arts in college. She agreed to work with the toddler.

The tutor spoke British English to Yuri and read storybooks each day. By the time Yuri started school, she was speaking English fluently.

Since Emi did not seem to bear any more children, she devoted her time to her daughter's bilingual education. She was somewhat obsessed with it. Every Saturday, she drove a long distance to a language school so Yuri could learn grammar, spelling, vocabulary, and to read and write just as an educated English-speaking person should do.

Yuri was making good grades in high school, so she wanted to take the tests for the exchange program to study abroad by using her bilingual ability, but Masaki wanted his daughter to go to the college where he graduated from—he knew that the scholarship program would not give her the choice of college.

It would cost him a lot, but he did not mind sending her to college in New Orleans. Masaki did not say much, but he was very appreciative of his wife who brought up their daughter as bilingual.

Masaki wished Yuri were a boy, but he knew his daughter was extremely intelligent and capable. Besides, Yuri expressed her intention of helping Masaki in his business by majoring in business and becoming his company's CPA after the college graduation.

He considered Jefferson and Marie as his best friends, so he asked them to be Yuri's sponsors. They gladly agreed and submitted the application to the college on behalf of Yuri. After Yuri's passing the language requirement tests at the American embassy in Japan, she was officially admitted to the college and a student visa was issued.

Masaki deposited Yuri's four-year tuition and more than enough living expenses into Jefferson's bank account. He simply trusted Jefferson and Marie. Besides, Masaki was wealthy.

At the arrival gate, Masaki and Yuri appeared. Masaki was tall and lean—rather too lean. Yuri was tall and beautiful. She was taller than Marie and Michelle.

Marie embraced Masaki and cried. Masaki and Jefferson had tears in their eyes too. The three best friends huddled, embraced each other, and chatted nonstop without introducing the girls.

Masaki had some gray hair, and his handsome face had a gentle smile. Jefferson's forehead receded a little, but he too was handsome. Marie looked much younger than those two. Her blonde short hair was nicely styled and looked vivacious. Her pretty face was radiant without any wrinkles.

All of a sudden, Marie realized she forgot to introduce Michelle to Yuri, but Michelle told her that they had already introduced each other. Yuri introduced herself to Jefferson and Marie with her polite British accent, which reminded Michelle of her nanny, Ms. Melissa.

Michelle had her mother's plump lips, pretty face, and short figure, but she was a little taller than her mother, Marie. As her father, Jefferson, and brother, Alan, were so tall, they practically bent over to embrace Marie and Michelle every time.

Yuri had fair skin, her big eyes were gentle like her father's, and her tall figure could be mistaken for a Caucasian. She was very friendly and even-tempered like Michelle. The girls seemed to be getting along nicely.

Jefferson's mansion had seven spacious bedrooms—four bedrooms upstairs, the master bedroom and two guestrooms downstairs. Yuri's room was ready. Jefferson and Masaki carried Yuri's two suitcases to her room upstairs. She started hanging up her clothes in the closet. Michelle helped her.

Masaki got one of the guestrooms downstairs. While being in New Orleans, he wanted to see Jefferson's headquarters, help his daughter register at school, and, most importantly, he wanted to eat half-shelled oysters, crawfish, and gumbo again.

The old college friends were sipping coffee and chatting nonstop at the kitchen table when Yuri and Michelle came downstairs. Masaki was ready to take everybody out for dinner in the French Quarter. He said he had never forgotten the taste of half-shelled oysters, crawfish, and gumbo. Jefferson was to show him his favorite seafood restaurant in the French Quarter.

Alan just came home when they were ready to leave, so Masaki invited him to join them. Jefferson introduced his son, Alan, to Masaki first and then to Yuri. Alan was stunned to see Yuri's beautiful face and hear her polite British accent.

His heart started pounding hard for some reason; he forgot to shake her hand and forgot to say, "Nice to meet you." He looked paralyzed for a minute. Perhaps, "a cupid's arrow" or "love at first sight" struck him in his heart.

They took a streetcar. Many restaurants prepare half-shelled oysters and crawfish in the French Quarter, but that particular seafood restaurant is very popular because of the freshness of the oysters.

The entire French Quarter was crowded for the weekend. All the narrow streets were so congested that Alan decided to maneuver Yuri through the crowd by holding her shoulders with both of his hands. They finally caught up with his family and Masaki.

Alan purposely held her shoulders because he felt a big love bite somewhere in his body and wanted to touch her. If she would let him kiss her, he would've already done it just as some young lovers were doing it in the crowd.

When Alan held her shoulders, Yuri was startled first, but she did not mind it at all. She rather loved it. He did not hold her too long, but for some reason, she felt his hands on her shoulders for the longest time. She, too, seemed to be experiencing a love bite.

There were many street entertainers—a clown pantomiming, a small group of musicians playing jazz, a magician playing card tricks, a solo saxophone player playing a familiar tune. Some storekeepers were shouting to lure some customers to their shops, the nightclub owners passing out some discount coupons.

They finally arrived at the restaurant. Behind the glass window, a couple of the shacklers were busy shackling oysters. The waiters and waitresses were practically running to get the orders. The restaurant was crowded, but they were able to get a large table in the back. The table had two wooden benches like a picnic table.

Yuri sat between Michelle and Masaki at one side. Alan sat between Jefferson and Marie at another side. Therefore, Alan was sitting at the exact opposite side of Yuri. He did it on purpose to observe his love at first sight while eating dinner. His heart was pounding louder than before by looking at Yuri directly.

Everybody ordered a dozen oysters including Yuri. It was the first time for Yuri to eat oysters. Her father showed her how to scoop up each oyster with a small fork and dip in the cocktail sauce. She followed her father's instruction to dip the oyster in the cocktail sauce before putting it in her mouth.

Alan was watching her, and he, too, put his oyster in his mouth at the same time she put hers. Alan's sexual fantasy was out of control—he wanted to kiss her mouth. As Yuri noticed his stare, she shyly smiled at him. After everybody finished their oysters, Masaki ordered a bucket of crawfish for the table and a cup of gumbo with rice for everybody.

Michelle showed Yuri how to eat crawfish. She got several tail meats out successfully, but she gave up on pulling any more tail meats; instead, she started eating gumbo with rice.

"Wow! It is delicious. I like this. Michelle, what do you call this dish?"

Alan answered before Michelle did. "Gumbo."

Michelle could not believe what a keen hearing her brother had. "Yes. It is called gumbo. It is a Cajun dish. I like gumbo too."

On the way home, in the streetcar, Alan was gazing at Yuri's beautiful face obliviously. His heart was still pounding and wanted to kiss her or hold her hand.

Michelle saw her brother's mesmerized look or lovestruck face when he was looking at Yuri. She was happy for him because after his messy relationship with the beauty queen, Alan was rather paranoid and often said to Michelle he could not find a girl to his liking any more.

The old college friends huddled by standing near the door in the streetcar, talking away without noticing the chemistry or love bites between their heir and heiress.

Alan could get in a conversation with anybody, especially with girls, but he was unusually quiet. Now he turned his face away from Yuri and Michelle, looking out the streetlights as though he was contemplating or daydreaming.

Alan was actually reminiscing about his English nanny. It had been long since he thought about his nanny until he heard Yuri's British accent—Yuri spoke just like Ms. Melissa.

When his sister, Michelle, was an infant, the housekeeper fed her and took care of her. The English nanny concentrated on Alan—reading picture books to him, teaching him how to read, how to count numbers, showing him to lift the toilet seat before urinating, showing him to brush his teeth in the proper way. He still remembered that he slept comfortably on her soft chest from time to time.

Whenever the housekeeper got busy cleaning up the house or cooking, his nanny had to feed his baby sister or change her diapers. Alan was usually left with a book in the living room alone until she came back. He was jealous of his baby sister.

When Michelle became a toddler, the nanny spent a lot of time teaching his sister how to read and how to count numbers. Alan was jealous again because his nanny spent too much time with his sister.

As the nanny noticed his jealousy, she told Alan to be a teacher, to read a picture book to his sister. As his sister intently listened to him by sitting beside him and looking at the pictures in the storybook together, he felt as though he became the greatest teacher like Ms. Melissa. His sister loved her brother's British accent and begged him to read more books. Alan indeed read many books to his sister each day. He was no longer jealous of Michelle.

The young nanny taught the children to wash their hands before each meal. The children learned the table manners. They ate in the European way, just as their mother, Marie, and the nanny did—by holding a fork with the left hand and using a knife with the right hand, and without switching the fork to the right hand, they ate with the left hand.

During the children's naptime, the nanny usually went back to her guesthouse in the backyard; she wrote some letters to her mother or friends in England. On the weekends, she took some classes in the nearby college.

When Marie was looking for a nanny for Alan, Ms. Melissa just graduated from college with a bachelor's degree in teaching. Instead of teaching in school, she decided to apply for a job as a nanny in the United States.

After reviewing Ms. Melissa's résumé and interviewing her on the phone several times, Marie decided to hire her because she liked Ms. Melissa's good personality and kind nature. The long-term visa was obtained.

Ms. Melissa liked Marie's generosity—she was getting a generous salary, a medical insurance, and a nice guesthouse. Additionally,

Marie was going to pay for her weekend classes if the nanny decided to pursue her further education at the nearby college.

When her children had grown up to be thoughtful, compassionate, and well behaved, Marie was very grateful to Ms. Melissa. Furthermore, when she found out that the children were learning advanced skills in reading, writing, and math, Marie knew she hired the best nanny for her children.

When Michelle started school, the nanny went home. Alan was devastated and heartbroken because she was his surrogate mother as far as he remembered. He cried in bed for many days, but at the end, he tried to forget all about her because he was very angry and almost hated her. He made up his mind not to think about her for the rest of his life. Indeed, he did not think about her until he heard Yuri's British accent today. He remembered Ms. Melissa's smile and missed her a lot.

Alan still could see Ms. Melissa's gentle smiles and could hear her British accent. He could also recall the things she taught him—not to take anything that does not belong to him, not to be arrogant or obnoxious, to be humble, and always respect grown-ups, parents, and teachers. Most importantly, help people with his genuine compassion without expecting anything in return, and always use the best common sense.

Ms. Melissa also taught Alan and Michelle to floss and brush their teeth in the morning and at bedtime. She warned them by saying that the cavity germs could eat up children's teeth during their sleep if they did not brush their teeth at bedtime. Therefore, Alan and Michelle had never failed to floss and brush their teeth twice a day, especially at bedtime.

When the streetcar stopped, Michelle tapped Alan on his back and gestured for him to get off.

Chapter 8
Alan and Yuri

When they arrived home, the old college friends each had an after-dinner drink with a slice of cheesecake. They talked nonstop and laughed too loud like some young college kids.

As Michelle saw her brother's lovestruck face when he was gazing at Yuri in the streetcar, she told Alan to give Yuri a tour of the mansion from the top to the bottom including the basement.

Alan's face lit up. "Yuri, welcome to our house. I am your tour guide today. Let me show you each room from the top to the bottom."

He showed his room first, which was surprisingly uncluttered and neat. His large bed was made up, and a bookcase displayed many books neatly. He also showed his bathroom. It was clean.

She did not know Alan's neat habit came from his English nanny's teaching. Ms. Melissa taught Alan to make his bed, shower every day, floss and brush his teeth twice a day, hang up his clean clothes in the closet, and put dirty clothes in the hamper. Of course, she taught Michelle the same.

Michelle's room was parallel to Alan's room across the hallway. Her room was as neat as Alan's. Yuri's room was next to Michelle's room with her own bathroom.

Yuri could not imagine having a huge mansion like this in Japan. Her father is considered very wealthy and has a big three-story house, but in relation to the size of each room, there is no comparison.

A room in a Japanese house has multiusage—a living room could be a bedroom at night by putting a futon bed on the floor.

In the morning, the bed must be stored in the closet so the room could be used as a living room or a dining room during the day. The floor of the Japanese house is very clean because they take off their shoes at the entrance of the house. House slippers are used to walk around the house.

They went downstairs. Alan showed a huge master bedroom and a marble-floored bathroom with a Jacuzzi. Yuri had never seen such an opulent bedroom with the magnificent bathroom before. Yuri saw two guestrooms next to the master bedroom, a humongous living room, a formal dining room, and a big kitchen with a wide window facing the backyard.

A large circular table was in the middle of the kitchen, and the old college kids were sitting around the table with Michelle and talking too loud. Even though the best friends were talking at the same time, Michelle was enjoying being with them.

Masaki was telling Michelle about her father, Jefferson—after Jefferson lost his father suddenly, he was going to sell the family business, but Masaki and Marie wanted to help save his company. In return, Jefferson offered his mansion for them to live. The three of them worked in the office after school until ten or eleven o'clock every night including the weekends.

They ate turkey or ham sandwiches three times a day for six months. Since Masaki preferred turkey meat, he only ate turkey sandwiches. Strangely, a live turkey often appeared in his dream and poked him in his eyes each time to blind him. He switched to ham sandwiches, but still the same turkey appeared, so he quit eating sandwiches altogether, lived on carrot sticks and boiled eggs.

Jefferson spoke loudly, "Because of his egg eating, Masaki's fart was a stink bomb. We had to run outside every time." The laughter of the old college kids was so loud that it echoed in the kitchen.

Michelle had never known her grandparents on her father's side, but she heard about them—that her grandfather died suddenly in the office, and her grandmother left the family for another man and moved to San Francisco, but she, too, passed away years later.

Michelle met her father's only sibling, Aunt Margaret, when she came to bury her husband in New Orleans. Michelle liked her very much, so she often wrote to tell her what was going on with her family in New Orleans. Aunt Margaret only had her brother, Jefferson, and his family as her blood relatives. She had no children of her own.

Alan and Yuri passed by the loud crowd in the kitchen and went to the backside of the mansion—there were a large sunroom, a patio, and a guesthouse in the backyard. Alan wanted to show the guesthouse, but it was too dark outside.

After passing by the crowd again, the tour guide stopped at a door and said loudly, "Now I will show you the basement. It is a little bit spooky like a ghost house."

"A ghost house?"

"Yes. My ancestors accumulated their antique furniture in the basement. We should donate the furniture to a museum, but so far, we are too busy to do anything about it. Some were made in the nineteenth century and should be very valuable. Many portraits of our ancestors are on the wall. Michelle and I were scared of seeing those old portraits when we were young. That is why we called our basement a ghost house. We never use the basement, but my father hires a professional cleaner to shine or wax each furniture once a year."

Alan opened the door to the basement, turned the lights on, and let Yuri walk before him. He wanted to hold Yuri's hand, before she started walking down the stairs, but it was too late. She slipped and went tumbling down to the bottom of the stairs. Her screams and the tumbling noise were so loud that everybody in the house heard the commotion. Alan saw Yuri flat on the basement floor. Luckily, the floor was carpeted, but she lay unconscious.

When an ambulance arrived, Alan jumped in the ambulance and rode with her. In the hospital, the doctors and the emergency staff were able to bring her consciousness back. She had several bruises on her arms and legs but no broken bones. When Yuri saw Alan, she smiled at him.

All of a sudden, Alan's eyes were filled with tears and felt the urge to kiss her mouth for some reason. The hospital staff probably thought Yuri was his wife or girlfriend. Yuri was shocked to be kissed by Alan, but she loved it and felt like kissing him back.

Michelle drove her parents and Masaki to the hospital. Masaki looked relieved when he saw his daughter conscious, and sitting in a wheelchair, ready to be discharged.

Michelle saw her brother's red eyes and could easily tell he cried for Yuri. Her brother was definitely in love with her. At the same time, she saw Yuri's sparkling and longing eyes when she was looking at Alan. She knew something had happened between them—they seemed to be mutually in love. Michelle felt happy for both of them.

At the airport, those best friends had tears again. Masaki was talking to Yuri in Japanese for a while and waved to everybody before he headed toward the departure gate.

* * *

The school started. Michelle and Yuri took a streetcar to school, waited for each other after school before coming home. Alan took his early classes and drove straight to work. Therefore, Michelle and Yuri hardly saw Alan during the weekdays, but they saw Alan and his best friend, Tom, at the family vacation home in Biloxi on the weekends.

Their antebellum mansion had six bedrooms. The boys slept upstairs and the girls slept downstairs. As usual, Tom cooked breakfast just as he did it in Paris with the help of Michelle. On Saturdays, Alan took flying lessons at the nearby airport. Tom studied alone upstairs with the books he checked out from the library. Michelle and Yuri did the same with the library books downstairs.

There were no such things as PCs or laptops, much less researching online. The library books were the only source they had for researching. Michelle owned an electric typewriter, and she was a trained typist as a future librarian.

Tom and Alan always depended on Michelle when it came to typing. Yuri was not a fast typist, but she did her own typing with her electric typewriter.

While their children including Yuri were in Biloxi on the weekends, Marie and Jefferson got together with Jake and Eunice. They went out to eat dinner at the French Quarter or invited each other for dinner or drinks. Sometimes, they visited the children in Biloxi and took them to a nice seafood restaurant there.

Teresa was still working for the Rousseau family during the weekdays. On the weekends, she often visited her friends and relatives. Whenever Jake gave her a long paid vacation, she went to see her mother in Mexico.

Jefferson and Marie wanted the boys to keep an eye on the girls and vice versa when they were in Biloxi because they knew there were many college students on the beach, especially on the weekends, who would rent a vacation home to have a wild party.

The weekend was the only time the boys could concentrate on their assignments because they both worked for their parents during the weekdays. Therefore, they hardly went out to meet other college students on the beach.

Yuri often prepared sushi for dinner. While watching Yuri, Michelle, too, learned how to fix sushi. Since Tom, Alan, and Michelle loved half-shelled oysters, raw fish was not strange to them at all. Eventually, they were rather addicted to sushi.

Even though Alan and Yuri had never displayed their affection in front of Michelle and Tom, their relationship was ongoing. One day, when Tom and Michelle came back from the grocery store, they witnessed a scene of their passionate kissing. They were so involved that they did not even know Tom and Michelle were already in the house.

Alan courageously told them that they have been madly in love since the first day of Yuri's arrival, but they have to keep their relationship a secret. Yuri is prohibited to get involved with any boy during her stay in New Orleans because she is supposed to take over the Tokyo branch of her father's business after her graduation.

However, they could not help loving each other—it was love at first sight for both of them. Michelle and Tom understood and promised them not to reveal their relationship to anybody, especially to Jefferson and Marie because Masaki already asked them to guard Yuri from any boy's advancement. He wanted her daughter to come home clean without any boy problems.

Delayed Justice

* * *

During the girls' first summer off from college, Masaki invited Alan, Tom, and Michelle to Japan with Yuri. Masaki sent the airline tickets for four. All of them were ecstatic.

At the Osaka airport, Yuri's mother came to welcome them. Masaki sent a limousine. He could not come to the airport, but he would be home tonight. Yuri's mother, Emi, introduced herself in English. She spoke some English. Yuri resembled her a lot with her fair skin and tall figure.

At the entrance of the three-story house, everybody had to take their shoes off and wear a pair of house slippers. As the slippers were too small for Tom and Alan, they decided to walk the wooden floor without them.

Yuri took the boys to the top floor, which had two bedrooms. She showed Tom where his futon bed was and how to spread the bed on the tatami floor at night.

Then she came to Alan's room and showed him the same. Alan tried to kiss her, but Yuri shook her head and whispered, "Be careful! You are in the enemy's territory."

On the second floor, there were two bedrooms. Yuri and Michelle each took a room. The master bedroom was on the first floor next to the living room and kitchen. Each floor had a bathroom.

When Masaki came home that evening, he asked the college students what they wanted to eat. They unanimously said, "Sushi." Masaki was very impressed by the answer. He took his wife and the college students to his favorite sushi restaurant and proudly introduced them to the chef and servers. They were surprised to see the American students eat with chopsticks. Some Japanese customers were watching them with smiles.

In the morning, Emi and the housekeeper prepared a traditional Japanese breakfast. Each student sat on a chair at the Western-style table in the kitchen. Emi served a bowl of rice, a bowl of miso soup, and grilled fish with some slices of cucumbers, tomatoes, and seaweed pickles on each tray. Green tea or coffee came with breakfast. Japanese breakfast was new to the American students, but they liked it.

Emi observed those young ones. All of the American students behaved well. They were friendly and courteous. Those young men are so handsome and tall that she thought her daughter, Yuri, would be a good match, especially with the tallest one, Alan. Her daughter always had a height problem in high school. She was the tallest among the female students and taller than most of the Japanese male students.

If her daughter, Yuri, would ever fall in love with Alan, Emi would encourage Yuri to follow her heart because Alan seems to be fond of Yuri, and he is also the son of Masaki's best friends, but Emi shook her head.

Masaki's business obsession for her daughter was beyond Emi's comprehension. Masaki strongly prohibited Yuri to fall in love with any boy during her stay in New Orleans because he wanted her to come home to manage the Tokyo branch.

Emi was often worried about her husband's health because he worked too hard without any breaks and traveled frequently between Osaka and Tokyo. This morning he left for work early in the morning.

While standing at the kitchen sink, Emi was watching Alan and Yuri and daydreaming—if Masaki sold his business, he could retire in his beloved city, New Orleans. Emi would be glad to follow him. If her daughter married Alan, it should be like killing three birds with one stone for Masaki—three birds, not two birds.

First, Masaki could retire in his beloved city, New Orleans. Second, he could live closer to his beloved friends, Jefferson and Marie. Third, he could live closer to his married daughter and her family. As a result, he should be the happiest person on earth.

Emi, too, should be the happiest person because she could get to see her beloved daughter and possibly many of her grandchildren every day. Furthermore, she might become bilingual just like her husband and daughter, whom she had admired for all those years. Emi heard Yuri's voice asking more coffee for the boys.

Yuri took everybody to Tokyo in a bullet train. They stayed in her father's second house in Tokyo. Yuri did not know it, but Masaki had already planned to give the house to Yuri after her graduation so she could live in Tokyo to manage the Tokyo branch.

They made a trip to see Mt. Fuji by riding a sky lift. After seeing the majestic Mt. Fuji, they decided to spend one night in a hot spring hotel at the foot of Mt. Fuji. The girls got a room and shared. The boys did the same.

The public bath had a huge bathtub, just like a shallow swimming pool, with hot spring water that was overflowing constantly to keep the tub water clean.

No bathing suits were allowed. Everybody must take off their clothes and shower before wading into the hot steamy tub to sit and relax. The hot spring water has some minerals, such as sulfur, which seems to be good for the skin. The hotness of the water was good for tired bones or sore muscles.

Yuri said that honeymooners or couples could rent a room with a private bathtub. Tom was daydreaming about having his own honeymoon with Michelle, soaking their naked bodies in the bathtub, making love to each other on the futon bed. Tom shook his head.

The students finished bathing in the separate public baths. They each wore a kimono called a *yukata* and sat at the dining room, which was set up for four people.

Many Japanese dishes were already on the Japanese-style table. They had to sit on a floor chair with a cushiony pad. Yuri showed them how to sit with their legs folded, but none of them could do it.

In the end, Michelle stretched her legs under the table. The boys did the same. They leaned against the back of the floor chair and stretched their long legs all the way to the other side of the table where Michelle and Yuri were sitting. Yuri could not help but laugh at their bad manners.

After dinner, a professional dancer dressed in a beautiful kimono came to their dining room and performed a Japanese dance with *shamisen* music. The boys thought she was a geisha, but Yuri said she was a *maiko-san*. She explained further—many decades ago, the geishas were trained in the geisha house. They perfected their mannerisms, dance performances, and played musical instruments. Moreover, they were taught to entertain wealthy male patrons at the exclusive restaurants. Because of it, many geishas became the wealthy men's mistresses.

After World War II, because of the stigma of the geishas, the word geisha became synonymous with prostitution. Therefore, the geisha business went under the scrutiny.

The college students visited Nara and Kyoto after Tokyo. They insisted on seeing Hiroshima because they heard about the city. Since Hiroshima is not too far from Osaka, Yuri decided to take them for a day trip, but she warned them not to feel bad about the tragedy.

In the museum of Hiroshima, they saw the photos and the documentary films about seventy thousand Japanese citizens killed by the atomic bomb on August 6, 1945. They knew about the tragedy, but viewing the horrific pictures with their own eyes—what America did to Japan—dampened their spirits. The American students were quiet on the train.

Yuri had to cheer them up. "It happened long before we all were born, so it was not our fault. Besides, America and Japan are best friends now."

At the shopping district in Osaka, Michelle bought several kimonos. Tom bought kimonos for his mother and Teresa, and for Jake, he bought a silk tie. Alan bought two pairs of pearl earrings—one pair for his mother and another pair for his love—and a silk tie for Jefferson.

At the airport, they thanked Masaki and Emi for the airline tickets and their hospitality. Alan saw a pair of pearl earrings on Yuri's ears. She was to stay for one more week with her parents in Osaka.

Chapter 9
Yuri's Decision

On the airplane, Tom and Alan sat together, but Michelle's seat was far from their seats. Tom almost asked Alan if he could switch his seat with Michelle, but he did not have the courage.

When it came to Michelle, Tom felt as though Alan was protecting his sister from any man's advancement, including his. Therefore, he was always hesitant to approach Michelle.

To Michelle, Tom was her surrogate or second brother who had been kind to her and had been protecting her since she was a child. Whenever they hung out together at any events in the French Quarter, Tom would protect Michelle against drunken young men who tried to approach her. Because of Tom's watchful eyes, those punks did not dare come forward. Of course, Alan was doing the same.

However, Tom's motivation for protecting Michelle was a lot different from Alan's. Tom wanted to save Michelle for himself, but he was often frustrated because he wanted to be Michelle's lover, not her surrogate brother.

Nevertheless, he felt fortunate because he could get to see his love every weekend in Biloxi—just like he is away from home for the weekdays and comes home to his wife for the weekends.

Besides, Michelle always asked Tom to come along to the grocery store, just as the wife would ask the husband. The weekends fulfilled Tom's make-believe marriage.

If someone at the grocery store ever questions Tom if the pretty girl behind him is his wife, Tom does not hesitate to nod his head in a hurry. He had never attempted to ask any girls out because he felt it would be unfaithful to Michelle. His father, Jake, was often worried about his son's sexual preference since he had never brought any girl home as a date.

After they came home from Japan, Alan and Tom started working full time. A week later, Yuri called Michelle and told her she would be arriving the following day, but Michelle had a doctor's appointment on that day, so she asked her brother to pick her up.

Alan gladly agreed. He worked in the morning and took the afternoon off. When he imagined Yuri's beautiful smile, her lips, her body, and kissing, he became aroused and felt warmth in his heart.

Even though they kissed, caressed, and touched, they had never gone beyond that. Yes, Alan's sexual desire was uncontrollable from time to time, but he kept his celibacy because of their forbidden love.

The beauty queen was his first sexual encounter when he was in high school. They made love in her place while her aunt was at the store. Her aggressive approach often made Alan the happiest teenager on earth, but several months went by, he started disliking her—actually, he was scared of her.

When Masaki brought his daughter, Yuri, to New Orleans, he sincerely asked Jefferson to guard his daughter from any boy's advancement during her stay. Jefferson agreed to do so, but he needed his son's help because Alan would be around Yuri much more than Jefferson would, especially on the weekends in Biloxi. Alan did not have any choice but to promise his father.

He felt guilty because it was too late. Alan was already in love with the girl whom he was supposed to guard. Yuri was genuinely his love at first sight. Yuri's feeling was mutual. Their chemistry was very strong. It was simply too late to do anything about it. That was why they had to be discreet and secretive about their relationship. Michelle and Tom were the only ones who knew about their relationship.

When Alan saw Yuri at the airport, he embraced and kissed her. In the car, they kissed again. Alan could tell Yuri was quite aroused just as he was. She was caressing Alan gently over his trousers for the first time. Yuri had never done that before. Alan's sexual desire was heightened.

Somebody honked at him, so he started the engine. Alan said, "Let's go to Biloxi." Yuri nodded without any hesitation.

Before Yuri left Japan, she had a long talk with her mother and told her that she was deeply in love with Alan. Her mother, Emi, was very happy about her relationship with Alan because he was the son of Masaki's dear friends.

She told her to follow her heart but to be discreet for a while until she could figure out what to do with her husband. If Masaki found out his daughter's relationship with an American boy now, he could make her come home instantly without her college degree.

Even though he was not prejudiced against American boys in general, his daughter's relationship with any boy, especially with an American boy, could be detrimental. His utmost fear was his daughter's possible marriage to an American boy. If it would happen, his business plan for his daughter would be wasted because she would never come home to take over the Tokyo branch.

The best solution that Emi came up with was to convince Masaki to sell his business first. After the sale of his company, she could tell him her theory of killing three birds with one stone.

If Yuri's marriage to Alan could take place, everything could fall into one place—New Orleans. Masaki could retire there, he could see his old college friends there, and he could get together with his precious daughter and her husband, Alan, there. Furthermore, later in the future, the old college friends might see many of their mutual offspring there too.

Emi knew it would be a difficult task because Masaki was stubborn, but she was determined to convince her husband when Yuri and Alan decided to marry. In the meantime, she wanted her daughter to nurture their relationship discreetly.

After her heart-to-heart conversation with her mother, Yuri was so happy that she embraced her in tears. She also promised her that she would be discreet.

On the airplane, she made up her mind—she decided to give Alan something very special. He was the only person in this world who would genuinely deserve her gift. When she thought about Alan, she, too, felt the warmth in her heart.

While driving, both of the lovers were quiet, but they both knew exactly what they were going to do. Alan ran upstairs to get his saved condom. Yuri prepared to consummate her love for the first time.

In bed, Alan kissed Yuri passionately and caressed her shoulders, back, and buttocks gently to arouse her. When she looked aroused, he gradually penetrated her, but felt some resistance and tightness, almost too tight as though she was squeezing him, so he kept caressing her buttocks. Yuri seemed to be relaxed. The tightness almost gave Alan a climax, but he kept stroking. Yuri's beautiful face looked flushed. It seemed Alan's warmth inside her was finally relaxing her.

Alan repeatedly whispered in her ear how much he loved her. Yuri said the same. Alan could not wait any longer. He felt guilty, but Yuri was nodding as though she was saying it would be all right not to wait for her. Alan collapsed on top of her with his flushed face. He was out of breath, but quickly went to the bathroom, came right back to hold Yuri tightly, and said, "I love you." He also whispered. "Thank you." He wanted to thank her for the precious gift she saved just for him. They both fell asleep in each other's arms.

When they woke up, it was already dark outside. They took a shower together in a hurry and headed toward New Orleans. His parents were already home. Alan told them Yuri's flight was delayed, and he had to wait for her for a long time at the airport.

Although the school started, the girls habitually came to stay in the vacation home every weekend. Alan and Tom joined them too. The lovers discreetly satisfied their sexual desires while Tom and Michelle were out to the grocery store or in the middle of the night in Yuri's room.

*　*　*

Henry Thompson's father owned a large seafood company in New Orleans and lived on St. Charles Avenue. Henry was the same age as Tom and Alan. He was as popular as Alan in high school, but he was not as smart as Alan.

He was known as a rich brat, a Casanova, and a drug user among his classmates in high school. Alan and Tom knew him very well as a Casanova who slept with any females including prostitutes and bragged about his conquests.

His parents were divorced when he was in high school, and his father had custody of him until the age of eighteen. After high school, he decided to live with his mother who was remarried to another wealthy man in Mobile, Alabama.

His father insisted for him to go to college in Mobile by paying his tuition, but Henry was kicked out of school because of his failing grades. After his bumming around for a year or so, in Mobile, his father made him come back to New Orleans and managed to put him in the same college where Tom and Alan were attending.

Because of his father's new marriage with three stepchildren, Henry was placed in an apartment closer to school. His father paid for his tuition and books as well as his allowance and the apartment rent. However, his father gave him an ultimatum—Henry must make passing grades to graduate from college.

His father repeatedly warned him that if he could not make it in college this time, he would be on his own. In other words, Henry would receive no financial support from his father. He also offered his son a part-time job in his company, but Henry had no interest in working. He was simply lazy.

His father could not stand lazy bums, but as Henry was his only biological child, he wanted him to be a college graduate or a respectable adult just like him.

When Henry was growing up, he got everything from his mother. Even now, when Henry needed some money, she would give it to him without asking any questions. Whenever he said he was doing well in college, she would give him a lot more allowance than he expected. His father did not know that, so Henry was getting double his allowance.

One day, Henry saw the beauty queen at his sports car, which was parked on the side of the walkway on campus, waiting for him. Henry Thompson was probably the beauty queen's second target after Alan.

"Hi, Henry. Do you remember me?"

"Yes. Of course. You are the most beautiful girl in high school."

"Would you please give me a ride to the French Quarter?"

"Yes. Hop in."

"Thank you."

As soon as the beauty queen sat on the passenger seat in his open sports car, she pulled her skirt all the way up to her panty line to expose her thighs, unbuttoned her blouse to show her cleavage, and fanned herself with her hands as though she was cooling off. Even for a Casanova, it was too much.

After high school, the beauty queen got a scholarship from the same college where Alan and Tom were attending. She was extremely smart. Her SAT score was almost perfect. However, the scholarship was only for the tuition. Her aunt paid for the rest. As her aunt had already invested a lot of money in her education; she wanted to see some fruitful results soon from her niece.

"Are you thirsty? I could make the best lemonade in town." Henry invited the beauty queen to have some lemonade at his apartment before taking her home. He had an ulterior motive.

She said, "Wow! I love lemonade." The beauty queen, too, had an ulterior motive.

She helped Henry make a pitcher of lemonade and sat at the kitchen table. By then, the beauty queen's aggressive move aroused Henry. They hardly had a sip of lemonade before they started peeling off each other's clothes.

They both were equally aggressive in bed. Their lovemaking was somewhat violent, but they seemed to be enjoying each other. Her beautiful body fascinated Henry.

He thought she was his type in many ways. She was probably the best love maker so far. He liked her aggressiveness—it was like a prostitute's. After their breathless activity, they went back to the kitchen in nude, sat at the table, and sipped lemonade.

The beauty queen was caressing his thighs and said, "Henry, what a great love maker you are! I am just flabbergasted with your great stamina. Wow! Thank you."

That was her way of boosting the male ego. Now both of her hands were holding him gently and caressing. Henry was again aroused. All of a sudden, he grabbed her buttocks and let her sit on him as though he was a bicycle. With his tremendous stamina, he leaned against the back of the chair and moved her buttocks up and down with both of his hands. When he again went limp, he unknowingly said, "I love you." She, too, said meaninglessly, "I love you."

The beauty queen was on the pill, so she was not afraid of being pregnant. "Henry, you like to make love like this, don't you? If we live together, you could do it as many times as you want and anytime you want."

Her ulterior motive was to marry a son of a wealthy family. Living together could certainly bring a great possibility of marriage, which could guarantee her the wealth that she and her aunt wanted. The aunt would be very happy because Henry was one of the wealthy boys on her list.

Henry gave her permission to move in with him, but he told her to be discreet. He simply did not want his father to find out that he was keeping a woman in the apartment.

When the beauty queen moved in, she was confident that she got a son of a wealthy family at last—a marriage could come very soon. Her aunt, too, thought she could see some kind of dividends from her investment. They did not know Henry could be penniless if he did not make it in college. Moreover, they did not know Henry was born a Casanova.

Henry had never slept with a virgin. His utmost dream was to make love to a virgin. He had always hoped at least once to meet a virgin and conquer her as the first man in her life.

One day, Henry saw Michelle, who was sitting on the lawn reading a book. He had seen Michelle in the same private high school and in the neighborhood when he was growing up. She was not that tall but now matured as a beautiful young woman and still appeared to be a virgin.

Henry sat beside her and introduced himself as her neighbor on St. Charles Avenue. She did not know him well, but she knew his name as Henry Thompson, who competed with her brother, Alan, for the student president in high school—Alan won the election.

He politely asked her to eat dinner with him. It was her first time to be asked out by any man, so she gladly accepted his invitation.

Besides, he was not a stranger. He was two grades ahead of her just like Alan and Tom in high school, and he was now a college student from a reputable family.

They were to meet at the steak house in an exclusive hotel on Canal Street at five. She liked the way Henry spoke to her courteously. He had a big charming smile on his handsome face. She was excited and felt some chemistry.

Michelle came home with Yuri. She showered and wore a nice dress and told Yuri which restaurant she would be dining in and whom she would be with just in case her family wanted to know.

As far as Yuri remembered, Michelle had never had a date with a man, so she called Alan at work and told him that Michelle would be meeting a college student named Henry Thompson. Alan knew Henry as a womanizer and a drug user. He panicked and needed Tom's help since they both knew Henry well.

Alan long suspected that Tom had feelings for Michelle since he was young, but he was not sure because Tom had never talked about his feelings toward his sister. If Tom told him how he felt about his sister, he was going to help him, but he had never confided in Alan. Tom was probably too shy.

Anyway, Alan wanted Tom to know Michelle was with the infamous Casanova, Henry Thompson. Alan also thought if Tom was in love with his sister, this might wake him up and would definitely try to save his girl from a vulture.

Alan told Tom to get to the steak house quickly, and Alan would be there to meet him too. They both needed to find Michelle and Henry before it was too late. Tom was shocked to learn that Michelle fell for the notorious Casanova. He blamed himself for not telling Michelle that he had been in love with her since he was a child. Tom became quiet on the phone.

"Tom, are you there?"

"Yes. I am listening."

"They must be eating dinner right now. We have to hurry up. Meet me there."

"Okay."

Chapter 10
Secret Engagement

When Michelle arrived at the restaurant, Henry walked up to her, held both of her hands, and kissed her on her lips as though she was his lover. Since she had never been kissed, Michelle's whole body was tremulous. Henry chose the table at the window so they could see the skyline of New Orleans at dusk.

They sat facing at each other at the four-person table. He reached for Michelle's hands and started caressing them. The skyline looked beautiful and romantic.

Soon, Henry moved from the opposite side of the table to Michelle's side and ordered two glasses of red wine. Michelle was not used to drinking alcohol but had several sips. The steak dinner arrived.

While eating, Henry often caressed her leg with his leg under the table. His caressing was magical. She felt a sensation in her body that she had never felt before. Michelle felt as though she grew up as a young adult who was fortunate to date such a good-looking man who seemed to know how to treat his date intimately.

She was waiting for Henry to ask her many questions, such as what her major was in college, what kind of hobby she had, what her father did for living, and so forth. If he asked her such questions, she wanted to ask him the same, but instead he seemed to be concentrating on her body by touching her arm, her back, and buttocks in silence. Occasionally he whispered to her ear saying how beautiful and sexy she looked. Michelle was too naive to know Henry's ulterior motive.

If Michelle knew Henry was a born Casanova or he was the gold digger's live-in lover, she could've never agreed to meet him in the restaurant as her first date.

Nevertheless, Michelle was happy to be discovered by a handsome young college student who was supposed to be a son of a reputable family on St. Charles Avenue.

In the past, Tom Rousseau was her sexual interest. From time to time, she wished he would touch her or kiss her, but he was always hesitant. She did not know why.

When they were spending almost every weekend in Biloxi, she really did not mind if they became intimate like Alan and Yuri, but he did not seem to know how to be intimate. Nevertheless, he gladly accompanied her to the grocery store as though he was her husband. Tom and Michelle were equally timid, naive, and sexually inexperienced. In other words, they both were virgins.

After dinner, Henry ordered two glasses of after-dinner drinks with some desserts. He told her to gulp down the drink to digest the dessert she just ate, so she did. It almost burned her throat and chest. Later, she felt dizzy and sleepy for some reason. The last thing she remembered was Henry holding her waist and walking past the hotel lobby.

Tom and Alan arrived at the same time, but no sight of Henry and Michelle in the steak house. They went to the hotel lobby to see if Henry Thompson was registered, but the receptionist said she was not allowed to give out any information on the hotel guests.

Nevertheless, she told them to use the house phone to call the hotel operator. If Henry Thompson had checked into the hotel, the operator could connect them to his room. Tom called the hotel operator and asked for Henry Thompson's room, but he was told that no such person had checked into the hotel yet. Tom and Alan were desperate to find Henry Thompson who seemed to be one step ahead of them, making the reservation anonymously or under an alias.

Alan saw Tom's distraught face, the lover's anguish—he looked heartbroken. Alan then knew how Tom felt about his sister. Alan said fiercely, "If I ever find out Henry touched my sister, I will kill him." Tom could have said the same thing, but he was quiet. They checked the nearby hotels, but the results were the same.

Michelle came home around ten. Jefferson and Marie were already in bed, not knowing that their daughter had had her first date. They did not ask Yuri where Michelle was. They assumed she was working in the library. She often volunteered to work in the library at night because of her major.

Besides, Yuri decided not to say anything about Michelle's date because Alan said something disturbing when she gave the name of her date, Henry Thompson.

In the hallway, Yuri asked Michelle how her date went. She had a faint smile on her face, said it was fine, and closed the door. Yuri heard the shower running in Michelle's room. Alan came home and asked Yuri about Michelle, but Yuri just shrugged her shoulders.

For several days after her date, Michelle was not herself, but she tried very hard to be cheerful in front of her parents and Yuri. Michelle was rather talkative in nature, but this time she had not said anything about her first date even to her best friend, Yuri.

At school, Michelle was looking for Henry Thompson, but he was nowhere to be found. She went to the administration office to find his class schedule, but she found out that he had already dropped out of school.

When Henry was making failing grades in school, he decided to drop out instead of being kicked out. His father was very angry and disappointed. He sternly told him that he must be on his own and had to vacate the apartment. Therefore, he decided to move back to Mobile, where his mother lived.

The beauty queen was very upset because she learned that Henry Thompson never intended to marry her, and his father's company or the family fortune could never be his in the future either. Now he had to vacate the apartment. Her aunt was disappointed as well, but again she took her in.

The aunt wanted the beauty queen to concentrate on the third target, Thomas Rousseau, who was accepted by a famous law school in Chicago. The beauty queen, too, passed the LSAT to be admitted in the same law school. Fortunately, she managed to receive a scholarship from the school where Tom was going to attend. She told her aunt that this time, she would definitely marry a wealthy one.

To the beauty queen, Tom was naive, shy, and an easy target. She rather liked the aggressive type like Henry Thompson or Alan Dubois, but she must go after Tom. She was somewhat doubtful about Tom's sexual preference since she had never seen Tom with a girl in high school or college. She just hoped he was not homosexual.

When the beauty queen saw Tom in school before their graduation, she told him she was also accepted by the same law school in Chicago where he was to be attending. She winked at him seductively and shook his hand. He did not know much about her except she was known as the beauty queen in high school. Nevertheless, her beauty and perfect body fascinated Tom.

Jake and Eunice were very proud of their son, Tom, who was accepted by the famous law school in Chicago, but on the other hand, they were emotional about their only son going to a faraway place and leaving them behind. Nevertheless, they were certain Tom would come back to take over the family business after his law school.

Jefferson and Marie were surprised to learn that their son, Alan, would be working as a pilot. A charter flight company in Gulfport had already hired him. Alan had obtained a pilot license while he was in college.

However, Alan promised his parents he would be back to work for them in the near future. Until then, Alan needed to live in the antebellum mansion in Biloxi because his work was in the next town called Gulfport.

Yuri and Michelle were still in college. Every weekend, they joined Alan in Biloxi. They missed Tom Rousseau a lot, especially Michelle did. Alan's flying schedule in the charter flight company was irregular. From time to time, he had to fly on the weekends and missed seeing Yuri and Michelle, but whenever Alan was home, Michelle gave the lovers some intimate time.

The gold digger and Tom were married during their law school, and after the graduation, both started working for a reputable law firm in Chicago. Jake and Eunice were not invited to their wedding. In fact, they did not invite anybody, even her aunt. It seemed they got married in a hurry.

The news upset Eunice because she always thought Tom had feelings for Michelle. She had been observing Tom's behavior toward

Michelle since he was a child. Eunice even told Marie about her suspicion, but Tom married someone else. She was sad for Michelle because she, too, acted favorably toward her son since she was a child.

Indeed, Michelle felt sad and heartbroken because the gold digger married her precious longtime friend who should've been her lover. She concluded Tom was so naive that he became a victim of a gold digger just as she became a victim of a Casanova. She could empathize with him for being so naive.

When Michelle learned about Tom's divorce six months later, she was elated and felt as though Tom could be hers again. Tom was supposed to come home and take over the family business after his law school, but he refused. Since the beauty queen wanted Tom's family fortune, she could not stand her husband who let the fortune slip away from her, so she decided to leave him.

Shortly after Michelle and Yuri graduated from college, Alan invited Tom to witness his engagement to Yuri in Biloxi. No one was invited except Michelle and Tom. Of course, their relationship was still a secret. By then, Tom was just divorced from his wife and estranged from his parents, so he came directly from the airport to Biloxi in a rental car.

Seeing Tom made Michelle so excited that she embraced him and gave him a quick kiss on his lips as though he was her lover or husband. Tom looked surprised, but he did not return the kiss. If he were alone with her, he probably would've returned the kiss, but instead, he just smiled and said, "It is so nice to be with you guys again. Thank you for inviting me to this special occasion."

Michelle and Yuri worked hard all morning to make some sushi, which everybody liked. Tom devoured sushi and said he had not eaten sushi for years.

After dinner, everybody sat on the sofa in the living room. Alan knelt down in front of Yuri and proposed. Yuri said yes and nodded several times with tears. Michelle took many pictures of them, including Alan putting a beautiful engagement ring around Yuri's finger.

In the end, Alan told Yuri not to wear her engagement ring in front of Jefferson and Marie. Their engagement had to be a secret until he could figure out what to do next.

Yuri told everybody that her student visa was extended for another year. Her father was reluctant, but he agreed because she needed to be certified as a CPA by passing the tests.

Alan had already moved back to New Orleans and started working as vice president in the family business. Since the mansion in Biloxi was given to him, he let Yuri live there so she could study for her CPA tests. Michelle, too, needed to finish her MLS degree, so she spent her weekends with Yuri in Biloxi. Michelle was determined to finish her degree within a year.

The next day, when Tom was leaving for the airport, Michelle followed him to his car and said, "Tom, it was very nice to see you again."

Tom embraced Michelle and whispered in her ear, "Michelle, I really missed seeing you. I often think about you and reminisce about how the great times we had in Biloxi. I will write you as soon as I get a new apartment."

"Tom, are you coming back to New Orleans sometime soon?"

"I don't think so. I am involved in a big case in Chicago. You may not know it, but my parents are not speaking to me. It is a long story, but eventually, I will be back home to help my parents, but I don't know when. Michelle, remember, you are always on my mind."

"Tom, try to reconcile with your parents soon so you can come home anytime you want. I will miss you. Come back soon."

Tom nodded and drove off.

The beauty queen quit her job in Chicago and moved back to New Orleans because she could not stand seeing Tom in the same workplace. Besides, her wealthy boss, whom she got involved with, could not make up his mind about leaving his wife, so she decided to come back to New Orleans.

The aunt was angry when she heard about her divorce, but she again took her in. However, this time, the beauty queen got her own apartment. While she was looking for a job, she decided to help her aunt at the gift shop.

The beauty queen always thought of her aunt as a savior who found her, rescued her from the foster care services, and sent her to the finest high school, college, and law school. She loved her for that. She sincerely wanted to pay her back in the future.

"Why did you leave Tom? He is the heir to the Rousseau Company. They live on St. Charles Avenue."

"Did you know that stupid husband of mine refused to take over the family business? He thinks his law practice is more important than the family fortune. Now his parents are not speaking to him. They offered the mansion on St. Charles Avenue and the entire business, but Tom refused. How stupid can he be!"

"Well, you are still beautiful and young. Work hard to find a wealthy man who can afford to buy a house on St. Charles Avenue. With your beauty, you should not have any problem marrying a rich man."

One day, when the beauty queen was rummaging through old newspapers that were saved to wrap up some souvenirs at the store, an old article caught her eye. "Alan Dubois, a son of Jefferson Dubois, was promoted to vice president at the Dubois Import Company." It was just one of the business notices in the local newspaper.

The beauty queen read the notice several times. She still remembered Alan's rejection, but she made up her mind—she had to see him. Alan was actually her first love, and she still had feelings for him. She was determined to recapture him and perhaps marry him in the future. This time she was going to show him how much she had changed and grown up.

Alan was surprised to see her. She still looked stunning just as before. She told him that she left Chicago and came back home, but she could not find a job in any law firm. She did not mention her divorce, but Alan knew about her marriage to his best friend, Tom. In the end, she practically begged Alan for a job.

The kindhearted Alan gave her a job, but he wanted her to look for a real lawyer's job. In other words, he wanted to hire her temporarily. She was to assist their company lawyer Jeffery Dubois. Jeffery needed someone who could type some legal papers and interpret the international tariff regulations. She promised that she would do anything—typing, copying, researching, interpreting, calculating, even making coffee. She was not a lazy person.

The beauty queen did not know Alan was already married. He married Yuri secretly in the city hall in Biloxi. Michelle witnessed their marriage. Her official name became Yuri Tanaka Dubois. Submitting the marriage certificate to the immigration office, Yuri got a permanent resident card known as a green card to live in the United States legally.

Alan went back and forth between New Orleans and Biloxi. He spent the weekends in Biloxi with his wife. Of course, Jefferson and Marie did not suspect their son's relationship with Yuri because Michelle was doing the same thing—spending the weekends in Biloxi to study. Besides, the mansion was already given to Alan when he became vice president, so they did not question Alan about his frequent visits to his own house.

Shortly after their marriage, Yuri became pregnant. Michelle was very happy about the baby, so she encouraged her brother, Alan, to tell their parents about his marriage and Yuri's pregnancy as soon as possible.

"Alan, you must talk to Dad and Mom about your marriage and Yuri's pregnancy. Since you both are officially married, there is no reason for you to hide the truth. You should be proud to tell them about the baby. I am very sure Dad and Mom could figure out what to do with Masaki. Do not wait too long. Yuri's stomach will be getting bigger and bigger each day."

Despite her pregnancy, Yuri passed all levels of the CPA tests. The certification paper should be sent to Yuri soon. Michelle, too, was scheduled to graduate soon.

The beauty queen was pressuring Alan at work. She made coffee every morning for the heads of the company, stayed in Alan's office all afternoon, and tried to seize the opportunity.

Michelle thought about telling her parents about her brother, Alan's, marriage, but she realized that Masaki told her father to guard Yuri during her stay in New Orleans.

If Masaki knew about his daughter's marriage to his trusted friend's son, Alan, their friendship might be jeopardized. Michelle, too, became hesitant.

Chapter 11
Tom Rousseau

In the morning, Mom fixed breakfast for Tom and me. Tom lived in New Orleans with his father, but while we stayed in his antebellum mansion, he did not mind commuting between Biloxi and New Orleans every day.

Several years ago, when Tom's mother, Eunice, got cancer, his father, Jake, decided to let his son, Tom, know about Eunice's terminal cancer. Tom was saddened and wanted to come home to see her. When he asked Jake if it was all right for him to come home, Jake was very happy to say, "Of course."

He thought his son was just visiting them, but Tom said loudly, "No, Dad. I wanted to come home for good. I hope your offer is still good. I will take over the family business and take care of you both. I have missed Mom and you a lot."

Jake could not believe what he was hearing from his only son after so many years of estrangement. He felt tears and could not speak for a while, but finally he said in a quivery voice, "Son, this is the greatest news ever. Mom would be very happy to hear that you would be coming home for good. We have missed you a lot too."

At that time, Tom was losing faith in the legal system. He saw his colleagues' unethical law practices and greedy legal maneuvering just to win cases. Most of the time, the money seemed to be the major motivation in his law firm. From his experience, justice was often bought.

Tom was too honest to maneuver or cheat the legal system. He felt dirty and wanted to start his life differently, so being a lawyer was no longer his interest. He wanted to come home. Besides, he wanted to see his parents. Another person he really wanted to see was Michelle Dubois, but he did not know her whereabouts.

He knew all about the Dubois family's tragedy. He had tried to write to Michelle, but all the letters he sent to St. Charles Avenue or Biloxi were returned, but he was determined to find Michelle once he moved back to New Orleans.

Before Eunice found out her terminal bone cancer, Teresa had already left for Mexico to take care of her mother who was very ill. Jake hired a daytime housekeeper for Eunice. During the night, he took care of her himself just as he took care of his son when he was born.

When Tom saw his mother after so many years, his face was wet with tears, and he was speechless. Eunice's wrinkled face was wet with tears as well. Tom knelt down on the floor to hold her hands instead of bending over to embrace her. Her skeletal hands were so tiny, like a child's hands.

Tom felt a pain in his chest from the guilt he had for all those years. When he was young, he thought his mother hated him because his birth almost caused her to die. As she hardly came out to play with him, or teach him the alphabet or numbers, he again thought his mother hated him.

He often wanted to be held in her arms, but she was too ill to do so. Instead, he remembered he slept on Teresa's soft chest most of the time. Because of all that, he had not been close to his mother. Now he was determined to rekindle his relationship with his mother. Of course, Tom always had the fond memories of his father and loved him very much.

He noticed his parents looked so much older than he remembered. Jake's brown hair was almost white and his height somewhat shrank. Eunice's black hair was all gray and thin.

Finally, Eunice spoke quietly by squeezing his hands, "Tom, it is nice to see you. You grew up to be such a handsome man."

"Mom, I came home to take care of you. I also came home to help Dad with his business. I am sorry that I did not come home sooner." Tom squeezed both of her hands.

Tom remembered that his parents begged him to come home to take over the family business, but he rejected them by saying that he had no intention of taking over a boring family business.

Because of the estrangement, Jake and Eunice had never met their ex-daughter-in-law.

Eunice had already told Jake that she was leaving everything to Tom—her life insurance, savings accounts, stocks, and all of her jewelry for her son's future bride. Jake agreed. He, too, named his son as his beneficiary of all his possessions including the family business.

When Teresa came to their lives, Eunice totally depended on Teresa. From time to time, she was jealous of Teresa because the baby would not come to her. Instead, he always cried for Teresa as though she was his mother. Eunice had never expressed her motherly love to Tom because deep in her heart, she blamed her child for her illness.

After Tom's return, Jake made him the president of the Rousseau Export Company. Tom had learned the company routine while he was in college, so it was not hard for him to manage the company.

After the family business was transferred to Tom legally, Jake decided to spend more time with Eunice at home, but since the housekeeper took care of Eunice during the day, he often went to the office to help Tom.

A visiting nurse came to check on Eunice every day and administered the pain medicine. The housekeeper helped Eunice walk around the house and gave her hot lunch. When Jake was home, he helped Eunice walk and ate lunch with her.

Whenever Eunice felt stronger, Jake drove her from Gulfport to Biloxi on the scenic drive because she enjoyed seeing the long white sand beach and the calm ocean from the window.

After Tom's return, the doctor thought Eunice was getting stronger for some reason, but he warned her to walk carefully with a cane or a walker and absolutely no stairs climbing.

When she was prohibited to climb the stairs, the guestroom downstairs became her bedroom. Jake moved some of her clothes and toiletries from their master bedroom upstairs to her bedroom downstairs. If she needed something from the master bedroom, Jake or the housekeeper was supposed to get them for her.

One day, Jake and Tom were at work, the housekeeper called them frantically and said an ambulance took Eunice to the hospital because she fell down from the stairs and became unconscious. The housekeeper apologized in tears. She explained what happened—when she was preparing lunch, Eunice climbed the stairs to get something from the room upstairs. She again cried loudly on the phone.

Jake consoled her by saying, "It was not your fault. You did the right thing calling for an ambulance. We will meet her in the hospital, so stop crying."

Jake and Tom went to the hospital. Eunice was in the emergency room unconscious. The doctor found some hairline fractures in her hip and leg.

The doctor said, "This kind of fractures cannot be treated by surgery. It will heal naturally by resting in one position from three to four weeks. I will arrange an orthopedic specialist to check her out tomorrow."

When Eunice made loud moaning sounds because of the pain, painkiller was injected. She stopped moaning, but remained unconscious.

After Jake sent Tom home because he needed to be in the office for the next day, Jake sat on a chair beside Eunice and decided to spend the night in the hospital. When painkiller was injected, Eunice stayed quiet and slept soundly. Jake dozed off by putting his head down on her bed.

In the morning, Jake wanted to hold his wife's hand, but her hand was ice-cold. Eunice passed away quietly without saying goodbye to Jake, who was beside her all night long. Jake sobbed.

Jake and Tom gave her a beautiful funeral service in a week. Her friends, office workers, and some siblings from Kentucky came. After the funeral, Jake gave his son Eunice's life insurance, several savings accounts, and stock certificates that bore the name of Tom Rousseau as her beneficiary.

Jake jokingly said, "I guess Mom loved you more than she loved me. No. I knew Mom would do that. It was her way of apologizing for not taking care of you when you were young, also a form of her love. She loved you very much. Remember that."

Tom was stunned by seeing the substantial value of his inheritance. Jake suggested for Tom to buy a house of his own so his mother's legacy could stay with him forever.

After Eunice's passing, Jake decided to dismiss the housekeeper. He wanted to retire from the family business completely, but he promised Tom that whenever he needed to be on a vacation or out of town, he would substitute for him in the office.

Jake started cooking breakfast every morning and waited on Tom with dinner at night. From time to time, Jake met Tom at a restaurant in the French Quarter and ate dinner just as he used to do with Eunice after work.

At the dinner table, Tom often talked about his childhood with Jake. He reminisced about how he enjoyed being on Jake's shoulders, watching the crowd from the top of Jake's head, eating beignets at Café Du Monde, and never forgot to take some beignets home because his mother loved them too.

He also told him he wished everyday were a weekend day because he hated to be cooped up in the house during the weekdays when Jake was at work—he had never gone outside because Teresa was always busy cleaning and cooking, and his mother was resting in the bedroom. The only thing he did was watch *Sesame Street* or cartoons on TV.

With his mother's money, Tom decided to buy one of the antebellum homes in Biloxi in the same neighborhood where the Dubois family used to own a vacation home. Besides, Tom knew how much his mother loved to see the white sand beach and the calm ocean from the scenic drive.

After Tom's mansion was bought and remodeled, Jake and Tom stayed in Biloxi almost every weekend and played golf together as though the long estrangement had never happened between them. They were bonded as father and son just as before.

One day, Jake asked Tom about his short-lived marriage and his ex-wife, but Tom just said, "It was a nightmare—nothing to talk about. It was a mistake. I want to forget all about it."

Nevertheless, Tom told his father boldly about his genuine love for Michelle Dubois. Jake was surprised to hear about it because he always wondered about his son's sexual preference and thought his marriage failed because of his son's possible homosexuality.

He felt relieved to hear his son's love for Michelle. They both did not know Michelle's whereabouts after the family tragedy, but at the time of Eunice's burial, Jake found out the funeral director was a cousin of Bob Turner, who eloped with Jefferson Dubois's only sister, Margaret, and moved to North Georgia.

Bob Turner was the heir to the Turner Funeral Home in New Orleans, but he gave the family business to his cousin and moved to North Georgia. When Bob Turner passed away, his wife, Margaret, brought her husband's body to New Orleans.

Jake knew that Jefferson's sister, Margaret, visited the Dubois family and learned that Michelle liked her aunt because her aunt had the courage of love to marry the Creole husband.

Jake remembered that Jefferson said something about Michelle and Margaret writing to each other. He thought it could be possible that Michelle went to live with Aunt Margaret after her eviction because Margaret was the only relative Michelle had in the United States.

Jake knew Yuri Tanaka moved back to Japan because she, too, tried to locate Michelle by calling Jake at work, but Michelle was nowhere to be found—vanished. After Michelle's disappearance, Jake and Eunice found out that someone already occupied the Dubois mansion on St. Charles Avenue, and so was the mansion in Biloxi.

When his son, Tom, confided in Jake how much he loved Michelle, Jake decided to locate Michelle himself for his beloved son. He went to see the funeral director named Rick Turner. He asked him if he knew Margaret Turner or Michelle Dubois.

"Yes. Michelle Dubois came to bury her aunt Margaret Turner several years ago. Margaret was my cousin's wife."

"Do you have their address?"

"Yes. Let me check the registry."

While checking the registry, he kept talking to Jake.

"Michelle said she lived with Margaret Turner after she lost her family in an airplane crash and worked as a librarian in college in North Georgia. One day when Michelle was at work, the neighbor called an ambulance to take her aunt to the hospital, but she died on the way to the hospital. She had a massive heart attack."

"Do you think Michelle still lives in North Georgia?"

"I think she does. I am sure Margaret gave the house to Michelle since she did not have any children. I visited my cousin Bob there and stayed in their house once. Here it is! I found it! Her address and phone number!"

"Thank you. We have been looking for her for years."

On that night, Jake cooked dinner, waited for his son's arrival, and surprised him with Michelle's phone number. Jake explained how he found Michelle's whereabouts. Tom was very grateful.

"May I speak to Michelle Dubois?" When Tom called Michelle on the phone after dinner, he heard a little girl's voice.

"Just a minute. Mom is in the kitchen."

"Who is this?"

"This is Tom Rousseau. Are you Michelle?"

"Oh my! Are you really Tom? How did you find me? Where are you? In Chicago?"

"No. I am calling from New Orleans. The funeral director, Mr. Turner, gave my dad your phone number. I came back home several years ago when Mom got sick. She passed away last year."

"I am very sorry. I remember your mother and my mother were such good friends."

"Yes. They were. After I heard about the airplane crash years back, I wrote to you, but all the letters were returned. All of your phones were disconnected. As my parents and I were estranged for many years, I just did not know how to find you. I missed seeing you for all those years. I would really like to see you soon."

Tom almost confessed how much he loved her since he was a child, but he did not.

"I am so glad you found me. We are on the summer break now, so you can visit us anytime. Do you know our address?"

"Yes, but you can give me a detailed direction when I get to Atlanta. In fact, I will be in Atlanta next week for a business conference with some vendors. By the way, who is that little girl on the phone?"

"My daughter. She will be nine years old soon. Her name is Lily."

"Michelle, are you married?"

"No."

"Are you sure it is all right to visit you?"

"Yes, I really want to see you too."

"I need to catch up with you before I see you. Is it all right to call you tomorrow night?"

"Yes, of course. Call me around ten. Lily would be in bed by then."

"Okay. I am so happy to hear your voice again. Talk to you tomorrow."

After the initial conversation, Tom called Michelle every night, asking her many questions and telling her about his life in Chicago. Michelle felt as though she gained a dear friend or a lover again. She felt comfortable telling him about the family tragedy, the disappearance of the family fortune, the evictions, and her life in North Georgia with her daughter.

She also told him about her suspicion of two lawyers who worked for Alan and her parents. She did not tell him one of the lawyers was his ex-wife. However, the grand larceny by those lawyers got Tom's attention.

"I will look into the property deeds in the courthouse—how the Dubois's business property and the home property were transferred after their deaths. Someone might have forged Jefferson's signature to transfer the properties. I had a case like that in Chicago. Anyway, I will help you find the crooks."

Tom told her about his marriage that lasted only six months and it was a mistake. Michelle asked him if he knew his ex-wife's whereabouts, but he had no clue. Therefore, Michelle had to tell Tom that his ex-wife moved back to New Orleans and got a job from Alan before the tragedy.

She said, "Tom, I think your ex-wife wanted to marry Alan so she could be the wealthy man's wife. That was why she approached Alan for the second time. Once in high school, she pressured Alan to marry her."

"I did not know that."

She also told him how remorseful she had been because she did not tell her brother about her findings when she was in high school. She found out that she and her aunt targeted Alan in their gold digging project because he was a son of a wealthy family on St. Charles Avenue. If she had told Alan about her gold digging project, he would never have hired her and then the family tragedy should've never happened.

Tom comforted her. "It was not your fault. My ex-wife was very aggressive, calculating, conniving, and, yes, she was a gold digger. I am sure Alan knew about her, but he was just kindhearted to hire her. It was not your fault." Michelle felt as though Tom was a godsend lawyer and a lover whom she had been waiting for the longest time.

Chapter 12
A Kid Detective

*M*om wanted to show me where Uncle Alan's mansion used to be after Tom left for work. She said it should be only two or three blocks away, so we decided to walk the street behind the houses. It was quiet and hardly had any traffic. The scenic drive in front of the houses was rather busy. Mom put sunscreen on my face and arms before putting a hat on my head.

When we came to an antebellum mansion that was fenced with the elaborate iron bars, Mom was confused, but after she saw the house number on the mailbox, she finally said while pointing to the mansion, "Lily, here you are! This is your birthplace!"

"I thought I was born in the hospital in Gainesville."

Mom was talking without thinking again, but this time, she looked remorseful.

"Right, I was confused. Sorry." She dismissed the topic of my birthplace and concentrated on the mansion.

"The iron-bar gate at the driveway looks very private. They must use a remote control to open the gate. I wonder what kind of people live in such a guarded place. We did not have anything like this before. We only had the iron-bar door in front of the house to prevent the burglaries."

While we were talking about the mansion, a girl who was probably my age was walking down the driveway with a bicycle. At the walk-in entrance next to the mailbox, she glances at us with a big smile. We smiled back at her. She was in shorts and looks pretty with her blonde hair. After she put her headgear straight, she rode toward the direction of Tom's house where we just came from.

After we walked past several more homes, we decided to turn around and head back home. While walking past the girl's mansion again, we saw a tall, glamorous, and movie-star-like woman with blonde hair walking down the driveway toward the mailbox. I assumed she was the girl's mother.

When Mom saw the woman, her face turned white. She quickly turned her face away from the woman and walked past the house as fast as she could. I turned around, saw the woman's good looks once more, and thought she looked just like a porcelain doll I saw at the antique shop. I did not think she saw my stare. By then, Mom was one house ahead of me, so I ran to catch up with her.

Mom's face was still white. She looked pensive as though she was trying to recall something or analyze something. I was very sure Mom recognized that woman. If she were Mom's high school or college friend, she might have yelled at her to say hello at least, but instead her face turned white as though she saw a ghost.

Is that woman the gold digger Mom was talking about? She certainly fits the description—a movie-star-like figure. Is she the one who stole Uncle Alan's house here in Biloxi, the mansion in New Orleans, and the family business? Did such a beautiful woman poison my grandparents and tampered with the aircraft, which caused the airplane crash to kill all three of Mom's family?

Mom might have thought I was too young to comprehend the family tragedy, but I knew what larceny meant and what poisoning and tampering did to my grandparents and Uncle Alan.

Many years ago, Mom and Grandma Margaret went to see a lawyer in Atlanta to find out how much it would cost to pursue the investigation on her family tragedy. The lawyer told her that the initial retainer would cost $15,000. Mom did not have that kind of money, so she gave up.

Before Tom visited us in North Georgia, I was sure that Mom had already told Tom about her suspicions on those lawyers. I heard the phone ring every night before I fell asleep. I knew the phone call was from Tom. They were rekindling their relationship because they had not seen each other for many years, and at the same time, Mom was probably asking Tom to help locate those crooks.

Tom was very kind to let us stay in his beach house. Mom had been reciprocating his kindness by cooking breakfast and dinner to wait on him. Tom liked that and jokingly said he felt as if he was married and having a wife and a child.

I owed Tom a lot too because I was able to see an ocean and a real beach, taste the ocean water, and see the endlessly moving waves for the first time on my ninth birthday.

While walking back, we saw the girl riding the bicycle toward us. She stopped in front of me and asked, "Excuse me. Do you live in this neighborhood?"

"No. We are staying in our friend's vacation home. I celebrated my ninth birthday here. Are you vacationing with your family here too?"

"No. I was born here. I will be nine at the end of this year. My name is Amy Dubois. What is your name?"

"My name is Lily."

When Mom heard the girl's last name, Dubois, her face turned whiter, again. Because of it, I did not exclaim by saying, "Wow! We have the same last name, Dubois!"

"Well, I have to go. Are you staying here for a while?"

"Yes."

"Come outside and play with me tomorrow. Which house is yours?"

"That one with brown color." I pointed to Tom's house, which was one house down from where we were standing. After putting her headgear straight, she waved at us with a big smile. *What a friendly child she was*, I thought.

Mom was quiet. I was quiet too, thinking about how such a friendly child could be the gold digger's child. I bet the child had no clue what hideous things her mother had done. I felt sorry for her.

While baking Tom's favorite chocolate chip cookies together in the afternoon, I asked Mom if the woman we saw was the gold digger. She nodded several times positively and looked anxious as though she could hardly wait to tell Tom about it.

After we finished dinner, she asked me to do the dishes and disappeared in the study with Tom. I did the dishes, but they were still in the study. I wished I were a grown-up so I could participate in their discussion and let them know I could help them with my inquisitive mind.

I sat on a chair in the porch contemplating while watching the scenic drive and the beach—I could be a kid detective for Mom and Tom. I will see Amy Dubois tomorrow and find out what her parents' names are, what they do for living, and other important information.

However, I have to lie to Amy Dubois about my last name—I will call myself Lily Turner, Grandma Margaret's last name, and tell her I live with a father and a mother in Atlanta, Georgia. My father is a famous lawyer named Thomas Turner—Thomas from Thomas Rousseau.

The reason I will call myself Lily Turner is that I do not want her to exclaim when she hears my last name, Dubois. I remembered I almost exclaimed when she introduced herself as Amy Dubois.

If I find out her parents are the crooks whom Mom has been looking for, I hope Tom as a lawyer will help Mom bring them to justice, but I understand a lawsuit would cost a lot of money.

Will Tom help Mom financially? In other words, will he help Mom without asking her for a $15,000 retainer? I know Tom is rich and generous, but Mom is the type of person who does not take anyone or anything for granted. She would insist on paying Tom even though she does not have much. However, if she is married to Tom, she does not have to pay her husband, does she? I do not mind having Tom as my father. He can be a good husband to Mom and a good father to me.

They are fond of each other, or probably very much in love, but they would not hold each other's hands or would not kiss. They seem to be out of practice in the romance department. They should see a romantic movie in the theater without me. That may bring their romantic feelings back. They surely act like a grandpa and a grandma who have forgotten how to be romantic.

I am a child, but I know what romance is—kissing and holding hands are romantic displays of affection. If Tom really wants to marry Mom, he has to hold Mom's hand and kiss her passionately. Then Mom agrees to marry him. After their marriage, they can make as many babies as they want. Being the oldest sibling, they can depend on me. I can teach the little ones everything I know so they are going to be very smart like me. I was daydreaming.

The next day, Mom wanted to go to the local library and the county courthouse to find something about the girl's family, but I did not want to go, so I told her I would rather stay home and read a book. Before she left, she told me to lock the kitchen door, not to go outside, and not to answer the door for any strangers. I nodded affirmatively several times.

Actually, I wanted to visit Amy Dubois or see her on the street, but I decided not to because of my promise to Mom. Nevertheless, I was determined to do my detective work soon—perhaps, this afternoon after Mom's return or tomorrow.

When I was reading a book, I heard a knock on the kitchen door. There stood Amy Dubois with a bicycle in the carport. She was waving her hand vigorously at me with her friendly smile. I opened the door and invited her in.

"I cannot stay too long. I just want to say hello."

"Come in. I am alone. Mom is running some errands."

I was glad Amy Dubois came to visit me. She was not a stranger, so I was not violating my promise to Mom. Even though I did not expect Amy this soon, I was thinking fast to keep her with me so I could get some information on her family.

I put two glasses of milk and some cookies on a plate and sat with her at the kitchen table. Amy thanked me and ate one. "Wow! I had never eaten such a big and moist cookie before. Does your mother bake cookies like this all the time?"

"Yes. From time to time, she let me bake cookies too. We made those yesterday."

"My mom would not cook or bake much, so I was not taught how to cook or bake."

While entertaining Amy with cookies, my detective mind is at work. My antenna on my head is alert. My secretarial skills to record the entire conversation are sharpened. My acting carrier as a movie star is about to launch. I am ready to read a script without any mistakes. I heard the director's loud voice, "And action!"

"Amy, my full name is Lily Turner. My parents and I live in Atlanta, Georgia. My father's name is Thomas Turner, and he is a well-known lawyer in the city. My mother's name is Michelle Turner. She is a librarian. Dad could not come with us because he has a trial this week. His lawyer friend let us use this mansion. My father makes very good money in his law firm, and we live in a big mansion. I think our house in Atlanta is much bigger than your house."

"My dad and mom both are lawyers too. Dad's name is Jeffery Dubois. Mom's name is Nancy Saunders Dubois. They own a company called the Dubois Import Company in Gulfport, next town."

"Wow! Your family must be very rich!"

"Yes. They make tons of money and are very busy. They have many employees too. We also have a big mansion on St. Charles Avenue in New Orleans. Right now, my mom's aunt lives there, but Dad told me when I get older, the mansion would be mine."

"Wow! What a lucky girl you are! Are you the only child?"

"I guess I am, but I have two stepbrothers and one stepsister in Houston, Texas. My father was married before, but for some reason, they hate Mom and Dad, so I have never met them. They probably hate me too. Are you the only child too?"

"Yes, I am, but I have two friends who are like a sister and a brother, and we play together almost every day."

"I envy you. I wish I had a friend who can play or ride a bicycle with me. There are no children in this neighborhood. I feel very lonely. As Mom would not hire a housekeeper, she expects me to clean the house. She works in the office with my dad most of the time, especially when I am at school, but during my summer breaks, she works on the typewriter at home."

She had another cookie with milk and continued. "When I once met a girl like you who spent their vacation for a week in this neighborhood, I invited her and her sister to play with me in our house, but Mom got very angry and sent the girls home. I cried, but she kept telling me not to bring any kids home. I think she does not like kids including me. On the other hand, Dad loves me and plays board games with me on the weekends. He bought me a bicycle so I could ride in the neighborhood. I love my dad. Does your father love you? What about your mother?"

"Yes. My parents love me very much, and they do not mind having my friends in the house. I am sure your mother loves you too, but she probably has lots on her mind."

"I hope so. Oh, I must go. Mom gets mad if I stop at anybody's house. Come outside to see me tomorrow. I may be riding a bicycle. Thank you for the cookies."

After Amy left, I sat at the table and analyzed what I found out about the girl's parents. I decided to tell everything to Mom and Tom. They could use my findings. I repeated the entire conversation in my head so I would not forget any of what Amy had to say about her parents.

Being a kid, I was a bit afraid of telling my findings to the grown-ups because most grown-ups would not take kids seriously. However, I was proud of my work as a kid detective.

At the dinner table, I told everything what Amy Dubois had said. Mom thought I went out to visit with her without her permission, but I told her Amy Dubois came to the house to see me instead.

I told them that I had to lie about my name as Lily Turner, and my father as Thomas Turner who was a well-known lawyer in Atlanta, Georgia. Tom and Mom did not say anything, but they were attentive.

"Her parents' names are Jeffery Dubois and Nancy Saunders Dubois. They both are lawyers and own a company called the Dubois Import Company in Gulfport. They are making tons of money from their business. They own a big mansion on St. Charles Avenue in New Orleans. Her mother's aunt lives there now, but in the future, the mansion would be hers."

I continued. "Amy thinks her mother hates kids including her. As her mother does not hire a housekeeper, she expects her daughter to clean the house. On the contrary, her father loves to spend a lot of time with her. He bought her a bicycle so she can ride in the neighborhood. She really loves her father."

After my reports, Mom was in tears and praised me for a great detective job I had done. She probably thought I was too young to comprehend the depth of the tragedy before, but now she saw me as a kid detective—a smart one.

She probably realized I was the only one whom she trusted, told me all about her suspicions and the gold digger. Of course, Grandma Margaret was included, but she was no longer with us. It seemed we had kept it as a secret for the longest time until Tom came along.

She praised me again in front of Tom by saying how proud she was to have a smart daughter like me. Tom smiled at me and said that I could be a great detective or a lawyer in the future. In fact, I do not mind becoming a criminal lawyer or a detective in the police department to catch all the crooks.

Now I was allowed to participate in their discussion in the study. Most of the time, we discussed our speculations, suspicions, thoughts, and suggestions. Tom informed us of his findings as well as his legal opinions.

Mom told us about Jeffery Dubois—he was the company lawyer as well as the family lawyer who made her parents' will and took care of the legal matters of the company and the international tariff calculation. He was not related to Jefferson Dubois, but he had the same last name. He was married to a nurse named Paula and had three children when he was working for the Dubois Import Company.

Mom speculated what went wrong with Jeffery Dubois: After the gold digger learned her beloved Alan was already married, she had no hope whatsoever to be a wealthy wife. Therefore, she probably decided to be wealthy herself without marrying any son of a wealthy family. In the process of avenging Alan Dubois, the gold digger had Jeffery Dubois involved in her plan because of his last name Dubois.

Mom did not think Jeffery was the gold digger's type, so she assumed their marriage took place just to share the Dubois fortune or the gold digger did not have any choice because Amy Dubois was born.

Nevertheless, Mom was puzzled because the faithful and honest man such as Jeffery Dubois got involved so fast in the grand larceny and married the gold digger by divorcing Paula.

However, Tom Rousseau understood how it happened and how his ex-wife worked with a man. A boneheaded man such as Jeffery or himself could easily be mesmerized by her sex goddess acts.

CHAPTER 13
MOM'S BIRTHPLACE

After Tom visited the parish probate court in New Orleans, he found something very important and told us all about it at the dinner table—the will of Jefferson and Marie Dubois, which was made a month prior to their deaths. It included the irrevocable trust, which could exempt most of the inheritance tax.

In that will, Michelle Dubois was not in it. Instead, Alan Dubois and Jeffery Dubois were in the irrevocable trust. After the death of Jefferson and Marie, all the properties were to be divided equally between Alan Dubois and Jeffery Dubois.

To Tom, the will itself was fraud because Jefferson and Marie would've never excluded Michelle from their will. Therefore, he concluded Nancy Saunders wrote the will and Jeffery Dubois forged the signatures.

Tom speculated furthermore on how they used the will—after Jeffery Dubois obtained three death certificates from Atlanta, he went to the probate court to show the death certificates of Jefferson and Marie along with a copy of their irrevocable will, and then he showed the death certificate of Alan. As a result, Jeffery Dubois became the sole recipient of the Dubois fortune.

By then, they found a warehouse in Gulfport. With the help of professional movers, they moved the Dubois Import Company over the weekend in a hurry. The employees were probably left perplexed by the sudden loss of their jobs when they came to work on Monday.

As soon as Jeffery Dubois obtained the ownership of the St. Charles Avenue property, the police department was asked to issue an immediate eviction notice against the tenant on that property. Later, again the police department evicted Michelle from Alan's antebellum mansion in Biloxi. Mom listened to Tom and nodded quietly with tears.

In the end, Tom said sadly, "It would be difficult to take this larceny case to the grand jury. If the executing lawyer of the irrevocable will testifies that Jefferson and Marie Dubois indeed asked her to write it with their sound minds, our claims of forgery and fraud would be thrown out instantly unless we have their genuine signatures to back up our claims, but we don't have it, do we?"

Mom shook her head by answering, "No."

"It seemed their plan was meticulously carried out, but let me speculate some flaws—if they wanted to be rich fast by using their bogus will, Jefferson and Marie must be eliminated fast. Nancy probably served the poisoned coffee to Jefferson and Marie in the morning. When they became very ill, knowing Alan was a pilot, Jeffery probably suggested for Alan to fly them to Atlanta. By then a doctor's appointment was made by him with CDC in Atlanta for a possible poisoning."

Tom glanced at Mom to see if she was agreeing with him. Mom nodded and gestured for him to continue.

"Jeffery and Nancy went to the airfield to rent a Cessna for Alan. They had already tampered with the aircraft before Michelle brought her parents and Alan to the airfield. Michelle, you said you saw both of them waiting for you at the aircraft, right?"

Mom nodded several times.

"They looked worried and genuinely concerned, but no incriminating scenes were there, correct?"

"Correct."

"Therefore, again, we have no witness, no proof of poisoning or tampering, but it is very obvious that they conspired to murder your family. The murder cases have no statute of limitations, so we keep hoping someone would come forward." Tom sighed and looked very frustrated.

Mom said, "I know one person who could be a witness or might know what was going on. She is Jeffery's ex-wife. They had three children together. After the gold digger got pregnant, I am sure everything was chaotic in Paula's life. Sorry to call your ex-wife a gold digger again."

"It is all right. The same gold digger married me because she thought I was going to take over the family business in New Orleans, but she found out I rejected the family fortune, so she left me. Michelle, when I saw her signature on the will as the executing attorney, everything came into place including poisoning and tampering. She seems to be a heartless and greedy murderer. I am very sure she murdered your family out of greed or revenging Alan. Jeffery Dubois probably did not know what he was getting into."

"Tom, I investigated her background when I was in high school because she was obsessively pressuring Alan to marry her. I found out that her aunt was the major culprit in their gold-digging project because paying her niece's expensive tuition was her future investment. She wanted her niece to use her movie-star-like figure to marry a son of a wealthy family on St. Charles Avenue so her investment could multiply. Their dream was probably to live on St. Charles Avenue like those wealthy people."

All of a sudden, Tom turned to me and asked, "Lily, did you say that Amy's stepfamily lives in Houston, Texas?" I nodded.

"Michelle, do you know Jeffery's ex-wife's name?"

"Yes. Paula Smith Dubois."

Tom jotted down her name on a notepad. "I will call the phone company tomorrow, but if her number is unlisted, I may not get any information on her." He looked pensive. We were quiet.

Suddenly, my detective mind made me speak out. "Tom, call Jeffery Dubois on the phone pretending you are a social security officer, and tell him you must contact his ex-wife to discuss her future social security benefits. I am sure Jeffery Dubois would give you her address and phone number."

"Wow! That's a good idea. Lily, where did you learn things like that?"

"From TV, and I read many detective stories too. I learned the inductive and deductive methods of the investigation too. By the way, Tom, are you doing this investigation as a labor of love for Mom?"

He did not hesitate. "Yes, because I love you both. You are like my family. My father will not mind working in the office while I do the investigation. He said he wanted to help your mom a long time ago, but he just did not know what to do at that time, so now he encourages me to catch the crooks as soon as possible."

Mom looked at Tom lovingly when he said, "I love you both. You are like my family." Tom should have added, "Michelle, I love you very much. Please marry me." No, he did not say it—he was simply out of practice in the romance department, and so was Mom.

"Michelle, do you think Nancy can recognize you after so many years?"

"Yes, she could. I recognized her instantly when I saw her in the yard the other day. I had to turn my face and walk fast so she could not recognize me."

Therefore, Tom told me not to see Amy anymore because things could be complicated if the beauty queen found out her ex-husband lived in the same neighborhood and Alan's sister, Michelle, was visiting him.

The next day, I saw Amy walking down the street with her mother instead of riding a bicycle. She did not see me because I squatted down to hide myself behind Mom's car.

After a week in Biloxi, Tom begged us to move into his father's house in New Orleans so he did not have to commute a long distance. Besides, he wanted me to see Mom's birthplace and the neighborhood they grew up in.

After we left Tom's beach house, Mom wanted to show me the twenty-three-mile causeway that was built to cross Lake Pontchartrain to New Orleans. She explained about the causeway—it took about eight years (1948–1956) to complete two lanes that became the southbound later and took thirteen years (1956–1969) to add two more lanes. The latter lanes became the northbound. The causeway is the shortcut for the workers who live on the other shore of Lake Pontchartrain. Many visitors who come from the north also enjoy the shortcut.

I did not know how far twenty-three miles was, but it took thirty minutes to reach the other side. The causeway was built so low that I thought the occasional high-wind waves or rainstorms could splash the highway or flood the low part of the causeway.

We finally came to I-10 again. The skyline of New Orleans appeared in the distance. Mom drove without getting lost or panicking in the heavy traffic.

We drove the one-lane street toward the university on St. Charles Avenue, which has the streetcar tracks in the middle and numerous Southern black oak trees on both sides of the street.

Mom turned into a long driveway to the back of the large mansion, which was neatly fenced with bricks and iron bars on the top. The front yard was rather small, but the manicured Bermuda grass and many flowers made the mansion very attractive.

At the back entrance of the humongous house, a nice looking old man welcomed us with a big smile. Mom introduced him to me as Jake Rousseau, Tom's father. Jake embraced Mom like his own daughter. He had some tears in his eyes and said, "I am glad we found you."

He turned and looked at me. "You surely look like Alan, but you look much prettier than him." Jake was talking just like Tom when he first saw me at our house—I looked like Uncle Alan. I rather wanted to be told that I resembled Mom, not my uncle who was already deceased and whom I had never met.

"Well, I put plenty of towels in the guesthouse, so please get situated there. In the meantime, I will be fixing dinner for all of us."

The guesthouse was big with a king-size bed that was big enough for both of us to sleep. Mom helped me wash my long hair in the sink before I took a shower.

When Tom came home from work, we ate crawfish and jumbo shrimp with red potatoes, corn on the cob, and some green vegetables. It was my first time to eat crawfish, so Jake showed me how to pull out the tail meat. Everything tasted great.

When I praised how great cook Jake was, he said, "Tom is a better cook than I am."

"No, Dad, you are the best."

The next morning after Jake and Tom left for work, Mom decided to show me the house she used to live in. As we assumed the gold digger's aunt lived there, we disguised ourselves with a pair of sunglasses and a hat.

At Mom's birthplace, we saw two women in the front yard planting flowers. They were probably the gold digger's aunt and her housekeeper or a friend. One of them saw us, but we paid no attention. She probably thought Mom was an unfriendly rich snob and I was a spoiled brat who lived in the neighborhood.

When we walked past the house, Mom started talking softly. I heard her quivery voice. "My family lived in that house happily for many years. My parents were happily married, and they were very good parents. Alan and I were very good kids too. I still do not understand why God punished us this way." Her voice was still quivery, but kept talking.

"We had antique furniture my ancestors accumulated in the basement. Some were made just for the Dubois family in many generations ago. I bet they sold them without knowing the values. When I was evicted from that house, I took all my mother's jewelry, my father's gold coin collections, and some other small antiques. Later, I was able to sell them to pay for the hospital bills when you were born."

We crossed the streetcar tracks to the other side of the street. Her face was flushed from walking or probably from the long-suppressed anger.

"I think the bad guys win most of the time in this world. I was Catholic like my Mom, but I no long believe in God. Many bad people and criminals go to church believing if they go to church, God would forgive their sins, but after church, they would commit the same sins again. I hate seeing the people who are hypocritical, especially in church. I believe in human decency and honesty. I also believe in the old adage 'What goes around comes around.' Sorry, I talk too much."

Mom realized I was still a child, but now I understood why she did not take me to church over the years. Mom was probably disappointed in God. Her belief in human decency and honesty was good enough for her to live happily.

We stopped behind one of the big oak trees to see Mom's birthplace again. The two women were still working in the yard. Mom said sadly, "I guess living on St. Charles Avenue was their ultimate goal of greed that killed my parents and Alan. I pity them for that. I hope they will see what goes around and come around soon."

Tom decided to call Jeffery Dubois at the Dubois Import Company in Gulfport from his office. He took my suggestion to get Paula's address and phone number.

"Hello. May I speak to Mr. Jeffery Dubois? I am calling from the Social Security office in New Orleans."

A secretary answered the phone. Tom waited for a while.

"This is Jeffery Dubois. What can I do for you?"

"Are you Jeffery Dubois who was the husband of Paula Smith Dubois?"

"Yes…ex-husband. Who is this?"

"This is Thomas Turner. I work for the Social Security office in New Orleans. We must send her a summary of her future social security benefits she requested, but she does not live in New Orleans. Instead, we got your company address and phone number."

"She moved to Huston, Texas, nine years ago."

"Do you happen to have her current address and phone number?"

Jeffery was hesitant, but answered, "Yes."

"If you hear from her, would you ask her to call our office?"

"Wait. I have not spoken to my ex-bitch and three brats since my divorce, but I have her address and phone number. I know the bitch's address by heart because I have to send the hefty alimony every month. I wish she would be killed in a car accident."

Jeffery talked angrily, but he realized he was talking to a government official, so he apologized. "Sorry for my language. I have been upset with her because I have to pay the inflating alimony every month."

"It is okay. By the way, are you allowed to give out her address and phone number?"

"Yes. I could give her address to anybody I want, even to a burglar or a killer." He was still cynical and angry.

"When you talk to my ex-wife, tell her to remarry or die soon so I don't have to pay the alimony."

"By the way, have you thought about hiring a lawyer to negotiate the amount of the alimony? You might be giving her too much. Are you deducting the alimony from your income tax? The alimony is deductible on your part."

Jeffery got quiet and did not reply, but gave Tom the address and phone number of his ex-wife. Tom thanked him and hung up the phone. Tom thought to himself—*Is Jeffery's ex-wife extorting from him because she has some incriminating evidence against him? Is that why he is reluctant to hire a lawyer to reduce the alimony?*

That night at the dinner table, Tom told us about his conversation with Jeffery, but he sounded pessimistic. "As Paula has been extorting from Jeffery, I am very sure she would not testify against her ex-husband."

Mom spoke, "I think Paula has my parents' original will that bears their genuine signatures. She might have a copy of the forged will as well. She is probably using those incriminating documents to extort from Jeffery. That is why Jeffery keeps paying her."

Tom nodded and said, "Wow! Michelle, you are right. I guess that is why Paula comes very strong and get whatever she wants from Jeffery. I wonder if Nancy knows about Paula's extortion. I also wonder if Nancy got the half of the Dubois fortune from Jeffery as his wife."

Jake joined, "Tom, did Jeffery Dubois become a sole owner of the Dubois fortune?"

"Yes. According to the will, he got everything."

"Do you think he was smart enough to get a prenuptial agreement before he married Nancy?"

"Wow! Dad, you brought an interesting point. Okay, this is my speculation. Please hear me out. After their meticulous larceny, Nancy wants all the loot for herself because the blueprint of the larceny was hers. She probably wanted to sell them all and be settled in an exotic island as a wealthy person happily ever after. However, Jeffery got all the loot."

Tom continued. "When Jeffery Dubois found out Nancy's pregnancy, he went to his wife Paula for a divorce. Paula was not stupid. She made Jeffery give her everything in order to grant a divorce—their house, their children, and savings, but later she wanted her children to live in a nice house in the nice neighborhood instead of living in an apartment, so she needed Jeffery's financial support, but he refused. Paula was angry, so she decided to use the incriminating evidence to start her extortion as a form of alimony."

Tom sipped tea and continued. "Now Nancy realized Jeffery got all the loot, but she thought about the marriage, which might give her at least half of the loot, so she accepted Jeffery's proposal. On the wedding day, Jeffery wanted her to sign the prenuptial agreement. She was outraged, but when Jeffery agreed to let her aunt live in the mansion on St. Charles Avenue, she signed the prenuptial agreement. What do you think?"

We applauded loudly.

Chapter 14
Jeffery and Paula

After college, Paula Smith Dubois landed a nursing job and supported her husband, Jeffery, in law school. They were college sweethearts and married in their senior year.

In college, Jeffery did not know how to talk to girls. He was always awkward in front of Paula, but his eyes told her he was in love with her. It took a long time for Jeffery to ask Paula out. He had a scholarship from the state, stayed in the dorm, and worked in the school bookstore on campus between classes.

Paula's parents were wealthy in Houston, so she had a one-bedroom apartment paid by them. In their second year, Paula let Jeffery move into her apartment without telling her parents. In the meantime, her father passed away, but her apartment and tuition were paid with her trust fund.

In the third year in college, she took Jeffery to Houston to meet her mother and her older brother. Since they liked Jeffery, she decided to marry him in front of the judge in the city hall. It was in their senior year. Their honeymoon place was their apartment—they stayed in bed all day to celebrate their wedding. They both were so much in love.

After Jeffery's law school, he landed a job with the Dubois Import Company. Jefferson and Marie needed a lawyer who could handle the international laws as well as the tariff regulations. In the past, whenever they needed a lawyer, they had to search for one. As their needs became so frequent, they decided to have their own company lawyer.

Jeffery Dubois was recommended by his law school. Jefferson and Marie liked Jeffery's humble disposition and his knowledge of the international laws. When Jeffery was hired as the company lawyer, many employees thought that Jeffery and Jefferson were related because of their same last name, Dubois.

Jeffery and Paula bought a house in a nice neighborhood after Jeffery's employment. The boys were born one after another, and later, a daughter was born. Paula's widowed mother from Houston helped Paula with the children, so she was able to go back to work.

As Jeffery grew up in an orphanage, he was glad his children's mother and grandmother cared for them. Whenever he thought about his mother who abandoned him when he was an infant, he always had tears in his eyes.

In the orphanage, he imagined his mother's face numerous times. One looked like a movie star in the magazine, one looked like his favorite caretaker, and one looked like an angel in the picture on the wall. He did not care how she looked but just wanted to be embraced by his mother.

From time to time, he drew a face of his mother who looked like him. He remembered he had never imagined or drawn a picture of his father, always his mother. Being a father, he wondered if his children thought more about Paula than him.

He did not hate his mother, rather felt sorry for her. He was going to forgive her for abandoning him if she ever came to see him. He remembered he had longed to see his mother a million times while he was in the orphanage.

Paula's mother was a kind and warmhearted person. She understood how Jeffery felt being abandoned and growing up without a mother. Therefore, she was extra nice to Jeffery. To Jeffery, she became the mother whom he never had. Even after she went back to Houston, he often called her to say hello and treated her like his own mother until her passing.

His devotion to his family, especially to the boys, was extraordinary. When they started school, he came home immediately after five and took them to baseball practice in the ballpark. On the weekends, he drove the family to the shopping mall, ate at the food court, and played some video games with the boys while Paula shopped with their daughter. Jeffery thought every child should have a family with a mother and a father.

Paula thought she was one of the happiest and luckiest women in this world—her children had no physical malady, their schoolwork was always excellent, they were well behaved, and her husband was stout and short but healthy. He still adored her body and satisfied her in bed every time.

Nevertheless, one day, with her woman's intuition, Paula suspected Jeffery's infidelity. He was often preoccupied at the dinner table as though he was daydreaming about somebody.

In bed, as Paula asked him what was going on, he finally told her that a new female lawyer was hired. Since there was no extra room for her, she came to share Jeffery's office.

He added admiringly, "That young girl brought her own coffee maker to fix coffee for us. She is a lawyer, but she does not mind serving us coffee every morning like a maid. She is amazing."

"How old is she?"

"I don't know how old she is, but she is very young."

Paula felt relieved. She strongly believed such a young girl would never be interested in her husband who was unattractive in general. She was very sure the young lawyer would go for young Alan instead of her husband. She did not know her husband was the one who got interested in the girl.

Even though Paula dismissed her suspicion against the young lawyer, she noticed Jeffery was continuously daydreaming. She thought he was having a midlife crisis.

Indeed, Jeffery was going through something—an infatuation. When he saw the young lawyer in his office for the first time, he was utterly mesmerized. He had never seen such a beauty in his life—her porcelain skin, beautiful blue eyes, a big firm bosom under her dress, and a perfect body. She looked just like a sex goddess he once imagined. He had never felt such a powerful feeling before—he felt very young.

Jeffery's office was big but crowded with some file cabinets, a copier, an electric typewriter, a disarrayed bookshelf with many law books, and other furniture. His office was rather in a mess.

As soon as the beauty queen's desk was placed at the corner slightly behind Jeffery's desk, she started tiding up the office with Jeffery's permission. The law books were displayed categorically; the file cabinets were moved to the corner of the office next to the workstation.

The beauty queen worked tirelessly all day long. When Jeffery came back from a meeting, he was very much impressed by the transformation of his office, especially the way the beauty queen put the law books in order categorically. Now his office looked like a big and respectable lawyer's office.

The beauty queen had a collection of law books in her apartment as well. Some people might have thought she was a dumb blonde, but she was extremely smart and studious. She had never been lazy. That was how she survived in college and law school.

All other employees worked on the open floor—some clerks typed the numerous invoices and some answered the phones. The noise of the phone conversations, telex, and electric typewriters were too loud, but nobody paid attention to the noise, much less the noise from the enclosed offices.

Many truckers downstairs were loading merchandise that was to be delivered to the airport, to the train station, and to various local department stores or specialty stores. The company was busy and prosperous.

Jefferson, Marie, Alan, and Jeffery as the heads of the company did all the planning, advertising, accounting, tariff calculation, issuing the payments, and writing letters to the customers.

Since they did not have their own secretaries, the beauty queen was willing to work as everybody's secretary and gofer. She also did not mind serving coffee every morning as a maid.

In fact, the beauty queen brought her own coffee maker and mugs. A can of expensive coffee was also brought in. With Jeffery's permission, she made delicious coffee in his office and served.

In the morning, she helped Jeffery write some legal papers, but in the afternoon after lunch, she disappeared into Alan's office and stayed there until five. She did that almost routinely every day.

Jeffery felt jealous for some reason. As he wanted to know what she was doing in Alan's office, he knocked on the door to peek in. She was busy using a copier. Alan was working on a big chart on his desk while standing up. He felt relieved.

Nobody knew her ulterior motive was to marry Alan. In Alan's office, she was actually sharpening her skills to capture Alan once more. She probably believed his hiring her was to rekindle their old relationship as well. This time she was going to act graciously and appreciatively without being aggressive or hysterical.

She remembered Alan liked her wild horse riding on his lap. Therefore, she stopped wearing her panties and stockings under her dress when she came to work. Nobody noticed, except Alan.

Nevertheless, Alan gave her no chance to sit on his lap; he stood up to work on a chart. He knew the beauty queen would hop on him if he ever sat down. Of course, he sat down when she was not around. While helping Alan, she kept watching him like a hawk because she did not want to miss any chance. However, Alan was determined to tell her something very important if she ever became aggressive.

She came to Alan's office every afternoon. One day, as she could not wait any longer, she approached Alan bravely and started unbuttoning his shirt. Alan gently held both of her hands and made her sit on a chair.

Then he said, "Nancy, I have a lovely wife. We kept our marriage a secret from everybody because our marriage could inconvenience my family and her family. Please understand that I am no longer available—I am legally taken. Please try to forget about me and move on."

The beauty queen was overwhelmingly shocked and heartbroken. She went in the restroom and cried. She realized she had been in love with Alan since high school. Even though she was rejected once, she kept remembering Alan's handsome face and his manly performance for the longest time. Now her love and her dream of becoming a wealthy wife were gone forever.

While crying, her love turned into hate. Now she became revengeful. Although her gold digging plan failed, this time she was determined to be rich herself without marrying any son of a wealthy family.

The beauty queen was born in Gulfport, Mississippi. When her parents were arrested for murdering a police officer during the drug trafficking, she was sent to the state foster care center. As a young child, she did not know the reason why she was sent to the center. She cried and cried for her parents for many days.

Finally, her aunt from New Orleans came to pick her up. When her aunt showed up at the center, her niece's face lit up as though she saw a savior or God. She held her young sobbing niece lovingly and told her that her parents were killed in a car accident.

The aunt was the sister of her mother. The niece believed whatever her aunt had to say about her parents. In any rate, the aunt promised her niece that she would take care of her like her own daughter for the rest of her life. The niece always loved her aunt for that.

The beauty queen stopped going to Alan's office. Instead, she helped Jeffery quietly in the office. She was actually planning on what she should do to be rich.

Her inborn criminal mind was at work. She made sure her plan should not alert the authority—it must be legally perfect. She used her legal knowledge and studied a lot. In order to execute her plan, she must include Jeffery Dubois because she needed his last name, Dubois.

She did not realize that Jeffery was already infatuated with her and daydreaming about her. She closely observed Jeffery from her desk. He was stout and short—not her type. She did not want him, but she needed him badly in her plan.

Although she stopped going to Alan's office, she still served coffee to Alan every morning and showed him some smiles so he would not be suspicious. Alan probably thought she was moving on like a reasonable grown-up.

Whenever Jeffery asked the beauty queen to write some legal documents, she did a superb job each time. Her legal vocabulary was vast, and her writing was just exquisite. Jeffery often praised her. At the same time, his infatuation deepened.

After recovering from Alan's second rejection, the beauty queen began working on Jeffery because she needed him in her plan. First, she wanted to capture him sexually. Again, she wore a dress without panties and a panty hose. As she brought her lunch to work, she ate in the office. So did Jeffery—he ate sandwiches his wife prepared.

One day, at lunchtime, the beauty queen locked the office door and saddled Jeffery's lap quietly as though he was a horse. Jeffery felt dizzy for some reason with his joyous anticipation. When she kissed his mouth, his sexual arousal was instantaneous.

She unhooked his belt, slid his trousers and underpants down to the floor, and carefully saddled him. He felt a slight pain, but they both safely hooked. Jeffery vigorously rocked with some noise, but the rocking did not last too long. His whole body limped with a climax. He was too excited like a teenager because the most beautiful girl was on top of him.

The beauty queen kindly kissed him, cleaned up Jeffery and herself, and tiptoed back to her desk. She knew he became her captive. Jeffery thought he was in the dream world. It did not look real, but his body told him he just made love to the most beautiful girl in the world. He was on top of the world.

After that, Jeffery became her sexual slave or captive. He was willing to do anything for her. As he was rewarded every day, he wanted to believe the reward came from her genuine love. He became the happiest stud in the world.

One day, Jeffery decided to satisfy the beauty queen in bed in her apartment for a change because he knew he was good in bed. He called his wife and told her that he had to work overtime on that day. He went to the beauty queen's apartment for the first time. Indeed, the beauty queen was satisfied.

Paula noticed Jeffery started splashing his expensive cologne every morning before he left for work. His phone calls for the overtime became frequent. Paula had to drive the boys to the ballpark each time when he called. In the past, he used to bring his work home instead of staying in the office because he wanted to take the boys to the ballpark himself.

Every day, the beauty queen sat on Jeffery at lunchtime. He did not wear any protection, but she told him it was all right because she was taking contraceptive pills.

One day, Paula decided to see if her husband was really working overtime or not. She parked her car at the corner of the shipyard inconspicuously and watched the parking lot. Everybody was fast gone home at five. Two cars including her husband's car remained in the parking lot.

There came a tall glamorous young woman who was probably the lawyer her husband was talking about. The woman drove past the corner where Paula's car was sitting. She could not believe how beautiful the young lawyer looked, but she still wanted to believe such a beauty could not be interested in her husband.

Now her husband's car was the only one remaining in the parking lot, but there was no sight of her husband for a long time. She thought he was telling her the truth—he was working overtime. As she started the car, she saw her husband coming out of the building and walking toward his car.

At first, she thought he was going home early without working overtime, but with her intuition, she decided to follow him. When he drove through the traffic and turned on to I-10 east, which was the opposite direction of their house, she stopped following him. Instead, she went back to the ballpark and waited for the boys to finish their practice.

On that night, in the beauty queen's apartment, after their satisfying lovemaking, she asked Jeffery to sign on the irrevocable will for Jefferson Dubois and Marie Dubois. Jeffery believed the beauty queen was asked to write the will because she was good at it.

From time to time, Jeffery was allowed to sign Jefferson's name including Marie's name when they both were out of office or on a vacation. They trusted him as their lawyer. Therefore, without thinking, he signed their names. Indeed, Jefferson and Marie were on a cruise vacation on that week. After Jeffery signed, the beauty queen put the will in Jeffery's briefcase and told him to proofread the next day.

She was going to tell Jeffery what she was going to do with the irrevocable trust that she worked on for several months, but she wanted to wait until he asked her about it. He might be shocked to learn that his name was in the will as a beneficiary. Because of his vulnerability or naivete, she was sure he would work with her if she said she did it for him just because she loved him, which was a lie.

Jeffery finally came home around eleven and said, "I worked too hard today. I had tons of papers to write. I need to take a shower."

Paula did not even ask whether he ate supper or not. After the shower, he came downstairs to kiss Paula and went back up to their bedroom.

Paula was just quiet and contemplating. Her imagination was at work—after leaving the parking lot, he went to the beauty queen's apartment. When she imagined their activity in bed, she became angry.

Chapter 15
A Sewing Basket

After Jeffery went to bed, Paula went to his study, shut the door, and opened his briefcase. Jeffery rarely locked the briefcase, which was his bad habit. She saw the new will of Jefferson and Marie Dubois. Nancy Saunders as the executing attorney signed and dated the front cover.

She sat at the desk, read every word in the will—including the irrevocable clause that named Jeffery Dubois and Alan Dubois as the beneficiaries of the Dubois Import Company, the mansion in New Orleans, and the mansion in Biloxi. She did not see the name of Michelle Dubois anywhere. She knew Jefferson and Marie would never leave out Michelle's name from their will.

Therefore, she immediately knew the will was a fraud. The signatures of Jefferson and Marie looked like her husband's penmanship. As she believed their signatures were forged, she decided to compare them with the old will Jeffery made for Jefferson and Marie many years ago. It was in her sewing room in the basement.

She carefully made a copy of the entire will by removing a paper clip. After putting the new will back in Jeffery's briefcase, she went down to the basement with the duplicated copy. The house was quiet. The children were sleeping soundly, so was Jeffery.

She tiptoed down to the basement. Her sewing room was just like her study. There were three sewing baskets in the sewing room. The largest one was her secret file cabinet, so to speak. It had two parts. The top part had all the sewing necessities such as needles, threads, a measurement tape, and so forth. The bottom part was like a big box that kept the important documents, including the old will of Jefferson and Marie.

Many years ago, when Jeffery landed a job in the Dubois Import Company, Jefferson and Mari asked him to make the family will. He got Paula's help at home because she was always good in writing. She often helped Jeffery with his writing assignments when they were in college.

After Jefferson and Marie were satisfied with the content of the will, they signed and kept one copy, and Jeffery kept another one as their lawyer. That night, Jeffery proudly showed it to Paula and thanked her for her help. After Jeffery went to bed, Paula made a copy and filed it in the sewing basket as her husband's first legal work.

She took out the old will and compared the signatures. She immediately knew the signatures were forged. That night, Paula could not sleep because she thought her husband was about to commit a crime with the young lawyer. Paula had loved Jeffery so much that she wanted to stop him, but she could not figure out what they were going to do with the bogus will.

Why did Jeffery and the young lawyer write the irrevocable trust for Jeffery Dubois and Alan Dubois excluding Michelle? The will would be useless unless Jefferson and Marie were dead. Even after their deaths, Alan would know the will is bogus because his parents would never exclude his sister Michelle. Are they conspiring to murder Jefferson, Marie, and Alan altogether so Jeffery Dubois could be the sole survivor to benefit from all of the Dubois fortune?

Paula had some awful feelings about the Dubois family. Marie had been very nice to Paula and her children over the years—she always sent her children the nicest birthday presents every year.

She thought about visiting Marie to warn her about Jeffery and Nancy by showing the bogus will, but she was hesitant because Jefferson and Marie had trusted her husband Jeffery for many years. Paula simply did not know what to do.

Jeffery did not have the time to proofread the will the next day, so he kept it in his desk drawer. In the meantime, the beauty queen was planning the next step.

Several days later, with the beauty queen's insistence, he proofread the irrevocable trust. He was angry with her at lunchtime. He demanded to know why she made such a will, excluding Michelle and putting his name instead.

She hopped on his lap and whispered into his ear sweetly that she did it just for him because she loved him dearly and her plan would never alert anyone's suspicion. She moaned and kissed Jeffery in his mouth. After Jeffery climaxed, somehow his anger went away.

That night, the beauty queen was extra nice to Jeffery in bed. While entertaining Jeffery, she explained what she was going to do next. She whispered the details into his ear.

Jeffery thought he was the luckiest man to make love to the most beautiful girl in this universe. He would do anything to keep her as his. It seemed an evil spirit already tainted his mind, or he probably had an inborn criminal mind just as the beauty queen had.

One day, the beauty queen was shocked to learn about her pregnancy. Now Jeffery became very happy because he could keep her to himself by marrying her.

One morning, after drinking the morning coffee, Jefferson and Marie became very ill and complained of a severe stomach pain. Jeffery called the CDC in Atlanta to report a possible poisoning. The CDC wanted to examine them as soon as possible, so they could get the antidote.

Knowing Alan was a pilot, Jeffery and Nancy went to the local airfield to rent a Cessna for Alan. When Alan called Michelle for emergency, she hurriedly drove her parents and Alan to the airfield. Jeffery and the beauty queen were already there and looked concerned. That night, Michelle heard from the FAA of the airplane crash.

When Paula heard the airplane crash, she immediately put the puzzling pieces together. She cried because she was regretful for not warning Marie. If she did, the tragedy could have been prevented.

After the tragedy, Jeffery did not come home and stayed in the beauty queen's apartment. They were planning something together. When Paula called him in his office, he came home that night and confessed to Paula about his love affair and the young lawyer's pregnancy. Paula did not know whether she should cry or be angry.

Paula told the children that their father decided to leave them because his girlfriend got pregnant. The children cried. When Jeffery came home to apologize to Paula and to the children, they were glaring at him with anger in silence.

If the children were not there, Paula could've screamed at him and said how dare he killed Jefferson, Marie, and Alan, but she was quiet. She remembered Jeffery was a law-abiding citizen, a good husband, and a good father before the beauty queen came into the picture. Now he became a criminal. Jeffery had no clue his wife had already figured out their crime.

After Jeffery left, she desperately needed someone like a police officer or a lawyer who would believe what she had to say—she could show them the bogus will and tell them everything she knew, including her suspicions and speculations. Most importantly, she wanted to tell them the airplane crash was not an accident. Her husband who was a mechanical genius probably tampered with the aircraft.

However, her speculation came without any witness or proof—it was just her logical speculation against the bogus will. Therefore, no one would believe her. It seemed they committed a perfect crime. No laws could touch them.

Shortly after the divorce, she quit her job, sold the house, cashed out all their savings, and moved to Huston, Texas, with her children. Her brother, Edward, helped her settle in an apartment. Paula wanted to tell her brother everything since he was a lawyer in the district attorney's office, but she did not know where to start, so she decided to wait.

Paula thought about Michelle Dubois often and wanted to hand over those two documents and explain her theory about the irrevocable will. If Michelle went forward to investigate the family tragedy, she was going to testify against her ex-husband, but Michelle was already evicted, and her whereabouts became unknown.

After the Dubois Import Company moved to Gulfport, the company operated just as before and hired local workers. Jeffery knew how to operate the company through his many years of experience with Jefferson and Marie.

The beauty queen was regretful and realized how stupid she had been. She made two mistakes—getting pregnant and losing the entire loot to Jeffery Dubois. Now she must carry a child of an unattractive stout man.

She was Catholic and went to church with her aunt regularly. She could not abort the child. Her aunt would be very angry. She did not want to upset her aunt because she was the most important person in her life.

When Jeffery heard about her pregnancy, he wanted to marry her soon. However, the beauty queen was thinking about how she could get the loot from Jeffery. She even threatened him to hand over the loot because the grand larceny was her idea, but Jeffery refused by saying he was the sole beneficiary and it was legal.

Therefore, the beauty queen had to think fast. The marriage might give her at least the half of the loot, and later, after Jeffery's accidental death, she could get everything as his widow, so she agreed to marry him.

However, Jeffery was not that naive or stupid anymore. He knew the beauty queen's ulterior motive—to get the Dubois fortune herself. When the beauty queen poisoned Jefferson and Marie, he became fearful of her. He imagined he might be poisoned during the marriage, so he had to think fast.

When they decided to marry and live in the mansion in Biloxi, they went to the courthouse to be married. Before their marriage, Jeffery took out the prenuptial agreement for her to sign. She was outrageously angry. Again, her plan went under the drain. She had to act fast—she told him that if he let her aunt live in the mansion on St. Charles Avenue, she would sign the prenuptial agreement. He agreed. She also asked him for a generous salary from the Dubois Import Company as the company lawyer. He again agreed. In a way, he was sympathetic about her situation, but he could not trust her.

He had already transferred several million dollars from the bank assets of Jefferson and Marie to an offshore bank. Jeffery was thinking ahead—*if the laws start suspecting him for what he and his wife had done to the Dubois family, he would disappear to the island so nobody could find him.*

As all the utility bills on both mansions were paid through the company, it did not cost anything for the aunt to live on St. Charles Avenue. Besides, she was getting some generous allowance from her niece every month. The beauty queen did not mind sending some money from her salary because she loved her aunt and cared for her.

Her aunt believed her niece finally married a son of a wealthy family. As Jeffery had the same last name as Alan, she believed her niece married Alan's older brother or the only surviving heir to the Dubois family. She knew none of their grand larceny or criminal activities, much less murdering the Dubois family or the prenuptial agreement.

Paula's extortion did not start until she decided to purchase a house in a nice neighborhood. She wanted her children to have some stability, but Jeffery refused to help her.

Therefore, Paula told him she could take the bogus will and the old will of Jefferson and Marie to the authorities to let them compare the signatures. She also told him she knew all about the grand larceny and the murder.

Jeffery was overwhelmingly shocked to learn that his ex-wife had a copy of the old will and the bogus will in her possession. Her speculation of their crimes was so accurate that he just became speechless and frightened.

Paula, however, told Jeffery that if he paid the five-figure alimony under the table every month, he should not be worried about being exposed to the laws. That was how Paula's extortion started. Jeffery indeed paid her the alimony without arguing.

With the alimony, Paula was able to buy a big house in the affluent neighborhood, and the children were able to enroll in the nice private school. Now she could plan for the children's college education too.

As the alimony payment was dealt under the table, so to speak, Jeffery could not deduct the payments from his income tax. Paula did not include the alimony as an income. It was a win-win situation for Paula.

Paula wanted to believe that Jeffery's alimony payment was a form of punishment that Jeffery should deserve. In reality, she was very angry with Jeffery, and at the same time, she cried for the Dubois family, especially for Michelle who did not benefit any of her parents' fortune.

She had been looking for Michelle Dubois for years because she knew Michelle could be the right person to prosecute those criminals. Paula wanted to hand over the incriminating evidence to Michelle, but she could not find her.

Her brother, Edward, looked after his nephews and niece while they were growing up. Jeffery never attempted to see his children because he had a tremendous grudge against their mother. Besides, he was scared of her.

Jeffery hired a certified accountant whom he could trust. The accountant accommodated Jeffery's request without asking any questions. He sent a money order to his ex-wife and wired money to the offshore bank every month.

He was also told that Jeffery's wife, Nancy, who worked as the company lawyer was prohibited seeing the company's financial records in any circumstances.

The beauty queen was working for Jeffery by putting their daughter in a nursery school. Jeffery once asked her to hire a housekeeper, but she refused to do so. She disliked having anybody in the house.

She was actually paranoid about having a housekeeper or neighbors who might ask her some questions—how they became so rich and how their business started. Therefore, she did not have any friends. Her aunt was the only one she would talk to.

Jeffery, too, was paranoid. His paranoia derived from Paula's extortion. The beauty queen's paranoia derived from the bogus will she wrote and putting poison in the coffee cups. As they were equally paranoid, they did not mingle with the neighbors or workers in the company. They built the iron-bar fence around the house to feel safe.

Their daughter went to a public school in the neighborhood. The beauty queen never went to meet her daughter's teachers or never attended the PTA meetings, but Jeffery did. He also nurtured his daughter by buying her a bicycle, toys, games, and books; spending some time with her, talking; or taking her to shopping malls to shop

Delayed Justice

or eat. Nevertheless, he did not invite her daughter's friends to their house just as his wife did not. He was afraid of the exposure.

After the prenuptial agreement, the beauty queen had been indifferent. The sexual activities were boycotted. Jeffery's sexual desire went somewhere else once a week.

Jeffery thought that without the prenuptial agreement, his wife could have already poisoned him. He knew how her mind worked. The reason he stayed married to the beauty queen was because of his daughter. He wanted his daughter to have a father and a mother.

The beauty queen knew if she divorced him, she could not get anything from her marriage. Even upon Jeffery's accidental death, all the loot would go to his daughter including the mansion on St. Charles Avenue.

Therefore, for her own sake, she was better off being married to Jeffery, save money from her salary, and let her aunt live in the mansion on St. Charles Avenue. That was best she could do to repay her aunt. Living on a paradise island as a wealthy woman was the beauty queen's dream, but she knew her dream would never come true.

When Paula's demand became unbearable, Jeffery hired a killer to kill his ex-wife. For years, he wished his ex-wife would be killed in a car accident, but it never happened, so he hired a killer.

One day, Paula was working in the yard. Suddenly, the small maple tree beside her broke off for no reason. The killer who was hired by Jeffery hit the tree instead of killing Paula. She called the police. They asked her if someone had a grudge against her. She said no, so they concluded the shooting was random.

However, she knew Jeffery had something to do with the shooting. She told the police later about her ex-husband, but she did not tell them why he might want to kill her. She did not want them to know about her extortion. The police questioned Jeffery on the phone several times, but as Jeffery denied the allegation profusely, the police dropped the investigation. After that shooting, Paula was afraid for her safety.

She wrote a five-page letter just in case. Her letter was addressed to Michelle Dubois. She stated her speculations about

Nancy Saunders, who probably poisoned Jefferson and Marie in the morning coffee, and Jeffery Dubois, who probably tampered with the aircraft because he was a mechanical genius.

Most importantly, she wrote that Jeffery Dubois agreed to pay her the alimony under the table because he was afraid of the exposure. That would prove he is guilty of his crime. Additionally, she wrote that she was almost killed by a hired killer in the past, so Jeffery might hire a killer again.

She made two copies of each document and her five-page letter. One large brown envelope had the name of Michelle Dubois in bold. Another one had no name on it. Each envelope looked bulky, but she made sure to seal each envelope tightly.

Paula decided to hide those envelopes in her sewing basket until she could talk with her oldest son, Gregory. She wanted her son to find Michelle and give the envelope to her in person in case of her death.

Chapter 16
Mom's Marriage

Mom and I already spent two weeks in the mansion on St. Charles Avenue. This meant we were away from home for three weeks including Biloxi.

Tom realized that he could not do much on the grand larceny or the family tragedy without any witness or incriminating evidence, but he promised he would keep working on the case.

Even though Tom had Paula's phone number, as a lawyer, he concluded Paula definitely would not testify against her ex-husband because of her years of extortion, so Paula was out of his witness list. Mom understood that.

However, murder cases has no statute of limitations, so when I become a lawyer, I would like to open the case and catch those crooks once and for all.

For the last-minute sightseeing, Mom showed me around New Orleans—we visited her college, drove to the other side of the Mississippi River, visited the famous cemetery, and went to the Lake Pontchartrain shore to see the ocean-like view.

On the last night of our stay with Tom and Jake, they took us to eat at Jake's favorite seafood restaurant in the French Quarter. After dinner, we four rode a horse-drawn buggy. I felt as though I were a daughter of a wealthy family who could afford to ride the expensive buggy ride.

It was time for us to go back home. After we put our suitcases in the car at the driveway, Jake embraced each of us and said, "Come back soon." Tom gave a peck of a kiss on Mom's lips and embraced her tightly, and then he bent over to embrace me too. He said, "I will see you soon in North Georgia."

We drove the endless highway and stopped at the rest area periodically. When I saw the skyline of Atlanta, I suddenly felt happy because we would be home soon.

The house smelled stuffy, so Mom turned on the central air conditioner. Ms. Norma brought mails and told us to eat dinner with them. Chris Gordon was on the road. Sharon and Toby came running to see me. I finally felt at home.

The rest of that summer was short, but we swam at the lake and talked about the real beach, salty water, bubbly waves, hot beach sands, and everything. I described Biloxi and Mom's hometown New Orleans to them. Sharon and Toby had never been to those places.

Furthermore, I wanted to tell them all about my being a kid detective, but I decided not to. They are probably too young to grasp Mom's complicated case. I would tell them in the future when we catch the crooks. Right now, Tom and Mom could not go forward because we have no evidence and no witness.

If I ever become a lawyer in the future, I would catch those crooks who got away with murder, but I must grow up first and study hard so I would be a smart criminal lawyer.

As Tom says, "There are many bad lawyers in the judicial system. Jeffery Dubois and Nancy Saunders are the typical bad lawyers." I would like to be a smart, honest, and compassionate lawyer. I don't want to be called a sleazy lawyer. I hope I could use my law degree to put those crooks away and keep the world safe.

*   *   *

Tom came to see us in North Georgia as he promised. Instead of staying in the hotel in Atlanta as he did before, Mom let him stay in the guest room in our house. He usually came to see us on the long weekends. Every fall, he stayed with us for a week because he liked the colorful foliage. We drove around North Georgia and all the way to North Carolina to see the colorful leaves on the mountains.

On the way home, we usually stopped at the roadside markets to buy apples and honey. The people in the market thought Mom and Tom were my parents and I was their kid.

When I was looking at the apple cider, the store owner told me to get my parents to buy one-gallon jug because he was going to offer a half price, so I got my parents. They bought two jugs of apple cider—one for Ms. Norma.

One day, I saw Tom kissing Mom passionately at the porch; I pretended I did not see them. Tom often sneaked into Mom's room at night. I felt relieved and happy because they finally learned how to be romantic.

In 1996, the city of Atlanta hosted the Summer Olympics. Shortly after I became fourteen years old that summer, Chris Gordon planned to take the children including me for a camping trip around the coastline of the Florida peninsula.

We three were so excited because we had never vacationed together in the past. By then, Toby became tall and handsome—no longer a mangy-looking boy. However, Ms. Norma was worried about Toby being with girls, but we did not care. He had been one of us since he was a child. Moreover, we taught everything that a girl should know including puberty and menstruation.

When Mom gave some money to Ms. Norma to cover my trip expenses, she kept saying, "No, this is our treat." As Mom insisted, Ms. Norma finally took it by saying, "We will buy some food." Mom made some sandwiches and tons of chocolate chip cookies for us to take.

The trip was for three weeks. Chris Gordon had a brand-new van. He attached a U-Haul container to the back of the van. The container had enough space for the camping necessities such as cooking utensils, portable stove, ice chest, a tent for the parents, a small tent for Toby, another large tent for Sharon and me; of course, each had a sleeping bag. The children helped pack the U-Haul container.

Mom was going to spend her summer with Tom while we were on a camping trip. Chris Gordon and Ms. Norma had already known Mom's relationship with Tom. Of course, we kids did too.

Keiko Palmer

After we got everything in the van, Chris Gordon told us to fasten the seatbelt. Mom was standing beside the van waving at us. Ms. Norma waved at Mom from the front seat. We waved, but Mom could not see us because the windows were tinted.

We kids sat at the swivel chairs and started sharing books and music tapes. We each had a cassette tape player with earphones. No CDs or compact CD players were available at that time.

When we came closer to the city of Atlanta, Chris Gordon was on the HOV lane that the DOT just completed for the Summer Olympics. The people from all over the world would be coming into the city soon. The city of Atlanta was ready.

He explained what HOV lane stands—high-occupancy vehicle—a vehicle with two or more people. Such a car could stay on the HOV lane. A car without any passengers could not use the HOV lane. If they did, they would be fined.

The HOV lane was to avoid the traffic congestion for the Olympic Games, and at the same time, the carpooling was encouraged to minimize the air pollution or congestion.

The skyline of Atlanta became much taller than I saw before. The city was cleaned up for the Olympics. I remembered the Atlanta Summer Olympics started in the third week of July and ended in the beginning of August because when we came back from Florida three week later, some games were still on.

The Interstate Highways 75 and 85 were widened to six lanes each side to accommodate the visitors. Ted Turner stadium became the Olympic Stadium to host the opening and closing ceremonies.

After Chris Gordon drove for about two hours, we stopped at McDonald's to use the restroom. Ms. Norma got some ice cream cones for the children. They both got a big cup of coffee between them.

The ice chest had water bottles and juice bottles for the kids. Another ice chest had Mom's famous sandwiches. We stopped at the rest area on I-75 and ate Mom's good sandwiches at lunchtime.

As camping was new to me, I wrote down the daily travelogue to note each campsite we stopped. Chris Gordon had a directory of KOA campgrounds. There were many campsites in Florida.

Delayed Justice

Ms. Norma put plenty of sunscreen lotion on our arms and faces each morning. We helped Chris Gordon set up tents when we arrived at each campsite, and the kids also did the dishes after each meal.

We kids explored the wooded area or beach area together before dinner. Ms. Norma did not tell the girls to keep an eye on Toby anymore; instead, she told Toby to keep an eye on the girls because Toby was taller than we were now.

We usually stayed two days in each campsite. If we liked the campsite, we stayed three days. We kids had a lot to do: swimming, walking on the beach, fishing, exploring the woods, and collecting some seashells.

Everybody at the campsite thought we were siblings. Chris Gordon did not bother to explain, just nodded. We certainly acted like siblings and got along well. We were inseparable, even at night.

Every night, Toby moved into our tent because he said he was lonely. We did not mind because three cushiony sleeping bags made a big king-size bed. It was very comfortable. We slept in pj's, so we did not need any sheets or blankets. It was hot even at night. In the morning, Toby was squashed by us, but he was sleeping soundly between us.

I remembered there were so many mosquitoes at the campsite, so Chris Gordon sprayed each tent from outside with Raid before we went to bed. Before we ate breakfast, we took a shower in the restroom facility. I remembered the location of the facility was too far.

Each campsite was located near the beach, river, creek, or lake, so we fished often. We kids knew how to fish because we did it many times at Lake Lanier.

Toby was a great fisherman. We ate Toby's catch almost every night. Most of the time, Chris Gordon grilled the whole fish on the campsite grill. Sometimes Ms. Norma fried in the skillet. Toby looked very proud when we ate his catch. He probably thought he was a breadwinner like his father, Chris Gordon.

Ms. Norma fixed balanced meals each day with canned vegetables and canned fruit. For dessert, we ate Mom's delicious chocolate chip cookies. We were eating well every day.

Keiko Palmer

We met many children at the campsite. Sharon and I exchanged addresses with some boys and girls. They, too, thought we were siblings. At the end of the trip, we three looked like brown munchkins. When we came home, Mom was already home. She exclaimed how dark we kids looked.

Our high school graduation was in 2000. The college in Athens, Georgia, already accepted Sharon. Chris Gordon and Ms. Norma were very proud of Sharon.

Mom wanted me to go to the college where she graduated, so I sent out an application form and I was accepted, but I did not think she could afford the tuition. So I was thinking about going to the local college by taking a part-time job.

However, Tom Rousseau volunteered to finance my college in New Orleans. He also offered a place to stay—in Jake's mansion because the college was nearby.

As I did not want to leave Mom alone in North Georgia, I talked to Tom on the phone about marrying Mom so we could live together in New Orleans. He thought that was a great idea. He gladly proposed to Mom on the phone and Mom happily accepted.

Jake Rousseau came with Tom for the wedding. After Tom and Mom got a marriage certificate in the city hall that week, Chris Gordon offered his house for their wedding reception. Ironically, it was on my birthday.

Chris Gordon hired a chef and a waitress to grill steak, corn on the cob, and shish kebab of fresh vegetables and mushrooms. Some fruit and cheesecake were brought in. Additionally, a white wedding cake was on the table.

We including Ms. Norma did not do anything. The hired chef and waitress did everything. They brought a long sturdy folding table with a nice white tablecloth to make a banquet table for eight people. The summer sun was strong, but the tall trees shaded Chris Gordon's backyard. We all looked like some VIP guests who dressed for the occasion.

Mom was in a white dress. Tom was in a dark suit. They both looked handsome and young. Jake Rousseau looked great in a dark suit too. Ms. Norma, Chris Gordon, and all teenagers looked great.

Toby was in a dark-blue suit and looked like a college student instead of a high school student. I was surprised that Toby grew tall and handsome with some muscles—looked sophisticated—no trace of a yucky-looking kid. When our eyes met, he winked at me with a big smile. Wow! What a charming smile he had!

Chris Gordon took many pictures of us including Mom and Tom alone as their wedding pictures. The chef took a family portrait of eight. He thought we were a family.

After Mom and Tom cut the wedding cake, Toby started playing guitar—it was soft and romantic. Mom and Tom danced slowly. Again, I was mesmerized by Toby who looked sexy. I felt as though I found somebody new instead of the Toby I knew. My heart fluttered.

My birthday was forgotten, but I did not care. I was just happy because they finally got married. They were probably forty or more, but I was very sure they could give me some siblings soon.

I really believed Tom and Mom were meant to be together. Most importantly, they had loved each other for all those years. They were definitely a good match, and their marriage would last forever.

Tom and Jake Rousseau went back to New Orleans after the wedding. Mom resigned from school. The realtor sold the house in time. We packed our clothes, books, and all personal things in several suitcases.

Mom gave away all of the furniture to Chris Gordon and all of the kitchen utensils including Grandma Margaret's Thanksgiving china to Ms. Norma because Tom told us not to bring anything except our personal items. Mom decided to leave all of the electric appliances in the house for the buyer.

We started filling up the trunk of her car and the back seat with our personal belongings including all the family pictures and jewelry boxes. The back seat was packed like a junk car.

Sharon and Toby looked sad; so was I. I embraced Sharon for a long time. Toby embraced me for the longest time and finally let me go with a kiss on my cheek. I thought I saw tears in his eyes. Mom and Ms. Norma were crying on each other's shoulders. Chris Gordon shook Mom's hand and wished her a good life in New Orleans.

Ms. Norma was waving at us in tears. Sharon and Toby came running after our car. I felt tears in my eyes, and I waved and waved at them until we turned the corner. Mom and I were very quiet for a while.

In Jake Rousseau's mansion, the master bedroom upstairs became the honeymooners' room. Jake moved to Tom's room downstairs. I chose the guesthouse.

Before my school started, Tom gladly paid for my tuition as my parent. Mom landed a great job in the same university I was attending as the director of the library. She was very happy.

I rode with Mom to school and back every day. I worked in the library for several hours a day between classes to earn some money. I wanted to save money for my own car. Tom wanted to buy a car for me now, but Mom said I could use her car whenever I needed.

Sharon and I got our driver's licenses before our graduation from high school, but I still had to get a Louisiana driver's license. Mom often let me drive her car when we went to the grocery store so I could get some driving experiences.

I missed Sharon and Toby a lot. I called her in her college dorm often. When Mom called Ms. Norma, I talked to Toby. I noticed his voice sounded like a grown-up.

Sharon told me she found a boyfriend who would be a medical doctor or a scientist like Sharon. She was interested in forensic science. Her other option was to major in science or math so she could be a high school teacher. Sharon and I were on the top ten list in high school at all times.

I told her I would like to be a lawyer in the future. She said, "Lily, you would be a great lawyer because you've always had an inquisitive mind."

When I said I would be a criminal lawyer, she got quiet and finally said, "Are you going to defend those crooks?"

"No. I will be prosecuting those crooks. I will be a prosecutor."

"Good. There are so many crooks in this world. Catch them all and put them in jail where they belong."

Sharon's boyfriend was from North Carolina, and he lived in the dorm just like Sharon. Ms. Norma and Chris Gordon met him and liked him very much.

Chapter 17
My Birth Secret

It was in May. My first year in college was actually over. I completed the final tests. Many out-of-state students were fast gone home, and the campus was very quiet.

One of my male classmates left for Europe. He was going to use a Euro pass to travel all over Europe until his money would run out. Some classmates went home to help their families by getting summer jobs. I did not know what I was going to do, but I was sure I would like to earn some money for my future car.

One night, when we were eating Jake's dessert, apple pie with ice cream, the phone rang. Tom answered it and brought the phone to Mom without saying anything.

As soon as she answered it, she left her seat screaming in a crying voice. I did not know what was going on, but I heard "Yuri" several times. Her quivery voice was too loud as though she was talking to somebody faraway. Finally, she sat down on the sofa in the living room and wiped her tears with a kitchen towel.

While eating dessert, we were actually eavesdropping on her conversation. Her quivery voice was still too loud. I put her dessert plate in the refrigerator because the ice cream was melting. After her voice got quieter, we stopped eavesdropping.

We all finished our desserts, but Mom was still on the phone. I praised Jake's cooking and said I would like to learn his Cajun cooking because he seemed to know how to use all the ingredients. I added—he probably could cook better than the famous Cajun chefs in New Orleans could. Jake said humbly, "No, I am not that good."

He seemed to be cooking more after Mom and I moved in because he wanted to be useful to his family. He did not want to be serviced by his family as most of the old people were accustomed to. In other words, he did not want to be a burden to his family. Instead, he wanted to be useful and do something helpful for his family.

If he lived alone, I did not think he would enjoy cooking or baking. Cooking and baking for his family members probably made him happy, young, and useful.

Jake knew how to make balanced meals with lots of various vegetables. He had probably learned from his longtime housekeeper, Teresa, who took care of his family. Mom was still talking on the phone.

I remembered that when I peeked into Mom's secret album years back, I saw all the pictures of Yuri Tanaka and Uncle Alan, but I could not ask Mom about their relationship because she had never told me about their engagement and marriage. I figured out their marriage from seeing the envelope that had "Yuri Tanaka Dubois" on it.

Finally, Mom came back to the table and told us it was Yuri—she would be calling her again at work tomorrow during lunchtime. She said Yuri had been looking for us for years. When she could not get touch with Mom, she called Jake years back. Today she was able to talk to Tom in the office. Tom told her to call home to surprise Michelle.

When Tom talked to Yuri, he told her everything—he came back to take over the family business, how he found Michelle and Lily in North Georgia, married Michelle last year, and now Michelle and Lily live with him in the same Rousseau house on St. Charles Avenue.

Tom also told her about his mother's passing. In return, Yuri told him about her father's passing shortly after the family tragedy and left New Orleans in a hurry. She also told him her mother's recent passing.

Yuri called Mom in the office during lunchtime almost every day. As she had an hour of lunchtime, she did not mind staying on the phone with Yuri. Besides, receiving the overseas phone calls did not affect the phone bills to the library. They both needed to catch up with many things—about twenty years of many things. Japan time was about midnight, and New Orleans time was noon.

* * *

When I was young in North Georgia, I could hardly wait for the summer because I could get to swim or fish in the lake with Sharon and Toby. When we planned to spend all day at the lake beach, we usually carried some picnic food and books. We ate and read while holding the fishing pole. Mom and Miss Norma read too while lying on the beach chair under the tree shade.

When Sharon and Toby went on a trip with their parents, I missed them a lot, but Mom and I spent a lot of time reading in the local library. They usually came back before my birthday, so again, we went to the lake beach to celebrate my birthday.

When I called Sharon at her dorm, I found out she was going on a cruise with her boyfriend and his family this summer. She was excited because it would be her first cruise. Toby joined the army right after his high school graduation in May, so he was already on his own and away from home for the summer.

Since I did not have any particular plan for the summer, I was going to work more hours or probably full time in the library. I wanted to talk to Mom first so she could help me with the job in the library. I knocked on the door. Before she said, "Come in," I was already in her office. She was writing something on a desktop computer.

"Hi, Mom. Are you busy?"

"Hi, Lily, I will be through in a minute."

I looked around her office. She had my picture and Tom's picture on her file cabinet.

"Mom, I like to work full time in the library this summer. Should I have to go to the personnel office or you can write a note to them?"

"Lily, I got good news for you. You are going to Japan this summer. Yuri will send you an open-air ticket to Tokyo, Japan, soon. She is anxious to see you and spend some time with you. She owns a big company in Tokyo. She is the president. Her mother passed away recently, so she lives alone in a penthouse. You would like Tokyo. We explored Japan many years ago. The bullet train ride was fun. Anyway, you will get a free trip to Tokyo. Yuri is a wonderful person. You will like her. I consider her my sister. She wants to see you and get to know you."

I do not understand why she wants to see me and get to know me. Did she see me when I was born? I know she lived with the Dubois family while she was going to college with Mom. I know they spent a lot of time studying together like sisters at Uncle Alan's mansion in Biloxi. I really think Yuri should spend some time with Mom instead of me.

Mom smiled and said, "Lily, Alan and I used to travel a lot when we were young because my parents were wealthy, but I have never taken you anywhere when you were growing up. I told Yuri about it. Traveling would open up your horizons, learn about your life and yourself, so go see Yuri in Tokyo and spend some time together. You know I love you."

"Yes. I love you too."

When I said it, she came to hug me. Mom and I often said "I love you" to each other and hugged a lot. Even now, she would hold my hand when we crossed the streets or in the crowd. She had been a caring mother and the best mother anybody would like to have.

"Mom, I don't speak Japanese."

"Oh, don't worry. You will have Yuri. She speaks perfect English. There are many Japanese who speak English because they learn English in school."

"Mom, do you think the airplane ride makes me sick?"

"I will get some medicine just in case. I did not get sick when I went to Paris for the first time, so you might be all right too. An airplane ride is not like a boat ride. It would not rock. It is a smooth ride. I remember the ride to Japan was too long but smooth, so I slept most of the time."

"I need a passport, right?"

"Oh, yes. You need a passport. The post office has a passport application form, so you have to fill it out first. You also need your birth certificate and two passport photos. I have your birth certificate at home. We have to do it as soon as possible because it would take several weeks to get a passport made. Let's do it tomorrow after lunch. If we do it now, you might get to celebrate your birthday with Yuri in Japan."

After she talked about the next day's agenda—going to the post office to have a passport made—she became quiet.

She finally said, "Lily, I need to talk with you before we go to the post office tomorrow. Remember, I told you I would tell you all about your father one day. It is the time. We talk tomorrow during the lunchtime. Are you through with your classes?"

"Yes, but I don't mind coming to school tomorrow because I have some books to return. I will take a streetcar. Do you have anything in your refrigerator for tomorrow?"

She walked to her small refrigerator near the window. I was observing her. *Is Mom shrinking, or am I getting taller? She surely looks much shorter than me.*

"Yes. Some apples. Tomorrow, I will bring Jake's sandwiches and bottles of water. Let us eat lunch together before I tell you all about your father. By the way, do you like your hair color?"

"Yes. I look prettier with the blondish color."

"Good. Anyway, you look pretty in either colors."

Mom's blonde hair was natural, yet she highlighted with the hair color solution. As my hair was very fine and straight, she could easily color my hair to blondish brown and highlighted just like hers. I really liked the way she colored my hair over the years. Now I looked like her, not Uncle Alan.

Tom and Mom usually made breakfast. Jake made sandwiches for us to take to work or to school. He made sure to make different sandwiches each day. My favorite sandwich was avocado with ham. Anyway, we all loved any of his sandwiches.

On that day, after dinner, Tom and Mom were in the study talking about something for a long time. They were probably talking about my father.

I could not sleep very well that night because I was anxious to learn about my father after a long wait. Mom would be telling me all about him once and for all. I was very sure she would describe how my father looked, how much she loved him, and how she felt when he was killed in an airplane crash before I was born.

The next day, after I returned the books, I walked around the campus and enjoyed the freedom from the classes. I saw very few students on campus. I explored the classroom buildings. Some classrooms were locked, some had carpet removed—probably installing new carpet during the summer.

The summer breaks seemed to give all college students some kind of freedom. They all seemed to have their summer plans such as getting full-time jobs, going overseas to see some foreign countries, climbing mountains, camping, going back to their families to help them in the farms, in the stores, in the restaurants, and some remain in school to take summer classes.

I read somewhere—during the long summer breaks, some students' lives would change dramatically—falling in love, losing virginity, breaking up, finding some new interests, changing their majors and future goals, dropping out of school, and so forth.

Finally, I went back to the library. Some students occupied the study hall—probably studying for the late tests. My work in the library between the classes was to collect the books that were left on the study tables and put them back to the correct shelves along with the returned books.

I knocked on Mom's office door and went in. She smiled at me and gestured for me to sit on a chair beside her chair. Her desk was big enough for two people to sit side by side. There were two plates of sandwiches, two bottles of water, and two apples. Her desktop computer was pushed away to the corner of the desk.

After we finished our sandwiches and apples, we both turned, sat face to face, and our knees were touching. She gave me a hug first and said, "I love you." I said the same. She held both of my hands. My heart was pounding loudly with the long awaited anticipation.

She looked very serious and somewhat nervous, but she looked determined to tell me all about my father once and for all. "Lily, when you hear what I have to say, you might feel sad, shocked, overwhelmed, feel like crying in the process, but remember, I love you very much and nothing would change between us. If you want to cry, I will cry with you. Just hear me out first."

Mom was looking at my long fingers obliviously. I heard her deep sigh. She started speaking slowly while holding both of my hands. "Yuri Tanaka and Alan Dubois were struck by love at first sight to each other on the first day they met, but they had to keep their relationship a secret from everybody for a long time. Tom and I accidently found out their relationship, so we knew they both were madly in love."

Mom had a sip of water and continued. "The reason they could not reveal their relationship to anybody was that my father promised Yuri's father, Masaki Tanaka, that he would keep an eye on Yuri and protect her from any American boy's advancement during her stay in New Orleans. See, Yuri was the only child and was supposed to manage the Tokyo branch, which Masaki had purchased just for her at that time. However, Jefferson needed Alan's help to protect Yuri from any boy's advancement, but it was too late. Alan and Yuri were already involved. That was why they kept their relationship a secret."

I did not know why Mom started talking about Yuri and Uncle Alan instead of talking about my father. I did not care to know about them because I had already figured out their engagement and marriage a long time ago. Right now, I wanted to hear about my father. I became somewhat impatient.

Mom had a sip of water again and continued. "Before our graduation, Alan and Yuri were engaged in front of Tom and me. Tom Rousseau lived in Chicago at that time but came to witness their engagement. After the graduation, Yuri was able to extend her student visa for one more year to take the CPA tests. However, they got married. I was the only one who witnessed their marriage."

Mom caressed my hands and continued. I was still waiting for her to tell me all about my father instead of Uncle Alan and Yuri.

"Shortly after their marriage, Yuri became pregnant. I told Alan to tell my parents the truth of their marriage and pregnancy, but Alan was procrastinating. Yuri's stomach was getting bigger. One day, when I was called by Alan urgently because of my parents' possible poisoning, I took the three of them to the airfield. That was the last time I saw Alan and my parents."

Mom's eyes were welled up with tears. "On that night, the FAA informed me of the airplane crash. Yuri and I both were devastated, heartbroken, and did not know what to do. Soon, the Dubois Import Company disappeared mysteriously and I was evicted from the family home in New Orleans for no reason. Before the eviction, I took all of my mother's jewelry and my father's expensive gold coin collections and moved in with Yuri in Biloxi. Yuri was certified as a CPA by then, and I was awarded with an MLS degree."

She wiped her tears and continued. "Soon, Yuri's emotional trauma and sadness caused the sign of early labor, so I took Yuri to the hospital. The baby was born on that day. Yuri named the baby Lily Marie Dubois. The baby's first name Lily in English is as same as Yuri in Japanese, so the baby got her mother's name. Therefore, Lily Marie Dubois was born as the child of Alan Dubois and Yuri Tanaka Dubois."

I was stunned. Now I was looking at my aunt, not my mother. Uncle Alan became my father, and Yuri Tanaka became my biological mother.

I did not expect this outcome. I wished she did not tell me anything about my birth secret because I did not want to be anybody else's child but Mom's.

Suddenly, I could not control my sobbing. Mom was probably expecting what would happen, so she held my face, kissed me on my eyes, and embraced me tightly.

My uncontrollable sobbing continued. She let me cry on her shoulder and whispered cheerfully, "Lily, no matter what, you are still my daughter. You just happened to have two mothers who love you very much. Yuri and I are lucky to have a smart and pretty daughter like you. Remember, no matter what, I am still your mom and you are still my daughter just as before. Nothing has changed between us, and nothing will change between us. You are my precious daughter just as always. I love you very much."

"I love you, Mom."

Chapter 18
Biological Mother

*N*ow I knew my father was killed in an airplane crash before I was born. My biological mother left me with Mom and never came back.

"Mom, why did Yuri desert me?"

"She did not desert you. It was my fault. Let me explain what happened. Shortly after you both came home from the hospital, Yuri had a phone call from Japan—her father passed away suddenly. She had to go back to Japan immediately, and her mother paid for the airplane ticket in Japan. Her mother did not know Yuri just had a baby."

She held my hands again and continued. "Yuri did not know what to do with the baby, but I courageously told her to leave the baby with me and come right back. At that time, you were just a week old. Your eyes were still covered with some films and could not see anything, but as Yuri had everything for the baby, I felt confident to babysit while she was away. I took her to the airport. You were sleeping in the baby basket between us. Yuri promised she would tell her mother everything and come back for Lily. She thanked me and left."

"What happened after that?"

"Shortly after Yuri left, I got the eviction notice. With my desperation, I called Aunt Margaret in North Georgia for help. I told her the family tragedy, the grand larceny, the baby, and the eviction. She thought the baby was mine. I told her about the baby after we moved in with her. Anyway, when I told her I would be homeless and almost penniless, she did not hesitate to take us in. By then, I sold all of my mother's jewelry and my father's gold coins to pay for your hospital bills. Indeed, I was almost penniless. I put all your baby stuff and my stuff in the car and left Biloxi in a hurry. It took almost eight hours to Aunt Margaret's house in North Georgia."

"Did I cry while you were driving?"

"No. Not at all. You were such a nice baby and slept almost all the way to North Georgia. I had to wake you up at the rest area so I could feed you, but after I fed you and changed your diaper, again you slept soundly."

"After you were evicted, did you try to call Yuri in Japan?"

"When I was going to call Yuri from North Georgia, I realized I left a piece of paper that had Yuri's phone number and home address. That paper was inserted in my address book. As I was such in a hurry, I forgot to retrieve my address book from the desk drawer. That was why Yuri did not hear from me for all these years. It was my fault."

Mom had some tears in her eyes. "According to Yuri, after her father's funeral, she told her mother about her marriage to Alan, his death, and a baby. Her mother wanted her to bring her grandchild as soon as possible. Yuri tried to call us many times, but no answer, and finally the phone was disconnected. She called Jake at his office, but he, too, did not know where I was. I could've called Jake or Eunice to let them know where I was, but my address book was left in the drawer as well. That was why I could not get touch with anybody including Tom."

Mom looked tired, but continued. "Yuri said your maternal grandmother wanted to meet you badly for years, but she passed away recently."

I sobbed again. Mom held my face and wiped off my tears and then cheerfully said, "Lily, remember Yuri did not desert you. It was totally my fault. I am glad Yuri finally found us. I was waiting for this moment so that I could reveal all the secrets I was hiding from you. Remember I told you I would tell you everything about your father someday. That someday came today. Yes, your father died in an airplane crash before you were born. Your father was the nicest man. Your mother, Yuri, is the nicest woman. Your parents genuinely loved each other. You are the product of their love. If your father were alive, you should be the princess of the nicest parents and should live happily ever after in that antebellum mansion in Biloxi."

"I am glad you told me everything."

"I am sorry I waited this long. Now let's go to the post office to get your passport made so you can see your biological mother in Japan. She is very anxious to meet you. I will show you your birth certificate so you can see who your parents are."

"Does Tom know I am Uncle Alan's daughter?"

"Yes, I told him about you before he met us in North Georgia."

"No wonder he said I looked like Uncle Alan. I guess Jake knew it too because he said the same thing." She nodded.

That afternoon, in the post office, I clearly saw my birth certificate with the names of my parents and the marriage certificate of Alan Dubois and Yuri Tanaka.

My passport arrived at the end of June. Mom helped me pack clothes, shoes, and some girl's necessities. She practically packed my suitcase as though I was still a young child who was going on a long trip without her. She gave me an old picture of Yuri and Alan.

"Lily, I had already sent your high school graduation picture to Yuri so she could spot you easily at the airport. Just wait for Yuri at the arrival gate. Do not stray away." Mom was talking to a small child.

She gave me Yuri's address and phone number in Tokyo just in case. I was to spend the entire month of July with Yuri so we could celebrate my birthday together.

Tom and Jake came to the airport with us. They knew this was my first airplane ride and my first trip to a foreign country. Jake and Tom gave me some spending money. I took some pictures of Mom, Tom, and Jake with my digital camera so I could show Yuri how they looked two decades later. Tom told me to take many pictures of Yuri and Tokyo. He proudly said he was there once.

* * *

My seat was at the window side. I was somewhat nervous when the airplane ascended but could not take my eyes off the land, the ocean, and the river below. Everything was getting smaller and smaller. Finally, we were above the white clouds.

I took out the picture of Yuri and Alan and studied the resemblance of me in them. My original hair color was a mixture of their hair colors. My facial complexion was definitely Yuri's. My eyes and eyelashes came from Alan. My height might be a mixture of Alan and Yuri.

I had to change the airplane in Los Angeles. I walked to the international terminal instead of taking a shuttle bus. On the airplane, I sat at the window side again.

A Japanese woman sat beside me and spoke some broken English to ask me if I were visiting someone in Japan. I showed the picture of Yuri and Alan and said, "My Japanese mother." She looked surprised to see the young mother in the picture. I told her the picture was taken many years ago. She nodded.

I was sleepy after dinner, so I put a blindfold to sleep. The Japanese woman was watching a movie. I did not know how long I slept, but I heard an announcement.

As soon as I went through the immigration and customs at the Narita International Airport, I was led to the arrival gate. It was so crowded with people who seemed to be waiting for the arrival of their relatives or friends. I saw some Asians in New Orleans, but this was the first time I saw so many Japanese or Asians at one time. They were rather short and I could see everything above their heads.

Yuri Tanaka spotted me and waved her hand vigorously at me. She had a pastel summer dress on and tried to come closer to me, but the crowd would not let her, so I pushed my suitcase forcefully through the crowd and went toward her.

I could not believe how beautiful she looked and more beautiful in person than the picture I saw. No wonder Alan Dubois fell in love with Yuri at first sight. Her smile was radiant just like a young girl. She embraced me with tears. We were about the same height. I did not know how to react to her embrace, but I embraced her back.

Yuri said, "You look so pretty. Michelle certainly did a beautiful job on you. You are tall like your father. In fact, you look like your father. I am so glad you agreed to see me." I just nodded with a smile.

She tried to pull my suitcase, but I did not let her, so she held my other hand to walk me through the crowd as though I was her little child who might get lost in the strange place. I did not mind my hand to be held because Mom did that all the time since I was a child. Her hand was soft and warm just like Mom's.

I was awkward in front of my biological mother, but Yuri seemed to know how to overcome the situation. She finally let my hand go when we came to a limousine outside the terminal. Yuri introduced me to the chauffeur in Japanese. He introduced himself in broken English with a big smile. His name was Mr. Nishimoto, who had worked for the Tanaka family for years. He seemed to know all about Yuri's long-lost daughter.

In the limousine, Yuri said, "Lily, Michelle told me all about you. I feel like I know you already. Now you have to know me. You can ask me anything and everything. I hope we are going to be good friends and get along well. I have missed you a lot for so many years." Her voice quivered.

I still did not know what to say to her, so I nodded with a smile. We came to a tall apartment building. Mr. Nishimoto stopped in front of the building, set my suitcase at the door, and said in English, "Good night. See you tomorrow." I thanked him. He was to park the limousine in the parking lot of the building and go home for the day.

Yuri opened the thick glass door with her coded key. I pulled my suitcase and walked behind her. The big open space with the marble floor reminded me of a hotel lobby, but no one was on the floor except a security guard at the desk near the elevator.

He acknowledged Yuri by nodding. We rode an elevator all the way to the top where her penthouse was. According to Yuri, many expatriated employees from the foreign countries lived in this apartment building.

When Yuri tried to open the entrance door of her penthouse, her housekeeper opened it from the inside and greeted us. Yuri introduced the housekeeper as Shigeko. Later, I learned that Shigeko took care of Yuri's mother, rather my grandmother, as a live-in housekeeper when she was ill. Now she became Yuri's housekeeper.

She helped me carry my suitcase without saying anything. I assumed she did not know any English just as I did not know any Japanese, but I thanked her in English. She smiled by nodding.

Yuri's penthouse was huge. She had three bedrooms, actually four bedrooms including Shigeko's room. After putting my suitcase in my room, Yuri gave me a tour of her penthouse.

The glass-roofed courtyard was in the middle of the penthouse. Many beautiful miniature trees were displayed artfully in the courtyard. I was mesmerized because I had never seen such dwarf trees in my life. Later, I learned the name of the miniature tree is called bonsai in Japanese.

According to Yuri, her father, Masaki Tanaka, collected them before he passed away, so Yuri and her mother, Emi, kept them for years by spraying water periodically. The courtyard was seen from the kitchen and the living room. The atmosphere of the courtyard was very tranquil.

My room was big and nicely decorated. The large window gave me the view of the city, streets, and a park down below. The neighborhood looked affluent with neatly built homes and a park.

It should be in the morning in the United States, but here in Japan, it was dinnertime. After I washed my hands and refreshed my face, Shigeko came and gestured for me to come to the kitchen. Yuri was already sitting at the kitchen table. She smiled at me and wanted me to sit across from her. The table had a big tray of catered sushi, fresh salad, and fresh fruit. Yuri was sipping green tea. I was hungry. When I was eating sushi with chopsticks skillfully, Yuri and Shigeko looked amazed.

Yuri probably heard from Mom how well I liked sushi—Mom and I used to drive a long distance to Atlanta to eat sushi for some special occasions. Mom told me Yuri used to fix sushi every time they stayed in Biloxi.

After dinner, we sat in the courtyard to have some dessert. Shigeko brought a slice of Japanese dessert called *yōkan,* which is made of sweet beans. Mom used to order it just for me in the Japanese restaurant because I like it so much.

Yuri started telling me all about what happened after she left New Orleans—after her father's death, her mother was emotionally devastated, and physically not well, but she managed the company headquarters in Osaka with the help of Masaki's faithful directors.

After the funeral, Yuri told her mother everything, including her marriage, death of Alan, and the baby. She wanted Yuri to go back to New Orleans and bring her daughter to Japan, but the phone was disconnected, did not hear from Michelle, and Jake, too, did not know Michelle's whereabouts.

Even after she came to Tokyo to manage the Tokyo branch, she tried to find Michelle's whereabouts, but she did not know how to find us. For several years, she and her mother operated both of the companies, but her mother's health was failing.

Therefore, they decided to sell the headquarters in Osaka and move everything to Tokyo. With the money from the sale of the house in Osaka and the second house in Tokyo, they bought the penthouse unit. Shigeko as a live-in housekeeper took care of her mother until her passing.

By using her business knowledge and accounting skills, Yuri's company had been sailing smoothly with profits. However, her mind was always on her baby, whom she left with Michelle. She often thought that Michelle and her daughter, Lily, had died and that was why she did not hear from Michelle.

"I did not think I would ever see my daughter in my lifetime. Thank you for coming to see me." Yuri said it in her quivery voice. I nodded awkwardly.

Before I went to bed, I showed Yuri the pictures of Jake, Tom, and Mom in the digital camera. She stared at each picture in her teary eyes. I left the camera with Yuri and said, "Good night."

"Good night, Lily. I love you." I almost said the same, "I love you, Yuri," but I could not say it. Yuri understood my awkwardness. That night, my dream was with Yuri and Alan at the beach, instead of Mom and Tom.

The next day, I woke up around ten. Yuri was already gone to work. Shigeko came and gestured with her hand to see if I were hungry. I nodded so she gestured for me to follow her to the kitchen.

There were a bowl of hot miso soup, rice, some fresh tomatoes and cucumbers, and a slab of grilled fish and fried eggs. When I ate everything on the plate, Shigeko looked happy.

After breakfast, I spent a lot of time in the courtyard to observe each bonsai tree. I was overwhelmed with the fact that they were so dwarf and beautiful. Yuri told me that some were fifty years old. In the afternoon, I dozed off in bed and slept until Yuri came home. I was probably suffering from jet lag.

The next day, Mr. Nishimoto greeted us at the entrance of the apartment building. His black limousine was a lot smaller than an American limousine, but it could accommodate at least five passengers.

We were to stop at Yuri's office before sightseeing. It took a while to get through the morning traffic. Her three-story office building was between the warehouse and the factory. We walked through the factory to reach her office.

About a hundred employees were already working with sewing machines. The workers covered their noses with white masks and heads with cloth caps to avoid the lint or dust from the fabric.

She had a private entrance at the back of the building. When she used a key to open the door, the steps appeared. The long steps reminded me of the emergency exit. She locked the door behind us. The long steps of the three stories did not bother Yuri, but I was breathing hard when we reached her office on the third floor.

Her office was big with a conference table with many chairs in the middle of the floor. While she was checking or reading some papers, I looked around her office. On her desk, I saw Alan's old picture and my high school graduation picture that was sent by Mom before my visit.

She had an upright computer on her large desk. Several file cabinets and a large bookcase were behind her desk. From the window, I saw the roof of the factory. Hundreds of sample garments were neatly displayed on the tables against the wall.

After she sorted out the papers, she called two people's names through intercom. A young lady in a dark suit and a fiftyish man in a suit and a tie appeared together.

Yuri introduced them to me as her secretary and accountant. I was introduced as her long-lost daughter who came to visit her. She probably said it in English for my sake, but they seemed to know English well too. They both smiled at me and said in English, "We are very happy because your mother finally found you. Welcome to Tokyo."

After our introduction, Yuri excused herself from me and started talking to them in Japanese—probably giving them some instructions what to do while she was away from the office. They were listening attentively.

While Yuri was instructing them, I peeked out to see what was at the other side of the door. I saw a dozen employees in the open floor. Since they did not see me, I closed the door quietly.

Chapter 19
Okaasan

Finally, we were out of her office. Mr. Nishimoto was waiting for us in front of the factory. He was to drop us off at Tokyo Tower this morning. His black limousine looked very shiny. He probably shined it just for us.

We drove through the city; the traffic was somewhat congested. In the center of the business district, well-dressed businessmen and businesswomen hurriedly crossed the streets.

After we were dropped off at Tokyo Tower, Mr. Nishimoto waved and drove off. Yuri probably told him she would call him on the cell phone when we were ready to go to the next destination. The cell phone was getting popular at that time in Japan.

From Tokyo Tower, I saw the north, east, south, and west of the city by walking around the observation deck. All the buildings looked very small, and the city was endlessly spread out to the horizon.

Yuri jokingly said that the view from Tokyo Tower could be the fastest way of sightseeing the city. I agreed because we learned the names of some notable buildings from the observation deck.

We also learned—The Tokyo Tower is 333 m (1,091 ft) tall, opened in 1957, and the highest observation deck is 250 m. The Eiffel Tower is 324 m (1,063 ft) tall, opened in 1889, and the highest observation deck is 273 m.

We came down to the lower observation deck that had gift shops and restaurants. We chose to sit at the coffee shop on the open floor that was like an outdoor café, so to speak. We had mid-morning tea with some doughnuts.

Yuri looked very elegant and beautiful. The Japanese tourists probably saw some resemblance in us and might have thought we were a mother and a daughter who came to visit Tokyo from a foreign country because we were speaking in English.

Mr. Nishimoto picked us up and dropped us off at our next destination—the Imperial Palace. The front part of the Imperial Palace has a huge white gravel garden. We saw the moat around the Imperial Palace with some pretty trees.

My black shoes got some white dust from the gravel garden. We took many pictures of each other. The view of the Imperial Palace and the Diet Building from where we were standing looked majestic.

The same roofing design of the Imperial Palace is seen in many Japanese temples. To me, the Chinese temple roofs or other Asian temple roofs look rather gaudy and busy, but the Japanese temple roofs look more subtle, tranquil, and modest.

We crossed the street from the Imperial Palace and walked into a hotel. We decided to eat lunch at a restaurant in the hotel. We chose a small sandwich shop. We ordered sandwiches with iced tea and continued talking—Yuri's first visit to Tokyo was when she was in high school. She took a field trip with her classmates to visit Tokyo Tower and the Imperial Palace. She liked the bullet train ride from Osaka.

She said she started liking Tokyo because the city was much classier than Osaka was. She even told her father to extend his business to Tokyo. Her father jokingly said, if he had a branch in Tokyo, he would die young from stress unless he had someone to oversee the branch, so Yuri volunteered to oversee the Tokyo branch for him. It was many years ago.

She also told me about her height. She was the tallest girl in the class, and she always felt self-conscious about her height, but when she met Alan, her self-consciousness disappeared. They were in love on the first day they met. Alan was kind, patient, well mannered, witty, handsome, tall, and he had everything Yuri liked.

I suddenly felt the urge to say something. "Yuri, thank you for bringing me into this world. Without both of you, I would not be here. I may not call you Mom, but I love you and I love Uncle Alan, no, my father too. Mom is right, you are a very nice person and I like you. I am glad you invited me to Tokyo to get to know you. Mom said our separation was her fault. Please do not blame Mom. I want you to know she took good care of me, even though she did not have much money."

I kept talking while holding her dainty hands just like mine. I did not explain in details, but I told her the two lawyers who worked for Jefferson and Marie stole the Dubois fortune. That was why Mom became penniless. Mom probably told Yuri about them, so she nodded.

I also said, "Yuri, Mom came to work in my school library after Grandma Margaret passed away. She used to work in the university library for a better pay, but she came to my school so she could be with me. We had the same holiday breaks and summer breaks. We were very happy."

"I wished I knew where you were so I could've helped Michelle financially. She said she has not taken you to anywhere when you were growing up."

"Yes. Mom took me to Biloxi on my ninth birthday. I saw an ocean and a real beach for the first time. She also sent me to Florida with Sharon and Toby."

"Who?"

"Sharon and Toby. They are my best friends, and we grew up together in the same neighborhood. I have many delightful memories with them. My childhood was wonderful in North Georgia because of them."

She looked envious because she had never lived in the countryside. She was a big-city girl. When I told her how beautiful the trees look in North Georgia in the fall, she again looked envious because there are no big trees or mountains in Tokyo.

She told me about my maternal grandmother who really wanted to meet her grandchild. She studied English herself because she wanted to converse with her granddaughter in English. She was a teacher in high school. I felt sad for not meeting any of my grandmothers or grandfathers who were all college graduates.

All of a sudden, I missed Jake who had been treating me like his own granddaughter since we moved in. I was determined to help him in the kitchen after my return so he could live longer.

One day, Yuri and I rode a tour bus to visit a famous temple. I learned how to sit in the Japanese way to drink Japanese tea. Yuri sat elegantly, but I could not fold my long legs well. There were many foreigners in the group, so I did not look like a sore thumb.

After the tour, Yuri called Mr. Nishimoto and told him that we would be taking the subway to Ginza, so he was dismissed for the day. At the subway station and in the crowded train, Yuri held my hand tightly as though I were her toddler. Yuri and Mom had the same maternal instinct.

In Ginza, I saw a big department store and famous brand name stores. While walking, she told me all about my father, Alan, who was witty and made her laugh often. He also did not hesitate to go to the first-time parent's class to learn about a baby before I was born and often shopped on the weekends to pick out the baby clothes himself.

In Ginza, the sidewalks were crowded with people. The neon signs started shining like Broadway in New York that I saw on TV. Some businessmen were in groups looking for some drinking bars or restaurants. Some young office girls were looking for a place to chat.

Yuri and I suddenly felt hungry, so Yuri decided to take me to her favorite restaurant. We walked one block off the main street of Ginza. The restaurant reminded me of the restaurant in Atlanta. It had a long sushi bar counter. The sushi chef recognized Yuri and tried to put us at a table, but she gestured for me to sit at the counter. We sat side by side.

Yuri did not introduce me to the chef; besides he was too busy. She wanted me to order whatever I wanted. I ordered a pair of tuna sushi first and added many more pairs of salmon, octopus, and shrimp sushi. I was hungry. Yuri was not surprised by my order. She probably heard about how crazy I was about sushi.

I learned how to use chopsticks myself at the Japanese restaurant when I was young. We only went there on the special occasions such as Mom's payday, or her birthday. Sharon and Toby had never been to a Japanese restaurant, so I taught them how to use chopsticks. We often ate cookies with chopsticks.

The chef came and talked to Yuri periodically in Japanese, but she still did not say anything about me. He probably thought I was one of her business customers from a foreign country.

Since Yuri encouraged me to eat more sushi, I kept ordering many more without thinking about the cost. I had never eaten that many sushi before. Mom could not afford it when I was young.

I told Yuri about how Mom had to make ends meet every month. In the Japanese restaurant, we had the limited budget to order sushi. Suddenly, Yuri started sobbing by covering her face with her cloth napkin. I was stunned. I thought I said something wrong to hurt her feelings. When I caressed her back to see if she was all right, she nodded several times and put her napkin back on her lap. I was glad nobody noticed her sobbing, but I was long puzzled by the reason of her sobbing.

One day, Yuri had a board meeting, so I stayed home with Shigeko. I learned many Japanese words such as *mother, father, grandfather, grandmother,* and some phrases such as *good morning, good afternoon, good evening, good night, goodbye,* and *thank you.*

She made me repeat each word clearly. If I did right, she clapped her hands. I wrote the words in Romanization so I was able to pronounce them.

That night, when Yuri walked in the house, I said, "Okaerinasai, Okaasan." Yuri's big eyes were wide open and welled up with tears. Shigeko was clapping her hands.

Yuri looked very happy. I was happy too because I was finally able to call Yuri, *Mother* in Japanese. I also pointed to the pictures of my grandfather and grandmother and said "Ojiisan" and "Obaasan." Again, Shigeko applauded.

I brushed my teeth and went to bed. That night, for no reason, I had a dream of Jake, who was working in the yard. He looked very tired and frail as though the yard work was too much for him. When I woke up, I could still see Jake in the yard. I did not know why I dreamed about him, but I remembered that I wanted Jake to live longer because he is like my only grandfather who is still alive.

The next day, Yuri had to stay in the office to meet some vendors from Osaka, so Mr. Nishimoto took me to Yokohama to see Japan's largest Chinatown. We drove probably a couple of hours to get there.

While driving, he explained in his broken English some American military words that derived from Japanese words such as *honki dori* and *hancho*.

He said, *honki dori* means "Honki Street" in Japanese. After WWII, during the military occupation of Japan, Honki Street in Yokohama's Chinatown had everything such as pawnshops, brothels, motels, restaurants, bars, grocery stores, dry cleaners, shoeshine stores, even candy stores, so American soldiers started using the words *honki dori*. "Everything honki dori" means "everything is there, everything is all right or fine." *Hancho* means "boss."

We rode the giant Ferris wheel together and ate late lunch at Chinatown before we headed back home. He spoke broken English, but I understood every word he said. He liked the way I listened to him attentively without correcting his English or without intimidating him. He often made me laugh with his jokes. He liked my laughter. We got along very well.

When Mr. Nishimoto dropped me off at the apartment building, Shigeko came downstairs to open the main entrance door because Yuri was still at work.

When I entered the penthouse, she gestured with her hands to see if I were hungry. I shook my head because I was still full, so she brought me a cup of green tea with a slice of sweet bean cake—my favorite *yōkan*.

I said, "Thank you," in English, but I remembered the word in Japanese so I said, "Arigatoo."

She clapped her hands and said, "Good," in English, so I clapped my hands for her. I learned many Japanese words and phrases from Shigeko during my stay. She was a good teacher.

On one weekend, Yuri and I took a bullet train to see Mt. Fuji and spent a night in an exclusive hotel at the foot of the mountain. There was a big hot spring pool for women, but I was too shy to take my clothes off in front of many women, so Yuri and I got a private hot tub. I took a shower before soaking in the tub. The water was so hot that my whole body looked pinkish afterward.

Whenever Yuri was busy, Mr. Nishimoto drove me to sightsee. By then, I knew exactly where I was. I took many pictures of the sights such as the highest waterfall in Japan and the emperor's resort house, some beautiful gardens, and temples.

I used some Japanese words with Mr. Nishimoto. He praised me for how fast I learned the language. Mom spoke fluent French when she was young, but after she moved to North Georgia, she said she had forgotten most of the vocabulary. Foreign language must be spoken frequently; otherwise you would forget it, especially vocabulary. However, the native language that you are born with or educated with may never be forgotten.

On my birthday, I received a "Happy Birthday" card from Mom, Tom, and Jake. Yuri gave me a beautiful Japanese birthday card with money and told me all about me when I was born—how cute I looked, how gentle I was—hardly cried.

For my birthday dinner, Yuri decided to take me to her favorite sushi restaurant again. The chef welcomed us. I said something nice in Japanese. He was impressed and said, "Arigatoo."

This time, Yuri asked for a table. She probably wanted to reminisce about the time of my birth privately. I was glad I was able to call Yuri "Okaasan" without any hesitation by then. We were getting along very well.

The chef brought green tea and checked to see if we were ready to order. When I called Yuri "Okaasan," he jumped. Yuri was laughing. I was very sure the chef wanted to know more details why I called her "Okaasan," but he realized I could not speak the language.

He turned to Yuri. Yuri was probably saying, "It is a very long story, but we are celebrating my daughter's birthday today." I could not figure out exactly what Yuri said to the chef, but he went back to the counter and got on the phone.

We ordered a tray of assorted sushi with miso soup. While eating, Yuri reminisced about the day before Alan's airplane crash. She remembered they ate sushi that night and talked about the name of the baby. If it were a girl, it would be Lily Marie after Yuri and

Grandmother Marie. If a boy, it would be Thomas Jefferson after Alan's best friend, Thomas Rousseau, and Grandfather Jefferson.

Alan was going to tell his parents about his marriage and Yuri's pregnancy on that very same day when the tragedy occurred. Yuri was very happy about Alan's decision, so everybody in Alan's family and her family including Masaki Tanaka might forgive them and bless the baby; of course, her mother, Emi, would be thrilled.

She also told me their marriage was a secret from Alan's family and her family. I knew that, so I nodded. Michelle was the only one who knew about their marriage. Again, I nodded.

She told me some funny episodes when she was pregnant—one weekend, Jefferson and Marie wanted to take Alan, Yuri, and Michelle to eat at their favorite seafood restaurant in Biloxi. Michelle usually drove her parents whenever they had to go to Biloxi. She panicked because Yuri's stomach was getting big, so she bought two opera tickets for her parents. Her mother, Marie, was crazy about the opera, so they went to see the opera instead.

Another time, they wanted to invite Yuri to eat dinner at the French Quarter and Michelle was to bring her there. Again, Michelle panicked, so she told them Yuri had been suffering from a sore throat and bad cold—might be contagious, so they gave up and ate at home. By then, Yuri's stomach was too big to hide.

We both laughed loudly. Yuri liked my laughter. She probably thought inviting me to Tokyo was the best idea because we got along so well. The people in the restaurant looked at us enviously because we were laughing like some loving mother and daughter.

After dinner, the chef brought a small birthday cake to our table. Yuri looked surprised because she did not order it. He was probably doing a favor for his regular or favorite customer. The chef started singing the "Happy Birthday" song in English, and his customers in the restaurant joined singing with him. I was surprised that they all knew the "Happy Birthday" song in English. After the song, I blew the candle, and everybody clapped hands for me, so I said loudly, "Arigatoo."

The chef sliced two pieces and put each piece on a small plate for us to have as dessert with green tea. After putting the rest back in the box, he gestured to me to take it home. The cake box was artfully decorated.

Yuri seemed to be explaining to the chef in Japanese—her long-lost daughter came to visit her from the United States. The chef glanced at me with a big smile and gestured with his hands that Yuri and I resembled. Yuri said "Arigatoo" to the chef. I, too, thanked him in Japanese.

Mr. Nishimoto picked us up although it was late. He greeted me by saying, "Happy birthday!" Shigeko was waiting for us. She, too, said, "Happy birthday!" in English.

Chapter 20
Going Home

By the end of my visit, surprisingly, I was able to walk around the shopping area in the neighborhood without being lost and shopped alone with the phrases I learned from Shigeko.

Shigeko and I once got up early in the morning and took a train to the biggest fish market in Japan. I had never seen such an enormous fish market with various big fishes in my life.

Shigeko and I also took many trains in the city for shopping, especially when Yuri and Mr. Nishimoto were busy with their customers. By then, I knew Tokyo very well. I told Yuri and Shigeko that I could take trains by myself to explore the city, but they did not think so.

I started packing some souvenirs Yuri bought for Mom, Tom, and Jake. My going home made Yuri sad even though she knew I must return home soon. Her eyes were puffed up in the morning—she probably cried in bed. I understood how a mother felt. Therefore, I assured her that I would write often to stay in touch.

I believed our frequent communication could assure her that she would never lose her daughter again and the long distance should be no problem.

I promised her to send my handwritten letters often so she could save them and read them whenever she wants, especially when she gets lonely. I also promised that I would call her on the phone from time to time so she could hear my voice.

Even though I have only known Yuri for a month, we successfully built great rapport. Moreover, I was able to call her "Okaasan" without any hesitation and embrace her without any awkwardness.

Before Mom sent me to Japan, she assured me that I was her forever daughter and she was my forever Mom, no matter what. Our wonderful mother-daughter relationship would never change.

She was right. My feelings toward Mom did not change even though I spent a month with my biological mother. I missed seeing Mom and wanted to hug her as I had always done. Besides, I love Mom, Tom, and Jake just as before. Nothing has changed.

I would never forget the day when Mom unveiled my birth secret. When she said it was time for her to tell me all about my deceased father, I did not expect anything else but the story of my father.

Nevertheless, she unveiled the devastating truth—Mom was not my real mother. I was the daughter of her brother, Alan, and Yuri. I was somewhat angry and wished she had never revealed my birth secret because I did not want to be anybody else's child but Mom's.

In the past, when I asked Mom about my father and their wedding pictures, she simply said she lost all the pictures when she was evicted, yet she hid the family album in her dresser with many pictures of her parents, her brother Alan, Tom, and Yuri.

Yes, as a child, I believed what she had to say about losing their wedding pictures and my father's pictures. Now I realized she had never been married and never had wedding pictures.

Grandma Margaret had never hinted that I was Uncle Alan's child and never said I looked like Uncle Alan when I was growing up. Therefore, I positively believed I was Mom's child for all my life. However, I was glad Mom waited to tell me all about my birth secret after I became an adult.

If she had unveiled my birth secret when I was young, I could have been more devastated and sad. Our wonderful relationship could have been destroyed, and then I might have become a difficult child who acted rebelliously toward Mom, definitely resented my biological mother, Yuri, who left me with Mom, and never came back to fetch me.

I was sure Mom wanted to tell me all about my birth secret many times in the past, but she did not have the courage because she did not know Yuri's whereabouts, so she probably decided to wait until she could locate her first. Besides, she probably wanted to enjoy me longer as her precious daughter.

If I were a minor, Yuri probably got the custody of me from Mom and let me move to Japan. However, in Japan, I could have faced all kinds of problems such as a language problem, a citizenship problem, and could never pass the entrance exam to college because of my language barrier, so I could have been nobody. Now I am an adult, so Yuri had no choice but to let me be American.

The night before my return, Yuri and I sat at the table in the courtyard and had my favorite dessert with green tea. Without saying much to me, Yuri caressed my hand lovingly from time to time.

It the end, when we both embraced each other to say "good night," she smoothed my hair and touched my face as though I were still the newborn baby she remembered.

"Lily, I will miss you."

"I will miss you too, Okaasan." We again embraced each other.

The next day, before we left for the airport, I thanked Shigeko in Japanese. She had tears in her eyes. In the limousine, Yuri sat beside me, and we held each other's hands without saying a word.

Mr. Nishimoto brought my suitcase and helped me check in at the airline counter. I thanked him in Japanese. After Yuri and I embraced each other, I walked toward the departure gate. They both stood there and watched me leave. I turned and waved at them for the last time. When I saw Yuri wave her hand vigorously at me, I felt tears in my eyes. I was sure she was crying too.

* * *

Mom was waiting for me anxiously at the airport. She held my hand all the way to the parking lot, and she kept saying she missed me a lot. Mom came alone to pick me up because Tom was at work and Jake was under the weather, so to speak.

On the way home in the car, Mom said, "Yuri called me to thank me how a great job I have done on you. She said you are very kind, smart, patient, and, most importantly, very understanding. I am glad you went to see Yuri. Now we have to include her in our family. Oh, another thing, Yuri wants to pay for your college from now on. She wants to help you graduate from college and help you get into law school. She will send you the allowance every month so you do not need to work in the library anymore. Instead, she wants you to study for the LSAT."

When we arrived at home, Jake came to the kitchen to welcome me. I was shocked to see Jake, how frail and thin he looked in a month. He looked just as the Jake I saw in my dream.

I asked him, "Jake, are you all right? You look pale."

"I am all right, but I just feel weak. I cannot sleep very well and get tired easily. I guess I am getting old. I am glad you are home safely. We missed you."

"Jake, have you had a physical checkup recently with Dr. Patterson?"

"No. I guess I should see him soon."

"I will take you tomorrow."

The next day, Dr. Patterson arranged Jake's physical checkup in the hospital. I waited in the lobby. They examined his blood, bone density, eyes, nose, ears, and chest by taking an X-ray.

Several days later, Dr. Patterson called me and said, "Nothing wrong with Jake, but he is a little anemic. Please help him take vitamins, eat more nutritious meals, drink more water, and, most importantly, do not let him do strenuous work or exercises."

After a professional mason built the short brick fence around Jake's mansion years ago, he planted pretty flowers and kept Bermuda grass throughout the yard. Maintaining the beautiful yard was hard work, but Jake had enjoyed doing it for years.

Typically, each mansion on St. Charles Avenue has a narrow or rather small front yard. Almost all the yards along the street are unanimously fenced with black iron fences. Very few like Jake's mansion have brick fences. The streetcars that run in the middle of the street and symmetrically planted numerous Southern oak trees are identified as St. Charles Avenue in New Orleans.

The yard work is a strenuous job—bending over or squatting down for many hours, but Jake had done it for years. Now he had to give it up. He said he would hire a yardman to do the work from now on.

Dr. Patterson prescribed some vitamins for Jake, so Jake and I stopped at a drug store. I decided to buy some essential vitamins for myself too. On the way home, we bought some fish, meat, vegetables, and fruit at a grocery store. I told him that cooking could be strenuous, so I should be the cook until he gets his strength back.

For the remaining summer, I became a cook under Jake's supervision. As Yuri suggested, I stopped working in the library and started studying for the LSAT at home instead. Yuri started sending me a substantial amount of monthly allowance through postal money order. I wrote a long letter to thank her and let her know about Jake's health. Most importantly, I let her know that I started studying the LSAT. I studied in my room most of the day.

In the evening, before Mom and Tom came home, I started cooking in the kitchen—washing potatoes, vegetables, and any other food needed to be washed. Jake was watching me. I told him I could peel, mince, shred, grind, chop, cut, mix, and mash anything; the head chef was laughing aloud.

One day, Jake brought his laptop to the kitchen to show me his stock portfolio. I did not know much about the stock market, but I did not mind hearing his successful moneymaking project. I saw the tremendous value in his portfolio. He said he tripled the value of his portfolio in twenty years.

He wanted me to learn the stock market and invest some money regularly. Since I had saved up my library paychecks for a car and now the allowance from Yuri, I decided to open a stock account by depositing some money and made an initial purchase of an inexpensive pharmaceutical company on that day. As Mom and Tom did not believe in the stock market, my moneymaking project was somewhat a secret between Jake and me.

When school started, Jake watched my portfolio while I was at school, and he had my permission to buy or sell stocks if necessary. I trusted Jake because he knew each company's profitability and P/E ratio. After I came home from school in the afternoon, we watched CNBC on TV together and then fixed dinner.

On the weekends, Tom often drove us to his summerhouse in Biloxi. We usually ate at the buffet restaurant in the casino instead of cooking for ourselves at the vacation home. The restaurant was huge, always crowded with many casino players.

One Saturday, we decided to eat dinner in the casino restaurant as usual and took a table for four. While Mom, Tom, and Jake were getting some food at the buffet counter, I waited at the table to order everybody's drinks. A waiter came—I ordered coffee for Tom, iced tea for Mom, milk for Jake, and cranberry juice for me.

All of a sudden, I saw the beauty queen with her husband and her grown daughter walking toward me. Her eyes met my eyes, but she had no clue who I was, much less I was Alan's daughter even though people say I look like him.

Jeffery Dubois was stout and shorter than his wife and daughter. Amy Dubois looked very pretty just like her mother with her porcelain skin. She could not recognize me either. They passed by me to exit the restaurant.

I was glad Tom and Mom did not see the beauty queen and Jeffery Dubois. My anger gushed out.

For almost twenty years, how could they enjoy living in my birthplace and operating the lucrative Dubois Import Company without any guilt? They might be enjoying a perfect crime now, but it should not be too long to face justice. I would do my best to put them away once I get my law degree. I thought Mom is the only victim in their crimes before, but now I know I am a victim as well. My father was killed by them. If they did not evict Mom, the long separation between the biological mother and the daughter should have never happened. Most importantly, Mom should have been married to Tom earlier and should have had her own children.

Mom said, "Lily, are you okay? Your face is flushed."

I nodded without saying a word, but I was not all right. I still felt anger toward the beauty queen and Jeffery Dubois.

Every day, I rode with Mom in the morning, and in the afternoon, I took a streetcar home. I tried to finish my assignments in the library between classes, but if I did not, I finished them in my room after dinner.

In any rate, I was anxious to be home to watch my money trees grow. While watching CNBC, Jake educated me with the company's P/E ratio, how to lower the average cost of the stock price. By then, my allowance from Yuri kept coming, so I put the half in my stock account and the other half in my savings account.

We traded online. I gave my password to Jake. He gave me his password too. We trusted each other. Later, he put my name as the beneficiary of his portfolio upon his death. I named Jake the same.

While trading stocks, we cooked a large volume of food such as beef stew, chicken stew, gumbo, and lasagna. We froze them for the future dinner.

I could tell Jake got stronger, gained some weight and stamina back. His face was not pale anymore. As Dr. Patterson suggested that Jake should get vitamin D from the sun for his longevity, Jake spent at least one hour to water flowers and stayed outdoors every day. As a result, his yard remained beautiful and his face got some tan, probably vitamin D, from the sun.

Jake and I were doing very well with our stock accounts until September 11, 2001. The two hijacked airplanes crashed into the Twin Towers in New York. Wall Street was shut down for four days including the day of September 11.

I was in class early in the morning on that day. The professor enlarged his laptop on the screen and let us see CNN news. We saw the Twin Towers smoking like two giant chimneys. The suicidal terrorists and the Islamic extremist Osama bin Laden were mentioned. We watched the chaotic scenes in New York for a while. Some students were wiping their eyes as thought they could not believe what they were watching. I could not believe it either.

The professor turned off the screen and told us to see the rest at the student center after class. At the student center, they were reporting the third crash in the Pentagon and the fourth crash in the wooded area in Pennsylvania. The suicidal terrorists used a total of four airplanes to kill three thousand innocent people in American soil. That devastated the American economy as well as the world economy.

It seemed the Bush administration was defenseless because all the suicidal hijackers vanished with the innocent passengers—the enemy country remained unknown, except some speculations.

On the screen, I saw people running with ashes on their faces, and screams and screeching sirens were heard. The debris were pouring and mounting at the foot of the Twin Towers.

Several hours later, the destruction of the Twin Towers to ground zero occurred. The sight of the Twin Towers vanished from the skyline of New York forever on that day.

After the last class, I went home straight. I saw Jake in front of the TV in the living room. I sat quietly beside him, watched the chaotic scenes and the destruction of the Twin Towers.

I felt angry with those despicable suicidal terrorists who took the lives of innocent people in American soil. When I thought about the people who lost their loved ones, I could not help but think about Mom and Yuri who lost their loved ones in an airplane crash, but those despicable crooks got away with murder. I interpreted those perished suicidal terrorists and Osama bin Laden who hid himself deep in the cave also got away with murder. I felt angry again.

Those crooks I know were driven by their greed, but what drove Osama bin Laden to such a hideous act? Was it his religious issue or his ego? Did Osama bin Laden brainwash those young suicidal terrorists under the Islamic belief? Does their God permit such a repulsive act? Do they think the suicidal act is the honorable thing to do in their religion? If it was the religious issue, couldn't they convince the world in the peaceful way? Now the world is angry and hates the Islamic religion. Isn't it counterproductive? Those hijackers must have had some kind of monetary compensation from Osama bin Laden such as their families would be well compensated after their deaths. Otherwise, no one would volunteer to die. In Japan, during WWII, the Japanese nationalistic government brainwashed young Japanese pilots to become the kamikaze pilots. The families of the kamikaze pilots were well compensated by the government after their deaths.

When the stock market opened the following week, we saw the huge drop on our portfolios. Jake and I lost a lot on the paper. He said it happened in 1987, but the market recovered in the '90s, so we should stay calm and buy more shares to make the average cost of the shares lower.

Tom's company felt some impact from the downturn economy after 9/11, but since he dealt with the staple food, it was not as bad as other companies' downturn.

Yuri's company seemed to be doing all right because she dealt with basic clothing such as socks, underpants, pajamas, and other necessary clothing for all ages.

Toby was deployed to an unknown location in the Middle East. Ms. Norma and Chris Gordon were worried about his safety. He could not disclose the location, but he called home from time to time. I wished I could write to him because I was worried about his safety too.

Sharon was still with her boyfriend. After her college graduation, she might move to Washington, DC, to get a job at the FBI forensic lab. Her boyfriend might go to the medical school there.

Chapter 21
Gregory Dubois

Several days before Christmas, when Paula Smith Dubois came to the shopping mall, the mall parking lot was full with Christmas shoppers, so she drove around the mall and finally found a parking space at the back of the mall buildings.

She had to walk around the storage areas and then to the front of the mall. It was a long walk, but she did not mind it at all. It was a sunny day.

After finishing her shopping, she pushed the shopping cart all the way to her car. She put all the shopping bags in the car trunk and left the cart at the curbside. She put a seat belt on and started the engine.

The sound of a big explosion was heard loudly. The front of the car was demolished, and the entire car was on fire. A fire truck came to extinguish the fire. The smell of flesh burning was detected.

The police and the ambulance came. The burned body was placed in a body bag and taken to the hospital morgue, and later the burned car was towed to the police station.

The name of the victim could not be identified, but from the car tag, the police finally identified the owner as Paula Dubois. The police got hold of Gregory Dubois, who lived in the same address and told him about the death of Paula Dubois in a car explosion. Gregory identified the burned body of his beloved mother.

Paula's daughter lived in California, and her second son lived in New York, but the oldest son, Gregory Dubois, who was an accountant, lived in Houston with his mother.

Gregory recalled his mother's desperate plea to find Michelle Dubois several days before the accident. She came to his room with a large brown envelope.

"Gregory, I want you to do something very important for me. Do you remember Michelle Dubois, who used to take care of the small children at the company picnics in New Orleans? You were still in elementary school."

"Yes, I remember Michelle. She was in junior high or high school. She taught us some card games. She explained so well that every child understood how to play. She also read some storybooks and showed us how to Hula-Hoop too. I heard all the Dubois family died in an airplane crash. Did Michelle die too?"

"No. She was not in the crash. I am very sure she is still alive, but I don't know her whereabouts. I have been looking for her for years. I know she does not live in New Orleans. This envelope contains very important information for her family. I would like to give it to her in person myself, but I could not find her. If something happens to me, please find Michelle and give this to her in person."

"Did the Dubois family live on St. Charles Avenue for a long time?"

"Yes. Generation after generation."

"Mom, I have a good idea. Perhaps, the old neighbors who still live on St. Charles Avenue might know Michelle's whereabouts. I am getting a week off for Christmas, so we both can fly there after Christmas and ask around. Somebody should know her or her family."

"Gregory, that is a good idea, but please keep this envelope just in case. I have the identical envelope just in case. I am very sure she has been waiting for these documents. Just remember those are very important to Michelle and her family. Please promise me you will find Michelle and give this to her in person."

"Okay. I promise. By the way, does Dad still live in New Orleans?"

"I don't know. I have not heard from your Dad since we came to Houston."

Paula knew exactly where her ex-husband lived. After moving the Dubois Import Company to Gulfport, she knew he and his new family lived in Biloxi by making tons of money, but she pretended she had not heard from their father for ages.

Gregory knew his mother was very upset at the time of their divorce because his father impregnated a young girl and married her.

"I wonder if he is still married to the same girl."

"I am sure he is. They had a daughter after their marriage."

"Do you know her name?"

"No."

Paula did not care to know their child's name or anything else about them. To Gregory, the girl was his stepsister, so he was curious. He was sure his brother and sister wanted to know their stepsister too.

Gregory's younger brother went to school in New York. After his college degree in finance, he was hired as a stock trader in the New York Stock Exchange. He made a lot of money. He met a girl and fell in love, so they both decided to live together, but Paula wanted them to be married so she could see some grandchildren. Gregory was the oldest, but he was still unmarried. He dated many girls, but no marriage yet.

His sister graduated from college in Los Angeles and was hired as a screenwriter in a movie production company. She met a young producer whose parents were famous movie stars.

He was wealthy himself and had a nice home. After they fell in love, he asked her to move in with him. Again, Paula wanted her daughter to be married instead of living together, but they did not want that.

Paula had been spending her extortion money for her children's education and the mortgage. Of course, she saved a substantial amount of money for her old age in her savings account. The money in the savings account was to be divided three ways after her death. The money in her checking account would be left for her brother, Edward.

Since her daughter was doing well in Los Angeles with her rich boyfriend and her son in New York was making tons of money from the stock market, she told them her house would be left for Gregory. They did not mind it at all.

Delayed Justice

Many years ago, when Paula bought a nice house in an affluent neighborhood, the children thought their wealthy grandparents had left her some money to buy a house and Paula's brother, Edward, thought his sister had invested wisely over the years to buy a house.

From time to time, her children wanted to see their father, Jeffery, but she did not allow them because she did not want her children to know how criminal-minded their father and their stepmother were. Moreover, she did not want her children to be associated with those murderers.

The reason Paula decided to leave New Orleans at the time of her divorce was that she wanted to seal her children from their father's despicable crimes. She was quite certain Jeffery tampered with the aircraft because he was a mechanical genius. He could fix cars, lawnmowers, and even airplanes. As his foster father was an airplane mechanic, he learned to repair airplanes from him.

Many years passed after Jeffery's first attempt on Paula's life. This time he hired a professional killer from an underground contact. It cost him a bundle, but the killer assured him the death of Paula.

The killer followed Paula for a week. He was determined to kill her in a car explosion. A small device of bomb was untraceable so it would look like a gas leak explosion.

When she parked her car at the back of the mall buildings, the killer knew it was the time of his work. Without being seen, he quickly installed a small bomb under the hood. If she parked in the crowded parking lot, among other cars, he could not do his job, but today, she parked her car where he wanted.

After the police's report, Gregory called his brother and sister in tears. They all came. Their uncle organized the funeral. After the funeral, he read his sister's will. The house was left to Gregory, and her savings should be divided in three ways. The share of each child was substantial. Her brother, Edward, got the money from her checking account that was also substantial. They wondered how Paula saved so much money, but they concluded she was frugal and invested her money wisely over the years.

The day before Christmas, the bank wrote a check for each child. Gregory's siblings were going home on Christmas Day. Gregory was to fly to New Orleans on the same day. He made sure to put the brown envelope in his suitcase to fulfill his promise to his mother.

At the airport, they embraced each other. Gregory told them whenever they wanted to come home, they should have the place to stay or live. They nodded.

When Gregory arrived at the New Orleans Airport, he rented a car and drove to the city of New Orleans. He was determined to find Michelle Dubois and give her the brown envelope in person. He just hoped he could find her in a week.

On Christmas night, Gregory was watching the skyline of New Orleans from his hotel room. He ordered Christmas dinner with a glass of wine. He was reminiscing about his mother and his childhood in New Orleans.

* * *

On Christmas Day, after we four exchanged our Christmas gifts in New Orleans, we went to our favorite casino restaurant in Biloxi to have Christmas dinner, and then spent the night in Tom's vacation house before we came home the next day.

I still had one more week off before resuming my last semester of my undergraduate studies. I would be taking the LSAT soon. I had studied for the test for several years.

I was determined to go to law school in New Orleans because I wanted Jake to continue helping me grow money trees, and at the same time, I wanted to help Jake live longer. Mom said I should not have any problem getting into law school in my school because my grade average was very high.

When I was in my room, I heard Jake call my name from the kitchen. In the kitchen, Jake was talking to a man who resembled somebody I saw or I knew, but I could not recall whom. He was sipping lemonade at the table with Jake.

When I walked into the kitchen, the man stood up and introduced himself as Gregory Dubois. I knew immediately whom he looked like—Jeffery Dubois whom I saw at the casino restaurant.

Delayed Justice

However, Gregory was much taller than Jeffery Dubois and attractive. I introduced myself as Lily Dubois. He shook my hand politely and asked me if I were Michelle's daughter. I nodded.

Jake explained how they met. When Jake was watering flowers in the front yard, Gregory drove into the driveway and came out of his car, and asked him if he knew Michelle Dubois or her family who once lived on St. Charles Avenue. When Jake said yes, Gregory screamed aloud as though he hit a jackpot in the casino. He had been asking around about the Dubois family in the neighborhood for three days.

When Gregory agreed to wait for Michelle in the house, Jake called me to meet Gregory. I sat at the table with lemonade. Jake had already explained to Gregory that the Dubois family and his family were very close and the children grew up together like siblings.

Jake probably explained to Gregory why Michelle could not get touch with any of her friends because she left her address book in Biloxi when she was evicted.

Jake said, "When we found Michelle and Lily in North Georgia, Lily was only nine years old. After Lily's high school graduation, she was accepted here in the university. Tom volunteered to pay for her tuition, and I offered the place to live, but Lily realized her mother, Michelle, would be left alone in North Georgia, so she begged my son to marry Michelle. My son was too slow when it came to marrying Michelle. He told me he wanted to marry Michelle since he was a child, but he was too slow to propose her." Jake laughed aloud.

"Anyway, Tom married Michelle four years ago, and now we live together happily ever after. Michelle has a great job in the same university where Lily is attending. She oversees the entire library system in that university. I am very proud of her. I am sure her deceased parents would be too."

Gregory said, "My mother, Paula Dubois, was looking for Michelle for many years and wanted to give the envelope to her in person, but she died in a car explosion a week ago. The police said no foul play involved—a gas leak caused it."

He brought a brown envelope from his car that had "Michelle Dubois" on it in bold ink. He wanted to wait for Michelle and give it to her in person, so he put it on the sofa in the living room.

Jake and I knew who Paula Dubois was because we had many discussions with Mom and Tom years back on how to indict Jeffery Dubois and Nancy Saunders, but we could not go forward without a witness or evidence. The only witness we thought we had was Paula Dubois, but as we learned she was extorting the large amount of money from Jeffery Dubois, we scratched her name from the witness list.

Nevertheless, Tom said if we had the evidence to prove Jeffery's forgery, we did not need a witness. Mom could go to the police or the district attorney's office with the evidence so the DA could indict Jeffery Dubois and the beauty queen. I was very sure that Gregory Dubois brought something Mom and Tom could use.

I called Mom at work to see if she could come home early because someone wanted to see her. In the meantime, Jake and I decided to invite Gregory to eat dinner with us. When Jake and I started cooking the pork chop dinner, Gregory looked surprised and watched us cook from the kitchen table.

Gregory Dubois was tall and had a likable face. In general, he was very attractive—clean haircut with plenty of hair, unlike his father. He looked sophisticated with a nice shirt and a jacket.

After college, Gregory had been working for a big oil company as an accountant. He had lived in his mother's house for all his life. He intended to move out after college, but his mother begged him to stay because the house was too big for her alone. Now he got the big house to himself.

I asked him, "How is your father doing?"

"I don't know. We had not seen him since we moved to Houston. I don't think he knows Mom's passing. I don't know how to contact him. I guess he is doing all right with his family. He has a daughter, but we have never met."

I almost said I met his stepsister, Amy Dubois, many years ago, but I did not say anything. Even though we frequented Tom's mansion in Biloxi after we moved to New Orleans, I never attempted to walk the neighborhood because I knew they still lived in my father's, Alan's, house, or my birthplace. However, I was very sure Amy Dubois was not living in Biloxi anymore. She should be in college somewhere faraway.

"How do you know about my father?"

He did not seem to know anything about his father who probably murdered the Dubois family. Paula Dubois did such a great job sealing her children from the crime their father committed.

"My mother told me. Your father worked for my grandparents for years."

After we put stuffed pork chops in the oven, we sat with Gregory again. He was still sipping the same lemonade. He talked about his childhood in New Orleans and his teenage years in Houston.

Mom came home in a hurry and went upstairs without stopping by the kitchen; probably she went to wash her hands. She finally came downstairs to the kitchen in her casual clothes.

Gregory Dubois stood up and introduced himself. "Hi. I am Gregory Dubois. I don't think you remember me, but I remember you. You always entertained us small children at the company picnic. You read many storybooks, played cards, and taught us how to Hula-Hoop."

"Yes. I remember you and your family too." She looked genuinely surprised to see the son of Jeffery Dubois. Jake explained how Gregory was checking each house on St. Charles Avenue to find her.

Gregory went to the living room to retrieve the envelope and gave it to Mom. She thanked him and held it tightly on her chest.

"My mother tried to locate you for years, but you no longer lived in New Orleans. She really wanted to see you and show you the documents in this envelope in person, but she passed away last week. Several days before she died, she gave me the envelope and made me promise to find you and give it to you in person. She said she enclosed her handwritten letter to explain how important those documents are for your family."

"I am sorry about your mother's passing. Was she ill?"

"No. She died in a car explosion. The police said a gas leak caused it."

"I am very sorry."

Tom came home but went upstairs just as Mom did and came back in jeans. He was surprised to see a visitor at the kitchen table. This time I introduced Gregory Dubois as Paula Dubois's son, told him how he found Mom, and brought the envelope his mother wanted Mom to have. I also added Paula died in a car explosion a week ago.

Tom shook Gregory's hand by giving him his condolences. Mom was pointing to the envelope on the stool. Tom glanced at the envelope before he sat down for dinner.

We made stuffed pork chops. Gregory devoured dinner by praising how great cooks Jake and I were. For dessert, we ate apple pie that Jake freshly baked this afternoon.

Before Gregory left, he gave us his home address and home phone number. He added his cell phone number and work phone number too. Mom gave him our address and home phone number.

Gregory said to Mom, "My mother should be very elated in heaven by now. I am glad I finally found you and fulfilled my promise to my mother. If you need me for anything, please do not hesitate to call me. I hope your family can use whatever you find in this envelope. Thank you for the delicious dinner."

Chapter 22
Paula's Letter

When Jeffery Dubois got the confirmation on Paula's death, he felt relieved. It was Saturday. He spent all day in the French Quarter celebrating his freedom with his favorite prostitute.

Years back, when the first attempt failed, he remembered he almost got in trouble with the law because Paula was alive to tell the police the assailant was probably hired by her ex-husband.

The police from Houston kept calling him on the phone to see if he had ever hired someone to attempt on his ex-wife's life. As he denied profusely, the police eventually dropped the investigation and stopped calling him. After that, Jeffery stayed low for years and kept paying the inflated alimony Paula demanded.

This time, the job was done professionally without any trace. Jeffery thought paying an enormous amount of money to the professional killer was the best investment he had ever made.

Now he had no more alimony payments to make, no more threats to hear, no more worry of having a witness to testify against him, and probably no more nightmares.

Nevertheless, he knew those documents were still in Paula's house. He did not want anyone to find them and give them to the police or Michelle Dubois. For years, he had the same nightmares of Michelle, who angrily appeared in his dream and gestured to a police officer to arrest him.

He had already told his accountant not to send any more money orders to his ex-wife. The accountant could not ask any questions, but he knew something had happened to his ex-wife; she died or she got married.

Jeffery again hired someone professional to break into Paula's house to retrieve the documents Paula said she had. Her belongings might be removed soon, so he had to retrieve them fast before somebody would find them.

He destroyed the original will and bogus will of Jefferson and Marie Dubois many years ago, but he still remembered how they looked. He told the burglars that the owner of the house was his ex-wife who passed away a week ago, so no one should live in the house. He instructed them to look for two wills of Jefferson and Marie Dubois. He emphasized the names of the policyholders.

Indeed, the break-in was easy—no security system. No one was home. They combed the house thoroughly, but they only found some unused checkbooks, car insurance, mortgage summary, mortgage insurance, credit card statements, monthly bank statements, savings account statements, and some printed letters in the study that was next to the enormous master bedroom. There were no file cabinets, no safety box in the study. They lifted the bed and searched between the mattresses, but again no such documents.

Her closet had nothing but clothes, shoes, some empty shoeboxes. They searched behind the pictures for a hidden safe or something, but no such thing.

In another room, they found a laptop with many spreadsheets, corporate letters, and bank statements, but no such documents they were looking for. In the closet, they saw some man's clothes, suits, shoes, and nicely ironed dress shirts. They realized that the deceased did not live alone in the house—probably a boyfriend was still living in the house. They started combing the house in a hurry because they were afraid the man might walk in on them in the middle of their burglary.

Finally, the two burglars came down to the basement. They saw a sewing room and a large playroom with a ping-pong table. In the sewing room, they saw some remnants of cloth, needles, scissors on a cutting table, and several half-made dresses on a portable clothes rack. On the floor, there were three sewing baskets next to a sewing machine.

They flipped the top of each basket, but they only saw various sizes of needles and many colored threads—still no documents. The closet was empty. The playroom was clean. When they heard some noise outside, they jumped and ran to their getaway car empty-handed.

The burglars told Jeffery on the phone that the documents might be secured in a safety deposit box in the bank, but Jeffery knew Paula did not believe in having such a safety deposit box—it was inconvenient for Paula to make a trip to the bank; besides, she did not own any expensive jewelry.

In the end, Jeffery concluded that Paula had been bluffing all these years by using her imagination or suspicion—it was just her way of extorting an enormous amount of money from him because she was jealous.

He felt as though he had been cheated or being stupid paying the five-figure amount endlessly without seeing the actual documents. At that time, when Paula told him about the evidence she said she had and her accurate speculation of his crime, he really believed his ex-wife was holding the winning card that could incriminate him and put him away.

If she were alive, he could demand to see the documents by threatening to cut off the alimony payments, but it was too late. He just needed to move on fast to his next project before the police would start sniffing around him.

His getaway fund was tremendous. Six months before Paula's death, he went to the island, bought a nice property near the ocean that was surrounded by the thickets of tropical trees. Nobody could look into the property.

A big two-story house was built. The large terrace in front of the bedroom on the second floor was facing the beautiful ocean with white sand beach and blue sky. The view from the terrace was exquisitely beautiful. However, the unpaved road to the house is muddy and narrow as though no one lived inside the thickets.

The Dubois Company was sold. The money was transferred to the bank on the island. Jeffery gave his faithful accountant an enormous amount of money and told him to disappear to a faraway place just as he was doing.

Nevertheless, the accountant, Joseph Miller, knew where Jeffery was disappearing to—to the island where his money was stashed away.

Jeffery only took his briefcase with the important bank statements and his laptop. He left his entire personal belongings home in Biloxi. He did not care what his wife would do with his expensive clothes and shoes. His female companion on the island already purchased new clothes and shoes for Jeffery. He obtained an alias passport from the underground contact. He was no longer Jeffery Dubois.

A young, tanned, and beautiful girl with black hair was waiting for him at the airport. They kissed passionately before they got in a red sports car and drove off. Some people might have thought they just got married and honeymooning on the beautiful island.

While Jeffery was planning his escape, the beauty queen was in the hospital in New Orleans. She had some unknown bleedings in her stomach. After the surgery, she was recuperating in the mansion on St. Charles Avenue under her aunt's tireless care.

When she came home to Biloxi, a brown envelope with Jeffery's letter was on the table. The two property deeds were enclosed in the envelope. In his letter, he granted two mansions to the beauty queen. The deeds were signed over to her.

However, he suggested that she should sell those mansions and disappear from the past just as he was doing. She knew what he meant. He also told her he would be living on an island under an alias so nobody could find him.

The beauty queen felt defeated—she was the one who was supposed to have the loot and live on a paradise island with her aunt happily ever after, but now Jeffery is doing it.

Nevertheless, she was thankful to Jeffery's generosity. Under the prenuptial agreement, she knew that she could not get anything from her marriage. She felt very happy for some reason; especially she was happy for her aunt because she could keep living in the mansion on St. Charles Avenue. Living on St. Charles Avenue was her aunt's dream or her lifelong wish.

After she received the ownership papers of the mansions, she thought to herself, *Now she can live like a wealthy woman who owns the beautiful mansions. One is in the affluent neighborhood called St. Charles Avenue in New Orleans and another one is a large antebellum mansion in Biloxi. Moreover, she now has a lot of money saved up from her salary over the years, so she is indeed wealthy.*

For some reason, she also felt free of her marriage, although she was still Jeffery's wife. During her marriage, she had no desire of making love to that short, stout, and unattractive bald man who took her loot and held the prenuptial agreement.

She was not interested in her daughter's well-being either because her daughter was always a daddy's girl since she was born. She did not even care to see both of them for the rest of her life because she did not love them.

Before Jeffery's disappearance, he transferred a substantial amount of money to his daughter's savings account so she could go to graduate school after her undergraduate degree. He also added enough money for her future house and wrote a goodbye letter. After the daughter read her father's letter, she cried in bed for several days. Her father did not explain why he was going away, but she knew he would never come back to see her.

She remembered when she came to Chicago for college. Her father came with her and rented an apartment, opened a checking and savings accounts by putting enough money for four years, and said, "Study hard and be somebody important."

Amy also had the porcelain beauty of her mother, but she always had smiles and warmth on her face. She was a genuinely likable person unlike her mother. When she was growing up, her mother refused to invite her friends; therefore, she did not have any friends while she lived at home.

Now in Chicago, she made many friends in school and invited them to her apartment. They studied together, walked, or bicycled together along the lakeshore.

While she was growing up, she noticed her parents did not talk to each other much; her father would spend a night somewhere once a week. She had never seen them kissing, being affectionate, or giving kind words to each other. Most strangely, they slept in separate rooms, yet they lived under the same roof for years. She did not understand that.

* * *

When Gregory came home from New Orleans, he called the police to report a burglary. The house was chaotically ransacked. Since nothing seemed to be missing or stolen, the police made a report as a malicious vandalism.

Gregory surveyed the house; the desk drawers were emptied in his mother's study; her bank checks, some cash, or credit cards were scattered on the floor. In her bedroom, the dresser drawers were left open, the top mattress was lifted, and all the doors including the closet doors were left open. Some pictures were taken down as though they were looking for something on the wall like a hidden safe.

Gregory's bedroom was ransacked as well. The desk drawers were emptied, and the contents were all scattered on the floor. The piggybank with tons of quarters was still there, the laptop, other electronic gadgets such as a portable CD player, an iPod, a digital camera were also on the floor among those spreadsheets he prepared for his work. Nothing was taken. They seemed to be looking for something specific—probably some documents.

Gregory was contemplating. *Were they looking for the envelope he just gave to Michelle? Mom said she was keeping another envelope just in case—did they find that envelope? What was in the envelope?*

After surveying the living room and kitchen, Gregory went to his mother's favorite room in the basement—the sewing room. The basement was not disturbed much. He noticed the tall sewing basket was tilted toward the doorway, so he tried to move it to the corner. It was heavy and the top part of the basket came off.

Delayed Justice

He looked into the bottom basket. It was covered with some remnants. Gregory sat on the carpeted floor to examine the basket. He saw some gold necklaces and bracelets, children's old report cards, birth certificates, and some pictures Gregory and his siblings drew when they were young. Finally, at the bottom of the basket, he saw the identical bulky brown envelope he gave to Michelle.

He took it out of the sewing basket and used a pair of scissors to open the envelope. A five-page letter came out of the envelope. It was addressed to Michelle Dubois. Two wills were also found in the envelope.

By stretching out his long legs on the carpeted floor and sitting against the wall, he began reading his mother's letter. It took a while, but after he finished reading the letter, the tears welled up in his eyes. Now everything became clear including his mother's death and this burglary.

He remembered his mother mentioned years back that someone tried to kill her in the yard. He thought no one would kill his mother on purpose because she was the nicest mother on earth. Even then, she never said his father hired a killer to kill her.

Her five-page letter stated her speculation, interpretation, and explanation of the grand larceny, poisoning, and tampering to cause the airplane crash twenty something years ago. Most importantly, she honestly explained why she had to extort from Jeffery Dubois, and she predicted she might be killed because of her extortion.

Gregory, as a child, wanted to remain living in New Orleans, even though his parents were divorced, but now he understood why his mother uprooted her children from New Orleans and came to live in Houston—she wanted to seal her children from their father's heartless, hideous, and greedy crimes.

He also did not understand why his mother was prohibiting the children to see their father who was the best kind of father. Now he understood why. She did not want her children to know what their father had done to the Dubois family as well as the fact of her ongoing extortion against their father.

Gregory now understood why they were able to live in the affluent neighborhood, went to the nicest private school, and to the expensive colleges. Paula explained in her letter—as she was raised in the affluent surroundings while she was growing up, she could not stand her children growing up in an apartment in the undesirable neighborhood.

She worked as a nurse in a small clinic and made much less salary than she made in the hospital in New Orleans. Therefore, she had a hard time making ends meet every month.

She had no choice but to use the assets she brought from New Orleans to pay for the three-bedroom apartment, three growing children's clothes, school supplies, and enormous food bills. The funds were getting smaller and smaller every month; she had no hope of buying a house and no hope for the children's college education in the future. She was depressed and became desperate.

When she called Jeffery for some help, he flatly refused. Paula became angry because she knew he got the Dubois fortune and was making tons of money from the Dubois Import Company in Gulfport. Therefore, she decided to use the documents in her possession to extort from her ex-husband. Her extortion worked well. Jeffery was scared and paid every month.

Paula's theory—if Jeffery was not guilty of poisoning or tampering to murder the Dubois family, he could've refused to pay Paula and he could've reported her to the authority instead, but he kept paying. That proves Jeffery was guilty of the grand larceny and the murder.

Nevertheless, when Jeffery could not tolerate the enormous alimony payment any longer, he tried to end Paula's life by hiring a killer, but the first attempt failed. Therefore, Paula predicted Jeffery might hire a killer again to end her life in the future.

Gregory gave his mother's letter to his uncle, Edward Smith, who was a lawyer in the DA's office. After reading his sister's letter, he, too, had tears in his eyes. He concluded his sister did not die in an accident—her ex-husband murdered her.

Edward told his nephew that his investigation would start immediately. If the crime lab could detect a bomb in the car, he would look for the hired killer and make him squeal on Jeffery Dubois. He felt sad for his beloved nephew because his father was the one who likely killed his mother and probably murdered three members of the Dubois family.

Paula's children were like his own because Edward had no children with his wife. He and his wife were fond of all her children because they were smart, well-behaved, and thoughtful. They always celebrated the holidays together as a family.

When Gregory became an accountant after college, he encouraged Uncle Edward to play golf with him so they could spend quality time together. When they were together, people thought they were father and son because they both were tall and their physical structure with plenty of hair on their heads was similar.

Edward told Gregory not to tell anybody including his brother and sister about Paula's letter for a while. Gregory nodded and put Paula's letter back in the envelope.

Chapter 23
Most Wanted Fugitive

Tom asked Mom to open the envelope that was addressed to her. She used a pair of scissors to open it. I was sitting beside Mom on the sofa to watch her open the envelope just like a little kid who was curious to see a Christmas present in a box. Jake and Tom were sitting together and waiting anxiously.

She took out a five-page letter and two sets of documents altogether. One of the stapled documents looked old and discolored. She gave those two documents to Tom and Jake.

Mom and I started reading Paula's letter quietly. Her writing was plain that average readers could understand what she wanted to say. She used simple vocabulary to speculate, interpret, and explain her thoughts logically.

Her inductive and deductive methods were used to conclude her hypothesis, such as Nancy Saunders, who served coffee to Jefferson and Marie every morning, probably poisoned them, and Jeffery Dubois, who was a mechanical genius, probably tampered with the aircraft to cause the airplane crash.

Tom and Jake were examining the signatures in the original will and in the bogus will. They did not say anything to each other, but they seemed to be witnessing the forgery.

When we finished reading the letter, Tom and Jake gave us the documents, and we gave them the letter. We were quiet for a long time. Perhaps, we were just shocked to learn things we did not know such as Paula predicted her own death because of her extortion.

Our speculation was very similar to Paula's speculation. If she were alive, we could have talked more to affirm each other's theories and speculations. Furthermore, she would be willing to testify against her ex-husband in the trial.

From her letter, she genuinely wanted to find Michelle Dubois for a long time. She knew Michelle was the one who needed the documents so that she could go forward to prosecute the criminals. She did not seem to care that her lucrative alimony income could end if Jeffery Dubois was exposed.

She was not afraid of her extortion because she did not leave any evidence behind her. It was carefully dealt under the table each time. No laws could have touched her. She knew writing the five-page letter could help Michelle in case of her death. She was actually testifying on behalf of Michelle through her letter. Now the perfect crime the crooks thought they committed was no longer perfect.

Many years ago, Mom wanted a lawyer who could pursue a legal action against the crooks, but she did not have enough money to hire a lawyer or an investigator. Besides, it was too late to dispute with the probate court. The crooks got them all. Additionally, she had no evidence to incriminate those crooks. Now Michelle Dubois got the evidence she needed.

Mom and Tom submitted Paula's letter and two documents to the DA's office to see if they could indict Jeffery Dubois and Nancy Saunders Dubois for the three counts of murder.

One of the state prosecutors said that they wanted to examine the authenticity of the evidence and conduct their own investigation first. After they Xerox-copied the evidence including Paula's five-page letter, they returned the envelope to Mom. They told Mom and Tom that the investigation might take a while because the crime took place so long ago. Mom and Tom understood.

While waiting for the lengthy government investigation, Tom found out that Jeffery Dubois was long gone and the beauty queen was enjoying the world cruise with her aunt. I was studying the bar exam and memorizing the Constitution and its amendments. Additionally, I was participating in a mock trial every week after school.

However, my letter writing to Yuri continued. I wrote her each time when I received my allowance. She knew what was going on with us in New Orleans because she and Mom had been talking to each other on the phone.

She did not write me much, but whenever she wrote me, she asked me to help Mom with the case. She also mentioned that she had to get a fifth shoebox to store my letters.

Because of my allowance from Yuri, I was able to save a lot of money in the stock market account and savings account. I considered myself rich, but Mom did not know how much money I saved and how much profit I made in my stock market account—I made a lot because of Jake.

When I bought a new car, Mom thought I spent all my allowance Yuri sent me over the years. Owning a car shortened my time of commuting, but as I was too busy preparing for a mock trial at school, cooking went to Jake without my help. Jake missed me a lot in the kitchen, but he understood how my law school schedule was, so he always left my dinner in the refrigerator.

Jake also kept an eye on my stock portfolio. If necessary, he had my permission to sell or buy stocks. Most of the time, we bought the stocks that paid dividends so we could buy more shares under the reinvestment plan.

Tom bought a cell phone for each of us under the family plan with unlimited long distance calls. Everybody felt safe having a cell phone in case we might get stranded on the road with a car problem. However, I used my cell phone to call Sharon and Toby most of the time.

After Sharon graduated from college, she landed a job at the FBI Forensic Lab Department in Washington, DC, and continued her graduate degree in science at night.

Her boyfriend was accepted to the medical school there too, so they decided to live together. I was told they would be married after his medical school. Until then, Sharon would be the breadwinner.

Since Sharon and Toby could not afford to have the cell phones, I did not mind using my cell phone to call them, but most of the time, they were not home. Mom used her cell phone to call Ms.

Norma often and let me know all about the Gordon family. Chris Gordon retired from the trucking company and was enjoying his retirement with Ms. Norma. They traveled a lot in a car, but when he was home, he taught at a local driving school.

One day I called Toby on the weekend. He was home. "Hello, Toby. This is Lily."

"Wow! Hi, Lily! I was just thinking about you! Do you know we have not seen each other since you left North Georgia six years ago? I really miss seeing you. How is your law school?"

"I graduated in May and passed the bar exam too. I applied for a job in the DA's office in New Orleans a month ago, but I have not heard from them. I hope I get the job."

"I just finished my undergraduate degree and passed LSAT. Now I have to find a law school."

"Congratulations! I am very proud of you, Toby."

After Toby was honorably discharged from the military, he went to a local college in North Georgia. He finished his undergraduate degree in three years.

I remembered he was a mangy-looking youngster with a running nose when he was young, but when he played guitar at the wedding party for Mom and Tom, I recalled my heart fluttered because he turned out to be such a good-looking and sexy young man.

"Lily, I sent an application to a law school in Washington, DC, but I have not heard from them. Sharon wants me to live with her and her boyfriend if I get accepted there. I want to study criminal law and work for the DA's office as a prosecutor like you."

"That is great. You would be a great prosecutor."

I did not tell Toby about my ulterior motive to work in the DA office. He did not know anything about my family situation including my birth secret. It would take a long time to explain. However, I was determined to tell Sharon and Toby everything next time we see each other.

"By the way, Lily, do you have a boyfriend?"

"No. I have been busy studying. Do you have a girlfriend?"

"No. I have been busy studying too."

I thought to myself, *Toby is one year younger than I am, but I do not mind having Toby as my boyfriend because he is handsome, thoughtful, and most importantly he is very smart. We got along well while we were growing up. Besides, Sharon and I taught him all about us girls, so he should know me well as a girl.*

"I am going to see Sharon soon and check out the law school there. I hope I can afford it. My GI Bill might pay for the tuition, but I am not sure."

"I hope everything would work out for you."

I received the notification of the employment from the Orleans Parish DA's office. I was to start working on the first week of September. Therefore, I have the whole summer to myself. My entire family including Yuri was very proud of me.

One Saturday morning, at the breakfast table, Tom showed us a big headlined article in the newspaper.

"The Grand Larceny and Murder
Nobody Knew for 25 Years"

Twenty-five years ago, Jefferson Dubois, Marie Dubois, and their son, Alan Dubois, were killed in an airplane crash. They owned the lucrative family business called the Dubois Import Company in New Orleans at that time.

After the deaths of the Dubois family, Jeffery Dubois, who was the company lawyer of the Dubois Import Company at that time came forward to claim the Dubois fortune. He submitted the irrevocable will that named him as one of the co-beneficiaries. However, since another beneficiary, Alan Dubois, was killed in the same airplane crash, Jeffery Dubois was to be the sole beneficiary.

As nobody came forward to dispute the will, the probate court awarded the Dubois fortune to Jeffery Dubois, which included the Dubois Import Company, a mansion in New Orleans, and a mansion in Biloxi. After Jeffery Dubois named himself the company president, he moved the Dubois Import Company to Gulfport and married the executing attorney of the will, Nancy Saunders. It was twenty-five years ago.

However, the Orleans DA's office received evidence that could incriminate Jeffery Dubois and his wife Nancy Dubois of conspiring to murder the three members of the Dubois family. Jeffery Dubois's ex-wife, Paula Smith Dubois, had kept the two wills of the policyholders, Jefferson and Marie Dubois, for twenty-something years until her death. Her genuine intention was to give those wills to Michelle Dubois, who is the only surviving child of Jefferson and Marie Dubois, but Michelle's whereabouts was unknown to Paula while she was alive.

However, after her death, her son Gregory Dubois finally located Michelle Dubois and gave her the wills with Paula's five-page letter. Michelle Dubois submitted those wills and Paula's letter to the DA's office several years back. It took a long time for the DA to conduct their own investigations since the crime took place so long ago. The investigation went all the way back to the thirty-year property registry of Jefferson and Marie Dubois.

The DA found out the irrevocable will was forged. The content of the will was also a fraud because Jeffery Dubois is not related to the Dubois family even though he bears the same last name. Paula's letter implicates the crime of Jeffery Dubois and his wife Nancy Saunders on poisoning Jefferson and Marie Dubois and tampering with the aircraft to cause an airplane crash to kill three members of the Dubois family.

Jeffery Dubois's wife Nancy Saunders was arrested at home, but her lawyer bailed her out. Now the FBI is looking for Jeffery Dubois's whereabouts. He seemed to skip the country under an alias several years back. Now he is posted as one of the most wanted fugitives. The trial of the two accused will begin as soon as Jeffery Dubois gets in police custody.

After we all read, everybody looked relieved. I was glad for Mom because her frustration would be eased soon, but Tom said the fugitive case would take for a long time.

"Tom, does Jeffery Dubois still own those mansions?"

"According to the bondsman, Nancy Dubois owns both of the mansions now."

"Amy Dubois said she was supposed to own the mansion on St. Charles Avenue."

"Well, Jeffery Dubois might have changed his mind or Nancy Dubois got greedy. Her daughter lives in Chicago. I talked to her on the phone to see if she knew her father's whereabouts. She said no and sobbed uncontrollably by saying she did not know anything about her father's crime. In the end, she asked me if her mother was involved. I said yes. She sobbed again."

"Tom, do you think Mom can get those two mansions and some of the Dubois fortune back?"

"I don't know. There could be many legal hurdles since the company was sold and the grand larceny happened so long ago, but if Jeffery Dubois and Nancy Dubois get convicted for the three counts of murder, yes, the court will award Mom with everything they own, and we have to prove Michelle Dubois is the only surviving child of Jefferson and Marie by her birth certificate. In the meantime, we could help the FBI look for Jeffery Dubois and keep an eye on

Delayed Justice

Nancy Dubois. Even though she is released on bond, it is possible she might escape."

"What is going to happen to Amy Dubois? She seems to be a very nice girl. I am very sure she did not know anything about her parents' crimes."

Mom spoke, "I am sure she should be all right. The judge and jurors should recognize her innocence once the trial starts. By the way, Tom, I saw a for-sale sign on the mansion today. The house looked vacant, no flowers, grass was high, no sight of her aunt. I copied the realtor's telephone number. Do you think her aunt moved to Biloxi? We should check what they are doing there."

* * *

On Friday, after Tom and Mom came home, four of us were heading toward Biloxi. We drove the backstreet inconspicuously to see the beauty queen's mansion. The summer sun was still strong. We also saw a for sale sign in their yard. Tom stopped the car and let Mom copy the realtor's name and phone number. I saw an old woman peeking through the window on the second floor. Mom and Jake saw her too. She looked like the beauty queen's aunt.

As usual, we ate at the casino restaurant. The next day, Mom and Tom got on the cell phone to call the realtors, but they would not give out the sale price by saying the owner would negotiate privately.

Tom said, "I will report the for-sale signs to the bondsman Monday. They might be planning some kind of escape."

In the afternoon, Tom drove us along the scenic drive to the city of Biloxi and explained that Biloxi draws many East Coast and Southern gamblers just as Las Vegas draws many West Coast gamblers. Many people may not know it, but Biloxi has a more charming atmosphere than Las Vegas has—the calm ocean and the ten-mile beach. There are many hotels and motels along the scenic drive for the family vacationers and beachgoers. He also said that Biloxi is becoming the largest casino city in Mississippi or in the south. Las Vegas is intimidated because they are losing their East Coast or Southern gamblers to Biloxi.

We passed President Casino far out to the water, a boat shaped Treasure Bay Casino, a tall classy building, Beau Rivage Casino, the humongous Grand Casino, Magic Casino, and Isle of Capri Casino. We also saw Imperial Palace Casino with Chinese temple roofs, and several small local casinos along the lagoon. I assumed each casino must be packed with gamblers because of the weekend.

We ate lunch at the casino buffet and headed toward home. It takes about an hour to New Orleans. Jake looks sleepy, so I give him a pillow that I always carry for Jake when we drive to Biloxi.

Chapter 24
Katrina

While waiting for my job, Mom helped me buy many office clothes, or rather business clothes. I had to practice wearing high-heeled shoes in front of her. She watched me stand up tall with a pair of black high-heeled shoes. As the shoes were well-cushioned, I was able to walk comfortably.

My car was checked out and I was ready to start my new job. I was also confident being a lawyer because I practiced my speech and delivery in the mock trials a lot. My law professors and classmates often praised my delivery.

However, the reality made me nervous—I was not used to wearing a suit and a pair of high-heeled shoes, but Mom sternly emphasized that the attire, posture, and speech pattern with good enunciation could gain the client's trust and respect.

I understand if a grown-up child starts earning income, the child usually moves out of the parents' house and lives independently. I, however, do not want to move away from my beloved family. I do not want to live independently. It would be too lonely.

Besides, I could not leave Jake now. He is getting too old and he needs me. When I helped Jake in the kitchen all this summer, I noticed he was slowing down, so I must help him more.

One day, I asked my family if it was all right for me to keep living with them just as before. They all gladly said yes. I told them I would keep helping Jake in the kitchen and buy some groceries from my income. Mom was looking at me proudly with her moist eyes.

She probably thought her precious young daughter finally became a responsible adult.

Jake looked happy because he knew I would keep helping him in the kitchen and watching the money trees grow together. Besides, I would help him live longer by keeping an eye on his health—reminding him to eat well, drink more water, take vitamins, and exercise. In return, he knew he could give me his advice or his wisdom anytime I needed.

One day, I told him about my nervousness or anxiety to face the first day on my job. He said, "Lily, once you meet your boss or other colleagues, you should feel better. It is going to be just like the first day in college, but this time, you will be learning many new things from your daily experiences, not from the textbooks. You might make some mistakes along the way, but you must learn from the mistakes. Then before you know it, you would be a great lawyer. Just remember, you must put away those greedy crooks or murderers where they belong so the world would be safe." I nodded several times.

Jake has been my mentor since I came to New Orleans. Mom had been my mentor when I was young in North Georgia, but now she has been busy, but Jake has plenty of time to nurture me or educate me at home.

Jake and I discuss politics a lot. I found out that Tom and Jake believe in government just as Mom and I do as Democrats. That is probably why we have been getting along so well. We are all very compassionate and understanding.

Jake would criticize the Republicans passionately by saying most of the Republicans are racists, bigots, militants, anti-government, self-righteous, pro-life, anti-women, anti-gays, anti-liberal, greedy, self-centered, and have no compassion whatsoever for the poor people. I always agree with him. I wished Jake would never get old—stay healthy and live forever.

Being the youngest one in the household, I was determined to take care of my beloved family when they get old. As Jake is the oldest, I often act like a nurse who reminds him to take vitamins and checks his water intake so he would not be dehydrated.

I also make him trade stocks and calculate the profits for me because I strongly believe the frequent use of the brains would prevent dementia or Alzheimer's disease.

When I thought about Yuri as an aged person like Jake, I wished she lived closer geographically or even moved in with us so I could keep an eye on her. Of course, I would do the same for Mom and Tom when they get old.

I know she has her devoted housekeeper, Shigeko, and chauffeur, Mr. Nishimoto, but they are her employees, not her relatives. I am sure Mom does not mind if she comes to live with us. They love each other like sisters. Besides, Mom says we have to treat Yuri as one of our family members.

* * *

August 23, 2005, Hurricane Katrina was formed at the sea near the Bahamas as a tropical storm. The people who lived along the coastline had experienced many hurricanes over the years; therefore, they have wooden shutters to protect the windows. We heard about Katrina when we were in Biloxi, so we secured each window with wooden shutters before we left.

On August 27, Katrina was predicted to become category 3 with wind power of 125 mph that could bring catastrophic damage to even well-built buildings or homes. Mayor Ray Nagin's voluntary evacuation was announced, but that afternoon, he changed it to a citywide mandatory evacuation.

The arrival of Katrina was estimated on August 29. All the businesses, schools, hospitals, and government offices should be closed on Monday. I was supposed to start my job on the first Monday in September, which was a week from August 29.

All the law enforcement, firefighters, military personnel, and emergency volunteers were allowed to remain in the city, but all other citizens were told to evacuate.

Jake reserved two rooms for three nights with one of the big hotels near the French Quarter. As the city of New Orleans tends to flood by hurricanes or severe rainstorms, staying in the hotel was one of Jake's evacuation plans over the years.

We each packed a suitcase with enough clothes for three days and put enough sandwich meats, cheeses, a gallon of milk, apples, oranges, and bananas in the large ice chest with enough ice. Candy bars, several bags of nuts and potato chips, a box of cereal, two loaves of bread, a large jar of peanut butter, and some can goods were put in a large carton box. Two cases of water bottles were already in Tom's car trunk.

As Jake's house is situated on higher ground than the street, we were confident his mansion would be all right. Besides, the brick fence should stop the floodwaters from the street, but just in case, the hired workers put enough sandbags at the front gate between the brick fences.

We helped put sandbags around the garage and my guesthouse. The hired workers nailed a sheet board on each window upstairs and downstairs. Jake said putting the sheet boards on the windows would also prevent burglary and vandalism.

Mayor Ray Nagin repeatedly announced the mandatory evacuation through radio and TV; the Superdome was already crowded. It was supposed to shelter 20,000 evacuees; 300 National Guards began dealing with the massive evacuees at the Superdome. Some meals and water were available, but Mayor Nagin emphasized to bring their own food and water for several days along with blankets.

It was estimated about a million people were leaving the city by using I-10, major roads, and the Lake Pontchartrain Causeway; the traffic jam was miles long. All the gas stations were almost out of gas. About 100,000 people were putting boards up to stay in the city. The Superdome was now filled with 20,000 evacuees—the maximum capacity.

The Superdome was chosen because it was thought to withstand the winds of 200 mph and 35 feet of water surge. The elevation of the Superdome is only 3 feet above the sea level.

It was Sunday, August 28; after Tom checked all the doors and windows, we drove to the high-rise hotel where we had our reservation and parked at the higher level of the parking deck in case of flood in the lower deck. The wind was getting stronger, the rain was pouring continuously, but the highways and roads were still passable.

Jake and I stayed in one room. Mom and Tom stayed in another. We ate dinner at the hotel restaurant. Some people seemed to have the same idea as ours to stay in the hotel. Some were stranded during their summer vacations.

Some restaurant workers had already gone home, and we had some limited orders. We were told that the restaurant should be closed if the power would go off. When we came back to the room, it was dark outside. The streetlights were still on, but no neon signs at the French Quarter or Canal Street. They probably turned off the power to prevent fire.

CNN showed Katrina's fierce movement at Pensacola, Mobile, the Mississippi coastline, and the southeast of New Orleans. Jake was worried about Tom's summerhouse that might not withstand the 125 mph wind. The Rousseau Company should be all right because the warehouse somehow survived from the numerous hurricanes in the past.

Mayor Ray Nagin was continuously announcing the mandatory evacuation. Governor Kathleen Blanco was mandating the immediate evacuation as well.

We were watching the TV late, but we fell asleep. Jake and I were awoken by the glass-shattering noises with some screams in the morning of August 29. Mom and Tom came to our room. No electricity was in the hotel, but we saw the daylight through the curtains. I went to the window to open the curtains, but the banging noise against the window by the rain and wind scared me. I hurriedly snuggled into bed with Mom.

Mom held me tightly in bed by covering my head with a pillow. Tom and Jake moved the sofa away from the window and sat tightly. The noises of splashing, swishing, banging, knocking, and rattling against the window were heard loudly and continuously. Occasional glass shattering noises with screams were heard nearby.

I really thought that the wind would break our window soon because the rattling noise was too loud. For almost an hour, we did not move, did not say a word, but our eyes were wide open in the dark.

When the wind stopped rattling the window, we all fell asleep. Tom and Jake were sleeping in Jake's bed. Mom and I were sleeping in my bed.

When we woke up, we saw the daylight through the curtains. The dark clouds and relentless rains obscured the view of the city, but we could tell the business district and Canal Street were flooded as well as the French Quarter.

We figured the hotel restaurant was closed due to no electricity and no water, so Mom spread a big bath towel on a table and prepared ham sandwiches. Luckily, Tom brought two cases of water bottles. We were thirsty. I told Jake not to be dehydrated. He had a dehydration problem before.

Later, I learned no one had ever predicted the city's levees, such as the Seventeenth Street Canal levee, the Industrial Canal levee, and the London Avenue Canal floodwall that were built by the United States Army Corps of Engineers, would be broken, but the water surge broke those levees.

The two-thirds of floods could be prevented if the levees around the city were built to withstand the water surge. Therefore, the poor engineering of the levees caused the floods of New Orleans. Now 80 percent of the city was under the devastating floods and over a thousand lives were lost.

On August 31, the floods measured 15 feet high in the Ninth Ward and Lakeview at the south shore of Lake Pontchartrain. The water did not recede in the low elevation area at all, and the dead bodies were floating in the water.

The Superdome was overcrowded and the surrounding was flooded as well. The situation was chaotic. The death toll by the floods was now over 1,400 and more bodies to be found. Some people were still waiting to be rescued on the rooftops at the Ninth Ward. In the meantime, lootings were just out of control at the dry areas such as the French Quarter, the business district, and the garden district.

On September 1, a curfew was issued, and 1,500 police officers were ordered to control the crimes in the city, instead of rescuing the stranded people or searching for dead bodies.

Delayed Justice

The Superdome became unsafe and unsanitary without water and electricity. Governor Kathleen Blanco pleaded to the neighboring states—Texas, Oklahoma, and Arkansas—to spare some public places to shelter the evacuees. FEMA with the help of the various bus companies including school buses provided almost 500 buses to transport the evacuees from the Superdome to the Houston Astrodome, and various places in Texas, Oklahoma, and Arkansas.

On September 4, the evacuation completed, but the floodwater remained the same in the low elevation area; water and electricity were still out. The city became inhabitable. The threats of diseases were mentioned.

The people including us who were stranded in the hotels or homes were mandated to leave the city due to the unsanitary condition of the city. By then, we were totally out of food and water. Because of no running water, the toilets looked filthy. We left the ice chest and all the trash bags in the hotel room, and we walked down the long stairs with suitcases. When we reached the hotel lobby, Jake was out of breath. A greyhound bus transported us to the airport.

At the airport, Mom used her cell phone to call Ms. Norma to see if she could accommodate us for a week or so; she was glad to do it. As Jake looked pale, I asked for some bottles of water at the rescue counter. Many volunteers were assisting the evacuees with water and food. Jake looked better after he had enough water and food.

When we arrived in Atlanta, Tom got a rental car and we drove to North Georgia. Ms. Norma and Chris Gordon were waiting for us. They said they were worried about us because of the chaotic situation in New Orleans.

In fact, the world was watching TV and saw the devastating areas in New Orleans, Gulfport, Biloxi, Mobile, and Pensacola. The floodwaters remained the same in the Ninth Ward area. They were planning to siphon the water soon.

Ms. Norma gave Mom and Tom the room that was used to be Sharon's room. Jake got Toby's room. I got a couch in the living room.

Ms. Norma said, "Toby went to see Sharon. He checked the law school there, but the tuition is too expensive for him, so he decided to come home and think about what he is going to do. Lily, you can encourage him to pursue his law degree. He is a smart boy. He finished up his college degree in three years after his military service."

"Is he coming home soon?"

"Yes, probably in a few days. He left Sharon's place yesterday. He might stop to see his friends on the way home. He does not know you all are here."

"When he comes home, where is he going to sleep?"

Chris Gordon said, "Don't worry. He could sleep anywhere—in his car or on the floor. He has a sleeping bag."

After dinner, we saw the flooded areas in New Orleans on TV again. Many military helicopters were searching for the dead bodies. The death toll now rose to 1,600. Some business people in the French Quarter area came back to clean their shops from lootings and water damages. The cleanup team started cleaning up the streetcar tracks and the long street of St. Charles Avenue.

The next day, when we woke up, Ms. Norma had already fixed breakfast for us. After we ate, Tom tried to call his accountant and secretary, but he could not reach them. Mom had no luck either. All the communication systems seemed to be shut down in New Orleans. As I did not know whom to call in the DA's office, I did not even try. My first day on the job had already passed, and the entire city was still in turmoil.

The TV also showed the most devastated area in Mississippi. It was Biloxi. Ninety percent of homes and buildings including casino buildings along the scenic drive were destroyed—over 200 dead, 60 missing. We saw the building of President Casino and the famous boat-shaped casino building, Treasure Bay Casino, were torn in half, blown toward the scenic drive like toy buildings.

Later, I learned that Biloxi's century-old lighthouse near Beau Rivage Casino withstood Katrina miraculously without any visual or structural damage. That lighthouse seems to be a symbol of Biloxi.

We knew Tom's summerhouse was destroyed and so was the beauty queen's mansion because those homes were too old to withstand the 125 mph wind, but Tom was not worried because he had a good home insurance.

I did not say anything, but I hoped the beauty queen and her aunt were smart enough to stay alive; in other words, they evacuated soon enough before Katrina's arrival because I really wanted the beauty queen to face the punishment without being dead. If she were dead, there should be no closure for Mom.

According to Tom, the FBI had been looking for Jeffery's accountant, Joseph Miller, who could probably tell which offshore bank he sent the company money to. They figured that Jeffery Dubois should be living closer to his money. Finding Joseph Miller was the key to finding Jeffery Dubois.

About 10,000 cleanup teams such as volunteers, law enforcement, fire fighters, FEMA, and the military troops including coast guards were concentrating on cleaning up the public places—streets, highways, parks, public buildings, schools, universities, hospitals, and clinics.

After the city was cleaned, the evacuees gradually came back home. In the meantime, the electricity was restored and the city water was running, but water boiling was mandated for two months until October.

The French Quarter was first to bring the normalcy to New Orleans. The destruction of the Ninth Ward area was so detrimental and irredeemable that all the residents fled to somewhere faraway.

Visitors saw the vivid flood lines on deserted homes in the Ninth Ward. Many homes in the Ninth Ward were unclaimed for many years—some homeowners deceased, some never came back to claim or rebuild, and some just deserted.

Chapter 25
After Katrina

My sleeping arrangement was not bad at all. The sofa had a hideaway bed. Every night, after everybody retired to their rooms, I pulled out the bed, put a bed sheet over, and slept with a blanket. The sofa made a queen-size bed. It was cushiony and comfortable.

The next day, Jake, Tom, and Chris Gordon went out to have lunch at Helen, Georgia, which is known as a German town. The town has many gift shops and restaurants. The visitors come to enjoy German hotdogs and beer. The annual Oktoberfest is very popular there.

Ms. Norma and Mom were baking something in the kitchen while talking nonstop. I did laundry for my family and folded them in the living room while watching TV. They showed a list of missing children in New Orleans who were misplaced in different evacuation camps. The parents were desperate to find their children.

At the Houston Astrodome, the city's Job Corps gave the able evacuees some jobs and placed them in temporary homes or apartments to avoid the overcrowded situation in the Astrodome.

Later, I learned that 250,000 evacuees from New Orleans decided to stay in Houston, Texas, instead of going home to New Orleans.

They knew their homes were under the floodwaters and destroyed. If they went back to New Orleans, they would be homeless. They rather wanted to start from zero with the new jobs and homes, which the city of Houston offered.

Some had no interest in rebuilding the totally destroyed homes in New Orleans. Some did not have any home insurances, so they just deserted their homes. Some had lived in the apartments, so it did not make any difference. They rather wanted to stay in Houston to start their new lives.

As a result, New Orleans lost 250,000 evacuees to Texas. It was a double jeopardy to New Orleans as far as the city population was concerned. The city lost a large sum of federal subsidy when the Census Bureau counted minus 250,000 in population. The city needed that subsidy money badly, but Houston got it.

In the evening, when we were eating dinner, Toby Gordon came home. He looked surprised to see all of us. He shook hands with my family, but he embraced me tightly and almost gave me a kiss. He went to the bathroom to freshen up before he sat with us at the dinner table.

He sat beside me and whispered, "It is so nice to see you. You look pretty." He caressed my thigh several times under the table. Ms. Norma gave him a plate, a fork, and a knife. He filled up his plate with vegetables and meat. He was devouring as though he had not eaten for several days.

Since I finished my dinner, I was observing him. Toby is a full-grown man now; his rugged face is handsome. His toned muscles are hidden under his cotton shirt—no trace of that frail-looking boy he used to be. His transformation fancied my female curiosity.

After he finished eating, he caressed my thigh several times again as though he could not contain his happiness to himself. He genuinely looked happy being with me. We had talked on the phone from time to time in the past, but we had not seen each other for many years.

Tom informed Toby about the situation in New Orleans, how we stayed in the hotel during Katrina, why we came to North Georgia. Toby was listening, but his attention was toward me as though he still could not get over me sitting beside him. I was probably a big surprise gift for him for some reason. He almost held my hand while listening to Tom, but he caressed my thigh instead. His touch was so magical, and I felt aroused.

I helped Mom and Ms. Norma in the kitchen to put away dishes in the cupboard. While everybody was watching TV in the living room, I took a shower in Sharon's room. Toby seemed to be taking a shower in his room too.

After everybody retired to their rooms, I shut the hallway door and pulled out the bed under the sofa. Toby brought his sleeping bag from his car, spread it on the carpeted floor beside my bed.

The house was quiet. As the hallway door was closed and the lights were turned off, no one could hear us or see us. I was at the edge of my bed watching Toby in the dark. Toby got a pillow and tried to lie on his sleeping bag, but he came closer to my bed, held my hand gently, and started talking softly.

He told me all about the time when he was in Iraq. I was shocked to learn that when he got lonely, he took out my picture and slept with it in the desert. My picture probably came from the wedding party of Mom and Tom.

He also told me how much he missed me after we moved away; he kissed my picture almost every night secretly in his room. Sharon and his parents had no idea how much he missed seeing me, and how he felt about me.

When he was in Iraq, his military friends thought I was his sweetheart who was waiting for him at home, just like an old war movie with a sweetheart picture.

He sat up straight on the floor, caressed both of my hands, and leaned over to kiss me. It was my first kiss. My heart was pounding. As Toby wanted to snuggle into my bed, I gave him some space. I was somewhat hesitant, but at the same time, I was thrilled to be in bed with Toby.

His toned body had overwhelmingly covered my entire body. He kissed me gently again and let me sleep on his muscular arm. He was wearing a T-shirt and pajama bottom. I was wearing summer pajamas.

My head was at his armpit. His other arm covered my whole body. I heard his fast beating heart and smelled soap fragrance. We did not say anything, did not do anything, but just snuggled together under a blanket, just like two sleepy lovebirds.

When I woke up in the morning, Toby was sleeping soundly in his sleeping bag. Ms. Norma was already cooking breakfast. I made the sofa bed without disturbing Toby and helped Ms. Norma.

In the afternoon, Toby and I decided to see the lake beach we used to go. He wanted to swim, but I did not have my swimming suit. Ms. Norma found Sharon's swimming suit. She made some sandwiches, put some water bottles in the ice chest, and told us to have a good time. She probably thought I was going to convince Toby to go to law school so his dream would come true.

At the lake beach, we spread a picnic blanket and start putting some sunscreen lotion to each other. We both looked like a married couple or lovers. No one was on the beach. It was a weekday. The children were probably at school.

While I was putting some sunscreen on his back, he put some to his face, front torso, and legs at the same time. When it was his turn to put sunscreen on my back, he told me to lie on my stomach so I did.

He started putting sunscreen with both of his hands gently to my back, arms, and down to thighs, legs, feet, and even toes. He was actually massaging my entire body with his warm hands.

My body was relaxing and felt sleepy. Mom put sunscreen on me when I was young, but this was my first time having someone like a professional masseur put sunscreen on me. Now he told me to lie on my back and started putting sunscreen on my face, neck, upper chest, stomach, and legs. He did not bother my bulged area in front, but I was sure he wanted to touch them. He kissed my fingertips from time to time.

His face was red from the sun. After he wiped off his hands with a towel, he lay beside me to kiss me. His kissing was so passionate that I could not breathe; I had to take a deep breath by lying on one side. He laughed, but he kept kissing me.

We kissed and kissed without saying a word. His hand was caressing my back and buttocks. I was aroused. I caressed his back while kissing too. When he touched me between my thighs, I moaned. His hand was almost touching my female organ. I thought my body was going to melt. I noticed Toby was hiding something between his legs by lying on his stomach.

When we were growing up, Sharon and I considered Toby one of us. We taught him the girl's anatomy, but one day, Toby told us that he had something between his legs that Sharon and I did not have. We wanted to see what it was, but he never showed it to us.

Suddenly, in the middle of kissing, Toby ran and submerged his whole body in the water, swam to the other side of the beach, and stayed there for a while. I was watching him. He finally swam back and came out of water. His swimming trunks and his sun bleached brown hair were all wet.

We ate sandwiches and finished a bottle of water. We kissed more by sitting up straight on the blanket. By then, I thought I had enough sun.

In his car, Toby asked me if he could come to New Orleans with us. He would do anything to help Mom, Tom, and Jake around the house like a houseboy so he could be with me.

I told him I would ask Jake. However, I remembered what Ms. Norma asked me to do. She wanted me to convince Toby to be in law school so his dream would come true.

Would Toby be interested in the law school in New Orleans? Will Jake allow Toby to stay in his house while he goes to school? I have enough money for Toby's school. However, if he is going to live with us, our love relationship has to be discreet. We cannot kiss in front of my family. We cannot reveal our relationship to anybody yet. Everybody thinks we are like a brother and a sister. Besides, I am a year older than he is.

Toby had some money saved up when he was in Iraq, but the school in Washington, DC, was too expensive, so he decided to come home without knowing what he was going to do. Now his beloved girl showed up unexpectedly. He was determined to follow his heart, not his dream. As long as he could be with her in New Orleans, he would do anything.

I told Toby if he wanted to be with me in New Orleans, he had to think about going to law school.

"Toby, did you hear what I said?"

"No. What did you say?"

"About going to law school. I am very sure Jake would let you stay with us in New Orleans if you decided to go to law school. However, our relationship has to be discreet."

He nodded several times. He did not mind keeping our relationship a secret as long as he could be with me. Toby kissed me passionately and said, "I love you very much. I hope you can convince Jake so I could come with you." Toby sounded desperate.

I took a shower and wore a pair of jeans and a top before seeing Jake. Mom and Ms. Norma were fixing dinner. Jake was watching TV. Tom, Chris Gordon, and Toby were outside talking.

I asked Jake to walk with me in the neighborhood because I wanted to ask him something. He was glad to do so. We started walking toward Grandma Margaret's house, where we used to live.

"Jake, Toby wants to come to New Orleans with us. I told him I would ask you first. I also told him if he wants to come with us, he must go to the law school in New Orleans. Ms. Norma wants me to convince Toby to go to law school so his dream would come true. He wants to be a prosecutor just like me. Is it okay for Toby to live in your house if he gets accepted to the same law school I went?"

"Of course! His parents told me Toby gave up on the law school in Washington, DC, because the tuition was too expensive. As you said, Toby has to think about enrolling in the law school if he wants to live with us."

"Do you think we can help him?"

"Yes, we can help him. If he goes to the same law school you went, I would be glad to provide shelter and food."

"Wow! Toby will be so grateful. He finished his undergraduate degree in three years and passed the LSAT. He is very smart. He should feel comfortable living with us because Mom and I know Toby very well. In fact, Mom changed his diapers when he was a baby. Toby and I are like a brother and a sister."

I did not want Jake to suspect our relationship.

"Okay. Tonight, I will tell Toby's parents what we are going to do with Toby. I heard the colleges in New Orleans have not started yet. Toby might be able to register for the first semester."

"I think Mom could help him get into law school. She is the director of the entire library including the law library."

"Lily, I have a good idea. Toby can work for Tom after school so he can earn his tuition. I will talk to Tom."

"Jake, Toby's parents would be very happy when you explain where we live and where the law school is. Toby does not even know that the law school is in our neighborhood. Thank you, Jake."

I gave him a kiss on his cheek. Jake was like my Grandma Margaret who was a warmhearted person and kind to everybody. I realized Jake's nurturing was the source of who I became. Of course, Mom, Tom, and Yuri did their parts, but my daily nurturing came from Jake. He was the ideal grandfather everybody should have. I was fortunate to relish his goodness and kindheartedness to myself for years. Now Jake could nurture Toby too.

Before dinner, Jake and Tom were talking. At the dinner table, Jake asked Ms. Norma and Chris Gordon if it was all right to take Toby with us. They did not know what Jake was going to say. Jake explained what Toby was going to do in New Orleans; he would be attending law school, work for Tom to earn his tuition, and live with us like a family member. The school is actually in the neighborhood, so it would be very convenient for Toby to commute.

Ms. Norma's eyes were filled with tears. Chris Gordon stood up, shook Jake's hand, and said, "Thank you." Toby stood up and yelped ecstatically like a kid. Everybody applauded for Toby and Jake.

That night, Toby snuggled into my bed, gave me a passionate kiss, and embraced me in bed for the longest time until I fell asleep. In the morning, he was in his sleeping bag.

Many evacuees were returning to New Orleans. The electricity and water system were restored. It was time for us to go home. Tom made the airline reservation. Toby and I were to drive his car to New Orleans.

Toby put his clothes, shoes, books, his laptop, most of his belongings, and his guitar in his car. I put my small suitcase on the back seat because his car trunk was full.

Ms. Norma put some sandwiches, several bottles of water, and some candy bars in the ice chest and told us to eat at the rest area, not in the car. She was probably afraid of the distraction if Toby ate while driving.

I embraced Ms. Norma and Chris Gordon and told them we would take good care of Toby. They nodded and thanked me. Mom and Ms. Norma were embracing each other with tears. Toby embraced his parents and waved before he started the engine. They waved at us by standing in the middle of the street.

We followed Tom's rental car all the way to Atlanta Hartsfield Airport. When they turned to the airport exit, I rolled down the window, waved at them. I saw Mom roll down the window and shouted something, but I could not hear her. She probably said, "Drive safely and see you later."

I remembered the way to New Orleans by heart because Mom and I drove to New Orleans several times. He had a road map just in case. When the Gordon family had a vacation in Florida, they always used I-75 south. Therefore, Toby had never been on I-85 south.

I told Toby I could navigate for him because I knew how to get to New Orleans, but he did not say anything. He seemed to be daydreaming. He was probably thinking about his new life in New Orleans with his beloved girl.

Toby held my hand and drove by one hand for a long time. He turned on FM and we listened to classical music. I caressed his hand that was almost twice bigger than mine was.

I remembered Sharon and I used to hold his tiny hands whenever we walked him on the street or at the lake beach. I still could not believe a frail boy like him grew up to be an ancient Olympic athlete—tall and muscular. Perhaps, his military training made him that way. Of course, I became taller and matured too.

When we stopped at the rest area on I-85, Toby passionately kissed my mouth and caressed my thighs before we used the restroom. After we washed our hands, we ate sandwiches at the picnic table. Ms. Norma's sandwiches were so fresh and delicious. After lunch, we walked around the rest area by holding hands like two lovebirds.

In his car, Toby inserted a CD of saxophone music. He said he used to play saxophone in a marching band, but he could play guitar better. I remembered he played a romantic melody for Mom and

Tom at their wedding party. He also said he often played guitar to entertain his friends when he was in Iraq.

He really looked happy when he talked about living in Jake's house with me and seeing me every day. However, we both understood our relationship must be discreet.

Chapter 26
Secret Relationship

While driving, I realized how peaceful I felt being with Toby. I have no problem being his girl. Toby confessed his love to me, and I realized I love him too.

Furthermore, we both really like each other. Because of it, we both feel very comfortable being together. I never had a boyfriend in my life, but now I have Toby as my boyfriend. Toby has me as his girlfriend.

Even though our relationship has to be discreet, living under the same house may give us some opportunities to exchange romantic glances, touches, or even kisses when my family is not around.

Toby's desire to touch me or kiss me might come too strong from time to time, but I am sure Toby knows how to control his desire. Seeing each other every day could nurture our relationship too. I cannot define what love is, but I could feel it in my heart. Love makes me smile and happy.

I am glad I went to North Georgia. It was like my fate. If I were not there, I could have never known how Toby felt about me, and Toby could have never known his confession awoke my love for him. Since we had lived so far apart, he probably buried his feelings for me, tried to forget all about me, and decided to move on without me. Katrina killed many people and caused turmoil and sadness, but I found my love because of Katrina.

When we came closer to Mobile, many trees along the highway were broken in many pieces like chopsticks. Broken trees and branches were piled high on the side of the highway. Seemingly, the DOT workers worked fast to clear the fallen trees to make the highway passable for the travelers.

On I-10, the situation was worse. We saw many caution signs at the fallen trees and blown debris along the highway. When I saw the exit sign to Biloxi, I was tempted to ask Toby to drive through the scenic drive, but I remembered how some residents described Biloxi on TV—Biloxi looked like Hiroshima, Japan, after the atomic bomb explosion. I was very sure most of the streets were closed including the scenic drive.

There were many detour signs on the streets when we came to New Orleans, but we managed to drive through the city. We saw many homes in shambles, some windows of the tall buildings and hotel buildings shattered.

Tom's blue town car was in the garage. They probably took a taxi from the airport to the hotel to retrieve his car at the hotel parking lot. The house did not show any damage—it seemed the sheet boards protected the house. The elevation of the land and the brick fence probably saved the house from flooding too.

Mom and Jake were cleaning up the refrigerator and discarding all the spoiled food in a trash bag. The electricity was back and the city water was running, but the water boiling was mandated for two months.

Tom had already taken off the sheet boards from my guesthouse, so I went inside to check the closet and bed. They were okay. No trace of mold or moisture, but I left the windows open in the bedroom and bathroom to get fresh air and sunlight for several hours.

Toby got a guestroom downstairs that has a bathroom. Jake used to have the same room, but he moved to one of the guestrooms upstairs. The reason he moved upstairs was to strengthen his legs by using the steps. Even though he had to hold onto the rail to climb up and down the stairs, his leg exercise was done every day. He believed the legs are the most important part of the body for the elders. He is afraid to be a wheelchair-bound old man.

After Toby brought everything from his car, he went outside to help Tom. Mom and I went to the grocery store to buy two cases of water bottles, meat, potatoes, vegetables, and fruits. On the way home, we bought three large pizzas for dinner because we did not have the boiled water in the house to cook. The mayor warned not to eat fresh vegetables—cook everything.

After Tom and Toby finished the work outside, they stored the sheet boards and sandbags in the shed. The shed was dry. The garage was dry too. It seemed our neighborhood dodged Katrina. The streets were cleaned up, and the streetcars started running.

On Monday, Mom went to work, Tom took Toby to work, and I stayed home because I was told to come to work on the first Monday in October.

Jake and I went to the university to get the enrollment application for Toby. After that, we walked to the library to see Mom. We saw some water damage on the campus yard and some shattered windows. However, all debris were already picked up.

Mom was working on the computer with a pile of folders. She stopped typing and looked up at us with a big smile. Without asking us, she got two bottles of water from her small refrigerator. Jake had visited Mom several times with Tom or me before.

She told us the library was all right, no damage, but it would be closed for another week. The computer technicians were checking all the computer systems throughout the university.

We told her we got Toby's application. She said, "I know Dr. Sinclair, who is the head of the law school. He is one of the board members in this university. We, the board members, meet almost every day to discuss all kinds of operational damages and problems, so I will talk to him personally about Toby. Since Toby passed the LSAT, he should not have any problem enrolling in this law school. If he needs a recommendation letter, I will write one. I'll also tell him I have known Toby since he was a baby. I am sure Toby will be accepted in this law school without any problem."

Before we left, she said, "Tom called and said everything in his warehouse is all right, the office is dry, Toby has been a big help typing those delayed invoices. Only a few employees showed up. The shipments were piled up, so they must work fast to ship the cargos out to the islands in a week. Oh, Yuri called too. I told her where we were. She said hello to everybody. Lily, write her a letter. She seems lonely."

"Okay. I will. See you later."

Jake and I stopped at the drugstore to get some vitamins. I wanted to drive to see how long it would take to commute from home to my work, but when we saw some detour signs, we decided to come home.

On the way home, we saw the beauty queen's mansion. A few windows upstairs were shattered; there was no sign of cleanup or repair. It seemed the beauty queen's aunt never came back. The grass was high; tree branches and debris were all over in the yard. The black iron fence was standing strong, but the long driveway to the back of the house looked filthy with debris.

I wondered whether the beauty queen would send someone to fix the mansion or not. I did not think she sold either of those mansions because of Katrina. We knew her aunt vacated the mansion and moved in with the beauty queen in Biloxi.

I thought that the beauty queen and her aunt were smart and greedy enough to be alive. I also thought that they might have escaped to a faraway place during the turmoil of Katrina. If they did, who would take care of those mansions? Amy Dubois?

I was sure Tom could call the realtor in Biloxi to find out her whereabouts. She could not desert such expensive mansions unless she stashed away money so she could afford to live in a faraway place. If she would become a fugitive, she could lose those mansions to the bondsman and the state.

When we came home, it was almost four o'clock. We had to start cooking dinner. The tall plastic container was already filled with the boiled water from yesterday. During the boiling water order, we boiled water in two big pots every night and leave them to cool off overnight. In the morning, Toby poured the heavy pots of water in the large plastic container. This ritual continued for many days until the boiling water order was lifted in October.

We could take a shower with the faucet water, but we were prohibited to drink or brush teeth with it. We put a pitcher of clean water in each bathroom for brushing teeth. The rest of the water in the container was used to wash vegetables, fruits, potatoes, rice, meat, and fish before cooking, also used to rinse dishes and utensils.

After putting chicken breasts in the oven to bake, we sat at the table and opened our own computers. Both of our portfolios were significantly low, but Jake said not to worry—the stock market would recover soon.

Toby and Tom came home at the same time Mom came home. Toby looked surprised because Jake was wearing an apron to serve dinner. When we first moved in with Jake, I, too, was surprised and impressed with the delicious dinner Jake cooked.

Toby sat beside me and devoured the dinner. He thanked Jake for the dinner. I had to remind Toby that I was one of the chefs in the house. "Toby, you should thank me too. Jake and I fix dinner together every day. Right, Jake?"

Jake nodded and said with a big smile, "I trained Lily for many years. Now she could be an independent chef."

Tom and Mom were nodding by glancing at me with a smile. Toby thanked me quickly by caressing my thigh under the table. If no one was around us, he probably kissed me passionately to thank me, but we had to be discreet.

After dinner, Mom helped Toby fill out the application and told him she would give the application herself to Dr. Sinclair at the board meeting. She put his application in her pocketbook.

I said, "Toby, I have some money in my savings account. If you need money for tuition, you can borrow from me."

"Thank you, but I saved some money when I was in Iraq, so I think I have enough to pay for the first and second semester."

Tom said, "Toby, I will pay you for your time in the office so you can save your wage for your future tuition. My dad paid me when I worked after school. Because of it, I did not get in trouble like other college students did, such as getting into drinking or drugs. Dad did the same thing for his father too."

Toby nodded and said, "Thank you very much. I really like being with you all. I feel at home. I will study hard and work hard too. Thank you for including me as one of your family members." Everybody nodded and welcomed Toby with a smile.

Jake turned to Tom. "Tom, Lily and I are thinking about going to Biloxi to check on your mansion tomorrow. Do you think the streets are passable?"

When we saw the beauty queen's mansion on St. Charles Avenue, Jake and I talked about going to Biloxi to find out the situation in Biloxi. We were sure that Tom's mansion and the beauty queens' mansion were destroyed, but we still wanted to see it for sure.

"I heard the scenic drive was cleaned, but most streets still have many detours. Lily, just be careful when you drive. I am sure many nails are sticking out from debris and wooden scraps." Tom knows I have been the designated driver for Jake since I bought my car.

The next day, Jake and I drove to Biloxi after everybody left for work. Tom gave me his digital camera to take some pictures of his house or remains from different angles. He needed the pictures for his insurance company.

The information we had from CNN was correct. Biloxi looked like Hiroshima, Japan, or a war zone. Some parts of the scenic drive were still blocked and many detour signs posted. We drove the detours.

We were overwhelmingly shocked to see Tom's property. His mansion was blown away without any trace of the building structure. His entire property looked empty. The cement foundation, some broken wooden poles, and part of the utility room were left. The destruction was far beyond my imagination. Amazingly, the heavy roofs were also blown away to somewhere faraway. That was just unbelievable. I took many pictures from different angles including several oak trees in the yard that had dangling branches.

We drove slowly toward the beauty queen's mansion. Almost all of the antebellum mansions along the scenic drive were gone. The beauty queen's mansion was totaled as well, part of the brick walls remained, and most of the black iron fence were gone too.

We stopped at the city hall to see the list of the dead. We did not see Nancy Saunders Dubois or her aunt, Sue Conn, but they said some of the dead bodies in the morgue were not identified yet.

We gave the address of the beauty queen's mansion to see if her daughter, Amy Dubois, came to look for her mother, Nancy Dubois, and her great-aunt, Sue Conn. They said, not yet. I also gave the address of Tom's mansion and told them the owner of that house, Tom Rousseau, was alive, but his house was totaled. They recorded everything what I said. They seemed to be collecting the information on the town's people as well as their properties.

On the way home, we ate lunch at a fast-food restaurant on I-10. Our favorite casino restaurant was closed. It seemed all the casino buildings and other businesses in Biloxi were shut down. They said it would take ten years to rebuild the city.

At the dinner table, I showed Tom the pictures of his property in his camera. He looked sad. I told him the beauty queen's mansion was totaled and their names were not on the victims' list, but some bodies were still unidentified in the morgue. Tom was going to call the bondsman to see if they knew the beauty queen's whereabouts. If she skipped town, the bondsman would send a body hunter.

Toby did not know what we were discussing. I told him I would explain everything later. He nodded. Indeed, he did not know anything about Mom's family tragedy, the grand larceny, most importantly, my birth secret.

On Saturday, Mom and Tom had gone shopping and Jake was watering flowers.

"Jake, I am taking Toby to the French Quarter and eat lunch there."

He waved at me as though he was saying, "Have a good time."

We took a streetcar. It was the first time for Toby to ride a streetcar. He was looking up at the tall buildings when we came closer to the business district.

We got off at Canal Street and walked on Bourbon Street. Some stores and restaurants were still closed. I showed him Jackson Square, but there was no weekend crowd. New Orleans had lost its charms because of Katrina. We climbed the steps to the Riverwalk.

The water in the mighty Mississippi River looked overwhelmingly full and powerful. Toby did not know how lively the New Orleans Riverwalk was before, so I explained—the Riverwalk used to provide some organized events, music, ice cream vendors, hotdog vendors, and mime actors.

It was sad to see what Katrina did to the walk and the city. There were hardly anyone around us, and we saw some caution signs along the walk.

I also told him how much fun every visitor could have in the French Quarter and in Jackson Square—listen to jazz music, see mime actors, enjoy a buggy ride, see a palm reader, visit St. Louis Cathedral, see some funeral procession with jazz music, and see some acrobatic performers and portrait artists.

I was talking like a tour guide. I also told him eating beignets at famous Café Du Monde next to Jackson Square is a must that every visitor should do. The visitors should also enjoy gumbo, crawfish, and half-shelled oysters when they come to New Orleans, but now the city lost its charms.

Toby held my waist so that he could hear me better. We both looked like a pair of lovebirds. Finally, we found a bench and sat closer. Toby cupped my face and kissed me passionately. Nobody was around, so I kissed him back. He was caressing my thigh, and I was doing the same to Toby. We both moaned while kissing.

We saw someone coming toward us, so we stopped kissing. A couple passed by us. They were an older couple who were holding hands lovingly as though they were still in love. I thought I saw the future Toby and me.

After they passed, Toby held my waist and started tickling my side. I tickled him back. As I tried to avoid his further tickling, I ran, but he caught me from behind, tickled my sides with both of his hands repeatedly—he did not stop. I laughed and laughed aloud until I could not laugh anymore. Finally, Toby stopped tickling.

The couple turned their heads and looked at us for a moment to see what we were doing. They probably thought we were fighting, but when they saw us play like children, they turned around and kept walking. I was breathing very hard from laughing. Toby embraced me tightly as though he was apologizing for tickling me so hard.

Chapter 27
A Long Story

After we came back to the bench, he cupped my face and kissed me gently. I was still breathing hard. He wrapped my shoulders with his arm and kissed my forehead several times. I was actually resting my head against his muscular arm.

As it was a cloudy day and the breeze from the river cooled our surroundings, we were able to sit on the bench without being hot for a long time.

We watched the Mississippi River quietly for a while. I caressed his other hand several times. He did not say anything, but I saw a smile on his handsome face. He looked very happy. I was happy too because we were alone and did not need to be discreet.

I sat up straight by turning my body toward him and decided to tell Toby all about my birth secret and other things he did not know. It was a good time to tell him since we were alone.

"Toby, I am going to tell you something very important about me. It is a long story. I hope you don't mind listening. My story might shock you, but I will be telling you the truth."

Toby looked puzzled, but nodded several times as though he was saying, "Shock me." His hazel eyes looked somewhat mystified.

I started telling him what happened to my father and my grandparents before I was born. It was difficult to tell Toby that Mom was not my real mother, but I had to tell him. Toby looked shocked.

"Were you adopted by your mom?"

"No. Mom is my father Alan's sister. My biological mother is Yuri Tanaka. She is Japanese. She had lived with Mom and her family during her college. Yuri's father and Mom's parents were dear friends and graduated from the same college. In fact, my whole family, including me, graduated from the same college. Yuri's father, Masaki Tanaka, or rather my grandfather, had the lucrative company called the Tanaka Clothing Company in Osaka, Japan, and just opened up a branch in Tokyo at that time. He wanted his daughter to manage the Tokyo branch after her graduation. Therefore, he told his daughter not to fall in love with any American boy while she was in college in New Orleans. He also asked Jefferson and Marie to keep an eye on his daughter. They agreed."

I took a deep breath and continued.

"Nevertheless, it was too late. My father, Alan, and Yuri were already struck by 'love at first sight' to each other at their first encounter. That was why they had to keep their relationship to themselves for a long time, but Mom and Tom accidently found out about their secret relationship. Tom was Alan's best friend. Actually, Alan, Michelle, and Tom grew up together in the same neighborhood just as we grew up together in North Georgia. Tom's parents and Mom's parents were very close like relatives, so they could know everything about their children. Therefore, Mom and Tom agreed to keep their relationship a secret from each other's parents."

Toby nodded without blinking.

"After Yuri and Michelle graduated from college, Yuri had to extend a year to stay for her CPA tests. Her father was reluctant, but let her stay one more year. Yuri stayed in the mansion in Biloxi to study. As the Dubois family's tradition, the mansion in Biloxi was always given to the heir who would take over the family business. My father, Alan, was already vice president in the family business, so he became the owner of the mansion in Biloxi. In the meantime, Alan and Yuri married secretly and Yuri got pregnant. Mom was the only one who knew their marriage and Yuri's pregnancy."

Toby was looking deep into my hazel eyes without blinking.

"When Yuri's stomach got bigger, Mom strongly suggested her brother, Alan, to tell their parents about his marriage and Yuri's pregnancy. She told him their parents would be very happy to know about their first grandchild so they could convince Masaki Tanaka to be happy with them. Alan promised Mom to tell them soon."

Toby nodded as though he agreed with Mom's suggestion.

"In fact, the day Alan was going to tell his parents about his marriage and the baby, Jefferson and Marie got very ill from drinking coffee in the office. Their company lawyer, named Jeffery Dubois, called the CDC in Atlanta and made an emergency appointment for a possible poisoning. Knowing Alan as a pilot, Jeffery Dubois and his assistant lawyer, Nancy Saunders, went to the municipal airport to rent a Cessna for Alan to fly. After Mom dropped off her parents and her brother at the airfield, she saw those lawyers leaving the airfield in a hurry. That evening, Mom heard from the FAA of the airplane crash."

Toby looked anxious to hear more about the airplane crash by leaning toward me.

"The FAA said the crash was caused by a gas leak. Anyway, after Mom's family died, the company lawyer, Jeffery Dubois, became the sole beneficiary of the Dubois fortune for no reason. He has the same last name, but no relation to the family. Mom went to see what was going on with the Dubois Import Company, but she found out the company vanished. She was just bewildered and did not know what to do. She also did not know Jeffery Dubois moved the company to Gulfport. He was probably afraid of Michelle because she was the only surviving child of Jefferson and Marie."

I wanted something to drink, but continued.

"Shortly after the disappearance of the company, Mom received the eviction notice at her family home where she was born and grew up. She was shocked, but as the eviction notice came from the police department, she had no choice but to move out. She was devastated because everything was changing so quickly. With her desperation and instinct, she smuggled all her mother's jewelry, her father's gold coin collections, and some valuable antiques in several pillowcases, and then moved in with Yuri in Biloxi."

Again, I took a deep breath and continued.

"One day, Yuri showed some signs of early labor—having severe stomach pains and bleeding. Mom took her to the emergency room and the baby was born on that night. The baby was named Lily Marie Dubois. Yuri and the baby stayed in the hospital for a week. In the meantime, Mom sold her mother's jewelry and her father's gold coin collections to pay for the hospital bills. After Yuri and the baby came home, Yuri had a phone call from Japan. Her father passed away suddenly. She was requested to return home urgently. The airplane ticket was already paid in Japan."

Toby looked very much interested in my talk. He was caressing my hand unknowingly.

"Mom told Yuri that she would take care of Lily while she was away. Yuri said she would be right back after the funeral and left in a hurry. Shortly after Yuri left, Mom got the eviction notice delivered by a police officer. She was to vacate the mansion in two days. If she had her parents' will, she could probably dispute the eviction, but she had nothing."

I caressed Toby's hands this time.

"Anyway, Mom had to vacate her brother's mansion in two days. She had nowhere to go and almost penniless. Out of her desperation, she called her aunt Margaret in North Georgia."

Toby seemed to be putting most of the puzzling pieces together now, why Mom and I came to live in North Georgia.

"On the phone, she told her everything, what happened to the Dubois family, how they died, her suspicion of those lawyers who worked for her parents. Most importantly, she told her aunt that she was with a newborn baby, almost penniless, and about to be evicted. Grandma Margaret assumed the baby was Mom's, so she did not hesitate to take us in. She gave her the direction to her house in North Georgia and told her to drive carefully. So Mom put all the baby clothes, her stuff in the car, made several bottles of milk, put me in a baby basket next to the driver's seat, and vacated the house in a hurry."

"What happened to Yuri?"

"This is our fate. Mom left her address book in the desk drawer. A piece of paper in the address book had Yuri's contact—address and phone number in Japan. She was putting everything in the car, but forgot all about the address book in the desk drawer. When she wanted to call Yuri from North Georgia, it was too late to retrieve it. Our separation was caused by not having Yuri's contact address. When Mom told me all about my birth secret, she apologized to me profusely by saying my separation from Yuri was her fault."

Toby finally understood why I was separated from my biological mother. He kissed me lightly and thanked me for telling him all about my birth secret. However, Toby wanted to know more about those lawyers who stole the Dubois fortune. I was tired, but continued.

"Mom had suspected those two lawyers from the beginning, but she did not have any evidence. Besides, Mom could not afford to hire a lawyer. After Tom found us in North Georgia, Tom went to the probate court to find the will of Jefferson and Marie that had Jeffery Dubois as beneficiary. He suspected the signatures were forged, but he, too, could not prove anything. Those lawyers probably poisoned my grandparents and tampered with the rented aircraft to kill them, but again, there were no evidence or no witness."

"So they got away with murder?"

"It seemed to be that way for twenty-something years, but Mom received an envelope from Paula Dubois, who was the ex-wife of the company lawyer, Jeffery Dubois. It contained two wills and Paula's five-page letter. In her letter, she wrote her logical explanation—why her ex-husband forged the signatures of Jefferson and Marie, why they put his name as beneficiary along with Alan Dubois, why they had to poison Jefferson and Marie, why Alan's airplane was tampered. If Mom did not get that evidence and the letter, yes, they could have gotten away with murder. Many thanks to Paula Dubois, those crooks will see delayed justice soon."

Toby nodded and asked, "Are they in jail now?"

"No, Jeffery Dubois sold his company and skipped the country several years back. Nobody knows where he is. His wife who conspired to write the irrevocable will and allegedly poisoned Jefferson and Marie was arrested, but her lawyer bailed her out. She is supposed to stay put in Biloxi to wait for her husband's arrest so they both could be tried together. Right now, Jeffery Dubois is on the FBI's most wanted list."

Toby asked, "Did Nancy Saunders skip country during Katrina?" Toby probably remembered our conversation at the dinner table.

"Yes. It seems. According to Tom, the bondsman could not locate Nancy Saunders. The body hunters are looking for her now. The FBI was already notified."

"Can Paula Dubois testify against her ex-husband once the trial starts?"

"Yes, she could, if she were alive, but she was killed in a car explosion several years ago. It could be coincidental, but Jeffery Dubois skipped country after her death. That made the Houston DA suspicious. Paula's only brother who works in the DA's office is investigating his sister's death. He thinks Jeffery Dubois hired a killer to set a bomb under her car."

"Whoa! Jeffery Dubois killed her too."

"It seems that way."

"Why did Paula wait so long to give the evidence to your Mom?"

"Well, Paula Dubois was looking for Mom for years, but could not find her. Mom was living in North Georgia. After Paula died, her son decided to check each house on our street to see if they knew Michelle's whereabouts. Luckily, he met Jake in the yard. That was how Mom got the evidence."

I paused for a minute and continued.

"Let me tell you more about Paula Dubois. She and Jeffery were college sweethearts and married while they were in college. She worked as a nurse to support Jeffery during his law school. When my grandparents hired Jeffery as the company lawyer, he was asked to write the family will for them. He wrote the will with the help of his wife Paula who was talented in writing. After finishing the will with the genuine signatures of Jefferson and Marie, Jeffery brought the will home because he wanted Paula to see his first legal work, at the same time he wanted to thank her for her help."

I paused again and continued.

"Paula made a copy of the will after her husband went to bed. That was how she had the original will with the genuine signatures of Jefferson and Marie. There were two wills in the envelope—the original will and the forged one."

"How did she get the forged will?" Toby was inquisitive.

"Many years later, when Paula discovered her husband was fooling around with his young assistant, Nancy Saunders, she suspected they were doing something else other than their assignation, so she looked into her husband's briefcase after he went to bed. There, she found the new will for Jefferson and Marie with the irrevocable trust clause that is known to avoid the hefty inheritance tax for the beneficiaries. She made a copy of the entire will and later compared the signatures with the original will. They did not match—she discovered the signatures were forged. She was also flabbergasted seeing her husband's name as a beneficiary along with Alan Dubois in the will that Nancy Saunders signed as the executing attorney. She could not figure out why Jeffery Dubois was in their will and what he and Nancy Saunders were planning to do with the forged will."

I paused. Toby was attentive.

"Shortly after the forged will, the tragedy happened. Paula knew immediately what her husband and Nancy Saunders did to Alan, Jefferson, and Marie. Jeffery did not come home for several days, but when he came home, he asked Paula for a divorce because Nancy Saunders was pregnant."

Toby had a scorn look on his face.

"After their divorce, Paula heard Jeffery Dubois became the sole beneficiary of the Dubois fortune. She knew then why they wrote the irrevocable will. The killing of the Dubois family was their main plan so the will could be effective. Out of despair, Paula uprooted her children from New Orleans and moved to her hometown, Houston, Texas. Even then, she was going to give the evidence to the only survivor, Michelle Dubois, but Michelle was already evicted from the family mansion in New Orleans. She knew those crooks evicted her. She cried for Michelle."

"Did Jeffery Dubois ever suspect his ex-wife had those incriminating documents?"

"Oh. Yes. Paula honestly explained in her letter what she had done with the evidence. Because of it, she predicted Jeffery Dubois might hire a killer to kill her in the future."

"What did she do with the evidence?"

"She decided to extort from Jeffery so she could give her children some stability they needed. When Paula moved to Huston with her three children, they lived in an apartment and her children went to school in the undesirable neighborhood. In order to get out of the neighborhood, she wanted Jeffery's financial help, but he refused, so she started extorting from him by telling him she knew all about their grand larceny and murder. She told him she had the evidence to prove their crime. Jeffery was scared, so he started paying the alimony under the table. As a result, she and her children were able to live in a nice neighborhood and all her children went to nice colleges."

"Do you think she was killed by Jeffery Dubois because of her extortion?"

"I guess so. Paula mentioned in her letter, she was almost killed by a sniper when she was in the yard many years back. She told the police to investigate her ex-husband in Biloxi, but eventually the investigation was dropped. After that, Paula Dubois was fearful of her life, so she put two documents and a five-page letter in a large envelope, gave it to her son, and told him to look for Michelle Dubois."

I really wanted to eat half-shelled oysters and drink some cold soda, but Toby changed the subject and asked me, "Are you getting along with your biological mother?"

"Yes. When I went to see her in Tokyo for the first time, I was nervous, but we got along very well. I was there for a month. I knew Yuri did not abandon me, so my feeling toward her was very amicable. Yuri accepted my position that Mom would be my mother no matter what, but I called her Okaasan in Japanese. She really likes that."

"What is *Okaasan*?"

"It means 'Mother' in Japanese."

"When did you go to Tokyo?"

"It was the summer after my first year in college, a couple of months before 9/11. Yuri paid for my trip. She owns a big company in Tokyo and lives in a penthouse with her housekeeper. She calls Mom often on the phone. I write her instead of talking to her on the phone. She loves to receive my letters because I address her "Dear Okaasan." She said she would treasure every letter I write. Yuri paid my tuition for college and law school. She loves to spoil me with her generous allowance. I told her since I got a job, I don't need the allowance anymore, but she is still sending me the allowance."

"How do you feel about having two mothers?"

"Wonderful. They are equally the nicest mothers. Mom and Yuri are like sisters. They are legally sisters-in-law. When they talk on the phone, mostly they talk about me. Oh, let me tell you something that happened in the sushi bar in Tokyo. Yuri was ordering all kinds of sushi for me to eat because I loved to eat sushi. They were expensive, but she did not care because she wanted to spoil me. When I told her that Mom had to count how much money she had before ordering sushi at the Japanese restaurant in Atlanta, Yuri could not stop sobbing in front of me. I was long puzzled."

Toby said, "Probably Yuri felt sorry for your Mom who lost her family and fortune. Besides, she had to raise the baby alone by counting every penny. She probably wished she could share some of her fortune with your mom if she knew where you were. That was probably why she could not stop sobbing."

I nodded. I thought Toby's explanation was very kind and moving. Toby Gordon was very understanding and genuinely a nice person.

Chapter 28
Became a Lawyer

I did not know how long we sat on the bench, but I felt thirsty and hungry.

"By the way, Toby, how is Sharon doing in Washington, DC?"

"She has a nice job in the FBI forensic department. I went to see her in her office. It is very impressive. The forensic department analyzes DNA of any kinds—blood, hair samples, skins, fingernails, and any sample of fibers. They also analyze fingerprint, footprint, shoeprint, tire tracks, bullets, and many other evidences collected from the crime scenes. Some countries would ask them to analyze their complicated evidences too. It is an advanced science in criminal justice. She works on the front line of forensic science. She said because of forensic science, many crimes could be solved accurately. Some unsolved cold cases could be solved through forensic examinations."

"How is her boyfriend? Did he finish his medical school?"

Toby hesitated for a minute, but said, "I think he did, but Sharon discovered that he was fooling around with a nurse in the hospital, so she made him move out. When I visited her, he had already moved out of Sharon's apartment. She said he directly moved into his lover's apartment. She was heartbroken and angry, but she was glad I visited her. She hugged me many times like I was still her little kid brother."

"I thought they were getting married after his medical school."

"I thought so too. Sharon wasted a chunk of her life for him. She told me all about her deceitful live-in boyfriend, but she said my visit did something good for her because she did not feel sad anymore. During my visit, she took some time off from her work, showed me around the city, took me to the different monuments, and ate dinner at the nicest restaurants. While eating dinner, she often talked about how wonderful the times she had with you and me. Sharon was genuinely happy to see me. I went there to check on the law school I applied, but it was too expensive for me, so I had to come home."

"Do you think Sharon would come back to North Georgia some day?"

"I don't think so. She is planning to finish her PhD while working. She was planning to get a smaller apartment so she can save some money."

"Do your parents know what happened to Sharon?"

"Yes. Sharon wanted me to tell them about it, so I did. They looked worried, but I told them Sharon has a great job as a forensic scientist and planning to finish her PhD while working. They finally looked relieved."

Toby held my hand and murmured with his moist eyes. "Lily, I won't fool around with anybody, so do not worry about me. I love you very much."

I nodded and said, "I love you too, Toby."

We held each other's hands and watched the river obliviously. Everything seemed to be quiet including the river flow.

"Toby, I am getting hungry. Are you hungry?"

Toby nodded. We decided to walk down toward Bourbon Street to Jake's favorite seafood restaurant. Toby had never eaten raw oysters before, but he wanted to try.

However, we learned that all the restaurants in the French Quarter or in New Orleans stopped serving raw oysters because Katrina contaminated the oyster beds around New Orleans. It would take at least two years to clean the oyster beds, so we decided to eat ham sandwiches with a cup of gumbo.

Toby liked gumbo by saying, "New Orleans must make the best gumbo." I nodded. He wants to pay for the lunch, but I reminded him that I am the wealthy person who does not know what to do with the money. He smiled and thanked me for lunch. In fact, I have saved a lot of money, many thanks to Yuri. I also own many money trees that were planted with the help of Jake.

We walked toward Jackson Square. I showed him the inside of St. Louise Cathedral. I also wanted to show him some street performances such as mime actors, magicians, jazz musicians, but no music, no performers, not even palm readers were there.

We stopped at Café Du Monde across from Jackson Square. We ordered some beignets with coffee. There were not many people, but the café was opened. I wiped Toby's chin with napkin because the white powder was on his chin. He wiped my chin too.

I gave Toby a history lesson of Café Du Monde—the café was established in 1862 by a French family named Fernandez. The entire family worked generation after generation and became well-known to the visitors over many decades. The café survived from the fierce hurricanes and floods since the establishment. All the visitors to New Orleans are told to visit Café Du Monde to taste French doughnuts called beignets. It opens twenty-four hours a day year-round.

We bought some beignets to go for my family and then hopped back on a streetcar, and got off in front of the beauty queen's house. I told Toby that house was the one the crooks stole from Mom. The house had no sign of repair yet. Nevertheless, the debris were picked up from the yard; probably the neighborhood cleanup team did it.

We walked home one block. Jake was busy preparing dinner. I put a bag of beignets on the kitchen table and started helping Jake. Toby was washing his clothes in the laundry room and ironing some of his shirts.

Mom and Tom came home. They told us they drove to Biloxi and saw all the devilish sights of the city. Tom said Katrina's fury was something that the residents of Biloxi would never forget. The recovery might take from ten to twenty years.

At the dinner table, Mom made a happy announcement—Toby's acceptance to the law school. She told Toby to register by paying the tuition by Monday. The school would be open the next week. She repeatedly said if he did not have enough money, she was going to help him. I volunteered too, but Toby said he has enough money in the bank in North Georgia, so he would write a check.

*   *   *

The first day of my work, I was extremely nervous. Mom checked my business clothes, high-heeled shoes, my hair, makeup, my posture, and smiles as though I was a kindergarten child on the first day of school. I used a large handbag to put my laptop, a notebook, several pens, and a bag of lunch with a bottle of water.

Mom and Tom make breakfast every morning and Jake makes a lunch bag by putting fresh sandwich, apple or orange, and a bottle of water for each of us. He knows his contribution would save a lot of money and time for his family. Now Toby is one of his family.

The DA's secretary was supposed to meet me at the lobby. While waiting, I read a pamphlet on the table that had the DA's message: "It is the mission of the Orleans Parish District Attorney's office to represent the interests of the State of Louisiana, to advocate for the victims of crimes, to protect public safety, and to uphold justice in an honest and ethical manner. This should be accomplished through the fair, effective, and the efficient prosecution of offenders of the law. The District Attorney's office is committed to being responsive to the needs of victims, witnesses, children, law enforcement agencies, and the citizens of this great community."

I was impressed by the message. The word *county* is used throughout the United States, except Louisiana. In Louisiana, the word *parish* is used to signify the county community. Since the Louisiana Purchase two centuries ago, the word *parish* remained in Louisiana for districting the local government. There are seven parishes in Metro New Orleans.

Finally, a middle-aged woman in high-heeled shoes came looking for me. She called my name and another girl's name, and gestured to us to follow her. After we went through the metal detector, we got on an elevator to the third floor, walked a long hallway to the district attorney's office.

Keiko Palmer

We were to meet the Orleans Parish District Attorney first. A tall and gray-haired man in the office welcomed us. The United States flag and Louisiana state flag were on the wall behind his desk. He smiled with tanned face that probably came from his outdoor activities.

He came from behind his desk and shook hand with each of us. His secretary stated our background such as law school and experiences. The other girl had four years of legal experience under a defense attorney, but I had none. She read my writing in the application—why I wanted to work in the DA's office. He nodded as though he agreed or liked my statement.

He said, "Welcome, hope you would like to work with us as prosecutors. If you have any questions, feel free to ask me." He shook our hands again before we left his office.

Again, the secretary gestured to us to follow her. When we came to the room that looked like a gathering room or a break room, she introduced us to several lawyers. They offered us some coffee, but we declined.

We walked farther to the very end of the hallway. At the last door, she inserted a key to open it. The room was large with wall-to-wall bookshelves with tons of case study books that reminded me of the reference room in the university library. The secretary said that we were to share the room for a while until some rooms would become available. She told us to rearrange the desks if we wanted, and then she gave a door key to each and left.

We like the way two desks were facing the door, so I let her choose a desk first and I took the one left. Each desk had an upright computer.

The large workstation behind our desks had a printer, a copier, a fax machine, a telephone, two file cabinets, and other small office tools. Some foam coffee cups and a roll of paper towels were there too.

After we were situated, we introduced each other as Angela Thornton and Lily Dubois. Angela said she worked under a defense attorney for four years, but she was so tired of defending prostitutes, pimps, Johns, hard-core criminals, and thieves. She did not like it because those criminals would lie, cheat, and bribe. She felt she was getting dirty just as those criminals were, so she decided to quit. Now she hopes she could prosecute those crooks for a change and put them where they belong.

Angela looks very attractive. When she smiles, her friendly eyes come with it. Today, she is wearing a pair of high-heeled shoes just like mine. We both are about the same height. Her brownish skin is very smooth.

She was born and grew up in New Orleans. She finished her undergraduate degree in one of the Ivy League schools in Boston with a scholarship. Her law school was in the same school, and she completed it with a scholarship as well.

I told her that I just graduated from the law school in New Orleans and being a prosecutor has been my dream, but I had no experience.

She said with a smile, "Every lawyer would start from no experience, but sooner or later, you would have tons of experiences because there are too many crooks in this world."

Angela and her family were evacuated to Houston for two weeks. As her house was on a slightly elevated property, there was no water damage, but some shingles were blown away from the roof. Her uncles came to put up new shingles to make her modest house livable again.

She bought a house when she became a lawyer and let her mother and sister live with her. As they all work, they divide the living expenses three ways.

I told her that we stayed in North Georgia for a week and our house was all right too. When I tried to tell her more about my family, the secretary put a boxful of case folders on my desk and told us to read and familiarize all of the cases because we might have to be in one of the prosecution teams. She also told us to have a one-hour lunch break at noon.

There were about ten folders in the box, so we took five folders each. We started reading all the documents, forms, letters, handwritten reports, the eyewitnesses' or criminals' handwritten descriptions or confessions. Their penmanship was so bad that I thought I needed a pair of glasses. My head started hurting. Angela Thornton said she rather wanted to observe the cases in the court instead of reading the cases. She, too, looked exhausted.

At lunchtime, Angela came back with a bag of potato chips and avowed she would bring lunch every day because she could not find any eating places in the building, except junk food in a snack machine. I told her I would share my sandwich. I was going to share a bottle of water too, but Angela brought a cup of coffee from the break room.

After I washed my hands in the restroom in the hall, I divided the sandwich in half and placed the half on Angela's paper towel. She halved the bag of potato chips with me.

She really liked Jake's sandwich. I shared an apple by cutting it half with a plastic knife. She thanked me several times with her friendly smile. I really liked her frankness and friendliness. I felt as though we were bonded.

In the afternoon, while we were reading the cases, Angela Thornton exclaimed, "Lily Dubois, do you know anybody named Jeffery Dubois? You have the same last name."

I was stunned, but pretended, "No. What are you reading?"

"This is a grand larceny and murder case. I read the newspaper article probably six months ago. It was about him. I was shocked because my boss and I knew Jeffery Dubois. He came to our office two or three times to bail out a prostitute named Maria Sanchez. He brought cash. The prostitute was a young Spanish-speaking girl from Puerto Rico. After he paid for her bail, he gave us some generous fees. He did that every time he bailed her out. We did not know his name, but knew his face."

Her chair was turned toward me. Her long legs were crossed elegantly like a well-trained lawyer. I crossed my legs just like Angela and listened to her attentively. Well, I was actually crossing my legs as a newly learned thing of the day. As Jake says, I am supposed to learn many new things at work every day since I am a brand-new lawyer.

Angela continued, "The newspaper article came with his photo as one of the FBI's most wanted fugitives. Then we learned his name. My boss was looking for Maria Sanchez for some time because she owed him a thousand dollars, but we could not find her. Her prostitute friend who shared a room with Maria Sanchez said she left to marry a wealthy man in Grand Cayman some time ago."

"Do you think someone wealthy could be Jeffery Dubois?"

"My boss and I thought so too, but Jeffery Dubois was much older than Maria Sanchez, so we were not sure, but we knew she moved to Grand Cayman, one of the Cayman Islands."

"Did your boss find her?"

"No. She was long gone. Her friend did not hear from her at all after she left."

"Angela, do you think we could work for the lead prosecutor of this case? I am very interested in this case because he has the same last name as mine."

I thought the superpower above me recognized me and gave me the opportunity to catch the criminals who killed my family. I could not let the opportunity slip away.

"Let me see who the lead prosecutor is… I found it!"

Angela brought the folder to me. The lead prosecutor was listed as David Simpleton, and the understudy prosecutor was Antonio Romano.

"Lily, personally, I am very interested in this case too because I met Jeffery Dubois two or three times. I want to find out if he is really the thief and murderer they say he is. Lily, we should work for David Simpleton before anybody does. This is a jury case. I had never done a jury case. I only bailed out some sleazy criminals. Let's talk to David Simpleton." I nodded several times with a big smile. Angela would never know the meaning of my big smile.

"I saw the name of David Simpleton on the door in this hall. Lily, let's go see him together."

The door of David Simpleton was half-opened. We knock on the door.

"Hi, Mr. Simpleton, may we come in?"

He gestured to us to come in. The tall man who was somewhat bald-headed stood up behind his desk. He looked very friendly.

"Mr. Simpleton, I am Angela Thornton. This is Lily Dubois. We are new employees. While we were reviewing some cases, we came to the Jeffery Dubois's case. We came here to see if you could put us in your prosecution team. We are very much interested in working with you."

David Simpleton said, "I have never had anyone came forward to help me before. I am the one who usually solicits to get some help in this office. Yes. I could use you both. As soon as we capture those fugitives, we will start the juror selection. In the meantime, we need to gather all the evidences including interviews, documents, FBI reports, arrest warrants, and so forth. The FBI is working very hard to locate Jeffery Dubois and Nancy Dubois. They both will be tried in the same court."

"Whatever you need, Lily and I will get them for you."

"Okay, thank you. May I call you Angela and Lily?"

"Yes, sir." We both nodded several times.

We were told to brief with him each morning. When we went back to the room, it was time to go home.

I felt guilty not being truthful with Angela Thornton, but I was elated thinking that Jeffery Dubois might be found soon in Grand Cayman. I could hardly wait to see Tom and Mom.

At that night, I told my family including Toby everything about my first day in the DA's office, sharing a room with Angela Thornton who, too, was newly hired, but she had four years of legal experience under a defense attorney.

Finally, I told them Angela Thornton knew Jeffery Dubois because he used to bail out a prostitute named Maria Sanchez several times anonymously. Maria Sanchez moved to Grand Cayman to marry a wealthy man. Angela and her boss thought the wealthy man was Jeffery Dubois. Tom thanked me and said he would be meeting an FBI agent the next day.

Chapter 29
The Trial

Because of Angela Thornton's information, the FBI captured Jeffery Dubois, seized his bank account in Grand Cayman, and he was extradited to New Orleans. Maria Sanchez was sent back to Puerto Rico, and Jeffery's house in Grand Cayman was seized. When he came to New Orleans, his bail bond was denied, so he had to wait for the trial in jail.

I felt guilty for not being honest with Angela and Mr. Simpleton, but I was determined to be in the prosecution team with them so I could help prosecute Jeffery Dubois and Nancy Saunders once and for all.

If Mr. Simpleton found out my relationship to the plaintiff, Michelle Dubois, he might remove me from his team. I did not want that. For all my life, I wanted to prosecute those crooks myself. That was why I became a lawyer. Mom and Tom understood that, so they pretended they did not know me even though they saw me in the DA's office.

Now the beauty queen became one of the most wanted fugitives. The FBI could not locate her. David Simpleton did not have any choice but to dismantle his team until her capture.

Angela and I worked separately under the different lead prosecutors. Mom and Tom patiently waited for the beauty queen's arrest. I was somewhat frustrated because it was taking too long to find her. However, in the meantime, I was getting many jury experiences as a prosecutor.

Almost a year later, the beauty queen was finally found in Canada. The border authority notified the FBI. She was immediately extradited to New Orleans. They put her in jail this time so she could not escape. Her aunt was arrested for aiding a fugitive, but she was released on bond.

The mansion on St. Charles Avenue and the property in Biloxi were long seized by the government. The accountant, Joseph Miller, was found in Canada soon after Jeffery Dubois was extradited a year ago, but he had to wait at home until the trial starts. He would be on the witness stand to answer some questions.

David Simpleton again regrouped his team. Angela and I were to meet with him in his office every day. The juror selection was scheduled. The judge was assigned. The media was in frenzy.

Angela and I worked hard. We went to the police department, the bondsman's office, the local FBI office to gather the necessary documents, also went to the parish archive to get a copy of the property registry, and contacted the border authority in Canada and asked them to fax a written statement of the beauty queen's arrest in detail. By then, we had many evidences to exhibit for the prosecution side.

The juror selection began. Angela Thornton and I helped select the jurors. As I made a mental note on each juror, I was able to tell which jurors could be picked out for the prosecution side.

The trial began on the following day after the juror selection was completed. Jeffery Dubois and the beauty queen sat separately with their own lawyers. Amy Dubois was sitting behind them at the first row of the spectator's seat. She was not talking to either of her parents, and she looked distraught.

Mom and Tom sat behind the lead prosecutor and the understudy. Angela and I sat against the wall closer to the prosecution side. We were to observe the defendants and the jurors. We were also to assist the team in the courtroom. If they needed something such as setting up an easel for some enlarged documents, we did it very quickly.

The courtroom was filled with the spectators who were all in business clothes. The media could set up cameras in court inconspicuously.

Jeffery Dubois lost a lot of weight, looked pale and sickly, probably a year of imprisonment did not agree with him. The beauty queen still looked stunning, but lost a lot of weight as well. Now she looked like a bamboo stick, her hair was somewhat disarrayed, and her porcelain skin looked rather yellowish.

When the beauty queen saw Tom sit beside Mom, she looked startled. Apparently, she did not know her ex-husband, Tom, married Alan's sister.

When the jurors walked in, everybody stood up including the judge. The judge told the spectators not to make any comments verbally or with body language—absolutely no noise and no obvious movements. The judge also instructed the jurors to be alert at all times, follow courtroom instructions, and use the best common sense or best judgment to bring justice to the court.

The defense attorney of Jeffery Dubois came to the podium in front of the jurors and delivered the opening statement.

"Ladies and gentlemen of the jury, my client Jeffery Dubois became the sole beneficially of the Dubois fortune twenty-seven years ago. The probate court examined the authenticity of the will and the death certificates of Jefferson, Marie, and Alan Dubois. The will of Jefferson and Marie Dubois clearly stated Jeffery Dubois and Alan Dubois were the co-beneficiaries. However, since Alan Dubois died in an airplane crash along with his parents, Jeffery Dubois became the surviving beneficiary. Since no one came forward to dispute the will, the probate court awarded Jeffery Dubois with the Dubois fortune. It was legal. As his lawyer, I am going to prove to you that Jeffery Dubois is neither a thief nor a murderer. Thank you."

The beauty queen's defense lawyer spoke. "Ladies and gentlemen of the jury, my client Nancy Saunders Dubois simply wrote the will because the owners of the Dubois Import Company asked her to do so. Their instruction was specific. They wanted her to add the irrevocable trust clause for their beneficiaries so they could avoid some of the inheritance taxes. After she wrote the will, the policyholders, Jefferson and Marie Dubois, signed the will with their sound minds. Unfortunately, the policyholders passed away, leaving Jeffery Dubois as the sole beneficiary. My client Nancy Saunders did not benefit from the Dubois fortune whatsoever. Therefore, I will prove to you the innocence of my client from any allegations that the state imposed upon her. Thank you."

Now the lead prosecutor, David Simpleton, spoke. "Ladies and gentlemen of the jury, you are here to find out the truth of the crime that happened twenty-seven years ago. You are also here to examine all the evidences that the state provides. We have already provided three incriminating evidences as exhibit 1, 2, 3 on the table. These evidences came from Paula Smith Dubois. Normally, she should testify as a witness in front of you, but sadly, she is no longer with us. She was killed in a car explosion several years ago."

He paused for a few seconds.

"Because of her passing, I would like to introduce her written testimony in this court. This case had neither a witness nor an evidence for twenty-five years, but after her death, her son delivered the evidence to the plaintiff, Michelle Dubois, who is the only surviving child of Jefferson and Marie Dubois."

He paused again.

"Because of no witnesses, this case requires your logical thinking and close examination of the evidences that the state provides. Exhibit 4 is a copy of the property registry of Jefferson and Marie Dubois thirty years ago. The state already investigated the authenticity of the signatures of Jefferson and Marie Dubois. The signatures on the irrevocable will did not match with the registry signatures. Therefore, the state concluded the irrevocable will was forged. This means the entire will is fraudulent including the irrevocable trust clause. Jeffery Dubois and Nancy Saunders committed a crime on writing a fraudulent document."

He paused and looked at the jurors to see if they were paying attention. Jeffery Dubois was stone-faced. The beauty queen looked somewhat defeated.

"Ladies and gentlemen of the jury, if you want Jeffery Dubois to be the sole beneficiary of the Dubois fortune, what would you do? Please remember, no will can be effective unless the policyholder of the will dies. Those defendants are trained lawyers. They know all about the wills, legal maneuvering, and many other legal things including a perfect crime."

David Simpleton glanced at Jeffery and the beauty queen, and continued. "If the defendants wanted the irrevocable will to be effective, what do you think they would do? They must plan to eliminate those three in the will so Jeffery Dubois could become the sole beneficiary. Elimination has to be inconspicuous or rather look like an accident. Nancy Saunders served coffee to Jefferson and Marie every morning, so she was able to put some kind of poison in their coffee to make them sick. Then Jeffery Dubois made an emergency appointment with CDC in Atlanta for a possible poisoning."

David Simpleton paused for a few second.

"Knowing Alan as a pilot, they went to the airfield to rent a Cessna for Alan. Michelle Dubois drove her parents and brother to the airport. The defendants were already there. They looked worried and deeply concerned. Why do you think they were there earlier than those three? They could've given them a ride instead of calling Michelle at school in the middle of her class. Please think. Yes. They needed time to tamper with the aircraft."

He paused for a second again.

"According to Paula Smith, her ex-husband is a mechanical genius who could fix cars, airplanes, bicycles, and any mechanical devices. His foster father was an airplane mechanic who used to take Jeffery Dubois to work and taught him all about airplanes. He knows how to make an airplane crash look like an accident. Even the FAA was fooled."

David Simpleton again glanced at Jeffery Dubois. Jeffery looked somewhat defeated.

"After the deaths of three members of the Dubois family, they were able to use the irrevocable will. Jeffery Dubois took the irrevocable will and the death certificates of the three deceased to the probate court. Do you see how they stole the Dubois fortune legally? If Paula Smith did not copy those wills, they should be still enjoying the lucrative Dubois fortune."

The beauty queen put her head down as though she has completely surrendered.

"Their meticulous plan was so meticulous that the probate court was even fooled. They almost committed a perfect crime. Well, actually they did for twenty-five years and almost got away with murder until we got the evidence. Ladies and gentlemen of the jury, the state is asking you to deliver a guilty verdict on each count—the grand larceny and three counts of murder. Thank you."

The courtroom was very quiet. The judge gave an hour break for lunch. Everybody stood up for the jurors when they left the courtroom. The beauty queen was escorted to the back door with a handcuff on, so was Jeffery. Their lawyers remained in the courtroom, seemingly discussing their cooperative strategy. Amy Dubois disappeared.

We gathered around David Simpleton. He was asking us who would testify next in the afternoon. We gave him the schedule and praised him of his opening statement. He smiled and looked confident.

The court resumed the afternoon session. The defense attorney of Jeffery Dubois called Amy Dubois for her father's defense, but as she was sobbing uncontrollably, the defense attorney had to withdraw her. I really felt sorry for her because she did not ask to be born between those criminals. I hoped she would be strong enough to survive the trial. I felt like going over there to embrace her. She put her head down on the rail all afternoon. Jeffery Dubois turned and looked very concerned, but her mother did not even turn to look at her.

The beauty queen's aunt was called to the stand. She defended her niece by saying how generous and kind she has been. Because of her generosity, she was able to live in an exclusive mansion on St. Charles Avenue and received a generous allowance from her niece every month. She believed her niece was physically threatened by Jeffery Dubois, so she had no choice but to put his name as beneficiary in the will of Jefferson and Marie Dubois.

David Simpleton called the accountant, Joseph Miller, to the stand. He told the jury that Jeffery Dubois asked him to do two things every month—to wire a large sum of money to a bank in Grand Cayman and send a money order of alimony to Jeffery's ex-wife, Paula Dubois. When the company was sold, he was given a substantial amount of money and was told to disappear somewhere faraway. So he moved to his wife's hometown in Canada.

David Simpleton asked, "Did you ever suspect Jeffery Dubois stole the company and other Dubois fortune?"

"No. I did not because his company had his last name—the Dubois Import Company. He was a very smart businessman, and the company was very profitable."

"Was his wife Nancy Saunders Dubois allowed to access the company account? Were they co-owners of the company?"

"Oh, no. The company solely belonged to Jeffery Dubois. His wife was prohibited to see the company bank account or the spreadsheet. She was just a hired company lawyer and did the legal letter writings for the company or calculating the tariff—Jeffery and I did the company operation."

"How was their relationship?"

"I guess they were all right, but never socialized with anybody. My wife invited them for dinner on many occasions, but they always made excuses. I knew they lived in Biloxi, but never been to their house. His wife did not like me and never spoke much to me. She treated me like a rival at work, but her legal work was meticulously good."

"Do you think they had a prenuptial agreement before their marriage?"

"I really do not know. Jeffery was very secretive about many things, but he was always kind to me and trusted me."

"Why did you think he was secretive? Did you suspect him for doing something illegal? That was why he was secretive?"

"No. That was just his personality."

"When did you stop sending the alimony to Paula Dubois?"

"Shorty before he sold the company. He told me there's no more need to send money orders to Paula Smith. He did not explain, but I thought either she died or got married."

"How much do you think he saved in the bank in Grand Cayman?"

"A lot, probably over two hundred million."

"Do you know a prostitute named Maria Sanchez?"

"Maria? Yes. I met her in the office. She came several times to thank Jeffery for something. Was she a prostitute?"

"Yes."

The defense attorney of Jeffery Dubois questioned Joseph Miller. "You said my client trusted you. Was he also generous and kind to you?"

"Yes, he was very generous to me and my family, especially to my boys. I have three. He used to buy some baseball outfits and other sports gears for my three boys every year. He had two boys and a daughter in Houston, but he had not seen them since his divorce. He missed them a lot, but he said his children did not want to see him."

"Was his wife Nancy Saunders kind to you?"

"She was always hostile toward me as though I was planning to steal the company money. Sometimes, I thought she was suffering from paranoia or some kind of mental illness. She was quiet, moody, and sneaky. One day, she was looking at the company book while I was out for lunch. I told Jeffery about it. He told me to lock the file cabinet and not to leave anything on the desk. Make sure to close the computer when I was out of office."

"So you did not like her?"

Joseph Miller shook his head, but he had to verbalize for the court recorder. "No, sir. I did not like her."

"You know all about the allegation against Jeffery Dubois?"

"Yes. I was told by an FBI agent who came to my house in Canada."

"Do you believe what the allegation says about such a generous man like Jeffery Dubois?"

"No, not Jeffery Dubois, but his wife could plan a grand larceny with her greediness. I think she was the one who planned the whole thing, and Jeffery Dubois was just mesmerized by her beauty and sex."

"Objection!" yelled the defense attorney of the beauty queen.

Joseph Miller was dismissed.

Michelle Dubois was called to the stand by David Simpleton.

"Do you know Jeffery Dubois?"

"Yes, sir."

"How well do you know him?"

"He had worked for my parents for many years as the company lawyer. He was a devoted employee and my parents trusted him. I knew his children and his wife Paula very well."

"Did you know Nancy Saunders?"

"Yes. She also worked for my parents. No, she actually came to work for my brother, Alan."

"How long did you know her?"

"Well, she was my brother's girlfriend for three months in high school. She was very possessive and talking about marriage, so my brother broke up with her, but she kept calling my brother at home, stalking him, and embarrassing him in front of his classmates, so I decided to investigate her background. I found out that she and her aunt were big-time gold diggers. Her aunt had a list of wealthy families' sons who went to the private high school on St. Charles Avenue. Her aunt wanted her niece to marry a son of a wealthy family so they both could be wealthy. I think my brother was their first target."

"Why did your brother hire such a gold digger?"

"He did not know she was a gold digger. I kept the findings to myself. She probably begged to get a job from my brother because she could not find a lawyer's job in New Orleans after moving back from Chicago. My brother was a kindhearted man. He probably hired her temporarily until she could find a real lawyer's job. He did not have an office for her, so he asked Jeffery Dubois to share his office. According to my brother, Nancy did everything to please Alan and my parents, including Jeffery Dubois. She served coffee to them every morning like a maid."

"Why do you think Nancy Dubois turned on your family?"

"I am not quite sure, but I think her ultimate goal was to marry Alan because she loved him. She thought Alan was still single, so she wanted the second chance to capture him, but when she found out Alan was already married, her love probably turned into hate. Her last hope of marrying a son of a wealthy family was forever gone. With her hopeless desperation, she probably wanted to steal the Dubois fortune so she could be wealthy herself once and for all. I think that was how she turned on the Dubois family."

"So you think Nancy Dubois's ultimate goal was to be wealthy?"

"Yes. I think that is usually a gold digger's goal, but I am not sure. Please ask her."

Chapter 30
Delayed Justice

The trial continued. The FBI agents and arresting officers testified. More exhibits were numbered on the table such as Jeffery Dubois's photo on the FBI's most wanted list, his extradition order and alias passport, Nancy Saunders's arrest warrant by the border authority in Canada, and so forth.

Finally, Jeffery Dubois came to the stand. His defense attorney asked questions.

"How long did you work for the Dubois family at that time?"

"For twelve years."

"Did you have a good relationship with Jefferson and Marie Dubois?"

"Yes. We were very close. They trusted me. Their family and my family got together quite often. Marie Dubois used to send many nice birthday gifts to my three children every year. They treated me like their own brother or son."

"Did you want to be wealthy like them?"

"No, sir. We were doing fine financially at that time. Jefferson and Marie paid me well, and my wife was working as a nurse in the hospital. My mother-in-law took care of our small children. We were financially strong and very happy."

David Simpleton cross-examined.

"Did you forge the signatures of Jefferson and Marie on the irrevocable will?"

"Jefferson and Marie let me sign their documents often, especially when they were out of office or on a vacation, so I signed without thinking."

"So you forged their signatures. Did you write the irrevocable will?"

"No. I did not."

"Who wrote that will?"

"My wife Nancy Saunders did."

"Did you know she was planning to steal the Dubois fortune putting your name as a beneficiary?"

"No. I did not."

"If you did not, why did you forge the signatures?"

"I was not thinking when I was asked to sign for Jefferson and Marie."

"Who asked you to sign?"

"Nancy Saunders."

"When did you realize she was up to something?"

"I realized when I was proofreading the will. I noticed the will had my name as co-beneficiary with Alan Dubois. I asked her about it. She said she was doing it just for me because she loved me."

"Did she discuss any details why she wrote such will?"

"No, but she kept saying I have the same last name, no one would know the difference, especially the probate court."

"When she was talking about the probate court, did you realize she was going to eliminate the Dubois family someway so you could be the sole beneficiary?"

"No. I did not."

"Why didn't you ask her to take your name off the will? Are you related to Jefferson and Marie?"

"No. I am not related to the Dubois family. I told her repeatedly that was not ethical, but again she said she was doing it for us because she was pregnant."

"So you became an accomplice because of your child. Did you realize Nancy Saunders's ultimate goal was always to be wealthy?"

"No. I did not know it. I guess I was swept up in the passion of the sex and the most beautiful woman on earth was carrying my child. Nothing mattered at that time. I was madly in love with her. I did whatever she wanted me to do."

"So you were madly in love and your ethical thinking was paralyzed, is that a fair assumption?"

"I guess so."

"Nancy married you because you got everything instead of her. Did you share the so-called loot with Nancy Saunders?"

"No."

"Why not?"

"The probate court gave me everything. I was the sole beneficiary."

"Don't you think that was why she married you because she wanted the half of the loot as your wife?"

"I guess so. She threatened me to hand over the Dubois fortune several times because the grand larceny was her idea. She made the blueprint. By then, I realized I was used by her because of my last name. It was not love. It was her greed. I was stupid to be brainwashed. It was too late to reverse what I had done, but I still wanted to marry her because she was pregnant with my child. By then I was wide awake."

"Did you have a prenuptial agreement before you married her so she could not touch the loot?"

"Yes. I was afraid if I married her without a prenuptial agreement, I could be poisoned just like she poisoned Jefferson and Marie."

"Objection," yelled the defense attorney of Nancy Saunders Dubois.

"Overruled," yelled the judge.

David Simpleton continued.

"Was your wife angry?"

"Yes. She was very angry."

"Where did you live at the time of your marriage?"

"In the antebellum mansion in Biloxi."

"That was one of your loot, wasn't it?"

"Yes."

"What did you do with the mansion in New Orleans?"

"I let her aunt live there. Because of it, she agreed to sign the prenuptial agreement. If she was not pregnant, I did not think I would have married her. I married her because of the child."

David Simpleton changed the subject.

"What kind of relationship did you and your ex-wife, Paula Smith Dubois, have after the divorce?"

"She hated me and was jealous of my becoming wealthy with my new wife. Because of her animosity or jealousy, I have not seen my children since my divorce."

"Did she extort from you?"

He nodded several times, but David Simpleton told him to say yes or no for the court recorder as well as for the jurors.

"Yes."

"Why didn't you report to the authority?"

"I cannot answer that."

"Why did you tell Joseph Miller that he did not have to send the money order to Paula Dubois anymore? Did anybody tell you Paula Dubois was dead or killed?"

"Objection," yelled the defense attorney of Jeffery Dubois.

David Simpleton's cross-examination ended.

Before the judge dismissed the jurors, he told them not to discuss the case with anybody, especially among the jurors.

I was exhausted. We went back to David Simpleton's office and briefed. We told him he did a great job cross-examining, but he said he almost crossed the jurisdiction. The death of Paula Dubois should be the Houston DA's job. He was glad Jeffery Dubois's defense attorney objected. He said he must concentrate on the grand larceny and three counts of murder, nothing else. David Simpleton looked exhausted.

Angela and I went back to our office and rested. Angela brought two cups of coffee from the break room, and we waited for five o'clock so we could go home.

The next day, after the oath, Amy Dubois came to the stand. She was calm this time. Probably, she had no tears left for her parents, but just shame.

Jeffery Dubois's defense lawyer spoke.

"Are you the only child of your parents, Jeffery Dubois and Nancy Dubois?"

"Yes, sir."

"How was your childhood like?"

"Normal as other children, I guess."

"Were you close to your mother or your father?"

"To my father."

"Why is that?"

"My father took time to talk to me, took me for shopping, walked in the park, studied in the library, sometimes we ate lunch together and saw movies. He bought me a tricycle when I was a toddler and then a bicycle. He taught me how to ride them. He was the best father."

"What kind of relationship did you have with your mother?"

"She was all right, but she did not allow any of my friends in our house. In fact, she did not invite anybody to the house. She seemed to be paranoid for some reason."

"Your parents got along well?"

"I guess they did, but I had never seen their affection when I was growing up."

"Were you shocked to learn about your parents' arrests?"

"Yes."

"When you went to college in Chicago, who took you there to get situated?"

"My father did. He set up my bank account there by putting enough money to pay for my tuition and apartment. He told me to study hard and be somebody important."

"Did your father tell you the house in New Orleans would be yours in the future?"

"Yes, but my mother changed the ownership to hers when my father disappeared."

"What do you do for living in Chicago?"

"I work for the city hospital in Chicago as a registered nurse."

"Do you believe what your father said in his testimony? Your mother made the blueprint of the grand larceny and murder?"

"Objection," yelled the defense attorney of Nancy Dubois.

The court recessed until tomorrow. We briefed with David Simpleton. In the meantime, we heard Nancy Dubois deny her rights to be questioned in the court the next day. Therefore, David Simpleton asked us to write a closing statement.

After we finished writing a two-page closing statement by integrating all the facts from the testimonies and cross-examinations, we let Antonio Romano and David Simpleton read it. They praised how observant we were and the fact-oriented write-up we did. They said we both could be great prosecutors in the future, and our closing statement was much better than they could write. Angela and I looked at each other and smiled.

The next day, Tom, Mom, and Jake sat behind David Simpleton and Antonio Romano. The verdict could be unpredictable, but I was very sure the jury would deliver the guilty verdict, which the state and my family would want.

Jeffery Dubois wore a suit and a tie, and looked clean. The beauty queen wore a nice dress and her hair was ponytailed. Her aunt and Amy Dubois sat behind the defense team.

When the jurors walked in, everybody stood up. The judge warned the jurors, "After you hear the closing statements, you go back and discuss the verdict. You only have two answers to the charged items: not guilty or guilty. Always use your best common sense and best judgment. Let's hear the closing statement."

The defense lawyer of Jeffery Dubois said, "The defense rest," so said the defense lawyer of Nancy Dubois. They gave up on defending their clients. David Simpleton delivered his powerful closing statement with his excellent enunciation, posture, and eye contact. I could not believe the closing statement Angela and I wrote was so moving and powerful.

The jurors went back to the sequestered room. Jeffery Dubois and the beauty queen were handcuffed and taken back to their jail cells. Amy Dubois was watching them leave. Their lawyers were fast gone.

When we came back to the room, I felt exhausted. Angela went out to get some coffee for us. After we ate lunch with coffee, Angela left the room to run some errands, but she said she would be right back.

I stood up at the window and thought about me with Yuri and Alan. If those crooks did not kill my father and grandparents, I could have lived with Yuri and my father, Alan, in Biloxi and they could have given me many more of my siblings.

Tom could have married Michelle when she was still young so they could have had many of their own children—my cousins. My American grandparents could have enjoyed many grandchildren.

Probably my Japanese grandparents could have settled in New Orleans with us and enjoyed their grandchildren including me. I know I could have been very close to them by speaking the Japanese language that I could have learned from my Japanese grandmother, who was a schoolteacher. I could have softened my Japanese grandfather's heart by loving him a lot.

I actually cried softly by watching the parking lot from the window. I was overwhelmed with the feeling of hatred against the beauty queen. I felt like slapping her porcelain face and screaming at her by saying, "How dare you kill my father and my grandparents!"

The justice is twenty-seven years late, but it is better than not having any justice at all. "What goes around comes around" is long overdue, but it is finally arriving.

Three hours later, the jurors delivered a *guilty* verdict on each count. Jeffery Dubois was not spared at all. They both were equally guilty of the grand larceny and the three counts of murder.

Mom and Tom were embracing. Jake was shaking hand with David Simpleton and Antonio Romano. Angela and I stood side by side and watched them from where we were. TV cameras zoomed around the courtroom.

The judge would sentence them in a few days. After being sentenced, each defendant would be sent to an undisclosed prison facility separately. The state did not ask for a death sentence; instead, they asked for a life sentence without any parole.

The government should assess the seized bank accounts and the seized properties. After deducting all kinds of taxes and fees, the probate court should award the remaining assets to Michelle Dubois. However, Michelle Dubois must provide her birth certificate and her parents' original will to satisfy the probate court.

Amy Dubois stood in tears and watched her parents leave. None of her parents turned around to say goodbye. The aunt was watching them in tears too. She held Amy's hand and left the courtroom in silence. I really thought Amy Dubois should stay away from that big-time gold digger aunt.

I felt sorry for Amy Dubois. Being born of the beauty queen was not her fault. I wanted to talk to her, but I realized it was not the right time. I wanted to give her the phone number of her stepbrother, Gregory Dubois. He could be a big help for her because she needed somebody to talk with. Gregory Dubois should be very kind and supportive of her.

When I came home, Tom and Mom were already home. Toby was still at work taking Tom's place in the office. I embraced Mom in tears without saying anything for a long time.

In the kitchen, Jake was warming up a pot of gumbo he made yesterday. I set up the table for dinner. Toby came home and congratulated us. He said he saw us on TV.

During dinner, Toby said admiringly that soon he would be standing in the courtroom like me. I told him I did not do anything, but Toby said I looked awesome like a well-trained lawyer in a TV series. I thanked him by throwing a kiss.

Tom said, "As soon as the probate court changes the ownership of the mansion on St. Charles Avenue to Michelle and the property in Biloxi to Lily, we have to clean up and repair some damages. It has been too long since Katrina."

The judge sentenced Jeffery Dubois and Nancy Saunders Dubois each to life without any parole. Additionally, the Houston DA indicted Jeffery and sentenced him to life for the death of Paula Dubois. Therefore, Jeffery Dubois was given two life sentences without any parole. The hired killer was caught in another killing, and eventually he was linked to Jeffery Dubois. The prosecutor was Paula's brother, Edward Smith.

I heard the beauty queen met her mother in prison. She did not know her mother was alive. Her father passed away in a jail cell from cancer. She always believed what her aunt said about her parents many years ago—they were killed in a car accident. They said the beauty queen looks just like her mother with her porcelain skin. That was probably how they found each other in the same prison facility.

The aunt went to Florida to live with her second cousin. It seemed Amy Dubois was smart enough to stay away from the big-time gold digger aunt.

Epilogue

Amy Dubois continued living in Chicago as a nurse. She apparently had suffered from psychological trauma and received some professional help at work.

I found Amy's address in the witness list, so I wrote to her. I gave her the address and phone number of her stepbrother Gregory Dubois that was listed in Mom's address book. In my letter, I introduced myself as Lily Dubois, a lawyer from the DA's office in New Orleans. I also told her that I met her many years ago in Biloxi and ate cookies together.

She wrote me back to thank me for Gregory's address and phone number and remembered me as the "Lily" who gave her some delicious cookies. She was surprised my last name was same as hers, Dubois.

I wrote her back to tell her that Alan Dubois, who was killed in an airplane crash, was my father, but I no longer have any animosity against her parents because now they are serving life sentences. I emphasized that their crimes were nothing to do with her, so she should lift her head up and move on.

She wrote me and apologized for the loss of my father. She mentioned that her stepbrother Gregory was very happy to hear from her and spent a lot of time on the phone to comfort her.

Later, Amy and I exchanged our email addresses. We wrote to each other from time to time. She wrote me about Gregory, who came to see her when he attended a convention in Chicago. It was the first time they met. She would be meeting two other stepsiblings soon. She thanked me again for everything. I felt happy for her because she was no longer alone—her stepsiblings would be with her. In fact, they need each other to forgive their father so they can move on.

The money in Grand Cayman was finally transferred to Mom's bank account in New Orleans. The government took all kinds of taxes, bondsman's charges, lawyer's fees, and some other expenses, but Mom was still a multimillionaire. The first thing she did with the money was to hire a building contractor to renovate the Dubois mansion on St. Charles Avenue.

She discovered that the antique furniture in the basement was untouched. The crooks probably did not know the value of the furniture. Mom said she might donate them to a museum soon.

After the renovation, Tom and Mom decided to live in the Dubois mansion. Jake looked sad, but Mom assured him that they would walk a block to see him often, especially at dinnertime. Mom was hinting something. She gave Jake a house key, told him to walk a block for exercise, and feel free to check their house. Jake nodded with a big smile.

Now Jake faithfully walks to the Dubois mansion every morning for exercise, tidies up their house, waters flowers in the yard, and walks back. He likes to be useful for Tom and Mom as well as for Toby and me because we are considered his family.

At lunchtime, he checks his stock portfolio and mine on his computer while eating lunch. In the afternoon, instead of taking a nap, he climbs the steps up and down many times. After that, he watches MSNBC or CNBC. He loves to read history books and political magazines. When I come home from work, Jake and I prepare dinner for three, or quite often for five.

Tom finally negotiated with the insurance company. They sent a team of workers to clear the debris off his property. After that, they sent a dozen workers to build a new vacation home with bricks this time.

Very few casinos resumed their businesses in Biloxi. People once thought Biloxi was a mecca of the casino business or a resort place, but Katrina wiped out its glory and charms. It might take many more years to revive the city of Biloxi.

Mom was able to transfer the property deed to me as the only surviving child of Alan Dubois by showing my birth certificate. Mom hired some workers to clear my property. When the property became bare, she had tears in her eyes. She probably reminisced about her family or thought about my birthplace that was now gone forever. The Southern oak trees around the property were still standing strong. Mom wanted to build a vacation home for me with her money, but I told her I would rather wait.

Toby was busy studying for the bar exam. I was busy prosecuting some misdemeanor cases with Angela Thornton in front of six jurors. We did the understudy separately with the lead prosecutors.

Angela and I still share the room and eat lunch together almost every day. While eating, we talk about our personal things. She told me all about her boyfriend.

"Lily, my boyfriend is white. His parents are against our relationship because I am black, but we love each other. He is a CPA in a big financial company here. We went to high school together. We were separated when I went to north, but every time I came home, we rekindled our relationship, so we have known each other for a long time. He wants to marry me, but I can't make up my mind."

I told her about my personal things too. "Angela, I'm a mixed race. My biological mother is Japanese and she lives in Japan. Actually, I have two mothers. It is a long story. I will tell you someday."

I was afraid that I might relate my birth secret to Jeffery Dubois's case, so I decided to wait until I feel comfortable telling her the truth. We have an unspoken message among my family members—never to bring up the names of the crooks who murdered my grandparents and my father.

"You don't have any trace of Japanese."

"Well, my mother here usually dyes my hair. Angela, if you love your boyfriend, marry him. Since you both have nice jobs, you should be all right financially. Forget about his parents. Later they would come around. Love always wins."

She nodded. "Lily, do you have a boyfriend?"

"Yes. We have known each other since we were children. After he finishes his law school and when he gets a good job, we might get married."

I did not tell her that Toby was living with us and a year younger than I am. Toby and I've been kissing behind the door whenever he came to see me at my guesthouse. The kissing was the only nurturing method we had.

Nevertheless, one night, I heard a knock on the door and a whisper. "It's Toby. Open the door." I got up and opened the door. He was in pajamas and tiptoed in bare feet.

After shutting the door behind him, he looked hesitant but snuggled into my bed quietly. He looked desperate to hold my body and started caressing me over my pajamas; soon he took off my pajama top, slid down my pajama pants and panties altogether. I was naked. He had never done that before, but I did not resist.

He caressed my buttocks, waist, back, and shoulders softly. When he inserted his tongue in my mouth, my sexual arousal was heightened. I wanted to take off his pajamas too so I could feel his body, but he would not let me. Both of my hands, actually my arms, were pinned under his armpits, yet he kept caressing me.

I felt something very hot and hard between his legs under his pajama pants, and he was stroking his hot object against my stomach. I wanted to touch it, but he shook his head. All of a sudden, he left the room. I was left aroused, but I slept like a baby that night for some reason. Toby came at least once a week in the middle of the night. He did the same thing to arouse my naked body, and then he would disappear in a hurry.

He passed the bar exam and got a job in the DA's office in Jefferson Parish. He no longer had the time to work for Tom, but he was able to help him on the weekends if Tom needed him.

Ms. Norma and Chris Gordon wanted him to come home to North Georgia, but he wanted to practice law in New Orleans. Jake told him he could live in his house as long as he wanted. He thought Toby was going to move out because he got a good job.

One day, Toby called me from his office and said, "Lily, let's unveil our relationship to your family this coming Saturday. I want to invite all of your family to a restaurant in the French Quarter and propose to you. I will explain everything and tell them we are ready to get married. What do you think?"

"Wow! We will be getting married?"

"Yes. Is it all right with you? I love you, Lily."

"Yes. I love you too, Toby."

When Toby came into my bed that night, I did not mind giving him my virginity since we would be getting married soon, but he told me to wait until our wedding night, and again he left in a hurry.

At the restaurant, Jake, Mom, and Tom were ecstatic about our engagement. Toby put a nice diamond ring on my ring finger and kissed me in front of my family for the first time.

Toby explained in front of my family. "Lily has been my love since I was young. She didn't know that, but when I told her that I kept her picture in my pocket and slept with it when I was in Iraq, she instantly fell in love with me. It happened when you folks came to North Georgia after Katrina. We have been in love since. We kept our relationship a secret from you because I was nobody."

Toby's eyes were somewhat moist. "With your help, I was able to finish school and landed a lawyer's job. Being a lawyer was my dream. Lily has been very patient with me and waited for me to be somebody without complaining. If it is all right with you, I would like to marry Lily on her birthday in July. It is only six weeks away."

Jake congratulated us, volunteered to pay for our wedding. In return, he wanted to give me away at the wedding. We all nodded. Mom and Tom volunteered to give us a honeymoon trip somewhere on an island in the Caribbean.

Mom said, "Yuri would be very surprised, but don't worry. I will tell her all about Toby, how handsome and smart a young man he is. Your wedding date on Lily's birthday is a great idea. Yuri would love that. I can hardly wait to see Yuri again. I have not seen her for almost thirty years. I want to show her the new Dubois mansion too."

I emailed Amy Dubois and invited her to my wedding. She was excited and asked me if she could bring Gregory and her boyfriend. She told me her boyfriend knows all about her parents. He works for Gregory in Houston. Actually, Gregory introduced him to Amy when they came to Chicago for a convention. I told her to bring them and, if possible, bring her other stepsiblings too.

Angela was so pleased that she said she would definitely bring her boyfriend to the wedding. All our guests were told not to bring any wedding gifts; instead, they could witness our wedding and enjoy the finger foods and drinks.

When Jake called Toby's parents, they were shockingly elated. Jake invited them to stay in his house before and after the wedding so they could explore the city of New Orleans. When Toby called Sharon, she was overjoyed and said she knew Lily was destined to be her family.

I was wearing a beautiful white wedding dress and Toby was in a tuxedo. At the wedding chapel, Jake gave me away. He looked so proud in a tuxedo. After the ceremony, all of the guests gathered at the reception room and watched us cut the tall wedding cake. The photographer took many pictures of our wedding ceremony and the family portraits with Yuri. Toby was very kind to Yuri and chatted with her from time to time.

Tom was in a tuxedo and supervising the servants replenishing the foods and alcohol drinks. There were plenty of finger foods including sushi. Many tables and chairs were placed in the reception hall so the guests can sit freely to enjoy drinking, eating, and chatting—some rather mingling.

I changed my wedding dress to a short white dress in the room next to the reception room. Toby changed his to a suit with a tie. Our suitcases for the honeymoon trip were already sent to the limousine we rented. I folded my wedding dress and Toby's tuxedo and put them altogether in a large box so Tom could take it home after the reception.

Toby and I held hands and mingled. I saw everybody I invited. Mom invited some of her colleagues from the library. Tom invited all of his employees and their spouses. Jake invited some of his classmates from his high school reunion. Toby invited some of his colleague friends from his work. Everybody seemed to be enjoying the finger foods and alcohol drinks while chatting.

Yuri looked very pretty in a long dress; so did Mom. Sharon looked thin and pretty. Her hair color got lighter just like mine. She just received her PhD. Now she is Dr. Sharon Gordon. She did not bring any date, but she looked very happy.

Toby had already told Sharon about my birth secret, so she knew all about Yuri. Sharon embraced me several times and kissed Toby as though he was still her little kid brother.

Ms. Norma looked young and pretty in a peach-colored long dress. Chris Gordon looked handsome in a tuxedo and resembled Toby a lot. Ms. Norma and Chris Gordon knew about Yuri because Mom had already told them. She explained everything including my birth secret, the grand larceny, the family tragedy, and the guilty verdict of the crooks.

When Amy and her boyfriend came to greet us, they were holding hands and looked very happy. Mom came to embrace Amy without saying anything, but Amy understood what her embrace meant, so she embraced her back. Mom probably tried to tell her that her parents' crimes are nothing to do with her so put her head up and move on.

Gregory brought his siblings who remembered Mom well from the company picnic. Mom was so thankful to Gregory and hugged him like her own brother and kept holding Gregory's hand as though she was thanking him for being her hero. She probably told him if he did not find her, probably no justice came to the Dubois family.

Angela and her boyfriend both looked stunningly handsome. He kept holding Angela's hand as though he was proud to be with Angela. Everybody could tell they were very much in love.

I was glad Angela did not recognize Mom as the plaintiff in the grand larceny and murder case. I was sure she did not recognize Amy Dubois either. As Angela and I have so many jury cases, we cannot recognize any plaintiffs or defendants once trials end.

I was wondering how Amy Dubois and her stepsiblings have been coping with the stigma of their parents so far. I hoped they would be able to bury them somewhere deep and never to bring up their names, just like my family has been doing, so the stigma would disappear from their memories and hopefully from their lives for good.

Yuri would be going back home to Japan in a few days while we would be on the honeymoon trip. I embraced Yuri and thanked her for coming all the way from Japan. Toby embraced her to thank her too.

When we were leaving for the airport, Yuri gave me two envelopes with money—one for the wedding, another one for my birthday, and said, "Happy birthday, Lily!" I saw some tears in her eyes, but she had a big smile on her pretty face. I embraced her tightly and said, "Thank you, Okaasan."

Mom was watching us with a big smile and shouted loudly, "Happy birthday, Lily!" The guests who heard Mom also shouted, "Lily, happy birthday!" We waved to everybody at the door and rode the limousine to the airport.

We flew to San Juan, Puerto Rico, for our honeymoon. We had the most gorgeous hotel room that was facing the beautiful ocean. Tom had reserved the room with the help of his business partner in Puerto Rico.

On our wedding night, Toby caressed and kissed my naked body until I was relaxed, and then he entered me for the first time. When I yelped a little, Toby stopped for a minute, but I told him to continue. He began thrusting vigorously. His performance was so superb that we both moaned at the same time. With his flushed face, he said, "Happy birthday, Lily. I am glad we waited for this moment."

* * *

After our honeymoon trip, we moved to the master bedroom upstairs where Mom and Tom used to occupy. Toby's lovemaking was so powerful and so arousing that my whole body melted each time. He did not disappear any more; instead, he held me with his muscular arms and let me snuggle against his chest.

I became pregnant soon after our honeymoon. Alan was born nine months later. Toby was so delighted to have a baby boy that he volunteered to get up in the middle of the night to change diapers. I took a maternity leave for one year. While staying at home, I got pregnant again, so I extended another year after Marie was born. I stayed home as a homemaker for two years.

Toby was prosecuting many cases. Jake was doing his daily routine to walk for exercise to the Dubois mansion. I was busy taking care of two small children who are a year apart. In the afternoon, after I put the babies in bed for a nap, Jake and I ate lunch together, checked our stock portfolios just as we used to do, and talked about politics a lot.

We were often frustrated with GOP (Grand Old Party—the nickname of the Republican Party) because they seem to be racists. Anything President Obama proposed to the Congress, GOP rejected just because he is black.

Osama bin Laden who masterminded 9/11 to kill three thousand innocent American citizens in 2001 was found and killed on May 1, 2011, almost ten years later by the US military forces under President Obama's command, but the Republicans would not give any credit to him just because he is black.

The notorious dictator of Libya, Muammar Gaddafi was killed on October 20, 2011, by the collective forces of the United Nations. It happened under President Obama's command, but GOP would not give him any credit just because he is black.

GOP's racism toward President Obama is so obvious to the American people as well as to the world. When GOP voted against President Obama's job bill, which was to create four hundred thousand jobs, Jake and I were outraged, so were most of sensible Americans.

Keeping the 9.1 unemployment rate until 2012 is the Republican's conspiracy because they would not want President Obama to be reelected.

However, President Obama is taking the matters to the American people directly himself because America can't wait for GOP to act together to help jobless people in America.

The massive Wall Street protesters known as the 99 percent movement are mostly jobless young Americans. Their demonstrations are so massive in many major cities that GOP is scared and very nervous, but they are still uncooperative with President Obama just because he is black.

The GOP's white supremacy attitude saddens most of American voters including Jake and me. We just hope "What goes around comes around" would arrive at the GOP's own reelection site in 2012 because American voters are not stupid.

Now Alan could walk and talk gibberish. His first word was *Dada*. Toby could not believe what he heard, so he wanted Alan to repeat it, but he gibbered "Dadadadada." Marie could crawl very fast like an alligator. Quite often, she would hide behind the sofa giggling, so Alan could find her.

I could afford to stay home to take care of my babies, but I want to go back to work. I want to find out who I am and what I want for my life. Staying home was not my dream. Toby understood how I felt about my career, so he avowed to help me with childcare and chores around the house.

I found a professional babysitter who was recommended by the Nanny Services. The young babysitter speaks with a British accent and loves to be with young children. Jake likes the babysitter because she knows Cajun cooking.

When I went back to work, I was able to share the room with Angela again. We ate lunch together in the room and chatted just as we used to do. Angela moved into her boyfriend's apartment; she said if she becomes pregnant, she would marry him.

Whenever Ms. Norma and Chris Gordon come to stay in Tom's vacation home in Biloxi, we take some time off to join them. Toby rents a boat and takes Tom, Jake, and Chris Gordon for a fishing expedition all day. Mom, Ms. Norma, and I take the children to the beach and teach them how to swim. Whenever the fishermen bring enough fish for dinner, we clean them, grill the big ones, and fry the small ones.

Mom sent Yuri many pictures of her grandchildren. I wrote Yuri a very serious letter recently, saying that she could retire in New Orleans or Biloxi once she decided to sell her business in Tokyo. I reminded her that she does not have any relatives in Tokyo, but she has many here in New Orleans—her grandchildren, Alan Gordon and Marie Gordon, her child, Lily Dubois Gordon, her son-in-law,

Toby Gordon, her sister-in-law, Michelle Dubois Rousseau, and her husband, Tom, and Tom's father, Jake, so she would never be lonely.

I also told her that the property in Biloxi belongs to me, but it should be hers because she was Alan Dubois's wife, so she could build her own retirement home there. She said she would think about it and let me know it in a few years. She seems to like my suggestion.

Justice for my family was delayed, but it came. "What goes around comes around" was delayed, but it came. The crooks were punished and the good people were rewarded. If the saying is the eternal law for humans, justice must come one way or another even after a long delay like ours.

Milton Keynes UK
Ingram Content Group UK Ltd.
UKHW050753210324
439796UK00015B/1450